Under the cover OF DARKNESS

TWISTED LEGENDS COLLECTION

EMMA LUNA

Copyright © 2022 by EMMA LUNA

All rights reserved. No part of this publication may be reproduced, stored or transmitted in any form or by any means, electronic, mechanical, photocopying, recording, scanning, or otherwise without written permission from the publisher. It is illegal to copy this book, post it to a website, or distribute it by any other means without permission.

This novel is entirely a work of fiction. The names, characters and incidents portrayed in it are the work of the author's imagination. Any resemblance to actual persons, living or dead, events or localities is entirely coincidental.

Emma Luna asserts the moral right to be identified as the author of this work. Emma Luna has no responsibility for the persistence or accuracy of URLs for external or third-party Internet Websites referred to in this publication and does not guarantee that any content on such Websites is, or will remain, accurate or appropriate.

Designations used by companies to distinguish their products are often claimed as trademarks. All brand names and product names used in this book and on its cover are trade names, service marks, trademarks and registered trademarks of their respective owners. The publishers and the book are not associated with any product or vendor mentioned in this book. None of the companies referenced within the book have endorsed the book.

First edition

Ebook ASIN Number - B09PPN4BKK
Paperback ISBN Number - 9798843086275
Hardback ISBN Number - 9798843086350

Editing: Rumi Khan
Proofreading: Emma Luna at Moonlight Author Services
Cover Design & Formatting: Raven Designs

Welcome...

Ten authors invite you to join us in the
Twisted Legends Collection.

These stories are a dark, twisted reimagining of
infamous legends well-known throughout the
world. Some are retellings, others are nods to those
stories that cause a chill to run down your spine.

Each book may be a standalone, but they're
all connected by the lure of a legend.

We invite you to venture into the unknown,
and delve into the darkness with us,
one book at a time.

TWISTED LEGENDS AUTHOR SERIES

The COLLECTION

Vengeance of The Fallen - Dani René

Truth or Kill - A.C. Kramer

Departed Whispers - J Rose

Hell Gate - Veronica Eden

Blood & Vows - Amanda Richardson

Under the Cover of Darkness - Emma Luna

Reckless Covenant - Lilith Roman

Bane & Bound - Crimson Syn

The Ripper - Alexandra Silva

Blurb

ADDY

I thought the suffocating loneliness of the last two year were bad, but then I was sent to Lakeridge Psychiatric Facility.

On the outside it's disguised as helpful brochures and friendly doctors who have vowed to help, but the real truth is just below the surface, lurking in the shadows, and haunting my dreams.

At night he comes—taunting and abusing me. Bending me to his will, and making sure no one believes me.

That is until Dylan.

I can touch him and see him, but if my mind is capable of creating such horrors like my nightmares, can I trust that he's real?

Blurb

DYLAN

I'm no stranger to breaking rules and living on the edge. I guess it kind of comes with the territory of being a rockstar. But when I'm forced to attend Lakeridge, to serve my time and get sober, I'm met with the one thing I know I can't have.
Addy.
I know we don't have a chance, not unless I want to get kicked out of here, and made to finish my sentence in a proper prison. Still, something about her calls to me. There is more to the marks on her pale skin than the doctors say, and her nightmares seem to be a little too real.
Digging deeper into the madness, I'm left to question, can nightmares really leave scars? Or am I becoming mad too?

Author Note

Under The Cover of Darkness is part of the Twisted Legends Collection, which is a series of standalones by different authors. It's a dark contemporary romance with rockstar vibes. This book contains scenes that may be a trigger for some people, and is therefore only intended to be read by a mature audience. If you would like more details on specific triggers, please don't hesitate to reach out to emmalunaauthor@gmail.com. Your email will be responded to swiftly and will be dealt with in the utmost confidence.

Please note - Under The Cover Of Darkness is set in England, and as the author is also British, it uses UK English spelling. If you think you have spotted an error, please email the address above. Please do not report it to Amazon as this can lead to the book being removed from sale.

Thank you to each and every one of you for taking the time to read Under The Cover of Darkness. If you enjoyed the book, I would be very grateful if you could leave a review. Reviews are so important to Indie authors, and make more difference than you realise. Thanks again for your support!

Love
Em
xx

Dedication

To my best and longest friend, Debra

Every day you wake up battling the darkness, trying to keep it at bay for another day.
Battling each and every day with your own mind is terrifying, but still you manage it.

You are so much stronger than you realise!

No matter the distance between us, or the days we go between talking, I know that our friendship is unwavering. If we can both fight against our own bodies and minds to survive, our friendship will always stand strong.

Keep believing in yourself, being strong, and never be afraid to reach out for help.

Nobody should have to fight the darkness alone!

Prologue
ADDY

EIGHT YEARS EARLIER

"Addison Mitchell, if you don't get your cute butt over here, I promise you we will stay here for an extra week," my dad yells from where he's sitting around the campfire with the rest of my family.

I stomp out of the large family tent we're currently staying in, and I pull the large blanket around my shoulders. Holding my phone up in the air, I continually check the reception, magically hoping I've suddenly got enough reception to connect with my friends.

"Dad, don't even joke about us staying in this hellhole any longer than is absolutely necessary. I will take part in this dumb-ass family holiday, but not for any longer than I have to."

I move towards one of the three logs that are

surrounding the campfire. Mum and Dad cuddle together on the largest log, while my little brother and sister are sitting on the other two. I'm the oldest of my siblings, at twelve years old. My sister, Arabella, is only eight years old, and my annoying little brother, Adam, is only five years old. I don't exactly mind being an older sister. There are just times when they are super annoying and I wish I could be an only child. Mum says it's just because I'm getting older, and that a time will come when I'll be grateful for having them in my life. Today is most definitely not that day.

We've been arguing on and off all day, and this is my dad's way of trying to save this horrible family holiday. I wanted to go somewhere sunny, where I could sit on a beach all day, read some books, and possibly meet some cute boys. Instead, Mum and Dad wanted to relive their younger days by bringing us to the campsite where they had their first holiday when they started dating. From the moment I arrived at this hellhole in the middle of nowhere, as I looked around at the run-down, shoddy wooden shacks that house the communal bathroom, I really questioned Mum's sanity. If this is the best he could come up with for one of their first holidays I don't know why she would stay with him. We are literally in the middle of nowhere. No electricity, no beds, and no phone reception. My worst kind of hell.

We'd spent the day on the lake beside where we had set up camp. I'm not even remotely surprised to find there's no other human life around us. Nobody else is stupid enough not to check reviews to make sure the place hasn't deteriorated significantly in the fifteen years since they last visited. But that's my dad for you, always wanting to relive his youth. To remember the better days, as he calls it. Actually, playing in the lake, canoeing, and paddleboarding was a lot of fun. I'm just not telling him that. I can't have him knowing that there are things I like about being here. The fact that I have to sleep on the floor in a sleeping bag, surrounded by my whole family—as we have only one large family-sized tent—is more than enough to overpower all the good.

"Addy, just sit down, I want to hear the story," Adam groans, as he shoves another marshmallow into his mouth.

Sitting down on the same log as Arabella, Mum reaches over and hands me a skewer with a marshmallow on the top for me to toast over the campfire. My dad has a cooler next to him, filled with drinks for us all, and on the top he's set up everything we need to make s'mores. I gratefully take the skewer and begin holding it over the fire, and Dad passes a can of Diet Coke along to me, which I accept with a sarcastic smile.

"What's the point? It's just going to be a stupid, made-up story," I grumble, but Adam throws me an annoyed glare as he shoves another marshmallow into his mouth.

"You know Dad tells amazing ghost stories, Addy. You used to love them. So stop pretending you are too cool and just listen to the story," Ara snaps from beside me as she grabs the phone out of my hand. "There's no point in keeping this if it doesn't even work. You can't charge it and there's no signal. Besides, you are hardly going to die if you can't stay in touch with those idiots you call friends."

I try to grab the phone back, pushing at Ara's shoulder as she holds the phone too far out of reach. "Give me that back, you bitch," I shout, slapping my hand around her shoulder when she doesn't give it to me.

Mum gets up from where she's sitting beside Dad, her long brown hair blowing in the breeze as she strides over to us. She snatches the phone out of my sister's hand and slides it into her back pocket, before turning to face me, anger etched across her beautiful face. "Do not call your sister a bitch. In fact, don't call anyone a bitch. Now, we are trying to have a nice family holiday. So, if you can't enjoy yourself, then the least you can do is pretend to be part of this family and fake the fact that you are having a good time."

Sitting back on the log, Mum pulls the blanket she shares with Dad back over her legs and takes a drink of the wine she has in a plastic cup beside her. My eyebrows furrow and I shoot daggers at my parents.

"When do I get my phone back?" I snap, and my mum just rolls her eyes.

"You will get it back when we leave the camp. Until then, you can't use it because there's no signal, and you will run out of battery before the night is over. We have four more days here, and we are going to have a good time." Mum sounds like she's trying not to lose her temper, talking through gritted teeth.

"Can we get on with the story now?" Adam moans, as he takes a big gulp of the Sprite can he has in his hands, no doubt washing down all the marshmallows he's just devoured.

"Yes! I've been practising my best spooky voice, especially for this. What urban legend do you want to hear about tonight?" my dad asks, as he picks up the torch he has beside him.

The sun has firmly set below the horizon, and the only light comes from the half-moon that sits high in the dark blue sky. As we're in the middle of nowhere, surrounded by trees on three sides, and the lake is in front of us. The moonlight reflects off the still lake, giving us a little more light, but mostly we are under the cover of darkness, lit up by only moonlight and the embers flying from the campfire.

Looking up at the night sky, I hate to admit that it's beautiful. Living in a big city, it's rare that there's complete darkness around me. Normally, lights from the building or street lamps illuminate the area, making it difficult to truly appreciate the beauty of the sky at night. The stars twinkle like little dots, and it looks almost magical.

I reach over to grab what I need to make a delicious s'more, and I catch the small smile on Mum's face that she quickly tries to hide. Clearly she sees me making a s'more as a small victory, like I'm taking part in the family event the way she has been nagging me to do.

"Ooh, can I vote for Bloody Mary?" Arabella shouts, practically buzzing with excitement. She may only be eight years old, but she loves all things dark and disturbed. She loves learning all about our bloody history, and anything involving folklore or the occult. I should have known she would have a list of legends she wants to hear about.

Before Dad can answer, Adam interrupts him. "No! I want to hear about the sewage monsters, or maybe the deadly chain mail legend." Adam is so hyped up on sugar, he's almost bouncing on the log he's using as a seat.

"What about you, Addy? Do you have a preference?" Dad asks, looking at me with those big green eyes that look exactly the same as mine. I may be the spitting image of Mum, but my eyes are definitely from Dad. Right now they're glaring at me, begging me to participate.

Rolling my eyes, I take a gulp of the Diet Coke can I have beside me, trying to make it look like I'm not remotely interested in participating. I'm trying to hide it, but I actually quite enjoy the ghost stories that Dad tells us. Though this is our first time coming back to this location, it's not our first time camping. We always have a family camping trip to somewhere new during the summer holidays. But, this is going to be our last year, or at least I hope it will be. After a lot of persuading, Mum and Dad have agreed that we can do a beach holiday abroad next year, which I'm already excited about. It's not like we can't afford it. Mum comes from a wealthy family, and when her parents passed away—I was only around six years old at the time—she inherited a vast amount of money.

Despite having the money, my parents are sticklers for sentimentality, and they like the idea of cutting off from the world for a week, giving us a chance to reconnect as a family. I used to enjoy these trips a lot. I guess as I've got older, it's become less fun. I hate not being able to be in touch with my friends, or miss out on the fun summer plans they have. But, mostly I miss dancing. It's my whole life, and to stop my training regime for a week is becoming increasingly more difficult. But whenever

I look back at previous trips, story time is one of my favourites.

I think we have heard all of Dad's stories before, but each time he tries to make them a little more animated and exciting. He will tell a different one each night. So, there's no real point in arguing. We stay for five nights, which means each family member gets to pick the story for one night. We all have our favourites, and I have at least three that come to mind, if I get to pick.

"Is it my night to pick, or are you just asking me to stop those two from arguing?" I snap, and I instantly regret it. Blame my puberty hormones, or at least, that's what Mum blames. She says the older I get, the more hormonal I become, which seems to make me more and more angry and irritable. Snapping at everyone for no particular reason. I try to dial it back, but it's difficult.

"Yes, Addy. You can have tonight's pick," Dad says, and he shines the torch in my face, to act as a spotlight while I make my decision.

Adam and Arabella groan loudly. They wanted to get the first pick. I chuckle, because who doesn't want to win? Besides, it's a moot point, since we will all get a turn to pick.

I move my hand to my chin and pretend to stroke my imaginary beard. This is what my family does to let everyone know they are deep in concentration. I don't miss the way my parents smile when they see I'm playing along.

"Okay, my choice is… drum roll, please." Everyone bangs their hands on their knees, making it sound like drums, building anticipation. "I want to hear the Legend of Slender Man."

Cheers ring out around the campfire, as everyone seems pleased with my suggestion. Adam jumps up, his blanket flying off his legs as he does a crazy happy dance. My family is so weird. Watching my little brother shake his bum whilst chanting Slender Man is one of the funniest things I've seen, and we all crack up laughing.

Once the laughter dies down, and my brother sits back on his log, Dad hands out some more marshmallows, and we all lean over to toast them in the fire. Dad holds the torch up, so the light is shining towards the sky. He holds it against his chin, casting shadows over all the features of his face. It's how Dad always tells his stories.

"Right, kids, gather around. I have a wicked story to tell. This is the Legend of Slender Man, and it will haunt your dreams." He pauses dramatically before continuing. "Once upon a time, on a dark and stormy night—"

Arabella interrupts with a tut. "Why is it always dark and stormy in all the stories?"

Adam huffs and throws one of his marshmallows at Ara, narrowly missing her head. "No interrupting story time, guys," Mum says, giving Adam that look that only mums seem to have. The one that says *if you do that again you will regret it*, and we all know not to test her on that one.

"Sorry," Ara and Adam both mumble, which makes me chuckle. Their heads are downcast, looking very much like children who have just been chastised by their mum.

"As I was saying… It was a dark and stormy night, the wind was howling, and thunder ripped through the walls of the big mansion. The large house sat on the top of a big hill, surrounded by eery-looking forests. Aside from the weather, all was silent. There were no birds or wildlife roaming the woods. They had fled long ago." Adam woos dramatically to add tension to Dad's story.

I notice my marshmallow has almost burnt; I was so enthralled with the story, I forgot to take it out of the fire. I place it on the biscuit I have ready, along with some chocolate, before sandwiching it together to make the gooey s'more that I love. Meanwhile, Dad continues his tale.

"The large, run-down, spooky-looking building wasn't just any house. It was the local insane asylum. Known to house only the most dangerous people, the ones who were not there by choice, but because it's for their own and everyone else's safety."

Ara cuts in with a mumble that I can only hear because I'm sitting next to her, but then again, I think she only meant for me to hear. "That's Addy's future home, then."

"Screw you," I snap loudly, which draws everyone's attention and earns me groans from Adam and Dad, and a very unhappy look from Mum. "She started it." I know it's not the best comeback, but it's the best I've got.

"Stop arguing, for Christ's sake." Mum sounds exacerbated, and she doesn't hesitate to take another mouthful of wine while Dad continues.

"There's a young girl in the asylum, sent there by her parents. She went mad after they murdered her husband before her very eyes. Most people who were committed to the asylum got better. The treatment was always very effective, except for this young lady. Every day she would sit by the window, staring out as though frozen. Yet, every night, she was tormented by the worst kind of nightmare." Dad spins his torch, shining it around the campfire, catching us all in its light as it passes us.

"Slender Man," I murmur, adding to the story I'd heard many times before, and earning an appreciative *ooooh* from Adam.

Dad chuckles before returning his torch to his chin, ready to continue the story. "Every night, the Slender Man would visit her dreams. He would torture her in the worst kind of way. Messing with the very make-up of her brain until she didn't know what was real and what were nightmares. She became convinced that Slender Man was real, and that each night when he came into her locked room without a key, he would tie her up, beat her, abuse her, and humiliate her, until she was left a shadow of her former self."

Dad passes the torch over to Mum for her to continue with the rest of the story, while myself and my siblings sit staring at them, completely enraptured by the story. Holding the torch in the same way Dad did, Mum continues.

"Every morning, the exhausted, broken girl, whose throat was hoarse from screaming all night, would meet with her psychiatrist. She would tell the same tale of a faceless man, tall and overpowering, dressed in a smart suit, who would enter her room. She did not know how he got in, but he did, and that's when her nightmare really began. She would scream and shout, begging for someone to come and help her, but help never came. The cruel, sadistic man would taunt and humiliate her, breaking her down piece by piece. Until finally there was nothing left of her."

"Ohhh, did she die?" Adam shouts, as Mum hands the torch back to Dad to finish the story.

"Why did nobody believe her?" Arabella asks before Dad can start again.

"They believed she thought the Slender Man was real. They thought her delusions had become so severe that she was now hurting herself, believing them to be true. No matter what medications or therapies they tried, her delusions got worse. She had started off telling anyone and everyone about the faceless man that haunts her dreams, but the more she told them, the crazier they thought she was. She would show them cuts and bruises, and they accused her of harming herself. So eventually she stopped talking. She cut herself off from the word, never uttering another word. During the day she stared out of the window, wishing for a better life, while on a night she screamed, begged, pleaded for her nightmare to be over. Eventually, the decision was made that she needed a lobotomy, the only way to rid her of her delusions…"

"Cool," Adam interrupts, earning a laugh from everyone except Mum, who just rolls her eyes. We all seem to lean forward, desperate to hear the end of the tragic tale we've heard so many times before.

Dad removes the torch from his face, turning it off, leaving us with very little light from the moon and the campfire. "After they removed a part of her brain, she literally became a shell of her former self. She could barely walk, she didn't talk still, and she simply stared out of the window again, drooling from her droopy mouth. That night, all she could think is she would finally have a peaceful night's sleep, safe in the knowledge that the Slender Man was gone. Except he wasn't. Of course, the Slender Man returned, his torture and abuse now a lot easier given her almost catatonic state. That next morning she broke her silence, using all her power to tell her psychiatrist that the Slender Man was still very real, and still featuring in her nightmares. They were at a loss for what to do, and simply brushed her off, upping her medication until she could not talk anymore."

"Shit," I mutter, chills running down my spine as I think of all the horrors that woman must have endured. Stuck in her body, having her brain torment her relentlessly.

"Language," Mum scolds me, but Dad just continues with the end of the story.

"One day, one of the nurses couldn't find the young girl, and they searched everywhere for her. Eventually they found her, hanging from the very same tree she'd spent every day looking at. Her stained, bloody bed sheets tied around the low-hanging branch, with the chair she obviously used to climb up to it now kicked over on the floor. They cut her down, but she was long gone, her body cold and lifeless. Strangely, it's the first time they'd ever seen her looking at peace.

"They found a letter in her pocket addressed to nobody at all. After all, she had nobody left to care about her. It said she wasn't going to apologise for killing herself, no matter how much God may frown upon it. She could no longer live in a world where evil was allowed to run riot, unattended, causing such hurt and pain. She asked them all to bury her with her husband, the man she never stopped loving. She also asked them to consider that maybe she was telling the truth.

"Maybe the reason Slender Man never disappeared, even after all the therapy, medication, and treatment, is because he wasn't a figment of her imagination. Maybe he wasn't a delusion created in her worst nightmares. Maybe the fresh injuries and wounds she had each and every day weren't the result of her hurting herself. After all, nightmares don't leave scars, yet he does. So, maybe after all this time, she was telling the truth. Maybe Slender Man wasn't a psychotic delusion. Maybe she never lost touch with reality and everything she said was the truth. Maybe the tall, faceless man who haunts her was real, and what's to stop him from moving on to his next target now she's gone."

We all sit in silence, listening to every word Dad has to say. He pauses for dramatic effect, taking a little too long, if Mum's eye roll is anything to go by, I think he's trying to add tension, but it only seems to be working with Adam, who appears to be frozen, in the middle of putting a marshmallow in his mouth, his mouth wide open while his body is unmoving. His eyes are latched onto Dad, just like the rest of us as we wait for the ending.

Sitting up straighter, Dad turns the flashlight back onto his face before continuing. "The staff at the asylum brushed off her letter, saying they were the ramblings of a mad woman, after all. They did as she asked and had her body buried with her love, hoping she'd finally found peace. For a while, all at the asylum was quiet—or as quiet as an asylum can be. Until one day, there's a new girl at the asylum. Committed by her family for mental health problems, she was given the other woman's old room. She'd only been there a few days when she first met him. She was lying in her bed, getting ready to fall asleep, when she heard a noise in her room. She looked up to find a tall, faceless man dressed in a suit standing over her. 'Who are you?' she asked, and the faceless man just stood completely still. The closer she looked, the more she realised his face wasn't completely missing. It's like she couldn't look at him properly, but she was sure she could see piercing blue eyes shining back at her. That was the first night he visited, and from then his abuse and torture continued, getting progressively worse. Nurses were shocked and stunned to hear the same tale again, occurring in a very similar circumstance. Some said the room was possessed, that it was the devil haunting that one room. But the girl knew he was real. Each and every night she would ask him the same question—'Who are you?'—hoping that one day he would speak, confirming her suspicions. It wasn't until she was completely broken, and a shell of her former self that he turned to her, and answered her question. 'I'm the Slender Man, and I'm your worst nightmare'. Hearing that had been all she wanted to hear. It confirmed that he wasn't all in her head; he was a real person. She died that night, never having got the chance to prove he was a real person. Some say he killed her, some say he isn't real. But the legend remains the same. He finds a shy, lost girl and he messes with her, twisting her consciousness until she isn't sure what's real and what isn't. He haunts her dreams, making her relive her nightmares night after night. Slender Man is the worst kind of nightmare. You don't know if he's real or if you have finally gone mad."

One
DYLAN

"I'M NOT GOING, JAKE. YOU CAN ALL FUCK OFF. I'VE MADE my feelings on this situation very fucking clear. I do not need to go to rehab," I shout at my best friend before taking a mouthful of the amber liquid swilling about in the glass I'm holding.

I'm very aware that taking big gulps of whiskey at ten in the morning, whilst arguing that I don't need to go to rehab, may seem like a bit of a contradiction, but I haven't been to bed yet, so it's still the night before for me.

I see the three guys I class as my brothers as their eyes continuously flit towards each other. Together we are The Catastrophists, one of the best rock bands in the world. We've had number one singles in over fourteen countries, and the world we live in now is a far cry from the group of scrawny kids we were, playing together in

Jake's basement.

Jake, the lead singer and frontman of our band, snaps at me, trying to grab my attention. "For fuck's sake, Dylan. This is not up for debate. This is a court order. If you do not complete the six-month rehab placement, you will go to prison instead. You are lucky our lawyer was even able to negotiate such a fucking good deal for you." He leans over and rips the whiskey bottle I'd just picked up out of my hand. I snap around to face him, fury etched across my face as I try to take the bottle back, but Louis pulls my attention.

"We are not playing around with this one, Dyl. You need help, and we're prepared to make good on our threats if you don't." I spin around to face Louis, my angry glare now directed at him. Surely after knowing me for just over ten years, he knows I don't respond well to threats.

"Don't fucking threaten me, Louis. This is my band, and you are not fucking taking it from me," I scream, louder than intended. They have picked one hell of a fucking time to confront me with this shit. We had a gig the night before. It was the last in a small string of gigs we organised to release our newest single. It went to number one instantly, and the gigs sold out within minutes. It's only been a bit of a mini tour, but I still treated it the way I always do. I would do the concert, then party all night, well into the early hours of the morning. Sometimes this involved finding a wet pussy or two that I could sink my dick into, but mostly it involved a lot of drinking. I usually won't go to bed until the sun comes up. Then I get a couple of hours sleep before one of the guys would wake me up and demand we do a sound check, or some promotional thing we agreed to. That's when I would start it all over again.

Henry, who is normally the quiet, chilled-back one of the group, and our bass guitarist, gently places his hand on my shoulder, trying to get me to calm down. "Dylan, we all started this band together, so don't start that bullshit. But this isn't just about the band anymore, Dyl. This is about you and your health. You need help, and if you don't take this opportunity, you may regret it. Not just because we will stick by our promise to replace you in the band, but we worry that you will kill yourself. You are twenty-three years old, and you can't go a fucking day without drinking or taking pills. You have no one else on your side looking out for you, which means you've always been able to run riot. But now we are stepping in. We genuinely believe you will end up in an early grave if you don't get your ass in gear."

Taking the glass of whiskey in my hand, I launch it at the wall, the glass shattering into a million pieces. Yelps from my band members fill the room, and they look at me in shock over my outburst. But Henry just hit below the belt. I don't need a constant fucking reminder that I have nobody in my life who cares about me. That's something I'm very well aware of, and they know I don't talk about it. Ever!

"Whoa. Fucking hell, Dylan," Jake yells, as they all take a step back from me, and I pace around the living room. I feel like a caged animal, and if they keep continually prodding me, it's not surprising that I'm going to lash out.

"Stop fucking pushing me. I've told you I'm not going!" I shout, making my feelings on the subject very fucking clear. As I look down at my now empty hand, I regret throwing the glass, because I could very much do with a drink right about now.

"Dylan, you have no choice. You either go to rehab, and you get yourself sober, or you will go to prison. That is what the judge made very fucking clear to you. But on top of that, our ultimatum remains the same. If you go to jail, you are out of the band. And, if you go to rehab, we expect you to pass several drug tests for the first three months after you finish there. If you fail even one, you are done. We will replace you. We cannot have another tour like this one, worried that you will get yourself fucking killed." Jake groans as the throws himself down onto the sofa, sounding exasperated and quite frankly, fucking exhausted.

I snap at him, my voice grinding through gritted teeth, my face distorted with rage. "You can't replace me. We started this band together ten years ago. We were thirteen fucking years old, and we've built this band up from nothing. I write all the songs. I am this fucking band, and you can all fuck off if you think you can replace me. This is my fucking band!" The last part I can't help but yell. These dickheads can fuck off if they think they can kick me out of my own band.

"Then you need to go to rehab, Dyl. Please... do it for us." The sad, almost pleading look on Henry's face is painful to witness. I may be pissed at these assholes right now, but they are still my best friends... my brothers. I hate that they are in pain, and that I'm the cause. I'm not going to admit I have a problem, because I don't think I fucking do. I admit that I take a lot of prescription pills—because I need them. Some call it addiction. I say a doctor gives them to me to alleviate my pain, and so I take them. Yes, I self-medicate on top of that with cocaine and liquor, but I'm not addicted. They make me feel good, and help me to forget about the black hole that is my past, and so I don't want to give them up. I've been living on booze and pills for the last five years, since the band started to hit the big time after we turned eighteen. I'm not entirely sure what my life will look like without them. But I guess if I don't find out, I will lose everything.

Defeated, I flop down onto the sofa beside Jake, who instantly throws his arm around my shoulder. The stroppy asshole in me wants to throw him off, but I don't. I have an awful feeling that these next few months are going to be the hardest of my life, and I'm going to need my brothers by my side.

Pulling up the long, paved driveway, my skin begins to feel itchy, and I can't sit still properly. Looking out the car window, I take in the countryside surrounding me. We are in the middle of nowhere, and all I can see around me is greenery and trees. The only sign of life occurs when we turn off the old country road towards the paved driveway.

Large iron gates stand almost ten feet tall, and they are intricately designed with a large metal letter 'L' in the middle of each gate. Next to them, in addition to a buzzer that I'm assuming we need to use to gain entrance, is a large sign that says: 'Welcome to Lakeridge Psychiatric Facility' and beneath that is the saying, 'In your well-being we care'. I want to laugh aloud, they clearly didn't have a great PR team on board when they came up with that shit slogan.

My driver, whose name I can't even remember, since he hasn't worked with us for long, buzzes us in. The gates slowly swing open, and the car pulls inside. To say the driveway is long is a massive fucking understatement. I can't even see the house from here. But the more we advance up the winding drive, the larger the house becomes as it slowly comes into view.

Lakeridge is fucking huge. It looks like a creepy old mansion, shrouded in gothic design features. The white bricks at the side of the house are almost all covered with ivy or other plants crawling up the external walls of the house. It looks to only have a ground floor and a first-floor level from what I can see out here, but if the amount of windows are anything to go by, there are a fuck-tonne of rooms in this facility.

The car pulls to a stop at the front of the large building. There are a few steps to get up to the front door, and on either side of it are two large pillars that make the mansion look even more elaborate. Even though the house is bright white, and should be light and inviting, it has a completely different feel. I don't know what it is about the building specifically, but it just gives off a dodgy vibe. It feels dark and eerie, but it's difficult to explain why.

The door beside me swings open and I'm greeted

by a young woman. "Hello, Mr. Matthews. I'm Dr. Amy Hughes, it's nice to meet you."

I run my gaze over the petite blonde standing in front of me, and I can't deny she's hot, in a posh kinda way. Her blonde hair sits in a neat bob, stopping just above her shoulders, and her dark-rimmed glasses cover her eyes. The black pencil skirt she's wearing stops around her knees, but clings tightly enough that when she turns around I know the curve of her ass will be visible. She's wearing a white blouse that's buttoned up high enough to be respectable, but the slight sheen to it makes it see-through, so you can see the white lace bra she's wearing underneath. She's wearing a matching black suit jacket over the top, and black stiletto heels that give her some extra height. She doesn't have many curves to her slight frame, which is usually my preference. I like to have something to grab hold of while I'm balls deep. Still, I wouldn't say no to this woman. She looks every bit the prim and proper professional, and if the past has taught me anything, it's the quiet ones that are freaks between the sheets.

The doctor holds her hand out for me to shake, and I don't miss the way a blush spreads across her cheeks as I give her my signature sexy smirk. "Hey, Doc. So, you're going to be my personal assistant during my stay in this hellhole?" I ask, as I shake her hand. Her gaze drops to the floor, and I notice the blush spreads deeper across her milky white chest.

It looks like she takes a couple of big, deep breaths before straightening her back, holding her head high, and addressing me again. "No, Dylan. I'm not your personal assistant, I'm your doctor. Your team has asked that I keep an eye on you during your time here, but that is the only allowance you will get. You're here under court order, just like everyone else. You will follow the rules, or we will inform the judge that you are non-compliant, and you will finish your sentence in a prison cell. Do not test me on this one, there will be no second chances. These beds are in high demand, and I won't have you taking one up if you're not serious about getting clean and sober."

She drops my hand, and I just stand there frozen, my mouth literally hanging wide open. I clearly misjudged this woman as shy and timid, but she's got a bit of a bite to her, which suddenly makes her more than just a pretty face. Still not my type, but if I have to be locked in here for six months without pussy, I will no doubt have to lower my standards a bit. I can already hear Jake's voice in my head lecturing me about how irresponsible it is to fuck my doctor. He's probably right too. But I don't know what other women there will be in this shithole. Maybe there will be a posh socialite with a coke habit and a nice rack that I can play with.

"I never said I wasn't committed to getting sober, Doc. I'm here, aren't I?"

She rolls her eyes at me. "Are you telling me you would have checked yourself in here voluntarily to get clean if the judge hadn't ordered it?"

My eyes cast to the ground as I scratch at the skin on my right arm. My fingers rake over the intricate ink designs, but it does nothing to alleviate the itch under my skin. It's like a million tiny ants are all worming their way beneath the surface, and there's nothing I can do to stop them. I haven't taken anything since yesterday. My bandmates pretty much stripped everything from me, under the instruction of the facility—although, I suspect they will repeat the process too. You can't have someone sneaking in a bag of pills and ruining everyone's sobriety—though that would be much more fun than what I'm about to face.

The truth is, I don't want to change. I know I take too many pills, or snort too much speed, and I drink pretty much all day. I know all of this. I've also heard what each and every doctor has said about my addiction and dependency causing strain on my heart, but I don't give a shit. There's a reason I do what I do. I use the pills and the booze to keep the darkness from creeping in, to stop all the harmful thoughts from overcoming me. I have a lot of shit in my past that I've never dealt with, and I don't ever want to think about it. So, I self-medicate. Yet, now, I only have two options. Letting in the darkness and hoping it doesn't consume me enough that I can finally get clean for the first time in five years. Or, I carry on as I have been doing and go to prison. My ass is far too pretty for prison, so I'm here, hoping like hell I didn't make the wrong decision.

"The judge may have issued the order, but I made the decision. So, since I'm here, why don't you show me around?" I say with a wink, and Dr. Hughes just rolls her eyes again. Apparently, the initial shyness she felt around me has resolved.

I notice behind us that another man comes over to my driver, takes my suitcase and my bag from him, before turning back inside. My driver doesn't hesitate, or even say goodbye to me, he simply gets in the car and drives off. Given I can't even remember his name, I don't blame him. Dr. Hughes pulls my attention back to her when she starts talking. "Don't worry, one of our assistants will take your luggage to your room. Let me be very clear about this, Dylan. We are not here as your personal staff. We're here to care for everyone in the facility equally. If you want a coffee in the morning before breakfast time, you get your ass into the kitchen and you make it. The only time we will do things for you is if you physically are unable to. I think, if what your friends and family have told me is anything to go by, you have spent the last few years surrounded by yes-men. People who will do whatever you want because they're frightened to say no to you. As a result you've become more than a little pampered and spoiled. Here we will strip you back to your roots. You're not famous here, and you most definitely don't have any more privilege than the person in the room next to you. I have agreed to be your personal physician, not because Jake asked me to be, but because it's in the best interests of the whole facility. Obviously we've had famous people come to us before for short stays, but you are the most famous long-stay patient. And it's my job to make sure that you get the right care, but also that the facility and the other residents remain protected. The only stipulation I had when I spoke to Jake was that the press do not know you're here. Our quiet tranquil existence cannot be threatened by you. Is that clear?"

As she talks, she begins walking me through the entrance into a room surrounded by large white and black marbled walls. I have never seen such a bright and airy room appear so dark and eerie. It's like things are just a little too still, with too many shadows. I had no idea what the facility would look like. I know Jake will have researched to make sure I end up somewhere good, but because this is a court-mandated stay, I wasn't given a whole heap of options.

Dr. Hughes walks me over to a large, dark mahogany desk, and a young guy is sitting behind the computer, tapping away whilst talking into the headset he has in one of his ears. He holds a finger up to let us know he's seen us, but he doesn't look up from his computer. Not that I needed a clue as to where we are, but sitting on the front of the desk is a wooden nameplate with a metal plaque over it saying 'Lakeridge Reception'.

"Hello, Dr. Hughes. Lovely to see you this morning. How may I help you?" the young guy asks, as he flashes the doctor with a smile I know all too well. He's trying to get into her pants, and given the way she barely acknowledges him, he's failing miserably.

The young guy only looks to be in his early twenties, probably not a lot younger than me. He's got shoulder-length blond hair, and dark eyes. He has that typical baby-faced look that women seem to love. My brothers call it stereotypical boy band good looks, and he most definitely fits into that category. I would have thought he'd be a perfect choice for my prim and proper doctor.

"This is Dylan, the patient I spoke to you about yesterday," she says, her voice sounding incredibly odd, like she's pretending to be a super spy, and I'm a big secret. I think I even see them share a wink.

"Oh, yes. The VIP," he replies, and I can't help

but chuckle. They obviously have a plan to admit me anonymously, so that anyone looking for me won't know who I really am. There are fucking paparazzi who will stop at nothing to locate me. My fall from grace, as the press is calling it, was very well publicised. Although the court case was a closed event, the press was informed that I was given a community order, and that I'd be taking some time away from the limelight to evaluate things and concentrate on the music. Or at least, that's what the official statement our manager Kevin put out into the world said. A few reporters speculated that it was code for rehab, while some believe I was sent to prison and we're just trying to hide it to maintain my reputation. So there are people out there doing deep dives on my name, desperate to find out if I've been sent down, or have checked in somewhere. Hence, the need to do this anonymously.

"Of course. He's checked in under Dylan Smith. I know it's not a great disguise, but it's also a common name that will be hard to flag. The room is all ready, and all the paperwork has been taken there already for him to look through. As soon as he's selected his options, and has completed his detox week, I will have his timetable completed," he explains to Dr. Hughes, and most of what he just said went in one ear and out of the other for me. But, when he turns his focus to me, I give him my attention. "Here is your access wristband. Dr. Hughes will explain where you need to use it and when. It's fully waterproof, and we expect you not to remove it under any circumstances. Give me your arm so I can secure it, please."

He holds his hand out, expecting me to just reach over and give him my arm. I look to Dr. Hughes for an explanation, but she's waiting for me to do as instructed.

"What the hell do I need it for?" I snap, and the guy behind the desk tuts, before reaching over and taking hold of my hand. I snatch it away, and look at him full of fury. "Do not touch me. Ever!"

"Okay, Dylan. Please, calm down. Lyle is sorry for touching you without your consent. Everyone at the facility wears a wristband. It's basically a security access card and will get you into the rooms that you need entry to. It is also the key to get you into your room. I will explain how it works as I give you a tour," Dr. Hughes explains.

I try to gain control over my breathing, the sudden panic of having someone touch me starts to cripple my body. I hear Dr. Hughes advising me on how to breathe, her voice sounding a lot farther away than she is. After a few deep breaths, I feel my heart beginning to slow down to a more normal rate. Why do people never respect other people's personal space? Just because I'm famous, it doesn't give people a right to touch me without my consent.

Dr. Hughes holds out her hand, showing me the wristband, making her intentions clear. I hold my arm out and let her attach the wristband, ignoring the way the other asshole beside me scoffs. She looks over at him and gives him a small smile. "Thank you for your help, Lyle. Is everything else all set up?"

"Yes, the room is ready," he answers Dr. Hughes before reluctantly turning to face me. He plasters a very fake smile on his preppy-looking face before talking to me. "This reception is manned twenty-four hours a day. If you have any issues, you can come to the desk and we can find the right people to help you. We hope you have a pleasant stay here with us."

He doesn't even wait for me to respond; he sits back down and turns his attention to the computer screen. "It's a court-ordered rehab stay, not a fucking holiday at the Hilton. I can assure you, I won't have a pleasant stay." I can't help snapping at him. What an asshole thing to say. Does he seriously think people are coming here for a fun little holiday?

Dr. Hughes obviously realises I'm losing my patience with Lyle, and she moves me on, thanking him for his help, before leading me down the corridor. Once we leave the large entrance hallway, we come to a thick door, and at the side of the door is an electronic lock. This is the first time that it becomes apparent this is a locked, secure facility, rather than an elaborate, beautiful mansion. Dr. Hughes gets me to try and swipe my new wristband across the keypad. It flashes red and gives off a loud beep, making it clear I don't have permission to open this door. She then takes me into the facility and begins the tour.

The more we walk around, the more overwhelmed I feel. There are rooms after rooms, and I have no idea how I'm going to keep track of them all. As we are going, Dr. Hughes explains how the day will be split, the idea of structure being crucial. Mealtimes are held in the cafeteria, and there's a large main room where people can congregate for downtime. There's obviously a little bit of free time, but the morning is mostly made up of group therapy, while the afternoon is split between art therapy or personal therapy.

"What the hell is art therapy?" I ask, as we go upstairs to where the individual dorm rooms are.

"There's a lot of research showing that partaking in art therapy is very healthy. Art therapy can be anything from painting, sculpting, or colouring, which are obviously the most obvious forms, but there are so many more options. We have music therapy, dance therapy, meditation, swimming, and even equine therapy. People react differently, depending on what makes them feel most calm. Your happy place may be while you are playing music, and so music therapy would be the most obvious choice for you, but I would personally advise you to try something new. You never know, you might find that sculpting is the thing that gives you the most peace," she explains, as she opens a door to a small room.

Taking in the very basic room. It's smaller than I would ever be used to, but the stark white walls make the room look bigger than it is. There's a small window that allows extra light to shine in, filling the room with sunlight. There's a small double bed in the corner of the room with a bedside table beside it and a small lamp sitting on top of that. There's a desk with a chair, and a wardrobe, as well as one soft, comfy-looking chair that is angled towards the window. Other than that, the room is bare. There's a plain blue duvet cover on top of the bed, and the blind that covers the window is the same colour. This room looks as sad as the people it has no doubt housed before. I note an extra door in the corner, that I assume leads to the en-suite. It was my only stipulation.

There's no fucking way I'm sharing a bathroom.

"Well, isn't this place homely," I gripe sarcastically, before turning to look at Dr. Hughes who just rolls her eyes. "How do I learn what art therapy works best for me? Can't I just have my drums or a guitar?"

I don't know why I'm bothering to ask. We have had this conversation numerous times. Apparently, I can only play the instruments in the music room, not in my room, and drums are most definitely a big no. There are people here with a nervous disposition, and me drumming may set them off. Personally, I don't give a shit about other people or why they're here. All I care about is what I need. Drumming is how I stay sane—well, that and pills and booze—I need to feel the pounding of my sticks on the skins, as it helps me to regulate my breathing and calm myself down. It's the same with when I'm playing on my guitar, writing songs, it's how I get the noises out of my head. At least I will be able to do this in the music room. I think if this wasn't an option, like my drums, I would most definitely go crazy.

"This week you will be exempt from the timetable, as you will need to take time for yourself while you detox. But starting next week you will have one week to attend as many art therapies as possible. Sample as many as you can, and hopefully that will then help you choose which one you think will help you the most. After that, the one you choose will be added onto your timetable, and you will be expected to follow your routine from then onwards. You'll have ample free time to use the music room, and we have leisure time when you can use the gym, go swimming, or even go for a run around the grounds. I want you to push yourself to try new things, but I know there will be things you need to ensure you still feel like Dylan. When you've been here for a short while, if I feel you're making progress, I may allow you to have your guitar, but that's a discussion for a later date."

I flop down onto the bed, and Dr. Hughes pulls the seat out from next to the desk and turns it to face me before sitting down. "That sounds easy enough. It's the detox bit I'm not exactly looking forward to," I say with a grimace.

"I'm not going to lie, Dylan, this week isn't going to be easy. But I'll be here for you each and every step of the way. There are meds that I can give you to help you get through a lot of it, but I won't be in a rush to give you them. Obviously, the aim's to get you off all your pills, and giving you more meds will not help the situation. I'll use my clinical judgement on this. I don't want you in pain, but I want to make sure you can kick this. I believe in you, Dylan. It's going to be hard, you are going to feel like shit, and you are going to want to quit. There will be times when you ask to quit, or to leave. Jail will seem like a holiday compared to this first week, but I will ignore you. I promise things will get better, but they will get worse for a while."

My eyes bug out as I listen to her explain the hell I'm about to endure. "Fuck, you aren't exactly selling this for me, Doc."

Her chuckle cuts through the tense atmosphere in the room. "I don't need to sell it to you, Dylan. You're stuck here now. But, I promise you, when this is all over, you will come out of this a better person."

"I don't know how you can improve upon perfection, babe," I joke, and she just rolls her eyes at me again. Looks like my doctor's no longer shy around me.

"Don't call me babe, Dylan. Doc is fine, even Amy is acceptable, but babe is most definitely unacceptable. Now, shall we get started? I'll give you a chance to settle in and unpack, then I'll be back in an hour or so and we will get you started with the detox. How does that sound?" She sounds stern, like she's talking to a child, chastising me over what is acceptable behaviour. I'm not used to people telling me I can't do things. It's quite refreshing.

At the mention of getting the detox started, I can't help but release a groan. This is probably the thing I'm looking forward to the least. I know how I feel when I go a little too long in between hits. I know how shitty it is. But in the past I've been able to remedy that with another hit, or a drink. I've never had to feel the full force of a withdrawal. I can't even remember the last time my body operated without the use of an illicit substance. This whole process scares the shit out of me, but more than anything, I'm worried I'm not going to like the Dylan that comes out the other side.

Two
ADDY

Walking into the large common area, I head over to the large bay window in the corner of the room. There's a small square table and a single solitary chair set up with the sole purpose of looking out over the vast expanse of greenery that surrounds this beautiful building.

This is one of the largest rooms in the entire facility, and I like to imagine that when this house was in its heyday, this would've been the ballroom where everyone would regularly congregate, dressed in their finery, ready to dance and meet people. This house is old enough, it's lived through so much of our history, yet now it looks as bleak and depressing as the people inhabiting the room.

Sofas line the outskirts of the room, so people can lounge as they please, or there are tables and chairs for people who wish to engage in activities. This is the room where you can watch television, play board games, read a book, or just spend some downtime. Everybody has their preference for where they like to sit or what they like to do, and they pretty much stick to that routine. After all, routine gets drilled into us nearly every minute of every day here. I think if we're allowed too much freedom, or time to think, that's when things get worse for us.

This table is mine, and everyone knows it. I staked my claim early in my sentence, making it very fucking clear that nobody touches my shit. I had only been here two days when I got a warning for hitting a guy around the head with a jigsaw puzzle box. Obviously, I didn't do any real damage. It was fucking cardboard; it did more damage to the box. But they clarified that violence wouldn't be tolerated. Not that I needed to get violent after that. I'd made my point and everyone knew to leave me and my table alone.

Sitting here, I alternate between staring out the window, and doing whatever jigsaw puzzle I've picked for that day. I wouldn't say I get any real joy out of doing the puzzle, although there's a brief moment of excitement when I complete it. I do it more to keep my hands busy. Without something to do, my hands are free to pick at the ants I feel crawling under my skin.

Dr. Manning, who is the psychiatrist they assigned me when I first got here, he thinks it's my anxiety manifesting as the feeling of ants crawling around under my skin, but he's wrong. I had anxiety and depression before I was sent to this place, so I know what they feel like. I know that all-consuming feeling of bleakness all too well. It's how I ended up here. I succumbed to a moment of weakness, and I allowed the black cloud that has shrouded my life for the last two years to get the better of me. I tried to end my life, to find the peace I so desperately longed for, but all I got was a one-way ticket to hell.

Lakeridge is supposed to be the place that I come to, under a medical order—which basically means I was committed and will be kept here until they believe I'm no longer a danger to myself—to battle my demons. I expected to be here for a few weeks while they pump me full of drugs until I'm basically a sedated zombie, have a few counselling sessions to talk about how I'm feeling, and then kick me out into the big, wide world again. Rooms in a facility like this are in extremely high demand, so I never thought that someone with crippling grief to the point of suicide would qualify for a room long term. Then again, people are supposed to come here to get better, not worse.

The itchiness that the doctor attributes to anxiety is a lot more to do with the revulsion I feel. I know what it's like to hate yourself so much that even taking one more breath seems like the wrong thing to do. But, since being in Lakeridge, that has increased tenfold. If I thought things were bad before, it's nothing compared to the hell I face daily while stuck here. I don't know why it happened, or what caused it—although I'm sure Dr. Manning has a few ideas—but I'd only been here a week when my condition worsened. I became psychotic, detached from reality. I see things that aren't there, but they're so fucking real to me. He is so real to me. He haunts my nightmares, and nothing I do will make him go away. Dr. Manning pumps me full of drugs, but all that does is make him more vivid, and while I'm asleep, I can't avoid him. He destroys me in the worst way possible, and what's worse is that it feels real to me. When I wake up, I can feel where his hands touch me, see where he's abused me. Fuck, it's almost like I can still smell his lingering scent.

Initially, I told Dr. Manning about him… about the Slender Man. I even told him the story I used to share with my family when I was a child. He thinks I'm being haunted by that childhood memory because of my family. He didn't believe me when I said he felt so real, and instead pumped me full of drugs and fobbed me off. So I stopped telling people. At least five nights a week he haunts my nightmares, and the other two I sit up all night waiting for him to find me. I deal with these horrors all alone, because it's the only choice I have. I've been alone for the last two years, with nobody to turn to, and that's the way I like it.

"Morning, miserable," sings the beautiful petite girl, who pulls up a second chair to sit opposite me.

Rolling my eyes, I try to hide back the slight smile I get whenever this annoying little pixie inserts herself into my life. Everyone else knows to stay the fuck away from me, but Lucinda Davenport—or Sin as she prefers to be known—has no sense of self-preservation. The first couple of weeks, no matter how much of a bitch I was to her, no matter how much I tried to get her to leave me alone, the more she stuck around. Now, we are used to each other, although I personally think she could do a hell of a lot better than me when it comes to having a friend. Even in the middle of a court-ordered psychiatric facility, there are better options.

I have been on my own for the last two years, and even though I don't think I will ever become used to that, I have got used to the loneliness. In fact, I would much prefer to choose to be alone rather than to let people in, only to lose them all over again. My heart is barely holding on. I feel like it's being held together by sticky tape, and one more heartbreak, and I won't be able to patch it up again.

"You are looking even more dreary this morning. You doin' okay?" Sin asks, as she flicks her shoulder-length mermaid hair away from her face, giving me that bright smile that she always wears. No matter how fucking shit this place becomes, she always has a smile on her face, and I'm kinda envious. I wish I could view life in a more positive manner, rather than allowing the crippling anxiety and darkness to rule.

"Shit, as always. You look perky," I groan, as I give her a small smile, before returning to do the jigsaw in front of me. It's a little Scottish West Highland Terrier in a field design, and although I'm sure I've done this jigsaw before, there aren't exactly a lot of options in this place, so I made do.

Sin is practically bouncing in her seat, looking even more spirited than usual. "I'm so frickin' excited. You will not believe what I just saw?" Her hands tap on the table, her legs jigging up and down, and she looks like she's literally about to burst. Her eyes are wide with excitement, and I can tell she really wants to share this gossip with me.

"How many Red Bulls have you drunk today?" I

ask, looking over at the clock on the wall that is covered by a metal grate. When I first got here, it shocked me, and I wondered why the hell anyone would destroy a clock, but after being here for just over four weeks, it no longer shocks me. Time is the bane of my existence, as it never seems to go by quickly enough. Yet the closer it gets to bedtime, the more I wish time would stand still.

"It's only ten in the morning," she scoffs, and I roll my eyes at that response.

"When has that ever stopped you?"

She chuckles, her bright smile lighting up her pale face. Sin has been here for around three months now and is making great progress with her eating disorder. There was a time when she wouldn't have gone near energy drinks because of the calorie content. Now, she's still very picky about what she eats, and definitely still calorie counts, but I think she's learning to get a handle on things.

"Why are you trying to ruin my excitement? I have exciting fucking news," she jokes, poking me in the arm repeatedly until I playfully slap her hand away. I can't help the little chuckle that escapes my lips. It's hard not to be affected by her infectious energy.

"You mean gossip? There's a reason people around here call you a gossip. It's why you volunteered to be Lyle's assistant on the front desk." Sin is one of the more stable residents that has been given the opportunity to take on a job role whilst here in the facility. She works a couple of hours a day during her free time, and in return, they add extra money to her commissary. This is like a virtual money bank that we have, and we use it to buy things in the store. It's only extra things like sweets, chocolates, crisps, or magazines. Just things to make our time here a little less shit.

The job will also help when the time comes to discuss Sin's release. She's here under a medical hold, the same as me. So they have to decide that she's no longer a danger to herself or others, but also that she will be a useful member of society when she leaves here. If she doesn't meet the criteria, they can keep her here longer. Sin is desperate to get out, which is why she asked for the job working with Lyle at the front desk. But that was only part of her reason. She's also a massive gossip, and working in the main office exposes her to all the scandals or news that are prominent in the facility.

She rolls her eyes, clearly not giving a shit that people refer to her as a gossip queen. I think it's a title she's quite proud of. "Have you heard of The Catastrophists?"

My heart skips a beat, and I freeze. It's been a long time since I've heard that name. They're one of the biggest rock bands in the country. I think everyone has heard of them. But, two years ago, I cut myself off from the world. The constant reminders of what I lost are too great. Not having someone to share in your excitement, or even have someone to talk to about things you have in common, it's crippling. Hearing the band's name brought back the heartbreaking pain as I'm reminded of the fact that I would normally have talked to someone else about the band we both loved. Why should I be allowed to keep enjoying their music when she never can?

I can't find the words and simply nod my head in confirmation. "Oh, my God. They are, like, one of my favourite bands. "I Need You" is one of my favourite songs of all time. I love them so fucking much."

"Is this part of the story, or have you gone off on a tangent now, Sin?" I snap, hating how irritable I sound. But the longer she drags out this subject, the more raw my wounds become.

"Oh yeah, sorry. Anyway… which band member is your favourite? I personally think Jake is the hottest. When he opens his mouth and sings with that delicious, raspy tone, I can actually feel my panties melting. I have an idea which member is your favourite, so tell me if I'm right," she sings, with a bright smile, oblivious to the knife she has just inadvertently stabbed into my heart.

I don't know what to say, I'm frozen to the spot. I know the answer I would've given, but that was a long time ago. I used to argue with her all the time over who was the best band member. Now I can't even say her name, it tastes like ash in my mouth. I shouldn't be able to live while she doesn't get to.

"Is there a point to this story?" I hate how vile my voice sounds, and I need this conversation to be over, but Sin either isn't able to read people, or she chooses not to. Surely she can see the pain etched across my face, but she simply ignores it.

I hate the way her face falters, that bright smile dimming, thanks to the darkness that consumes me. I have an incredible fucking ability to bring down everyone around me, and I warned her of this many times, the more she tried to make friends with me when I got here. I didn't want a friend—I still don't—but I can't deny that having Sin in my life can sometimes be nice. Other times, like now, it's torture.

"Yes, of course, there's a point. Now, stop being a miserable bitch and tell me who your favourite is," she snaps, that smile returning to her very thin face. Even though she has put on some weight since being here, in an attempt to reach a healthy weight, she still has more to go to stop her features looking so pronounced. I hate when I can see all her bony structures. It makes me mad she was so beaten down she got to that stage. Nobody stood by her side to support her. I may have nobody in my life, but that means there's no one to hurt me.

Groaning, I reply. "Fine. I quite liked the drummer, Dylan. The one who writes all their songs. But that was a long time ago. Apparently, he's a massive twat now." Just because I try to keep away from anything that might trigger old memories, doesn't mean I don't see the news. His fall from grace over the last year has been well documented. His addiction and his volatile, spiralling behaviour have been put out there for all the world to see. I actually feel a little sorry for him. I would've hated to fall apart and have the whole word watch, which is exactly what's happening with him. Then again, he doesn't exactly do a lot to avoid the press' attention, from what I've seen.

Sin's excitement seems to peak and her eyes widen as she continues to bob up and down with joy. "I knew Dylan is who you would pick. That's why I knew you would like this news so frickin' much."

I pause, giving her the opportunity to go on, but she just stares at me like I'm supposed to guess the track her mind is now on. Getting her to focus and just tell the story is like trying to get a kid to sleep after giving them a shitload of Halloween sweets and let them stay up late to eat it. It's almost an impossible task, which is why I speak through gritted teeth, trying not to lose my temper with her, "Sin… for the love of all that is holy… get to the fucking point!"

She lets out a huff, like she's annoyed, but she's still smiling so she can't be too pissed. "He's here!"

My brow furrows, and my brain hurts trying to keep up with her ranting. I feel like I'm getting whiplash trying to follow what she's saying. "Who?" I ask, when she doesn't appear to be continuing with that particular train of thought.

"Dylan Matthews. He was admitted here around five days ago. He's detoxing at the moment, so he's confined to his room…probably more out of choice. I remember how awful I felt during my detox period, and he sure as fuck is on more than I was," Sin explains, giving me a rare insight into her story.

Although we have been friends for just less than a month, she doesn't really say much about her story. I know the basics, most of which I've learnt from group therapy. She's had a shit life, which culminated in her self-harming to the point she needed hospital care. She's been here ever since.

Sin clears her throat, pulling me back to the present as I try to forget about all the pain this young girl has gone through. Especially since she's only two years younger than me. "What do you think?" she asks, and I try to rack my brain to think of what question she could have possibly asked that I missed.

"I don't know." I hope she can't tell that I don't have

a fucking clue what I'm talking about.

Sin rolls her eyes. She knows! "Dylan. What do you think about Dylan fucking Matthews being here in our facility?" she screeches, before looking around to make sure nobody else has heard her.

Although she's a massive fucking gossip with me, she doesn't actually share these secrets with anyone but me. Everyone in here has a story, and it's one that should only be shared on their terms. So, sometimes hearing it from Sin feels wrong and invasive, but I made her promise the only way she could tell me all the juicy details—as she refers to it—is if I'm the only person she tells. I know I will maintain their confidentiality, and she gets to have her gossipy moment.

"I guessed he would be in rehab. I just didn't know which one. I saw on the news they said he was taking some time out of the public eye to concentrate on his songwriting, and to take time to reflect on his recent behaviour. It couldn't have sounded more like bullshit if they'd actually tried." Sin laughs, nodding her head in agreement.

"Yeah, it was all a bit hush-hush about what actually happened. I'm not even sure the media knows why he was arrested. Not properly. It's all been very cloak-and-dagger," she explains, and I agree.

"Hopefully, he gets the help he needs." I try to keep the scepticism out of my voice. There are many people who get admitted here, spend a few days, or a couple of weeks in the facility, and they become well enough to go home. Every time a new person comes and goes, my heart aches. It makes me feel like there's something wrong with me. I can't be the only person who comes in here to get help and gets worse.

"I can't wait to see if he's as hot as he is on television."

"I thought you said you saw him?" I ask, wondering where she got this information if she didn't actually see him.

"So I overheard Dr. Hughes talking to Lyle about him. Apparently, she's going to be his personal psychiatrist. Lyle was saying he shouldn't get any special treatment, and that he should be treated the same as everyone else in here. I think he sounded jealous, if I'm being honest," she explains, getting worked up about the possibility she's stumbled on another piece of gossip. But it's hardly fresh news. Anyone with eyes can see Lyle has a thing for Dr. Hughes. He watches her like a teenage boy watches their favourite porn film.

"I would imagine they need to keep him away from everyone. This place will be like a fucking circus if word gets out that he's here," I muse, more to myself than to Sin, but she nods her head and replies, anyway.

"Well, in all the paperwork, he's registered under a different name. I think many people here wouldn't have a clue who he is, anyway. Most are either too old or too drugged up to know who he is." We both look around the room as she says that, and I can't help but agree. This place is like a fucking zombie town. People are in their own little worlds, so spaced out on medication to even know where they are, or they are too old to remember they've just eaten breakfast.

"Well, I hope everyone gives him the space he needs. He clearly needs help. I hope this place can give him it. So, try to hold back your fangirling when he starts to participate in group stuff. Give him a chance to be a nobody for a while. It will probably be a nice break for him, out of the public eye. I just hope this place can help him…" I let the end of my sentence go unfinished. But I think Sin knows I was about to say… *Since they can't help me*.

I seem to be the only one in this hellhole that is getting worse. Each day, I feel as though I am losing touch with reality more and more. I don't know what's real and what isn't. I can't remember the last time I had a good night's sleep. Slender Man haunts my nightmares. While I sleep, he destroys my mind and body, but now he's started to destroy my soul, both while I'm asleep and awake. I feel like I'm losing the Addison I was before, and he's stealing me away piece by piece. I know I should tell my therapists about him, but I don't want them to know I'm getting worse. I will never get out of here. So, instead, I am suffering in silence. Hoping that one day soon, Slender Man will go all the way and end my pain. I don't know how much longer I can live like this. Not living is looking like a pretty fucking good option.

Three
DYLAN

They say time flies when you're having fun, so it should've been obvious that these last few days would drag out longer than a toddler trying to avoid going to bed and requesting just one more glass of water. I can't even joke about it. The last few days—I don't even know how many it's been—have been fucking horrendous. Obviously, I knew detoxing was going to be tough, but I was nowhere near prepared.

The feeling of ants underneath my skin worsened, and I scratched my skin until it bled. My stomach felt like it was tied up in knots, and nausea soon turned to physical vomiting. I threw up so much I didn't even bother getting up off the bathroom floor, choosing to lie there with my head resting on the toilet seat in between bouts of sickness. A sheen of sweat covered my trembling body, and I felt like I was dying. In fact, I remember asking

Dr. Hughes to let me die during one of her visits.

I have to give Dr. Hughes credit. She was here every day, sitting with me and helping me through the pain. There were a few times she asked me if I wanted medication to dull the detox effects, but we both knew that if I took them, it would prolong the detox and I would still need to learn to live without them. So, I continually told her no, and she sat with me, holding my hand to help me through it.

Today is officially the first day I've been able to stand upright without feeling dizzy and sick. I've managed to shower, which is a fucking win because I haven't been able to do that since I got here. I had no idea how weak I would feel without the drugs and booze. I hate the fact that it's left me feeling vulnerable and exposed. Dr. Hughes says that being raw is exactly where she needs me to be. It's like wiping the slate clean, and now's my chance to re-write my story. To forget the past, and to learn how to survive without relying on illicit substances to survive.

Lance, one nurse that's been looking after me, sticks his head into my room. I've been stuck in this room since I got here, which means I've had everything I need brought to me. Normally, Lance brings me the new antidepressant medication they started me on, and my breakfast. So, I'm shocked this morning to see he only has a little pot of pills.

"Morning, Drummer. How are you doing this morning?" he asks, and I can't help but roll my eyes. He uses the nickname *Drummer* in a sarcastic tone. Apparently, while I was off my tits when I first got here, I asked Lance to do something, and when he refused, I may have said that dreaded phrase, 'Don't you know who I am?' I may have also said, 'I'm a drummer'. Hence the sarcastic nickname he's been using ever since. I know he's joking, and actually, it makes him a lot more relatable to me. He's seen me at my worst over the last few days, and has never even looked at me in a judgemental way. Even after I pissed myself as I lost control of my entire body. He helped to wash me down as best he could, given I couldn't even climb into the shower.

"Nurse Lancey, you look like shit, as always. How are you doing?" I joke, deflecting his question back to him. When he started using Drummer as a nickname, I started making fun of the fact that he's a male nurse. Don't get me wrong, I'm not sexist. I actually think he's a fucking great nurse who works far too many hours and gets very little reward for all the hard work he puts in. But I have to have something to take the piss out of him about if he's going to continue calling me Drummer.

"Don't deflect, asshole. I'm here with your meds, so I actually need to know how you feel. I'm not asking because I care," he grunts, with the hint of a smile. He may come across as unprofessional, or even rude, but in reality, he's exactly what I need. I've spent my entire adult life surrounded by yes-men. People who would rather tell me everything's okay, and give me whatever I want rather than challenge me. So, no matter how much I fucking hate him arguing with me, it's a relief.

"I don't think you're allowed to call me an asshole," I state, and he just laughs.

"I am if you are one. Now… stop deflecting and tell me how you feel."

Taking a big, deep breath and releasing it in a huff, I open myself up like he's spent the last few days teaching me how to do. "I'm feeling better than I was yesterday. There are still times when the pull is strong, and I'm so fucking desperate for a drink or some pills. It has me antsy and on edge. I've almost stopped scratching at my skin until it bleeds. It's only when the itching becomes uncontrollable. Mostly, I feel a bit caged. But it's a bit of a catch-twenty-two. I want to get out of this room so fucking much, I'm done looking at the same four walls.

"At the same time, the idea of what could be on the other side scares the shit out of me. At least in here I hold a certain level of control and I know what to expect, but out there is unknown territory, and that's fucking terrifying." Once I talk, I can't fucking stop. I hate opening up, but over the last few days, we've had the same routine. Lance comes in to give me my medication. We banter for a bit, and then he forces me to tell him how I'm feeling. It's not something that comes naturally to me, and he really had to work at getting me to open up. He can tell when I'm bullshitting and just telling him what he wants to hear. Eventually, telling him what I'm feeling became the norm, and I've learnt to trust him.

He smiles, a big, genuine smile that lets me know he's proud of the fact that I not only told him how I felt, but I told him the truth. I opened myself up to be vulnerable, which is not something I feel very comfortable with. Lance hands the pills over to me, and while I'm taking them, he talks. "I know it's scary. You're so used to being the one in control of everyone else. But the one thing you need to learn is that it was all a lie. How can you be the one in control, when pills and booze had control over you?" he asks, and I have an 'ah-ha' moment where I realise what he's saying is true. I've never really had control of anything, and that's a fucking terrifying thought.

Sitting beside me on the bed, Lance continues. "Look, Dyl. You're stronger than you realise. You have just spent the last nine days in detox, and not once did you let Dr. Hughes help you or take anything to help you get through it. That was your first real taste of control. You took your detox by the horns and you owned it. You should be really proud of that. But now it's time to move on to the next stage of your rehab."

Brow furrowed in confusion, I ask, "What next stage?" I thought detoxing and getting clean was the whole reason I'm here. So now I'm clean, what could be next? I thought I would go home now that I'm sober, but Lance looks like he has other plans.

"Now you've detoxed, we'll expect you to follow the scheduled timetable that's over there on the wall." He points to the noticeboard near the door, and sure enough, there's a piece of paper stuck to the board. Has that always been there, or did someone just put it there? In fact, I'm not even completely sure I remember the noticeboard being there.

Lance must see my confusion and continues to explain. "Everyone here follows a schedule. It will tell you on there what times we expect you to arrive. There will be group therapy, solo therapy, and art therapy scheduled, along with mealtimes, downtime, and sports or recreational opportunities. We'll also update it whenever we have special occasions. So, in a few weeks, there will be a talent show, and we expect everyone to take part. It'll be a whole-day event, and you will spend time in art therapy preparing. I know you haven't chosen an art therapy yet, which is perfectly fine. You will see on the schedule that just for this week we've assigned you a session in each, so you can try them out. We have not assigned you to music therapy, as we want to push you out of your comfort zone. You've always had music, and it's never been enough to keep you away from your vices, so we need to find something that will. You will still have free time to play, and you can even ask for music time instead of something like sports or even rec time. It's your choice. By the end of the week you have to tell Lyle on the front desk which therapy you want to stick with, and he'll draw up your permanent timetable. Keep your eye on the timetable, as it can change when other important events come up, or if a staff member is unavailable. Things like that. Do you have any questions?"

I sit there in shock, not entirely sure what the fuck to say. The idea of doing any of it is terrifying, and I'm not sure I want to. But, like Lance said, I'm stronger than I think. Besides, if I stay in this room any longer, I may really go insane.

I walk over to the timetable and take it in. So, I should be having breakfast now, and then I need to go along to group therapy in meeting room three.

I feel like a child on their first day of school. I skipped breakfast because I was too fucking nervous to eat anything. I don't want to do any form of counselling, but the idea of sitting in a group is fucking terrifying. I think it's the unknown. I have no idea what they will expect of me, or what I'm supposed to contribute to the group. Nerves bubble in my stomach as I make my way to meeting room three.

The door's wide open, and I tentatively lean my head around the doorframe to peek into the room. It's not a large room, but there's a big window along one wall, which floods the room with light, making the room seem a lot larger than it really is.

Along the opposite wall, to the right of the door, is lined with two large tables. One holds a large hot water holder, which, given the mugs beside it, I would guess they are to make tea or coffee. The table beside it seems to have some pastries—croissants, pain au chocolat, cinnamon rolls, and more. There are also some doughnuts and biscuits. It's not a bad spread, and normally I would be straight into them, but I barely have an appetite after the detox. Add in the nerves I feel bubbling under the surface about this session, I'm far too nauseous to eat—for now. Once I've got used to this event, I no doubt will want to sample some of the delicious-looking pastries. I didn't have any breakfast, after all.

There are no other people in the room, and at first I wonder if I've got the wrong damn room. Until I look at the clock on the wall above the food and drink table. I choose to ignore the fact that the clock is covered over with bars. I'm around fifteen minutes early. Before attending this group session, my timetable stated I should be at breakfast, and so I imagine that's where everyone currently is.

In the centre of the room, there's a circle of chairs, all facing inwards, so when we're all sitting down, we'll be able to see each other. I debate sitting down, but I can't bring my legs to move. I simply stare at the chairs, hating the idea of sitting so close to people, and being so visible. I'm supposed to be hiding who I really am to prevent the media from finding out where I am, but being so open and visible in a room full of people doesn't feel like the way to do that.

Coward! I think to myself. The nerves have nothing at all to do with fear of being discovered, or someone leaking my location. My anxiety is more to do with having to open my soul and let people see the gaping hole and darkness inside. Maybe I can just bullshit my way through? Make people think that I'm miraculously healed so I can get the fuck out of here. My biggest worry is that when I finally get outside of this facility, I may not be able to stick to the sobriety I've worked so hard to achieve over the last ten days. I think this is the longest time I've been without a substance fuelling my body since I was around sixteen years old.

"Are you just going to stand in the doorway, or should I push past you? There are only a couple of jam doughnuts, and I need to get one before Billy eats them all," says a voice from behind me.

Turning, I step out of the way in time to see a middle-aged woman with ginger hair walking past me into the room. Her shoulder-length hair looks neat and freshly cut, and her face is obviously done up with as much make-up that's allowed here. Her black trousers are pressed perfectly to create a line down the middle, and her emerald green silk shirt goes nicely with her hair. If it wasn't for the wristband on her arm, I would have no idea this woman's a patient here, instead of one of the counsellors.

The few people I've passed around here so far are either still in their pyjamas, or they're wearing typical lounging clothes. I haven't come across anyone so well dressed. I mean, we're allowed to wear whatever clothes we want, whatever we feel comfortable in. So, if this is what makes her feel best, that's all that matters.

"Do you want anything, or are you not joining the group?" she asks, before adding, "I'm Sally-Anne, by the way." She has a big smile on her face as she picks up one of the jam doughnuts and bites right into it, sugar coating her mouth.

I give her a small smile, my heart racing as I decide whether or not I need to lie. I know Dr. Hughes admitted me into the facility under a fake surname, but I'm still Dylan. As I feel my palms sweating, I panic and realise I should've spoken to Dr. Hughes about this before just turning up at the group session. I settle for simply being polite. "Hi, I'm Dylan… I'm new."

I didn't really need to add the fact that I'm new. I may as well have a giant fucking sign on my forehead. She doesn't comment and just continues to munch on her doughnut. Before either of us have a chance to say anything more, two more people arrive. One's a large, white man with broad shoulders and a big beer belly that his t-shirt is only just able to contain. I'm not even sure he knows I'm standing here. He's hyperfocused on the doughnuts. This must be Billy.

He's followed closely behind by a tall, thin black man who walks with his eyes downcast, not looking around. He almost looks twitchy and doesn't even look at the food table. He just makes his way towards one of the seats and sits down. His hands are in his lap, and he laces his fingers together, as he picks at the skin around his nails. His eyes continue to be downcast, refusing to make eye contact with anyone else in the room.

Dr. Hughes is next to appear, and as she walks past me, she tugs on my arm. "Come inside, Dylan, and take a seat. You're making the place look untidy," she jokes, as she heads over to the coffee machine. She pours herself one before looking over at me. "Want one?"

I look around and see that Billy and Sally-Anne have both taken their seats, and they appear to be arguing over the last jam doughnut. The other guy looks like he's trying to watch what they're doing without actually raising his gaze. Once I see they are out of earshot, I whisper my concerns to Dr. Hughes. "I don't think this whole group thing is a good idea. I mean, who do I say I am? What is my story? Obviously, I can't tell them the truth."

Dr. Hughes takes a gulp of her coffee and releases a little sigh, like she's been desperate for it. She reaches over and makes a cup for me, before handing it over with a smile. "Dylan, you don't have to hide or put on an act. Everyone in this room signed a non-disclosure agreement the minute they walked into this building, as did you. And when the session starts, we'll remind them that this group's a safe space. Whatever is discussed in the group stays in the group. You have to be prepared to open up and show the real version of yourself, Dylan. Or this process won't work. So, no hiding. No stories. No lies. Just the real you. Understand?"

My heart races and I can feel myself hyperventilating. My palms are sweating and my skin's starting with that horrendous itching sensation. This is more than just panic, this is an overwhelming urge to have a drink or to pop a pill. I can feel my brain working overtime, thinking about where I could get something I shouldn't. I'm even considering breaking into the medication cupboard, as I'm sure they will have exactly what I'm looking for.

"Breathe, Dylan. Listen to my voice and take some deep breaths." I can feel Dr. Hughes' voice, although it sounds as though I am hearing her through cotton wool in my ears. She seems far away, and it's not until I feel her hand on my arm that I'm brought back to the present.

My breathing slows, and I feel like I have control over my body again, but only just. Dr. Hughes holds out the coffee she made for me, and I reach up to take it, hating that my hand has a slight tremor to it. "I don't think I can do this," I mutter.

Dr. Hughes reassures me, as well as telling me to help myself to food. She's concerned my blood sugar is too low if I'm not eating. As I reach for the croissant, we are all halted by a screeching noise.

"Holy fucking shitballs. Dylan fucking Matthews. Is it… are you… I mean, real?"

I look over to the door, where the high-pitched squeal came from and a petite girl with bright blue and green hair is staring right at me, her hands held up to her mouth in shock. Her eyes look like they are bugging out of her head. It's almost comical. Clearly, this little pixie of a girl knows who I am.

Before I have chance to stress over her knowing who I am, and that she could break the nice little bubble I've created here, I notice the beauty standing next to her.

Long brunette hair that appears to fall in waves past her chest and down her back. She's taller than the little pixie standing next to her, but she's probably around five foot four compared to my six feet. The dark leggings and off-the-shoulder t-shirt give us a slight hint of the curves that are lying underneath. It's hard to tell for sure, but the slight patch of skin that's visible between one side of her t-shirt and her leggings shows she's in good shape. That little patch of silky, creamy skin is sexier than anything I've seen in a long time.

I'm used to women with their tits and asses hanging out as they throw themselves at me. And I don't say no… why would I? But this woman, despite the haunted look on her pale face, she's the epitome of beauty. Her emerald green eyes fix on me, as is everyone around me, I'm sure, after the pixie's little outburst aimed at me. I don't know what it is, but there's something in the way she looks at me. Her broken, desolate soul is visible to me in her haunted stare. I connect with her in an instant. My darkness recognises hers, and there's nothing I want more than to find out more about this beauty.

"Okay, Sin. Please, can you take your seat? I will do the introductions, if that's okay with you?" Dr. Hughes says, the note of authority taking over her voice. I don't think I've heard her use her professional, stern voice. I guess I have been relatively well-behaved so far.

The pixie girl—Sin—goes to take her seat next to Billy, and Dr. Hughes takes the seat beside her, continuously sipping on her coffee. I'm watching what they are doing out of the corner of my eye, but my focus is on the beauty who is currently frozen in the doorway.

I watch as her gaze trails over my body, taking in my ripped jeans and dark t-shirt. I don't miss the way she bites her lower lip, and fuck is that like an instant connection to my dick. Those plump, pink lips are puffy and the more she bites her lower lip, the harder my cock becomes. This is the last fucking thing I need. Getting a hard-on in the middle of a group counselling session is not the smartest move, but it's not like I have a choice in the matter. This girl is fucking gorgeous, even with her pale skin and haunted gaze.

"Okay, guys. Please, can everyone take their seats so we can get started? If you need a drink or anything to eat, please get it now so we can begin," states Dr. Hughes, breaking the trance we appear to be in.

Billy gets up and heads towards the pastry table to grab something else—since he and Sally-Anne ate all the doughnuts—and he piles a couple of items onto his plate. The girl walks quickly and slides into the nearest empty seat beside Dr. Hughes. The little pixie girl, whose eyes I can feel watching my every move, goes over to the drinks table. She makes two coffees and hands one to the beauty with a smile. The way her face lights up as she tastes the delicious caffeine, I wish I had a camera to take a picture right now, as it's the perfect shot. I may only be a bit of a hobby photographer, but I can appreciate beauty when I see it.

Once everyone is seated, I sit down in the only free seat. I'm directly opposite the stunning brunette, with Sally-Anne on my right and the shy black man on my left. As soon as we're all settled, Dr. Hughes begins the introductions.

"Morning, everyone. I hope you're all well today. As I'm sure you have seen, we have a new member in our group and I hope you will all join me in making Dylan feel welcome within the group."

Mumbles of *hello* or *welcome* cut through Dr. Hughes' speech, but she looks pleased everyone wants to welcome me. I enjoy the way the brunette says welcome, that hint of a smile just gracing her face.

"Before we begin the introductions, I want to remind you of the non-disclosure agreements you all signed when you were admitted to Lakeridge, and the confidentiality you promised to maintain. I believe that every one of you has a right to privacy, but some need it more than others. Dylan has people on the outside world who would give anything to find out information on his whereabouts and his condition. We've worked hard to give him anonymity. He has the right to heal, in exactly the same way you are all doing, without the threat of people finding out hanging over his head." She pauses to take a sip of her coffee, but nobody moves. They're all enraptured by what Dr. Hughes is saying.

"This group has always been, and will always be, a safe space for every one of you. So, I need promises from you all that nothing discussed in this group will ever leave it. Nobody on the outside world can ever know Dylan is here, and I need your word that you will honour his anonymity and respect his right to privacy."

Everyone nods their heads, and some even say they give their word, and I can't help but smile. I don't know why, but I feel like maybe I can trust this group. As I look around, I can tell they all have their own issues. I mean… of course they do, otherwise they wouldn't be here. What I mean is they are just as desperate to find the same safe space I crave.

"Right, since we have got that out of the way, let's start with the introductions. We're going to do names, one fact about yourself, and one thing you want to get out of being here at Lakeridge. Who is going to start?"

Sally-Anne's hand flies up into the air, while everyone else seems to cower away at the idea of talking. "My name is Sally-Anne. I have two beautiful children, five and three. They're my life, and when I'm not being their momma, I love to paint. During my time here, I would like to become as strong as I was before my husband left and took my children. I want to be the strong, independent woman I used to be so I can get my kids back." She sounds so light and positive, right until the end. Upon the mention of getting her kids back, her voice breaks and you can see tears collecting in her eyes, giving them a glassy appearance. She clearly loves her kids, but there's obviously a lot more to the story. I know from experience that children's social care is more concerned with keeping children with their mothers, and taking them away is incredibly fucking difficult. So, I'm guessing Sally-Anne was given more than enough chances, but I don't want to judge her until I've heard the whole story.

Dr. Hughes thanks Sally-Anne for her contribution

and turns to the other side of the circle, looking towards the pixie girl next, who grimaces before she starts. "I'm Lucinda, but everyone calls me Sin. I was one of six children and my parents barely knew who I was. They kicked me out at fifteen and I lived on the streets for a few months. I celebrated my sweet sixteenth in a cardboard box with a cup of soup from the soup kitchen. While I'm here, I want to learn how to cope with stressors better and build up my self-esteem. I never want to be in a situation again where I settle, simply because I can't do any better."

I see the beauty opposite me smile at Sin, like she's so proud of her, and I can tell they're real friends. I didn't even consider the possibility of making friends whilst I'm here. Other than my bandmates, I don't think I have anyone I could really class as a friend. I have people I pay to be part of my life, like my assistant and my manager. But if I have to pay for them, they aren't really friends.

Then, in no particular order within the circle, Dr. Hughes instructs Billy and who I now know to be Lenny to give their introductions. But I have to confess I'm not fully paying attention. I'm distracted by the girl opposite, but I'm also overthinking exactly what I'm going to say.

Thankfully, Dr. Hughes indicates she should go first, and I wait with bated breath to hear her name. "Hey, so my name is Addison, but everyone calls me Addy. I'm a loner and enjoy doing jigsaw puzzles by myself. I would love to just get out of Lakeridge… I mean to take with me what I've learnt to live a happier life."

What a steaming pile of horseshit. I think the only honest thing she said in that statement was her name. Her tone was dry, her voice monotone. It's like she was reciting a speech from a brochure. When she said she hopes to just get out of here, I could tell she meant it. She really doesn't like it here, but she feels the need to hide why. I mean, everyone is here by force, and so we all have some issue with being here. It's probably something we all have in common, so why hide it? It's like she's trying to be the perfect patient. I wonder if everyone else can see how fake she is, or is it just me?

"Excellent, now it's your turn, Dylan." Dr. Hughes points at me, which is unnecessary as everyone in the group knows who I am at this point.

I give them a big fake-as-fuck smile before starting the speech I've been preparing over the last few minutes while everyone else has been speaking. "Hey, I'm Dylan. As I'm sure you guessed by Sin's outburst, I'm famous on the outside. I'm the drummer for a band called The Catastrophists. I'm grateful for you all giving me my privacy. I would like to leave here as sober as I am now and continue down this path for good."

I don't know why I decided to be so honest. It just felt like the right thing to do. I know I shouldn't trust them, but I don't really have much choice. If Dr. Hughes reports back to the courts that I'm not co-operating in my rehab journey, I will need to finish the rest of my sentence in prison. I'm too fucking pretty for prison.

"Great, now we have everyone introduced, I think we should talk about why opening up in a group session is so important. I know most of you have had a lot of group sessions, so this may feel irrelevant to you, but it isn't. Who wants to start by telling us what we can gain by talking in a group?" Dr. Hughes asks, and despite not knowing these people very well, I could have predicted that Sally-Anne's hand would shoot up before Dr. Hughes has even finished her sentence.

Dr. Hughes nods for Sally-Anne to give her answer. "Well, I think one of the main benefits to talking in a group is that it's great to hear that you are not alone. I enjoy hearing that there are other people around me that have experienced similar or worse things than me. I don't mean to sound harsh, but knowing someone else is worse than me makes me feel a little better."

I can't help the sarcastic comment that drips out of my mouth. "Well, I'm glad you are benefitting from our shitty lives." I know I shouldn't have said anything, and I wait for Dr. Hughes to chastise me, but Sin interrupts us.

"That's not entirely fair. I know what you mean, Sal. Sometimes seeing what other people are going through, knowing they can beat worse things than you are living with, it pushes you. If they can do it, so can you."

I don't know why I'm in such an asshole mood today, and it's not even that I don't agree with what they're saying. They're probably right, but my anxiety's in full swing, and sadly, when my body feels as though it's in fight-or-flight mode, it responds with sarcasm.

"So, other people need to go through shit just so you can pull your big girl panties up and get on with life? You don't need to rely on other people to know you are strong. You shouldn't ever rely on someone else. Just live your own fucking life and don't concern yourself with other people's shit, as you never really know what they're going through."

I regret it the moment it leaves my mouth. As soon as

her little pixie face scrunches up and tears fill her eyes, I'm filled with shame. I don't even know what my point is. I just wanted to clarify that what you see someone going through might not be the real deal. I can put on one hell of a show, so nobody knows what's really going on beneath the surface. It's hard enough trying to stop myself from sinking into the abyss, without knowing someone else is relying on me too.

Dr. Hughes chastises me, not only for snapping at Sin, but for swearing. Though, before she finishes, Addy cuts in. "Who the fuck do you think you are telling people how they need to get over their own shit? I happen to agree with you when you said that people should only be concerned with their own issues, not someone else's battle, but there are much better ways of voicing it. You might be new here and not know how group sessions work, but you are a functioning member of humanity. You know how to communicate like a normal guy. So why don't you put your cock away along with your ego, because there's no need for a pissing contest here. We know you're a big deal to the outside world, and every single person in this room has promised to give you anonymity. The least you can do is show us some respect, you pretentious asshole."

Everyone around the room looks stunned. I get the impression that Addy's speech may well be the most this girl has ever talked. I know exactly how I should respond to her comment. I should mumble an apology and just let it go to move on. But, my pride is butthurt, and my cock is straining at the fire in her emerald green eyes. I like a girl with fight and she sure as fuck just showed plenty.

"Believe me, sweetheart, you would know if I had

my cock out, and there would be no need at all to measure it," I reply with a cocky grin on my face. I may as well be holding a sign saying, 'I know I'm an asshole, I can't help it'.

Her face scrunches up in distaste, and her eyes glare at me. If she could shoot laser beams, I would be six feet under by now. "Typical asshole. Fuck you. Stop thinking it's all about your cock. Grow the fuck up, or get the hell out of our session." Her voice cuts through the air like a knife, and everyone in the circle appears frozen, just waiting to see what happens next.

I don't know what it is, but I'm enjoying this way too much. When she first walked into this room, Addy was shy, vacant, almost empty, yet now her eyes are full of fire. It's like arguing with me has lit a fire inside her, and suddenly she's burning bright, finding her strength. If I have to play the role of an asshole to watch her come to life again, that's something I don't mind doing.

"You can fuck me anytime you want, sweetheart. You just have to ask." I pucker my lips and blow her a kiss at the end, the cocky grin spreading across my face afterwards.

Addy falters when she sees my lips pucker. It's a more exaggerated movement than I would actually use, but given the way she bites her lower lip, nibbling it between her teeth, I think she enjoyed it a little too much.

Before we have a chance to argue any further, Dr. Hughes steps in. "Okay, enough of that. Dylan, if you can't behave, say nothing at all. Same for you, Addy. I'm shocked at you. Most days I can't even get you to tell me how you feel, and now you are shouting and swearing, the most animated I've seen you since you got here."

I knew it. I knew I was having a positive effect on her. Now she's looking at me with pure hatred in her eyes, and fuck does that go straight to my cock. I know there are a million reasons I shouldn't pursue this girl, but that just makes me want her even more. Maybe if we do a little more arguing, she will be ripe for a bit of hate-sex.

I don't know if sex between residents is banned, but I'm guessing since nobody has told me, I can claim plausible deniability. Don't get me wrong, I know it's probably not a good idea to fuck someone who's an inpatient in a secure mental facility. Fuck knows what she did to get admitted. But that's the thing, I only want one night. Right now, thoughts of her are filling my brain, and I'm thinking of more ways I can piss her off, just enough that the sex will be steamy and full of anger. So, when I fuck her and get her out of my system, I can stop thinking about her.

Admittedly, it's not a great plan. Winding up a crazy lady until she is pissed enough that her only option is to fuck her anger out on me. But, it's the only plan I have. I've only been in the same room as this girl for around half an hour, and already I can't get her out of my head. No girl has ever flooded my senses the way she does. It's like she's everywhere, and my body craves her. My darkness calls out to hers, and we can dive into the abyss together.

Four
ADDY

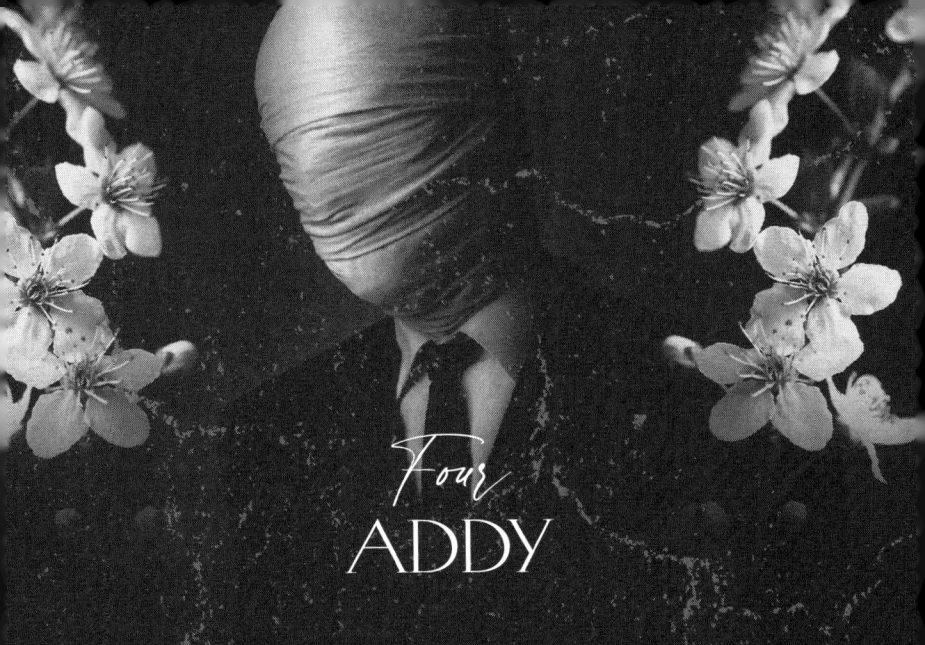

I SPEND THE REST OF THE DAY SEETHING, TRYING NOT TO FOCUS on that pretentious asshole. They always say not to meet your idols and they sure as fuck were right. Dylan is nowhere near what I was expecting. Don't get me wrong, it's obvious that Dylan would need to have more than his fair share of issues to have ended up here. But that doesn't mean he has to be a dick about it.

Dr. Hughes has made it clear after our group session she plans for Dylan and me to have a short session, just the two of us, to hash out our issues. Apparently, the hostility I have towards him will only cause problems within our group sessions. Once the groups are selected, they try not to swap them around too much, as we all kinda develop a bond together, and that's when we are more likely to open up and see improvements in our mental health. However, if our animosity continues to bubble over, Dr.

Hughes feels it will continue to muddy the waters and make it difficult for our group to function effectively.

So, tomorrow, instead of being in the group session, Dylan and I are expected to sit down together and sort our shit out. The problem is, I don't really give a shit. It is irrelevant to me if I like him or not, nor would it impact my engagement with the group. What Dr. Hughes doesn't realise is that—except for my outburst today—nothing in the group session is real for me. I have done the whole honesty thing, and nobody listened. In fact, they thought I was getting more mentally ill, and as a result, they pumped me full of more drugs until I became a zombie. But even then, I didn't get better. So, when I meet Dylan tomorrow, I will do what I have been doing for the last couple of weeks—I will put on my best mask. I will pretend everything is well between us, and I will make sure nobody doubts that I'm on the path to healing. I worry if I don't do this, I will end up committed here indefinitely.

As the day goes on, and the sun sets, my heart starts to race and the panic I feel every night before I'm expected to go to bed cripples me. I sit in my room, not wanting to be near other people. The closer it comes to the nighttime lockdown, the more terrified I become.

Not everyone in the facility is on a full lockdown. Most can leave their room and go to the kitchen area to make a drink, but the majority are so drugged up that they sleep until morning. Some are locked away… 'for their own good'. Which I find incredibly hard to believe. Given the reduced staffing levels overnight, it's more to do with the fact that they don't have enough to adequately care for everyone if they're moving around. Whereas, if they are locked in their room, one person can monitor everyone from the security cameras.

Initially, I begged and pleaded to be locked down, convinced the Slender Man couldn't get to me if the doors were locked and there were security cameras watching my every move. I even got myself put on suicide watch for a while in the hope they would find something when they check on me, but it never helped. But, as Dr. Manning so helpfully reminded me, delusions are not something that will show up on a camera, and a locked door won't stop them. I know he's right. I know there's no way the Slender Man could be real. There are no fucking faceless men roaming around the halls, after all. But, when he's near me, my delusions are so strong, so prominent, I can't help but be convinced they are real.

Sitting on my bed, I stare blankly at the white walls, wondering how long I will be able to stay awake for tonight. I ponder ideas for how I can make it look like I'm taking my medication, whilst secretly not taking them. They make me go to sleep, and that's the worst thing in the world to me. But, the problem is, they are used to residents refusing to take their meds, or faking taking them. So they stand there and watch you swallow them. They even check your mouth to make sure you haven't stashed them under your tongue. If it looks like you aren't compliant, they inject you with them, anyway. There's no escaping them. I've thought of everything.

A knock on the open door pulls my attention to Dr. Manning, my assigned psychiatrist, who is standing in the doorway, waiting for my permission to enter.

"Evening, Addison," he greets me, as he walks into my room and pulls the desk chair around so it's facing me and he's sitting beside the bed.

"Dr. Manning, I thought you would have gone home by now. And how many times do I have to ask you to call me Addy?" I say through gritted teeth. I don't know what it is about this man, but there's something about him that sets me on edge. I don't know if it's because I know that every single time he interacts with me, he's judging me. Whatever it is, I can't help but feel like I'm walking on eggshells around him. I feel a shiver travel down my spine, that ever-present reminder when I'm around him, my subconscious' way of telling me we aren't sure if he's really the friend he makes out to be.

"You know I like to check on my patients before I go home for the evening. I also know that the last couple of nights, the staff have reported you have been having nightmares. You wouldn't go into detail when they asked you about it, but they reported screams." He looks almost disappointed in me. Like screaming while I'm experiencing the worst nightmare of my life is something to be ashamed of. Maybe this is why I feel like I don't like the guy. His judgemental attitude isn't helping right now.

I can't help but snap at him as the anger bubbles away under the surface. "If they heard me shouting and screaming, why didn't they bother to come and check on me? To wake me up?" I hear the plea in my voice at the end. I want them to wake me from the nightmares, and when they don't, it just prolongs them.

"They have instructions not to wake anyone in the middle of a night terror. It can be very harmful to people.

It can result in people becoming dissociated, confused between reality and delusions. That is the last thing we want to happen to you. Because your delusions already feel so real to you, it wouldn't be too difficult to push you over that edge, and you end up living your delusions."

Ha. I want to laugh and tell him it's too fucking late for that. I'm already living with them. Slender Man may haunt my nightmares, but the idea of him, the suffering he puts me through, that consumes my every waking minute and I fucking hate it. At this point, I'm not sure waking me up could do any more damage.

Dr. Manning can see I'm not happy with his decision, but I keep quiet anyway. If I say any more and he realises I've been lying to him this whole time, nothing good will come from that. I tried telling him how real my delusions felt. I tried showing him all the marks Slender Man left on my body, but he was just convinced I was living my delusions or having a psychotic breakdown and was self-harming myself. He put me on meds that made me a zombie, but they didn't help. So I pretended they did until I could come off them again. The last thing I wanted was to be so docile I was an easy target for Slender Man. So, I hide the fact that my delusions are very real. It's the only way I ever stand a chance of getting out of here.

"I have a new sleeping medication for you to try. There have been good studies showing that it can lessen the impact of night terrors. In some patients, it even reduced them completely. Will you try it?" Dr. Manning asks, a hopeful look on his face.

I give him a fake smile and reply as politely as I can. "Of course. What do I have to lose?"

Dr. Manning stands up, and he walks towards the small fridge in the corner of the room, pulling out a bottle of water before returning to his seat. When he stands, Dr. Manning is tall, probably a little over six feet, but he's a little on the skinny side, making him look more lanky than lean. His dark pressed trousers and crisp white shirt hang loosely off his frame, giving the impression that there are no muscles in sight. He has a baby face, and when I first met him, I was astonished to learn he was my primary doctor. He doesn't look old enough. But he has one of those faces that looks like he couldn't grow facial hair, even if he wanted to. His thin-rimmed glasses make him look smart, but ultimately makes him look more geeky. The pocket protector he wears in his shirt breast pocket tips him over the edge into nerd.

I don't mean to judge him, but this is the guy responsible for my mental well-being. He's the one who makes all the decisions regarding my medication, and it will ultimately be his decision to release me. He will decide when I'm well enough to be let back into society. And since I'm very aware that my delusions aren't going away anytime soon, I need to work on getting to know all there is to know about Dr. Manning, so that I can effectively manipulate him into thinking I'm well enough to be released.

With a bright smile on his face, he hands the bottle of water over to me and removes a small tub of pills from his pocket. I can't see the label, but that hardly matters. If I refuse treatment, that will set us back and I need to get out of here. He pops the lid off the pill bottle and hands over one capsule. "We will start with one tablet, but there is some leeway to increase if needed. It may make you feel a little tired and drowsy when you first take it. So I recommend you get into bed straight away. I will let the nurses know we are trying this medication tonight, so you won't need any of your other ones. That way, you can go straight to sleep without being disturbed. How does that sound?"

Staring at the indistinct pill, I take a deep breath as fear of the impending sleep overwhelms me. "Can you ask them to please wake me up if I'm screaming? If the nightmare goes on for too long, please wake me up," I beg, desperation dripping from every word. I try to hide the tremor in my hand, but I'm sure he sees it. I can't help it. The fear is real and crippling.

"Because this is a trial medication, and I want to see how you respond to it. I will stay on-site tonight. I will monitor you from the security room, and someone will be able to see your camera at all times. If your nightmares look to be going on for too long, or you are in real distress, I will look at bringing you out of the nightmare safely. But I hope that won't be necessary." He reaches over to stroke down my arm, and I can't help but flinch. The gesture is completely innocent, meant to be a comfort, but I don't like being touched. The feel of another person's skin against mine repulses me, and I can't help but pull away. I've only just learnt to tolerate Sin hugging me. I guess that's what happens when you are deprived of human contact for so long, and then the only contact you have gives you pain.

His smile brightens as he watches me swallow the pill, and before he can ask, I open my mouth and wiggle my tongue around, making it very clear I swallowed it. From the moment he confirms that the pill has, in fact, gone, my panic begins—heart racing, sweating in places I don't normally sweat from, buzzing in my ears. I feel like the fear is going to consume me and I don't know what to do.

I try to remember the breathing exercises that Dr. Hughes taught us in group, but each time I try to take a big, deep breath in, my lungs burn and I start to panic again. The feeling of not being able to breathe properly, my heart racing in my ears, consumes me. That's when I remember Dr. Manning is still sitting there. He must be able to see me panicking. My chest is rising and falling about a million times a minute, and I can only imagine what my face looks like, yet he just sits there. His face is serene, like this is exactly what he expected would happen. Then again, it's the same every night, but normally the nurses fuck off as soon as they see the medication has gone, allowing me privacy to freak out by myself. So, it surprises me he knows my routine.

"Get into bed, Addison. Just let sleep take you. Don't fear it," he mutters, before getting up and walking to the door. Just before he's about to leave, he stops and turns to face me. "I have a feeling tonight's going to be a good night for you."

With that, he closes the door and leaves me. As I look around the room, loneliness consumes me. Now it really is just me against the world. I force myself to get up, and to potter around as much as I can, putting off sleep for as long as I can. But it doesn't take long for me to succumb to the darkness. I can feel the medication blurring the edges of reality, and I sink further and further into the darkness.

I don't know how long I've been asleep, it feels like only a few minutes. I'm still exhausted, yet my mind feels clear. There's the telltale jingling of the keys against the door, and that's when it hits me; I'm not awake, I'm still asleep, and he's here.

The door swings open, revealing a tall man, dressed in dark trousers, a crisp white shirt, and a smart black suit jacket buttoned at the front. His shoes shine bright, and his suit is perfectly pressed. He's tall, appearing to be well over six feet, but it's hard to get a proper read on him as his head is blurry. Sometimes I think he has no face at all, just pale skin that matches the rest of his body, covering where his face should be. But then sometimes it feels like the picture clears up, and the surrounding haze becomes less confusing and it looks like it's a bandage covering his face.

It's hard to explain, and I gave up trying a long time ago, but it's like there's a hazy aura around him, one that makes it incredibly difficult for me to get a proper read on what he looks like. Though, I'm not ashamed to admit, after a while, I stopped trying to see him.

When he first started visiting my nightmares, I wanted to know everything about him, convinced that memories of my father's story were fuelling his existence. But then things happened that were nowhere like what my father would say. Even on his wildest night, he never came close to scratching the surface of what the Slender

Man is capable of.

"Hello, my little slut. How lovely to see you again." His voice sounds almost robotic, like one of those voice changers you see in spy films. I don't know why my head can't just give him a voice, make him seem more normal, more real. I can beat normal. But he's something else.

I don't bother to reply. He makes it sound like he hasn't seen me in ages. He saw me just last night. He terrorises my dreams four to five times a week, and has done since I first got here. He's nothing new. He's been calling me his little slut or whore since then, too. Probably because that's exactly how I feel. Like I'm prey and he's hunted me until he finally has me trapped.

"You know better than to ignore me, little slut. Don't make me punish you so early in our evening. You know the rules by now."

Before he even finishes the end of his sentence, I scramble off the bed. The mere mention of him punishing me has me moving quickly. I drop to my knees in front of him, arms clenched together behind my back. I arch my back, sticking my tits out into the air, and I drop my head. The ultimate subservient position, as he calls it. It's also what he expects of me every time he enters my room. I'm surprised he hasn't punished me for not doing it straight away. It's the same every day. I'm so terrified that he's here, I forget, and he has to remind me. I think the sadistic twat loves to punish me.

Fuck, I need to stop thinking of him as a person. He is not real, just a figment of my overly active imagination.

"Now, tell me, have you been a good girl today?" he asks, the same way he does every evening. I learnt pretty early on that it's a fucking trick question. It doesn't matter if I've done absolutely nothing wrong, he will still find some way to punish me. However, remaining silent and ignoring him are two of the worst things I could do.

Taking a deep breath, I try to push the fear out of my voice as I answer him in the way he has trained me. "I've been a very good girl. Just for you, Sir."

"Mmm, I love the way you call me Sir." Somehow, even through the mechanical voice, it's like I can hear the deep rumbling of his tone, and it's not hard to miss the fact that he's turned on.

Fisting his hand into my long brown hair, he pulls hard until I'm looking up at him, my scalp burning. I keep my eyes downcast, trying not to look directly at him—that will earn me a punishment. At this position, I find myself looking down at his very tented crotch and a shiver of revulsion ripples down my spine.

One hand pulls firmly on my hair, causing my scalp to burn, while the other reaches down to cup my cheek. The feel of his ice-cold touch against my skin causes my stomach to flip in disgust. I hate each and every time I feel him lay a hand on me. It feels so real, and I curse my imagination for being able to create something so lifelike and so fucking terrifying.

What starts off as an almost gentle, comforting gesture doesn't remain that way. Before I even have a chance to register what is happening, I feel a blast of pain spread through my cheek as his hand slaps against the side of my face, my head exploding in pain. I try to reach up to cup my cheek, hoping the feel of my touch could soothe the ache, but he beats me to it. Grabbing my hand, he throws it backwards, making it clear it should remain in position behind my back, and to make sure I got this message loud and clear, he delivers a few more slaps across my cheek. Each one harder than the last.

I know what he wants, and it's not until the fifth slap that I give it to him. I can't help but scream from the pain of having my head rattled around. Not to mention the way his firm grip on my hair pulls my scalp farther each time my head rocks around. I try not to give him the satisfaction of seeing my pain and suffering, but he just continues to push until he breaks me. My resistance dwindles quicker with each passing visit. I don't know how much more of this I can handle.

"Now, little slut, you were telling me what a good girl you have been, weren't you?" He pulls my head back, causing me to yelp, more out of surprise by the unexpected tug. I know he wants me to make eye contact when I talk to him. It's the only time I'm permitted to look at him.

Slowly, I rake my gaze up over his smart suit until I get to his face. There's a haze around him still, but now, the longer I stare, the more I can see that there isn't a blank, skin-covered face. It looks like bandages cover his face. A flicker of a memory flashes in my brain, and I can't help that feeling that I've thought this before.

If you asked me to describe Slender Man before this moment, I would have said he looks just like the legend, a faceless man. But now he looks like a man wearing a bandage over his face. It feels as though he has real eyes beneath, like I can feel him staring at me with them. What really confuses me is that I know I've thought this before.

I've seen the bandage before and questioned if he really had a face beneath them. So, why when I'm awake do I forget this little detail?

Before I have chance to think about it any further, he pulls me up from the floor onto my feet before dragging me over to the soft, cushioned chair next to the small table that is sitting below the only small window in this room. The facility controls the blinds, and they are closed at the same time every night, and opened the same time every morning. The windows won't open, even if I want them to. Once he has me in position, standing next to the table, arms behind my back, eyes downcast, he begins the first stage of his humiliating torment.

"You know what to do. Don't make me wait," he sneers, sitting down in the armchair I have come to hate.

When I first arrived here, there wasn't a lot to look forward to about being here. So, I tried to find positives in the little things. When the blinds are open, the window looks out across the beautiful greenery of the grounds, and there are woods in the distance. I liked the idea that I could sit in that chair. It was big enough that I could curl up with my legs tucked under my ass while I cover myself in a blanket and read a book. It really felt like a tranquil place to relax. But, all that changed the first night Slender Man appeared. Now, I can't even look at the chair without thinking of this moment. This humiliating ritual he has me go through each and every night.

Slowly, I peel the clothes from my body. If I go too fast, he punishes me. If I go too slow, he punishes me. So, I focus on remembering how he likes it. I strip the vest top first, revealing my naked breasts to him. The cold hits my skin and I hate the way my nipples pucker, making it look like I'm enjoying this. That couldn't be further from the truth.

Sticking my chest out as far as I can, presenting my tits to him as instructed, he reaches over and tweaks each nipple in turn. He squeezes so hard I can't hold back the cries of pain, which is exactly what he wants to hear. As soon as he releases them, I move on, peeling the pyjama shorts off next. Once they are off, I stand before him completely naked, and although I can't see any facial expressions, I can hear his appreciative groan. It's almost like I can feel his gaze burning into me as he rakes his eyes across my naked body.

Reaching out, he rubs his hand across my pubic area, his finger just touching the top of my slit. I bite my lip to hide the revulsion I feel, as I take some small breaths to control the vomit that is threatening to make an appearance. It wouldn't be the first time that happened, but the memory of the punishment I received is enough to keep it at bay for now.

"Oh, little slut! Tut tut. Can I feel some hair threatening to make an appearance? You know how I feel about that," he snaps, and flashbacks of the very first time he came to me assault my mind.

I didn't exactly have an unkept pubic area. It had a small landing strip that was well maintained, but that's not what he likes. He made me shave it off in front of him, ensuring I remove every strand of hair from my neck down. I've never been so humiliated, or so I thought. Then every night since he runs his hand over the area, making sure I'm maintaining it to his standards. Each time he touches me, I want to curl up and die.

I know I just earned myself a punishment. With all the crap going on with Dylan, and all the memories of him being here has evoked, I was completely out of sorts today, and I forgot to prepare myself. Normally, I shower and shave before bed, but then Dr. Manning interrupted my normal process, and now I'm going to pay for his intrusion.

"I'm sorry, Sir. I didn't do it intentionally. I was busy and then I had to take some new medication that completely threw out my routine." I don't know why I'm grovelling. I can almost hear the elation in his voice as he informs me of how very fucking screwed I am.

"Do you think I give a shit about all of that? I am your priority. Your only job, the only reason for your existence, is to please me. You are my slut, my whore, and your job is to keep me happy. No more excuses. You know what to do." His voice is harsh and unwavering. Even though he sounds mechanical, I can pick up the subtle changes that are the same as a human voice. I can tell when he's pissed, or when he's playing with me like an animal toying with their prey before they devour them whole. That's exactly how I feel.

Slowly, I lower myself over the small table, a blush spreading across my cheeks as I'm filled with humiliation. My tits crush against the cold surface of the table, and because of the angle, and the way my back arches, my ass sticks out in the air. My feet remain shoulder-width apart, and when I feel the cool breeze against my pussy, I know I'm completely exposed and vulnerable. Just the way he likes me.

I close my eyes, sending a silent plea to whoever is listening, begging for this to be over. I try to will myself to wake up, shouting as loud as I can in my mind, telling me I have to wake up now. But, it's no use. It never helps.

I hear his clothes ruffling and I know that my punishment, whatever method he opts for this time, will be humiliating and painful. His specialty. I don't even get time to prepare myself.

CRACK!

CRACK!

I hear the whoosh of air before the sound of leather on skin assaults my ears. I think I hear it before I feel it. The crack of his belt against my ass cheeks. Two welts, one on each side, and the pain is unbearable. He doesn't hold back, his belt connecting with my ass at full force, causing pain and burning to spread over my ass. I can't hold back the screams. Not cries of terror like before. These are full-on screaming as loud as my lungs will allow screams. My throat burns, and tears fill my eyes as I beg him. "Please, Sir. No more. Please show mercy."

I don't know why I bother begging, it just turns him on even more. He enjoys seeing me in pain, and he loves when he has complete control over me. Which is why he doesn't stop when I ask him to. On the contrary, he continues to rain down blow after blow with his leather belt.

His aim is all over the place. Some hits get their target, landing on my ass cheeks, whereas others hit my upper thighs, my lower back, and the odd one lands on my exposed pussy, which really fucking hurts. I'm holding on to the edge of the table in front of me, as instructed by him, but now I feel like I need it to keep me upright.

The pain ricochets through my body, and everywhere hurts. My ass feels like it's on fire, and my legs are wobbling more than jelly at a kids' party. He must have hit me twice with the buckle of his belt, because I can feel small amounts of blood trickling down my legs. My throat is hoarse from all the screaming, my eyes sore from the tears. Now he's having a break between whips, I take quick breaths, desperate to fill my burning lungs. While he's beating me, I can't concentrate enough to breathe, and as a result, when he stops, I feel like I'm running out of air. I gulp down as much as I can in quick, short bursts, but hyperventilating only makes it worse. The edges of my vision blurs, and my body becomes weak. I try to focus on my breathing, but I can't focus on anything except the pain.

Before I have a chance to panic more, to think I might be about to pass out, that's when I feel his touch again, and I'm back to high alert. The feel of his cold finger running through my slit repulses me. He presses his finger against my clit, rubbing it frantically, trying to get a reaction. Normally my body responds the way anyone's would when stimulated, but this time my body is too focused on the pain to get wet. Not that it bothers him, he just pretends.

"Little slut, you wouldn't be getting wet, would you? You like being punished and humiliated, don't you?" I've learnt that when he asks a question, I answer. No hesitations, no defiance. Just obey him.

"Yes, Sir. I like anything you give me." I feel like a robot, just reciting the words he has pre-programmed into me.

"Why is that, little slut? Tell me what you are."

Gulping down the vomit I can feel in my throat, through gritted teeth, I say the words he wants to hear. "I enjoy when you inflict pain and punish me because I'm a slut. I am your dirty whore. I belong only to you, and I'm here with the sole purpose of pleasuring you."

I try not to let the words get to me, to believe them, but it's hard. Obviously, there isn't a single fibre in my body that enjoys the pain and suffering that he implements, but there are still times when my body betrays me. When he plays with my clit enough to get a reaction out of me. No matter how much I try to stop it, sometimes I have no control over my body. They're the times when I really feel like his whore.

"Yes, you are a dirty little slut. Tell me, which of your holes should I use first?" he asks, as he reaches out with his cold hand and massages my sore ass cheeks. The feel of his hand against the sensitive flesh is both a blessing and a curse. Even just the lightest touch is enough to burn and sting, but the cold temperature of his hands acts almost like an ice pack, and it soothes the sting. I hate that I like the relief it gives me.

Before I have a chance to answer, he grabs hold of my hair, my tender scalp burning again, and he drags me until I'm standing in front of him. I see that when he removed his belt, he also took all his clothes off, folding them neatly on the edge of my bed. His skinny body is hair free, and he has no muscles to be seen. The only thing of note about his body is the V that leads down to his average-sized erect penis. Normally I drool at the sight of a guy's V, but this one repulses me.

He sits back down in the chair, and all I can think about is his bare ass pressed against the soft, grey fabric of the chair. He pulls me until I'm sitting on his lap, straddling him. Gripping the back of my neck, he holds me in place. I'm currently sitting on his thighs, my bare pussy pressing against them, while his cock sits erect in front of my stomach. If I were to shuffle a few inches closer to him, it would impale me, which is why I stay still. I'm already closer than I want to be.

Pulling my head down, at first I think he's going to kiss me, and then I remember. Thank fuck he doesn't have a mouth. Instead, he whispers in my ear. "I asked you a question. Don't make me punish you again, little whore."

Fuck! While he was pulling me around and manhandling me, I was too busy thinking about what he could want to do next, that I completely forgot he asked me a question. I rack my brain, trying to think of the question. Then it hits me. "You can use any hole you want, Sir. I'm nothing but a disgusting cum-dump. You can fill all my holes. It's your choice, Sir. They belong to you."

It feels like a million tiny ants are crawling under my skin and I'm disgusted by myself. I hate the fact that I'm telling him what he wants to hear, but what choice do I have? Believe it or not, what he's about to do to me, while it may destroy my soul piece by piece, I know I can survive it. But the beatings, the pain he inflicts, there's only so much a body can take. I know he's capable of killing me, if I let him.

It sounds stupid to think that a delusion is capable of

killing me, but it's true. My mind can only take so much, and I can only bend so far before I snap completely. I'm not sure how many more nights of this I can tolerate. I know exactly how tonight is going to go, and as he has me take his cock in my hand, getting it nice and hard while his fingers probe about in my pussy, I try to block it out. He's going to rape and assault me in the worst ways possible. He's going to impale his cock in all my holes, pounding away, taking what he needs without a care in the world about how much pain I am in. This isn't about my pleasure, which is good because I don't get any. This is about him taking what he wants and humiliating me in the process.

Each time he slams into me, he calls me a whore. As he pushes his cock down my throat, he laughs and calls me a slut. As he forces his fingers into my ass while his cock is buried deep in my pussy, he tells me that only really dirty bitches do that. He calls me names; he tells me I like it when he knows I don't. He spits on me and degrades me as he plasters his handprint all over my skin.

When he finally leaves, my throat is raw from all the screaming. My face is covered with a mix of my tears and his spit. My pussy and ass are gaping, sore, and leaking cum. His handprint is just one of the many marks and cuts adorning my already tarnished skin. A light sheen of sweat covers my body, but that's nothing compared to the sensation of drowning in humiliation.

I don't know when I'm aware that I'm now awake. It all feels the same to me. But as I look around and see he's nowhere to be seen, that's when I know for sure. I wish I could trust my own mind. It's so fucked up that I can't even tell what's real and what isn't. I don't know what is a hallucination, what's a delusion, and what's real. He feels so real. That entire experience has never felt more real. Which is why I wasn't aware I woke up, because I never felt like I was asleep. I hate that my mind can mess with me in such a way. It makes me question everything I ever see or encounter. Is Sin real? Did I really meet Dylan from The Catastrophists? Am I really as alone as I think I am? I wish I knew the answers, or I at least knew who to turn to in order to get the answers. But for now, I just have to keep going.

Walking as quickly as my stumbling legs can carry me, I get into the shower. I turn the water to the hottest setting, hoping the steaming water will burn away all traces of him and my shame. It never does, but at least it's worth a try.

I stay in there, letting the water wash away all traces of him until the water runs cold. I must have stayed in the cold too long because my teeth chatter. I pull on a large, oversized hoodie and some baggy sweatpants before tucking my feet into my slippers. I need to warm up, and the best way to do that is with a hot drink.

Walking to the door, I try the handle, and just as I suspected, it's locked. I press the nurse call bell next to the door and wait for a voice to answer. "What is it, Addy?" a female voice answers, but it's not one I recognise.

"Please, can you open my door so I can go to the kitchen and make a hot drink?" I ask, trying to keep the shaking out of my voice. I wrap my arms around my trembling body. Though I'm not sure if I'm shaking because of the cold or because of the pain I can feel engulfing my body.

"Okay, but back in your room straight after. I'm very busy tonight, so don't make me regret this." Before I have the chance to thank her, the intercom disconnects, and a buzz sounds as my door is unlocked automatically. There is a keyhole where you can override all the access restrictions to get in the room, but they mostly rely on the electrics. I guess they have to have a secure option available if the technology crashes. It is a secure facility, after all. There are people a lot more fucked up that me in here, and that's saying a lot.

I quickly run to the kitchen, and as I approach, I'm shocked to see the light on. There aren't many people allowed to leave their room at night, and of the people that are allowed, most don't. Preferring to get a good night's sleep, usually a happy side effect of all the pills they are on. So, when I walk into the kitchen and see Dylan standing there, I'm shocked.

He's leaning against the kitchen cabinet, wearing only a low-hung pair of grey sweatpants. His rock-hard body is layered with muscles and etched with beautiful ink. I can't help but compare his body to that of Slender Man, and there is no fucking comparison. This guy's built like a real man should be. Whereas we should rename *him* Slender Boy.

I know I'm staring, and yes, there is a part of me that is admiring how insanely hot he is, but I already knew that. What really shocks me is the way he makes me feel. I don't know where the feeling comes from, as it's been two long fucking years since I last felt this, but the more I stare at his arms, the more I want him to wrap them around me. I don't know whether it's my completely vulnerable state, or the fact that I can't remember the last time I was hugged, but as I stare at the beautiful asshole in front of me, that's all I can think about.

Fuck, if I thought I was messed up before, now I know I am. My brain just took me down one of the darkest routes to date, subjecting me to horrors I didn't even think I could possibly dream up. Then the first thing I do when I see the asshole I argued with just yesterday is stare at him like he's the water I'm craving in the middle of the desert. I don't know what it is about him, and at this point, I'm not entirely sure I can trust my brain, but I get the impression I will be safe with Dylan. Even if he is an asshole who speaks before he thinks, but that doesn't mean he isn't capable of caring.

Now I really know I need to shut my overly active brain down right now. I don't know this guy, and the one interaction I have had with him wasn't the best. I need to hold on to that, not the imaginary Dylan my brain has dreamt up. The one who will hold me and make me feel better. He's fictitious, just like Slender Man. I have enough hallucinations to last me a lifetime. I need to focus on what I know is real, and this guy has shown no real signs of being a decent guy, but I'm going to give him a chance. I really hope my brain is right on this one. For the first time in two years, I actually want someone to care for me.

Five
DYLAN

Given that it's just after three in the morning, the last thing I expected as I stood in the kitchen making myself a hot drink, wearing nothing but my grey sweatpants, was to turn around and see someone else standing there. I had to blink a few times and wipe the sleep out of my eyes enough to focus on who it is. The bright, luminescent lights that adorn the kitchen ceiling are shining far too bright, and she's shrouded in light, making it difficult to see her properly. I can tell it's a female by the petite curves of her body, even hidden beneath the baggy clothing, as she stands in the doorway.

I take a step forward, and that's enough to change how the light hits her face. It's Addy, but she looks different. Her face is white as a sheet and her eyes look almost vacant. She's frozen, unmoving, just staring straight at me. I don't know if she's shocked to see me here, or if I've scared her, but she looks genuinely terrified.

I want to go to her, to check that she is okay, but even just from that one small step forward, I can tell she's skittish and will run at the slightest little thing. So, I try to act normal, like I'm not genuinely worried by the scared look on her face. The way she holds herself is different. In the counselling session yesterday, she looked shy and quiet, until she had a reason to argue with me, and then I saw the fire in her eyes I think should always belong there. I felt like I got a glimpse of the real Addy in that moment, and if me being an asshole is what she needs to find herself again, then call me the villain. I don't mind being the villain of the story, and long as she wears her crown and doesn't shy away.

Realising walking towards her may spook her, I settle on being friendly instead. "Would you like a hot chocolate, Addy?" I ask, my voice calm and gentle as I try to sound as non-threatening as I can.

I don't miss the way her gaze travels all over my body. Enough women have checked me out for me to know that's what she's doing. But there's something different about her, about the way her eyes feel like they are setting my skin alight. It's like I can track the path her eyes take just from the feel of how my skin heats under her watchful gaze. Usually when women look at me like that, they are getting ready to pounce—something I am more than happy to accommodate. I like it rough, hard, with no feelings or complications. I don't want to do repeats, and I sure as fuck don't call or text the next day. I don't even want to know their name most of the time. There's no point getting close to people. They always leave in the end, anyway.

Addy's stare is different, and it causes a shiver to ripple through me. Don't get me wrong, I'm turned on by this gorgeous woman, but this is more than that. If I was a pussy who over-analysed his feelings, I would say we were sharing a connection. But, since I'm not, I push all that soppy shit to one side. I want to make a cocky comment, like I normally would. Something to cut through the chemistry like a knife, but I can't bring myself to do it. It's clear given the haunted look on her face, she needs more than sarcasm and witty banter. The only problem is, I'm not sure I'm still capable of being a normal human being. I've spent so long drugged up and high on whatever substance I can get my hands on. They don't exactly make you behave like a kind, caring guy. There's a reason the media refer to me as a bad boy rock star who has fallen so far off the wagon, he's sitting in hell with the devil beside him. I've spent the last few years behaving like a selfish, spoiled brat, and I'm not entirely sure I remember how to be nice. But for this girl, I think I need to try.

She takes a small step forward, but I can see her hands trembling as she picks at the skin around her fingernails—an anxious gesture I know only too well. It's like the closer she gets to me, the more confused she becomes. It's like her legs are carrying her closer, but her body is screaming at her to stay away.

"Do you want to sit down?" I ask, pointing to the chair on the opposite side of the table from where I planned on sitting.

Although she hasn't answered me yet, I waste no

time pouring some more milk into the saucepan that is sitting on top of the stove. It's a longer process, boiling the milk, but I prefer my hot chocolates made with milk. They are so much creamier that way. While I'm seeing to the milk, I hear Addy pulling the chair out from the table and when I turn around, she's sitting down, hands resting on the table. I don't know what it is, but I can definitely see a wince on her face, like she is in pain, but I can't see anything obvious that could cause it.

"I would love a hot chocolate, please." Her small smile shoots me in the heart, and for the first time, it's like I can feel my heart beating. If you'd asked me before, I would have said my heart doesn't beat. It's cold, black, and dead, encased in as much stone as possible. I've never felt it beat, never cared for anyone—except for my bandmates who are like brothers to me. So, I'm very surprised to feel a slight flutter as she looks at me.

Addy's voice is hoarse, almost sounds like she has a sore throat, and she talks so quietly it's almost a whisper. Maybe she is sick? She looked like she was in pain earlier, and even though I've only been here a few days, I know it's not normal for residents to be walking around out of hours. I have special privileges because I'm a spoiled asshole who insisted on them. I've only ever heard of a couple of other residents being allowed out, and they are usually the ones that are getting ready to go home imminently. Even then, I have seen no one else at night. This place pumps everyone so full of medication they are all in drugged-up comas. I never wanted to be like that. I'm trying to get off all the damn pills. So, I've always declined them, and every night when I wake up after only a couple of hours' sleep do I regret my decision. Yet, I still never let Dr. Hughes prescribe anything for me.

"What are you doing up so late at night?" I ask before giving her a smile. "Or should I say so early in the morning, since it is, in fact, Tuesday now." I try to keep my voice light and airy, to appear as unthreatening as possible. The corner of her mouth rises slightly, and I will take that as a win.

Turning around when I hear the milk begin to bubble, I work on making our hot chocolate before reaching into the kitchen cupboard with my name on it. We all have one. It's accessed using the electronic tag in our bracelet, and we can use it to keep our own food stored here. Mine springs open, revealing all the sweet things I store in here out of the way of other people. Some people put their food in the communal cupboards to share with everyone, but I have a massive sweet tooth, and my treats are mine. I grab the mini marshmallows and drop a couple in my cup before topping it off with whipped squirty cream from the fridge.

"Do you want marshmallows, cream, or chocolate on yours?" I ask, as I sprinkle chocolate over the top of my masterpiece. It already looks delicious, but as I crumple bits of Flake over the top, that's the moneymaker.

Addy licks her lips as she eyes up my creation. "Can I have the same as you, please? I can give you some stuff back when I do my next commissary order," she mutters, looking almost shy to ask.

I can't help but scoff. "Fuck that. It's my treat," I say, as I push the completed drink before her.

Reaching into the draw beside me, I grab us both

a spoon, as we may need to dig into it with cutlery. My creation really is that big. She doesn't hesitate, scooping the cream and chocolate onto her spoon and straight into her mouth. Her responding moan is music to my ears. It's like she has a one-way connection to my cock, which springs to attention at the sexiest fucking noise I've ever heard… and all she's doing is eating some fucking cream. Imagine how she would moan when I eat her, I think, before pushing that thought out of the way.

Dr. Hughes had obviously heard of my reputation before I arrived, and as she went through all the admission paperwork with me, she made it very clear to point out the no-fraternising clause in my contract. If I so much as touch another resident, or a member of staff, in a sexual way, I'm straight to prison. I always knew going six months with just the company of my left hand would be tough, but I didn't realise I would have to avoid this. I thought everyone here would be so fucking mental my dick wouldn't know how to stand tall, yet here he is.

Not only do I not want to break the rules, I don't want to scare Addy off. There's something strange about her, and I'm inexplicably drawn to her. Like I have to help her—but with what, I have no fucking clue. I need more sleep.

"This is so good. Thank you," she says, looking straight at me with a genuine smile. Fuck, there goes my heart beating again. What the hell is wrong with me?

"No problem. It always helps me get back to sleep for an hour or two." I take a sip of the hot, delicious chocolate and I know why she's moaning. It tastes fucking delicious. "Are you always up in the middle of the night? I haven't seen you here before."

I may have only been here a short time, but my inability to sleep properly is an ongoing issue. I'm up around the same time every morning. This is almost a routine for me, and I know that over the last couple of weeks, I haven't seen another soul while I've been making my drink. Until tonight.

"This is the first time they let me out. I don't know why they did, but I'm glad," she says, hugging the hot chocolate mug closer to her, as she tries to pull warmth from the drink. Though, I'm starting to think her shivering isn't related to the chill in the room. After all, she's wearing a large hoodie while I don't have a shirt on, and I don't feel cold.

"Obviously you don't have to talk to me, but are you all right? You don't look so great." I don't want to spook her, but I want her to know she can talk to me if she needs to. There's a ghost of a smile on her face, and that's enough for me. She may not be ready to talk, but she appreciates my gesture.

"I have night terrors. Tonight just happened to be a pretty bad one," she mumbles, barely above a whisper.

Her hands are resting on the table, and she's fiddling with her fingers like she can't allow her hands to stay still, even for a moment. I reach forward and lay my hand on her wrist, just to stop her movements and let her know she can relax with me. Instead, she flinches, releasing a hiss from her mouth as she pulls her hand away. Acting on instinct, she pulls the sleeve of her hoodie up and rubs the sore area on her arm. I barely touched her, and I definitely didn't grab her hard enough to cause this reaction.

That's when I see the blood. Her wrists look like they are covered in rope burns, and there's a cut across her wrist that she's bleeding from. Crimson red blood seeps from her wrist into her other hand, and as soon as she realises that I've seen it, she quickly pulls her sleeve down.

Standing up, I walk to my cupboard, open it with my wristband, and pull out one of the clean tea towels I keep in there. Call me weird, but I don't enjoy using ones that the other residents have used. You have no idea what the fuck they've used it for, or if it should have gone into the wash three days before. So, I keep a stash of my own in there, and I know the one I grab hold of is brand new, as it still has the label on.

Pulling the label off, I throw it away before pulling my chair closer to Addy before I sit down. Our knees are almost touching and I can hear her sharp intake of breath as she takes in how close we are. Moving very slowly, so she can see that I'm not a threat, I gently take hold of her wrist. She resists at first until I make it clear I'm not giving in. Eventually she allows me to pull her wrist so that it's lying in front of me, and I pull her sleeve up before applying the tea towel to the fresh wound.

Addy hisses as I press hard on the wound, knowing it needs pressure or it won't stop. Her eyes remain averted, like she doesn't want to look at me. Her cheeks are flushed, and it's almost like she's ashamed.

Reaching out with my free hand, I gently touch her chin, and it breaks my heart when she flinches. I'm persistent and she doesn't pull away, allowing me to move her head until she is looking at me. Her eyes are glazed over with unshed tears and I can see she is fighting them back. I don't know this girl, but at this moment, I can tell this girl is a fighter. She looks broken, like she's holding herself together with tape, yet she still puts on a brave face. But, it's her eyes that give her away. She looks lost, lonely, and so fucking broken. I want to hold her—I have no idea where that fucking thought came from, but it's true. I want to pull her against me and wrap my arms around her, protecting her from whatever is putting that look on her face. I've never felt protective over someone before. In fact, I think for the last few years, I've barely thought about anyone except myself.

"How did this happen?" My voice is barely above a whisper, sounding deep and rumbling. I expect her to look away, or to not answer me, but she doesn't. Her eyes lock with mine, and there's that damn beating again.

She gives me a small, one-sided smile. "Would you believe me if I told you it was an accident? I was thrashing about during my nightmare. Nothing exciting."

I pull the cloth from her wrist and am pleased to find that the bleeding is slowing down. We will need a first aid kit, as this will need to be properly bandaged to ensure it doesn't get infected. But the more I look at her wounds, the more I can tell that her story is bullshit. There are definite rings around her wrists, like they had been tied up using something. The cut itself is straight and deep, like it was done by a knife, instead of the skin being caught on something, which is what would have happened if it was an accident.

"What would you say if I said I didn't believe you?" I ask, adding my award-winning cocky grin to let her know I'm not trying to be threatening. When I say award winning, that's not an exaggeration. I've been featuring in the sexiest man line-ups for the last few years, and they always seem to comment on my cocky smile. Apparently it's panty-melting, and although that is most definitely what I'm going for with Addy right now, I want to put her at ease. If she's anything like me, talking to someone else, trusting someone else, doesn't come easy. But, I've never met someone who is more in need of a shoulder to lean on. If you'd told me before this damn rehab stint that I would give a shit about this girl enough to want to help her, I would have laughed at you. I barely can be arsed to learn the girl's name, and I sure as fuck don't care if I upset them when I'm kicking them out of my bed. Yet, with Addy, there's nothing sexual; I just want to comfort her. Obviously I can't deny that I think she's hot as fuck. I'm not blind. But, at the same time, the way I'm feeling right now is more about making sure she is okay as opposed to fucking her. Shit, maybe I am evolving emotionally!

"I would ask, why do you care?" she mumbles.

"Honestly, if you'd asked me before I got here, I would have said that I don't care. But, strangely, I do. Maybe I recognise something in you I see in myself." What the hell am I saying? This is supposed to be about getting her to talk to me, not me talking about myself.

"What do you see?" She looks up at me through hooded eyes, and there's hope reflected there. She wants to know if we really are the same, and I know why. Nobody wants to think you are alone.

"You are lonely and lost. You know what it's like to

lose people and so you push people away before they have a chance to hurt you. You wear your mask well, but we share the same darkness. I can see it clouding your pretty emerald eyes, and it shouldn't be there. You deserve to have people on your side," I say, as I move my hand from her chin and gently stroke across her cheek. I expect her to flinch or to pull away, but she doesn't. Instead, she leans into my hand, closing her eyes for a second, allowing herself to just feel my touch. For a fraction of a second, she looks so serene.

She doesn't allow herself that feeling for too long, and as her eyes open, the glazed look returns. "You don't know me. I'm nothing like you," she spits, as she pulls away from my touch, pulling her arm away from the cloth I had been holding against it. Thankfully, the bleeding looks to have almost stopped. Her mask is back, and this is something I completely recognise.

"You may not be like me, and you are right. I don't know you. But, they always say like will always recognise like, and that's what I see in you. We share the same pain, and we both push people away."

Her voice becomes harsh as she snaps at me. "Well, if you push people away too, why are you trying to talk to me?"

I'm asking myself that very fucking question. Normally, I would be so far away from this fucked-up situation. If she wants to be alone, fucking let her. I know that's what I would want, but I can't leave it alone. If she's anything like me, she's pushing me away, but she doesn't really want me to go. She wants me to fight for her, and given the wounds I can see, I think she needs someone to fight for her.

"Because you need someone. Before I started all this rehab shit, I would have told you to drown your feelings in booze and push it all down. That was until I just spent the last several days feeling like I was dying while trying to detox. Leaning on someone will be nowhere near as painful as that was." My body shudders at the mere memory of the pain I went through. I'm not saying I'm healed or cured, because there isn't a fucking hour that goes by when I don't think about using. After the argument with Addy, I felt like shit, and I wanted to drown myself in substances to help me forget. I talked it through with Dr. Hughes, and I can't deny that having someone to listen to me when I'm in that crisis moment really helped. I've never wanted anyone to listen before, but now I think I see the benefit of it. Sadly, I don't think Addy agrees with me yet.

"Maybe for you. I'd be worried they think I'm fucking insane."

I can't help but chuckle, and her brow furrows as she glares at me. "Addy, we are in a fucking secure psychiatric facility. I think by that definition we are all fucking mad here," I say with a cheesy grin and a chuckle. My stomach does little fucking somersaults when I hear her sweet little laugh. I think she even shocks herself as she smacks her hand up to cover her mouth.

"I guess that's true," she says through her hand. "So, you're trying this whole opening up to people thing, are you?" She looks at me like she's genuinely interested, like she is thinking that if I can treat my issues, maybe she can too.

"Don't get me wrong, it's not easy and I've only been attempting it for a couple of days, so I'm hardly an expert. But Dr. Hughes made it pretty fucking clear that if I didn't engage in her sessions, she would fail me, and that would result in me being kicked out of the facility, which I can't allow to happen." I take a sip of my now cooler hot chocolate, loving the taste as it helps with my dry mouth. Detoxing literally sucks all the moisture out of your body, and I constantly feel parched.

"I've spent so long not talking about the deep stuff, I don't think I could," Addy mutters before she takes another sip of her drink. Fuck, there's that moan again. I had just got my dick under control and now he's back again.

With a shrug of my shoulders, I explain what I've been doing. "I wouldn't exactly say we have covered any of the big shit yet. I don't think it's realistic for two people who have never met to suddenly start talking about the heavy stuff. I've spent years keeping all my shit bottled up, and it will take a lot before I'm able to open that bottle. But Dr. Hughes basically said that the only way for me to truly feel like I can tell her all the bad shit is to be able to trust her with the little stuff. Basically, it's like having a friend. You talk to them about the everyday stuff until you trust them enough to tell them the rest. It's fucking embarrassing as hell to know that I need therapy just to learn how to make a friend, but it's true. I've spent years consumed with myself and what I want. I haven't given the people who call themselves my friend a second thought, which I think by definition makes me a terrible fucking friend." I wince, thinking of my brothers.

When we became friends in school, we really were best friends. Particularly Jake. He was there for me through everything, and I would have taken a fucking bullet for him. But, as cliché as it sounds, fame really changed me. I hated that the media was obsessed with finding out about my life, exposing my secrets. People I thought I could trust betrayed me, and so I stopped trusting people. I pushed them away before they could hurt me. Even my brothers, who I don't for a second think would hurt me, but substance clouded my decision-making process, and I didn't care who got caught in the crosshairs.

Lifting her mug of hot chocolate until it's resting just in front of her face, I see just behind the edges that she's trying to hide the tiniest of smiles. She looks fucking gorgeous when she smiles. Even though it was barely a smile, it was enough to light up her face, and that carefree glow should always be on her pretty face. Instead of her looking like she has the weight of the world on her shoulders.

"So what you're saying is, I need a friend? And since you need one too, we should be friends with each other?" she asks, her voice rising to make it sound like just saying the words out loud is reason enough for her to question her sanity.

Nodding, I agree with her. "Yes, I do think that. Why the hell not?" I can't keep from sounding shocked that she would not want to be friends with me. Then again, she's only met me once, and I was an asshole to her. So, maybe I would judge her more if she wasn't hesitant.

"Erm… maybe because you were a twatwaffle to me just a few hours ago."

"Hey, now. That was past me, and there's no need for us to be living in the past now, is there?" I joke. What else am I supposed to say? I was an ass to her, and now I have to try to put it right.

"How do I know that future Dylan won't be a jerk too?" I can see the hint of a smile is still there. She's enjoying sparring with me, just as much as I am. I like that she's allowing herself to have a laugh and a joke because the Addy that walked in here not too long ago looked like she wasn't capable of smiling.

"Oh, he will. But that's okay because the more you get to know me, the more you will love me. Everyone always loves me." Fuck, that statement actually used to be true. When the band started becoming famous, everyone wanted to hang out with me, everyone wanted to be my friend, and I loved it. I loved feeling wanted and needed for the first time in a long time. But the more people I let in, the more hurt me, and so I stopped trying to make them like me. Hell, I think I even went out of my way to stop them from liking me, but before I became an asshole, I really did know how to be a good guy. Surely it won't be too hard to find him again, will it?

Addy laughs at my response, and as she sits the mug down, I'm blown away by how different she looks. There's a flush to her cheeks, stopping her from looking too pale, and there's a smile across her face that makes her eyes sparkle. She no longer looks dead or haunted in her gaze. She looks young and carefree, like she's supposed to.

"You're not big-headed at all, are you?"

Now it's my turn to laugh because she's right. I

guess after years of people blowing smoke up my ass, I started believing it. "Is it being big-headed if it's true? Everyone loves me. I've won awards that basically agree with that. I bet you even had my poster on your wall a few years back. When you were a teenager, back when The Catastrophists first started out?" I throw a sexy, cocky wink in her direction, and she honest to fucking God blushes. Shit, did she really have my poster on her wall? I was just being a cocky twat. I didn't actually imagine she would have been attracted to me enough to put a giant poster of me on her wall.

"Erm... that's not... not the p-point," Addy mumbles, before taking a big, deep breath and continuing, sounding more sure this time. "I had, like, one picture of the whole band, maybe one of you. I don't remember. It was Arabella who had the pictures all over her wall. Her bedroom was covered from floor to ceiling with Catastrophists posters. You couldn't even see what colour the paper was behind them."

Throughout all our conversations, including the group session where she became animated standing up for Sin, I've never heard her sound as happy as she has been telling this story. Whoever Arabella is to her, she's important. I'm not sure if asking Addy about her will burst this bubble we've created, or if she's really looking to talk about her. She is the one who brought her up, after all. "Who is Arabella? She sounds like someone I would love to meet. You know I will get along with anyone who adores me in that way?" I try to keep my tone light, to not scare her off too easily.

Addy's face falls. The smile that lit up her face has

gone and is now replaced with pain. Fuck, if I could go back, I would take back every word. I reach over slowly, giving her enough time to see what I'm doing and to pull away if she chooses to, so when she doesn't, I gently lay my hand over hers. Addy's breathing hitches, and I feel like I'm holding my damn breath constantly around this woman. Scared that the slightest little thing will have her running for the hills, and that's the last thing I want.

"Arabella was my younger sister, and even though she liked you, most of the posters were of Jake." Every word sounds painful, like her heart is breaking just by uttering the words. I can see tears welling in her eyes, yet she isn't running. She's sitting here, telling me about something that's obviously painful for her. We could make progress here.

"Fucking Jake. Everyone loves the damn frontman. I write the songs. I put the damn band together, and I play drums. All that pretty boy does is sing and look good and he's everyone's fucking favourite," I chunter, more to myself than to Addy. I love Jake. He's the closest thing I have to family, but I've always resented him for the attention he gets.

People look at our band and because Jake's the frontman, the voice of The Catastrophists, they think he's the leader. He's the most outgoing of the group, and he has the perfect vocals for the songs we do, and that's all that matters to our fans. I think if you were to line the four of us up, before we got famous, we would all have been able to get our fair share of girls. Jake's not the only good-looking guy in the band, and like I said, I have won awards. But, everyone thinks Jake is our leader, songwriter, and general boss man. When in fact, I put the band together and I write all the songs. I could have been the frontman. I can sing and play the guitar, but I didn't want that. Although, it's funny what you want when you can't have it. Once we chose Jake as the frontman, there was no going back, and it was a decision I never thought I would regret. But the longer time went on, the more I resented him, and the more I wanted to take credit for the hard work I put into the band. Some of our songs, I literally cut myself and bled all over the pages. They're raw and heartbreaking, and when they became a hit, I was over the fucking moon. Until everyone assumed Jake was our songwriter, or that we hired someone. So, I stopped putting all of myself into the songs. I wrote the generic shit people wanted to hear, and I let Jake take credit for them. By that point, I fucking despised the songs, anyway. They weren't in line with the music we wanted to create.

"I never knew you wrote the songs. I should have guessed, really. The songs got shitter, the more you dived into drink and drugs."

Fuck, nobody has ever put that link together. I mean, it's true, but nobody else has ever put the pieces together and realised my addiction was causing the downfall of The Catastrophists.

"Wow, talk about kicking a guy when he's down," I joke, or at least part of it's a joke. Her words really hit home harder than I was expecting.

Her face wrinkles, suddenly seeming uncomfortable about the situation. "Sorry, sometimes I say mean shit, so it deflects the conversation away from me."

I can't help but chuckle, and she looks confused. "A

bit like I did yesterday in group. It's easier to take stabs at someone else, as opposed to looking at yourself. Isn't it?"

"Fuck, this is why we shouldn't be friends. We're just going to keep pissing each other off," she groans, and she may be a little right, but I'm not ready to throw the towel in just yet.

"I don't know about you, but for me, that's exactly what I need. I need someone who will push me into talking about the hard shit. I've confessed more to you in the last half an hour than I have to my best friends in years. We might piss each other off in the process, but maybe we just have to accept that's how the other person deals with pain. I want to help you, and if the only way to do that is by hurting myself, then I will put up with that. Who knows, I might help myself in the meantime. And since our main goal is getting out of this hellhole, maybe this is our way out?"

Nodding her head, I feel her squeeze my hand, and I realise our fingers were still laced together. I had put my hand on hers and forgot all about it. I hadn't even felt our fingers lace together, until now. The feel of her soft skin against my hands is amazing. I feel connected to her, and it's not terrible. I'm still terrified she could hurt me, but I have to trust people, eventually.

"Okay, we will try the whole friends thing, but you have to respect my boundaries. If I say I'm not in the mood to talk, you have to give me space. Obviously, don't let me push you away completely, just try to find that middle ground. Deal?" she asks, voice sounding full of hope, and I'm so pleased she no longer sounds like the scared little girl who walked into the kitchen not so long ago.

"Deal. But you have to promise that you won't hurt me. The last girl I trusted sold all my secrets to the media. I've never let anyone in since." Shit, I hadn't meant to tell her about Maggie. That bitch is the reason I don't know how to trust and why I've avoided anything more than one night with a woman ever since. Maggie took my trust and shit all over it, hurting me in the worst way possible. She is the only girl I ever thought I loved, and she was using me as a stepping stone to reach the career she dreamt of.

"Looks like we both just got ourselves a friend. Sin will be jealous," Addy jokes, and I can't help but chuckle. I don't know much about Sin, and have only really met her a few times, but each time she's had a bright, bubbly smile on her face. I get the impression it's hard to truly piss Sin off. Even in group therapy yesterday when I snapped at her, she didn't really get upset. That was all Addy.

"And Arabella. She will be jealous too, I'm sure," I joke, remembering how she just told me her sister loves my band. But it soon becomes clear I said the wrong thing. But, as is typical for men in situations like this, I have no fucking clue what I did wrong. She's the one who told me about Arabella liking my band, and since she mentioned her first, I thought that meant I could mention her. But, apparently not.

Addy drops my hand like it's suddenly burning her skin, and she slides her chair back from the table. The grinding noise as it scrapes across the linoleum floor hurts my ears. She's got that deer in the headlights look again, and I realise I need to stop her before she spirals further.

"Hey, whatever I said or did wrong, I'm sorry. Please, sit and finish your drink."

She shakes her head. "You have done nothing wrong. I shouldn't have brought her up. I'm not ready to talk about her yet. I thought maybe I was, but I'm not."

"What do you mean?" I'm confused as shit.

"Arabella died two years ago, along with my entire family. I am the only one left. I should have died that day too, but I didn't and I've regretted it every single day since. I have no right to live when they can't. That's why I'm so nutty. That's why my brain is manifesting the biggest punishment I can think of and is haunting my nightmares. There's a reason I can't be helped, no matter how many fucking pills Dr. Manning shoves down my throat. I'm haunted because it's what I deserve." Her eyes fill with unshed tears, and she looks so lost. I think she genuinely believes every word, and fuck, does it break my heart. I'm not ready to tell her yet, but I'm probably the one person in the world who can relate to her. I know what it's like to have no one.

"Addy… I'm—"

She cuts me off before I have a chance to say anything more, holding her arm out, palm facing me in the universal sign for stop. I want her to hear what I have to say, but clearly she isn't ready for that yet. So, I listen to her.

"I'm going to go back to my room and try to get a little more sleep. Rome wasn't built in a day, as they say. This whole friendship thing will not happen overnight. But I'm willing to give it a go. For now, let's just leave it there. Is that okay? I understand if you don't want to be my friend." Her voice sounds so small, and I can hear the pain in her voice. She thinks her darkness is enough to scare me away. It isn't.

Standing, I walk over to her slowly until I'm standing so close to her I can feel her breath on my face. She tries to hide her slight gasp, but I catch it. She didn't expect me to come so close, and now I am. She's frozen. I move slower than I would with anyone else, letting her see that I'm not a threat. I reach around, wrapping my arms around her back before pulling her towards me for a hug.

At first Addy stands completely still, frozen and as stiff as a board. But I just hold her against me, resting her head against my chest. After a few very long seconds, she finally relaxes, and it's like she deflates in my arms. I just keep holding her, and when she wraps her arms around my back, pulling me impossibly closer, I feel myself begin to relax. When I first went to hug Addy, I did it because I could see she needed a bit of human comfort; I hadn't realised how much I needed it too.

I don't know how long we stand there, just holding on to each other tightly, and simply embracing the feel of taking comfort from someone else. I try not to think about how perfect she feels in my arms, or how the feel of her against my skin is a massive fucking turn-on. I also try not to think about how much calmer I feel, just having her this close. I try to take this for what it is, a hug between two blossoming friends. Nothing more. Well… maybe I will fantasise about more with my left hand later on, but for now… this is perfect.

Six
DYLAN

It's been a couple of weeks since that first night in the kitchen, and with every passing day, my friendship with Addy has grown stronger. Each and every night, roughly around the same time, we both meet in the kitchen for a hot drink.

Whenever we meet, I turn a blind eye to the way she looks, the fear in her eyes, and I simply provide a shoulder for her to lean on. Every night since that first one, we have hugged more and more. We don't exactly talk about anything deep or meaningful, but we're getting closer and more comfortable with each other.

Every night when she comes into the kitchen, she looks even worse than the night before. She holds herself up by wrapping her arms around her slight frame. When she walks, she winces, like every bone in her body hurts. She tries to cover her body using baggy clothing, but I know the wounds are there. Sometimes the blood seeps through the hoodie she wears, and other times it's just obvious she's in pain given the way she holds herself. After the first couple of nights, I stopped asking to see them, to help her. No matter how much I wanted to keep pressing her to show me the wounds, I could see how badly she wanted me to drop it. I'm hoping that the longer we spend getting to know each other, the closer we will grow, until one day she feels comfortable letting me see the wounds.

I can't even begin to tell you how much it pains me to know she has wounds adorning her body, and it's even worse knowing she did them to herself. It's obvious she's the only person who could have caused them, and it's clearly something she's embarrassed to talk about, but in the time I've been getting to know Addy, I wouldn't have said she was capable of self-harm. Don't get me wrong, I know it's hard for me to truly know a person after just a couple of weeks, but I just don't get that feeling from her. I know she's depressed, and her dark side can overtake her often because I've seen it. There will be times, more so during the daytime, where you can see her mind shutting down and she just stares off into space. And during our group therapy sessions, she often says that sometimes she feels it would be easier to leave this world than to have to fight every day just to survive. But suicidal ideation and physically self-harming yourself are two very different things.

Last night was one of the worst nights I've ever witnessed, and for the first time since our evenings together began, she curled up in my arms while we sat on the sofa in the adjoining living room, and Addy just sobbed. She cried for what seemed like hours, and my heart broke for her. I tried to hold her as much as I could, to let her know that I was there for her, because that's all I can do. I don't really know what caused her to be like that, and without knowing all the details, it's impossible for me to even try to help her.

I hate the way she winces when I touch her, even though she's used to my touch and actually seems to crave it now. But she clarified that our friendship can only happen on a night, away from prying eyes. Obviously, at our counsellors' requests, we spent some time working out our differences, after that first day when we had our falling out. They did not know we'd already solved the problem, so we had to make it look real. Since then, Addy has allowed us to be civil in public, even getting along in our group sessions, but she insists we hide our friendship. I have no idea why she's insisting on that, but I respect her decision.

"Morning, Dylan. How are you doing today?" Dr. Hughes shouts to me as I'm strolling down the corridor towards her clinic room. I'm expecting her to be in her office, as opposed to running up behind me. This morning, I have my solo session with Dr. Hughes instead of group therapy. When I first started, this used to be one of my favourite days as I had a couple of hours' free time after seeing Dr. Hughes, while others were having their solo therapy. Now, it's just more time I don't get to see Addy.

"Good, Doc. You?" I ask, as she swipes me into her room. I flop down onto my usual comfy chair, and Dr. Hughes gets settled into the one opposite me. She puts down the mug of coffee she must have just been collecting and picks up the notebooks laying on the table next to her.

"I'm good, thank you, Dylan. So, have you had any more thoughts about what you want your art therapy to be? I've had several messages from Lyle saying you are refusing to commit to just one therapy. Apparently, he gave you an additional week's grace period and allowed you to attend more sample sessions, but you still haven't committed. Why is that?" She places her pen against her lip and gives me that judgemental stare I've grown used to. It's the one she always gives me when she disapproves of something I've said or done, but she obviously can't come straight out and chastise me. So instead she gives me the look that most mums around the world have perfected. It says I'm pissed, but I'm giving you the chance to put it right without me yelling at you, so don't make me regret it by getting it wrong.

I simply shrug my shoulders and tell her what I told Lyle. "Honestly, I'm not trying to be difficult. I just don't feel like I've connected with any of your therapies."

"Lyle also said he offered you a slot in music therapy, which you declined. Normally we don't allow people to do therapies we know aren't useful to them because the whole point is, if that therapy was enough to help you cope, you wouldn't have ended up here in the first place. But I think at this point Lyle just wants you to pick one. Which obviously is not ideal. I want you to find something that works for you. So, why are you declining to try music therapy?"

Running my hands through my jet-black hair, I don't do a very good job of hiding the anguish I'm feeling over the music session. I've missed two now, and that's seriously frowned upon. The last thing I need is to get kicked out of this damn place over something so trivial. "Look, writing music has always been something that's personal to me. I never write with anyone else, it's always been something I do by myself. Then playing music became something I did for all the world to see. I had to share it with millions of people, and I loved it, but it's also something I heavily associate with my addiction. I can't remember the last gig I played without being high, and I haven't even picked up my guitar since I detoxed. I guess maybe I'm worried I won't be able to play the way I used to." Fuck, saying that aloud really hurts.

Obviously, when I started playing the drums when I was eight years old, I wasn't hooked on substances. In fact, it was my teacher who told me to do it. I was a pretty angry kid, and given the way my childhood had panned out, I had every reason to be. Yet, I was struggling to know how to deal with my feelings, and so my teacher gave me some sticks and told me to beat my anger out on the skins. At first, that's exactly what I did. I just smacked the skins as hard as I could with my sticks, letting out all my rage. I loved it so much I decided I wanted to learn how to play for real.

The only problem was that I had no parents to pay my tuition money. My teacher believed in me so much, she petitioned the school for a scholarship, which they gave me. It's the first time anyone had ever believed in me, and she started my career that day. My music teacher didn't just teach me to play the drums, she taught me music. How to read music, how to write it. How to break it down and understand all the little facets that make up a song. I fell in love, but I struggled to practise, given I didn't have a stable home. There weren't a lot of foster families queuing up to take in an angry eight-year-old and then buy him a drum set. So, the school loaned me a guitar. That way I could still play music, and use it as a way to chill, without it causing too much noise. Some families still hated it and banned me from playing, so I left and found another family. I lost track after the tenth home.

Shaking her head, Dr. Hughes fixes me with that stare I've grown used to over the last couple of weeks. "That's rubbish and you know it. You were playing music long before your addiction came along. So what else do you think is holding you back?"

Biting at my lip, I war against my nature, which is to shut my mouth and hope she drops the subject. I know from experience she's like a fucking dog with a bone when she thinks there's a chance I might actually open up to her about something important, so there's no chance of her dropping it. I have this war with myself during every session, as I slowly become more used to baring my soul to this complete stranger. Well… she used to be a stranger. Now she knows me better than anyone else, I think. "Erm… I don't know?" My voice hitches at the end, making it sound like I'm asking her a question.

"Dylan…" Dr. Hughes' disapproving tone forces me to groan.

"Fine. I'm worried that playing music again will make me want to use. While I'm here, I can avoid drugs and alcohol. It's not available to me. Yet, when I go back to my normal life, I will be surrounded by it. Fuck, people will throw it my way, and I don't know how I'm going to be able to say no. There are times now that I crave it, but I don't use it because it's not available. Yet out in the real world, when it's available, it will be harder for me to move away," I answer honestly, but we both know I'm not fully answering her question. I see Dr. Hughes begin writing and I know while she may focus on this, she will come back to the other stuff. She always does.

"Do you think you are not strong enough to battle your addiction?" Her steely gaze remains fixed on me, and I almost want to squirm under her judgemental looks.

"Honestly, I have no idea." My head sags as I confess something that has been worrying me for a while now. The fact that I have been clean for twenty-five days now is a massive achievement, and it's the longest I've been clean since I was maybe seventeen. But, the fact remains, I've never had to test myself. I am clean because I have no choice here. But if someone put a bottle of beer in front of me, I don't know if I would be able to simply walk away from it, and that scares the shit out of me.

"Well, I will make a note of that, and will be sure to test you before you leave here. But this is a long-term process, Dylan. This first part was getting you clean, and you've done that. The next part is giving you the tools you need to stay clean. That's why we are teaching you ways to deal with your addiction, but also coping strategies. You are not alone in this thinking. Everyone in here is battling addiction worries whether they will be able to stay clean when they are back surrounded by things that made them use in the first place or not. And a time will come where we need to look at what type of things made you use, and evaluate whether they should remain in your life when you leave here. For example, if your best friend is your dealer, I would advise you to not see him ever again. There's a high probability that he won't be able to just be your friend, and having regular contact with someone who can supply you with drugs is a factor you can avoid.

"Obviously, music is a big stressor, but you can't cut music out of your life, so I want to turn it into a positive factor. I want music to be something you turn to when you want to use, not something you do while you are high. Music is so personal, you can tap into your emotions and really put it all out there. You just have to be brave enough to let it in, like you used to."

Fuck, I know what she's saying is true. And she's absolutely hit the nail on the head there. It's not that I fear using again—although that fear will always be real—it's more that I'm scared to allow myself to be vulnerable. The songs on our first album, they were our best for a reason. I wrote them while I was sober, and they come straight from my soul. I wrote what I knew and people really got it. Then fame hit, and people started letting me down. I used pills and booze to numb everything, but that had a knock-on effect on the music I wrote. I wrote what people wanted to hear, but it was never as good as our first album. I didn't put my heart and soul into each song, and that showed. Yes, they were still good, and we hit charts and won awards for them, but I knew they didn't even compare. The original had something so raw and beautiful, and it's what got people hooked on us. That's what I need to get back to, and it scares the shit out of me.

"I don't know if I can be vulnerable for the world to see, only to have my heart smashed all over again." I sound so dejected and fucking miserable. But I'm trying to sum up years of being used and let down by people I thought I cared about.

"Does any of this relate to Maggie?" she asks, as she takes a sip of her coffee.

I can't hold back the groan that escapes my lips and I run my hand through my hair again in frustration. "Haven't we talked enough about that bitch?"

We must have spent two hours talking about her in my last session. I felt like my heart was being ripped out all over again as I went through all the details of how I gave her my heart and she obliterated it. She sold my personal stories to the press, leaked our locations so she could be photographed, and she cheated on me as a lovely cherry on top. She's the only girl I ever thought I cared about, and who cared about me, and the whole time she was using me for a leg up. She dreamed of being a model. Hell, she would have been happy with being a cheap, nasty reality television celebrity—which ironically is what she does now. She used me to get famous, and it worked. But she broke me in the process.

"We've talked about how she hurt you, and I've listened to the songs you wrote after your break-up. You clearly used music as a way of getting over her. Or was it revenge? I don't think you ever said anything real in the songs, did you?"

"I told people what really happened. You don't get any more fucking real than that, Doc." I can't help the angry growl that slips out as I snap at her.

Dr. Hughes just rolls her eyes before replying, "I mean, about your real feelings. All the stuff you told me about how she broke your heart left you feeling vulnerable and unsure if you could ever care about anyone again. You went into a lot of detail about what she did wrong, and you made it very clear you were pissed at her, but did you ever try writing a song about how you felt, or how you still feel? You say you are over her, but the anger and resentment you hold towards Maggie still makes me think you still hold a grudge. People who have moved on have usually let those feelings go."

Fuck, she's totally right. All the songs I wrote about Maggie were telling the world what a bitch she was, and so many of them weren't released to the public. The band wouldn't even record some of them. They were that bad. But none of them looked at how I feel, and I think Dr. Hughes could be right—shocker, I know—about some of it, but not all.

"You are right when you say I'm not over what Maggie did to me, but I am most definitely over her."

Now Dr. Hughes is looking at me with interest, her pen scribbling away on her little notepad. I'm actually impressed she can write while maintaining eye contact with me. I would need to look at the notebook. I guess women really can fucking multitask.

"How do you know you are over Maggie? Have you started having feelings for someone new?"

"I wouldn't call it feelings. I don't really know how to explain it, other than to say, I don't think about Maggie anymore. I hadn't for a while before coming here, but since the detox, she's rarely on my mind at all. It's like my mind is free to notice and appreciate other women now." So, I know that's an out-and-out lie. There's only one girl I'm thinking about, and she's on my mind all the fucking time. I wouldn't say I have feelings for her, but I'm attracted to her, and I guess you could say I'm caring about her in a friendly way. Fuck, what I think about her is anything but friendly, but I'm hardly going to say that to Dr. Hughes.

"Do you mean, think about women in a sexual way, or as friends?" she asks, her eyebrows raising as she waits anxiously for my answer.

"Don't get me wrong, Doc, I'm still a man with a dick. Of course, I see women in a sexual way, but that doesn't mean I like them or have feelings for them. I can look at a woman and admire her without it meaning anything. But I am trying to let people in, as friends."

"Like who?" Fuck, I should've known this question was coming.

"A few people from the group therapy session. I think it's easier to form a connection with them because they already know all the heavy stuff without me having to tell them. It means I can just form normal friendships with them, which is something I haven't done for years." I try to keep it as vague as possible, but her steely gaze tells me she's not buying it.

"That is true. Forming connections with people in your group sessions could be great for you. One of your biggest issues is struggling to make connections and trust in others. So the fact that you're willing to try that is brilliant. Would you like to tell me about one connection you've formed?" she asks, trying to pull as much information out of me as possible.

"Not really," I mutter.

"Okay, why don't I tell you what I already know, and we can go from there? The nurses have told me you have been spending time with Addison and look to be forming a solid friendship with her. Would you like to elaborate on that?"

Fuck. I don't know why, but whenever I'm with Addy, I forget that we're surrounded by nurses and security cameras. No matter how much she wants our friendship to remain a secret, it won't ever be because Big Brother is always watching us.

"What is there to say? She's one of the people in group, and I've had a few nice conversations with her outside of our group sessions. You forced me to get to know her and to apologise for being an ass to her, so I did. We started talking, and I didn't hate her company, so we hung out sometimes. Not a lot. Addy still prefers her own company most of the time, but it's a start. I think we both need to learn to be around other people, to have people we trust in our lives, and so this is a pretty good start for us."

I take a sip of water as silence fills the room. The only noise is the scratching of Dr. Hughes' pen against the notepad in her hand. She clearly has a lot to write down, and that worries me. I know the rules. But I don't want her to take Addy from me.

"I agree. Can I ask, do you care for Addy? And before you snap at me, that doesn't have to mean sexually. I just mean in a platonic and friendly way. You can be friends with someone without really caring for them," she inquires, and it makes me think.

"Honestly, I think I care. Not in a sexual way, or in a crossing the boundaries type of way, but I do think about her. She's clearly going through a lot of personal shit she doesn't talk to anyone about… unless she confides in Dr. Manning. Every day she has new wounds that she tries her best to hide, and I want to help her, but I don't know how. I'm concentrating on just being there for her, so that when she feels strong enough to talk about whatever she's going through, I will be here for her, and she will know that."

Dr. Hughes' face changes from her usually professional mask, and her brow furrows in confusion. I'm sure I see worry on her face, but she hides it so quickly I question if it was ever really there to start with.

"Dylan, do you mean that someone else is harming Addy, or that she is harming herself?" Dr. Hughes asks, concern dripping from every word.

Fuck, I knew I shouldn't have talked about Addy. Me and my big mouth. I take a big, deep breath and try to calm my racing heart. "I'm sorry, Doc, but if I'm trying to build up a friendship with Addy, one of the worst things I could do is break her trust."

"I understand that, Dylan, and I can assure you that our conversation will remain private. But, I have to know that my patient is safe. I promise, I can help, and I will do it discreetly in a way that doesn't mention you."

I can't stop my leg from jigging up and down as anxiety runs through my body. The urge to drink flows through my brain, and I can feel that itch just under the surface of my skin. It's familiar, and it tells me I don't have to feel anything. One sip of alcohol and I can be numb from it all. Only problem is, I don't have anything near me I could use to numb the emotions. Then I remember what Addy told me when I told her I wanted to be numb and not feel. She told me that owning your feelings means you have power over them; they don't have power over you. So, I will own my feelings, and I will use them to make us both stronger.

"She says she does it in the night while she's having nightmares, but I don't think she's telling the truth. Some of the wounds are not consistent with a self-inflicted injury. A couple of weeks ago she had rope burns around her wrists. She can't have done that to herself. Apparently, Dr. Manning has her on an experimental drug, but it doesn't seem to be helping," I explain, while I send a silent prayer to whoever the fuck is listening, that I haven't just ruined my friendship with Addy.

Dr. Hughes looks confused, and she even sets her notepad on the table beside her so she can lean in closer to me. "Are you sure Addy said the drugs were experimental?"

I rack my brain trying to think of the answer, but I remember her conversation plain as day. "Yes, she didn't know the name of the drug, but he definitely said it was experimental. I'm not sure if she said it was a trial drug. I know he gives it to her himself every night, instead of the nurse giving it when they do the final drug round."

Dr. Hughes tries to hide it, but I see the look of concern and confusion on her face before she replaces it with her professional mask. She picks her notepad back up and begins making notes. The silence is deafening, and I almost want to say something just to cut through it.

After she finishes writing, Dr. Hughes looks at me, her serious expression now firmly in place again. "I will look into this, and I promise I will do it discreetly. But I wouldn't be doing my job properly if I didn't give you a warning…"

I cut her off before she begins her lecture. "Look, Doc. You don't need to give me the lecture. I know what you are going to say, and I promise nothing is going on between Addy and I, except friendship."

Shaking her head, Dr. Hughes continues what she was about to say, anyway. "I understand that, Dylan. But, I have to say this because it's my job, even if you think you already know it. I have to remind you of the rules. You cannot form a relationship with anyone in this facility past the realms of a friendship. You cannot have feelings for Addy. You cannot do anything romantic or sexual with Addy, or anyone else in the facility. We have a no-fraternisation rule for a reason. You are all classed as vulnerable patients, and you are all at a very emotional time in your lives. To form relationships while things are so raw would be very dodgy ground, particularly surrounding consent. You are all here by court order, and some are here because they have been declared medically unstable. That means they are not capable of making important decisions. That's why we have the no-fraternisation rule. If I believe at any point that you've taken your friendship with Addy further, there will be no warnings. I will kick you out of the facility, and the judge will declare that you need to finish your sentence in a normal prison. Do you understand?"

She sounds stern and professional, like this is a rule she's recounted so many times before. Maybe she even told me about it when I first got here? Not that I would have listened, which is probably why I don't remember. I'm guessing it's a rule she needs to remind people about often. When you throw a load of vulnerable men and women into close confines and teach them to open up to each other, bonds are going to form. And I completely understand what she's saying about us being at our most vulnerable, and that it's the perfect time for people to take advantage of others. But that's not what's happening with Addy. Believe me, she's the one with all the fucking power. I'm just along for the ride.

I allow her words to sink in, and hearing them again, linked to Addy and the friendship we've started to form, I can't help but feel deflated. I can't risk being kicked out of this facility. Not only that, but I'm also guessing it will be possible for me to get access to drink or drugs in a prison facility, as people will go to any lengths to get what they want in somewhere like that. So, it's a massive risk to my sobriety if I get kicked out of here. But the problem is, I can already feel myself starting to like Addy. Each time I spend time with her, the longer we talk and the more we open up to each other, the more I like her. She's stunningly beautiful, even with the wounds and scars adorning her pale skin. There's potential for me to really start to feel something for her, and I think maybe she might feel the same way. I catch the little glances she throws my way, and the way she tries to check me out without me noticing—but I always know. It's like her eyes burn into my skin, and I can feel whenever she's near.

I'm starting to like her and that means we are both fucked. Nothing can happen between us, and I can't let these feelings grow. I want to be there for her, but I need to make sure it doesn't go further than that because I can't risk prison. Looks like asshole Dylan is going to rear his ugly head again, just enough to keep her at arm's length. I need her to talk to me, but not fall for me. Fuck, I'm so screwed.

Seven
DYLAN

I SPENT ALL DAY YESTERDAY TRYING TO COME UP WITH A WAY to keep Addy at arm's length. To still be there for her, and to be her friend, without developing any feelings. What I've basically summarised after an evening of deep contemplation is that I'm so fucking screwed. I want to have my cake and fucking eat it all, but that's just not realistic. So, I have come up with a plan. It's not a plan I like, or am proud of, though.

I realised that my biggest issue isn't me developing feelings for Addy, or her developing feelings for me. It's that I opened my stupid big mouth and told Dr. Hughes that we had formed a friendship. That meant all eyes immediately turned to us, putting that relationship under a microscope. So, I've decided, the best thing to do would be to let Dr. Hughes know that Addy and I are no longer friends, and therefore she has nothing to worry about.

Granted, the only way to do this is to very publicly fall out with Addy, and since I need for it to look super real, I've decided not to fill her in on my plan. I can apologise for it afterwards.

I'm very aware that this plan doesn't really address the whole feelings thing, and I know that the more time I spend with Addy, the more I like her. I guess I'm just going to hope I can get control over it. I've spent the last few years keeping women at arm's length, so why should she be any different? Yes, I know I'm bullshitting my brain, but it's the best I've got right now.

The night before last was the first time since we started meeting that she didn't show up, and I hate to admit that I was gutted. I really missed her, and I didn't realise how much I fucking love our time together until it went away. Logically, I knew it was most likely a one-off, but that didn't stop the loneliness from engulfing me.

When she came to group therapy the next morning, I was pleased that she looked better after having some extra sleep. The dark bags under her vacant eyes had diminished and were more of a shadow than anything else. But it was the glittering in her eyes that made me feel like a massive dick for making this about me. Her eyes glimmer with hope, and I know she's questioning whether this could finally be the day that the medication Dr. Manning pumps into her body truly works.

Fuck, I'm such an asshole. She's starting to have hope, which is fucking crucial in this place, and there's me feeling sorry for myself. Obviously, I want her to get better, and to get more sleep. I just don't want to sacrifice our time together. So, last night, as I sat in the kitchen making my hot chocolate, I was torn between wanting her to appear, and wanting her to be safely asleep in her room because that means the medication is finally helping, and she's getting better.

As she walked into the kitchen, tears streaming down her red, puffy face, my heart broke for her, whilst secretly being over the fucking moon that she was here. Last night, she made no effort to hide how much fucking pain she was in, and my heart was torn. I hated seeing her agony, but the fact that she was actually there, crawling into my arms, did unspeakable things to me.

I held her last night for longer than normal. At first, she just wanted me to wrap my arms around her, to hold her close to my chest as she curled up into a ball on my lap. You have no idea the things I had to think about to stop my cock from springing to life. I didn't need her thinking I was an asshole who got off on her pain. But, at the same time, I had the most beautiful girl I've ever met wrapped around me, her soft, silky skin touching mine. It was nearly impossible for me to keep my cock under control.

When she finally stopped crying, we just talked. She didn't want to talk about that night, and even though I asked her repeatedly, she told me to drop it. I hate that she still doesn't trust me enough to open up to me. There were so many times as we sat there, just getting to know each other, making each other laugh, where I could have told her about my plan. I should have told her, but I didn't, and now I really fucking regret it.

"Morning, Dylan," Sin shouts as she bounds over to the table where I'm preparing my coffee, pulling me out of my head. I can't stop thinking about Addy and the plan I need to implement today. I'm starting to think I should have warned her. She's clearly a good actress, she's been hiding the nightmares she has each night, and our time together, so I'm sure she can act surprised by my plan. Sadly, it's too late now.

"Morning, Sin. How you doin'?" I ask, trying to get my voice to sound like Joey's signature saying from *Friends*. It's been a running joke between us since the first day we met. She joked that she expected me to be a lot more flirtatious, given the way I'm portrayed in the media, and so now I don't disappoint. What I love about Sin is that she has no filter. She literally says whatever she's thinking, fuck the consequences. Few people would have ever said that to me, yet she did without thinking. I've liked her ever since.

"Shit, that gets sexier each and every day, rock star." I can't help but laugh at her cheesy, unoriginal nickname for me.

"I try to please," I say with a wink as I take a sip of my coffee.

"Who are you trying to please this morning?" Addy asks, sneaking up on me from behind. Although she still insists on us keeping our distance from each other during the day, we still talk a little, particularly during the group sessions.

"Can I say you?" I give her my best cocky grin, and she just rolls her eyes, reaching past me to pick up the coffee jug.

As she leans over, her chest presses against mine, and she's so fucking close I can almost taste her. She smells like vanilla and honey, the body wash she uses causing me to drool like a hormonal teenager.

"You can, but I would save it for someone you stand a chance with."

"Oh, you wound me with your vicious tongue," I joke, as Sin jumps in with another example of how she should think before she speaks.

"I bet there's a lot she could do with her tongue." As soon as the words leave her mouth and her brain catches up, she slams her hand over her mouth. Her eyes widen in shock as a blush spreads across her cheeks. "I didn't mean to say that out loud," she mutters from behind her hand, as both Addy and I laugh.

"Right, guys. Please, can you take your seats so we can get the session started?" Dr. Hughes shouts, grabbing all of our attention as she points to the circle of seats in the centre of the room.

We're all creatures of habit, and we all move to sit in the same seat every morning. I remember on my second day, when I tried to sit in Lenny's seat, having not realised we had an unofficial seating plan. He kicked off so badly, and I learnt my lesson. Once we are all in our seats, the door springs open, and Dr. Manning walks in. He has this pompous air about him, and I'm sure I hear Sin groan when she sees him. We all hate it when he sits in on our sessions. There's only Sin who isn't afraid of showing her annoyance. Though I'm sure that was completely accidental.

Pulling up a spare chair from the side of the room, Dr. Manning drags the chair into the space between Sin and Addy, who automatically shuffle their chairs farther away from him. Which leads to the whole circle shuffling around, moving their chairs back to make the circle big enough to add in an extra person.

"Good morning, everyone." Dr. Hughes pauses to allow for the echoes of everyone returning her greeting. "Dr. Manning has agreed to join us for this session, as it's a particular area of interest to him. As I mentioned at the end of the last session, we need to look at causation. You all have a 'go-to' for when you are struggling to cope. Maybe you fall into depression and sleep all day, you may look for solace at the bottom of a bottle, or you may opt to self-harm yourself. These are all coping mechanisms we need to change. We need to give you the tools to make better decisions on how to handle your emotions, so that when you face a complex situation, you know how to deal with it. But before we can even think about retraining your brain, we have to look for the catalyst. What is it in your past that created your response?"

Groans echo around the group, as we all know there's no way we are getting out of today without talking. Most days, the majority of us can get away with just a little share, just enough so Dr. Hughes doesn't stress out about us not taking part. But on the whole, we leave it to people like Sin and Sally-Anne who love fucking talking.

Dr. Manning puffs out his chest, something I've noticed he does when he's trying to portray his importance. He's an arrogant asshole, who is about as slimy as the gel he wears to slick back his hair. He can't be more than ten years older than me, but he carries himself with a level of self-importance that even outdoes me, and I'm a fucking award-winning, loved all around the word, millionaire rock star. So, the fact that he can come across as more arrogant than me really is a warning bell.

"As Dr. Hughes mentioned, this is my area of expertise. I specialise in looking at traumatic past events, and how they can impact our future. One of the main things my current research is looking at explores the idea of whether we should treat the here and now, or whether we need to look to the past. Can we teach you coping mechanisms to just get past your current issues? Or is that pointless unless we fix the past?" Dr. Manning sounds like he's reading from the most boring academic journal in the world. When I'm dealing with Dr. Hughes, she never makes me feel like a patient. I know ultimately that's what I am, but she never makes me feel like that. She just makes me feel like I'm someone she's trying to help, and each approach is individualised. There isn't a one-size-fits-all approach. Yet, in the space of one monologue, that pretentious asshole has made us all sound like fucking lab rats. He has a theory, and he's testing it all out on us. I suspect he already knows the answer, and he wants us to fit into the perfect box he's creating. The more this guy speaks, the less I like him.

"Surely that's a given. Even without looking at mental health specifically, our past shapes us. Our past defines us and makes us who we are," Addy says, shocking us all, as she doesn't normally speak in the group sessions unless they force her to.

I agree with every word she just said, but I see an opening to begin my plan, so I take it. "I think that's a cop-out. Yes, our past influences us, but to say it's the reason we act the way we do feels like a bit of an excuse.

If I were to drink a bottle of vodka now, surely it's my choice and I have to own that, rather than blaming the shit that happened to me fucking years ago while I was a kid."

All eyes turn to me, and I can see Addy looks confused as to why I would challenge her. Even though this was supposed to be my way of starting an argument with Addy, I actually believe what I just said is true. Obviously, I'm not going to deny that my shitty upbringing didn't play a part in why I'm here, but to dismiss the choices I made would be a definite, easy cop-out where I didn't have to take full responsibility for my actions.

Dr. Hughes aims her massive smile at me as she supports my statement. "That's an excellent point, Dylan, and it's actually a discussion Dr. Manning and I have had on numerous occasions. Even though the past plays an important part, is it our choices that define us, rather than our pasts?"

Dr. Manning claps his hands together once, as though he's trying to get all eyes back on him once again. "I think that's the perfect place to start. I want each of you to tell us why you're here, what negative traits you have that you feel you need to change, and how that relates to your past. Then, as a group, we're going to explore which element is of most importance."

Lenny, who is usually the most silent in the group, gingerly raises his arm, asking for permission to speak. He's looking at Dr. Hughes, his terrified look visible to anyone paying attention. His hand shakes as he moves it into the air. "What if we don't feel comfortable talking about our past in the group?"

We all look with bated breath, as it's a question on all our minds, we just never expected Lenny to be the one to say it. In fact, right now, even Lenny looks shocked, if his wide eyes are any indication. Before Dr. Hughes can address him, Dr. Manning chips in. "This is group therapy, and the whole point of it is to open up. You have been working together as a whole group now for a few weeks since Dylan joined, and the rest of you will have been here a little before that, too. By this point in your therapy, I would expect you to be comfortable talking in front of each other. Otherwise, what has Dr. Hughes been doing with you?" Dr. Manning practically spits the last part, his voice dripping like acid off his tongue. His face is crinkled into a look of pure disgust, and I've never wanted to punch him more.

Dr. Hughes' face falls and a pink tinge spreads across her cheeks, embarrassed that her boss is essentially calling her out on her performance in front of the whole group. I like Dr. Hughes. She's a big part of why I feel like I'm getting back to an old version of myself, and I will not sit here and let this asshole drag her down.

"Dr. Hughes has done amazing things with this group, I will have you know. Have you ever thought maybe it's you we don't feel comfortable talking in front of? You've been here five minutes, and you basically called us lab rats you are experimenting on to get the research results you need. You don't see us as people the way Dr. Hughes does. She gets to know us and treats us as individuals. You, on the other hand, just want the research so you can publish and have other people blow smoke up your ass to make you feel more self-righteous and important." As soon as I finish, Sin claps and laughs, which then seems to set everyone else off. Dr. Manning's face morphs into an angry glare as his fixed glare aims directly at me.

"ENOUGH!" he yells, silencing everyone in an instant. "I will not be spoken to like that in my hospital, Dylan. We will discuss this matter later. Until then, I think it's best you simply speak only when spoken to. Understand?" His pale green, murky eyes glare straight into mine, and his eyes look almost completely black, like you would expect someone possessed by a devil to look. Obviously, I know he isn't really a demon—I'm not quite that insane yet—but there's no denying his eyes look evil right now and they're fixed on me.

Rolling my eyes, I want to fight back. I'm a fucking world-class, chart-topping, millionaire rock star, and I can't remember the last time someone chastised me in this way. He's making me feel like a naughty schoolboy being punished as a child. I'm about to snap back until I see Dr. Hughes looking directly at me. She's trying to get my attention, and I watch as her mouth moves, and her hands make small gestures—small enough that Dr. Manning can't see what she's doing—and I try to work out what she's saying. It's not until the final hand movement that I understand what she's asking.

"Yes, I understand. I will keep quiet," I drawl, trying to sound as unconvincing as possible. I may be doing what Dr. Hughes asked, but that doesn't mean I can't be rebellious at the same time. She was telling me to just agree with him, not to kick off, and so I agreed.

"Good. You," Dr. Manning says, pointing to Sin.

"You can begin. I want to know your background, your vice, and why you are here. Tell the story in any way you like, but be sure to give us plenty of detail that we can then pick apart."

Fuck, I hate how clinical he's making it sound. Surprisingly, I found that I quite like group therapy. I know I was very against it when I first got here, but now they're a regular part of my day and I like everyone in the group. But, as much as I like them, I don't like the idea of them picking apart the details of my life. I hate when I do it with Dr. Hughes and she's a fucking professional. This just feels like getting a bunch of amateurs with their own issues to pass judgement on my life. I, for one, don't feel in any position at all to be commenting on other people's lives.

Sin takes a deep breath and pauses for a second before she begins to talk. We're all a bit stunned, as Sin is most definitely not known for thinking through what she's going to say. I think whatever is about to come out of her mouth will not only be the truth, but it will terrify her, too. "I guess the easiest place to start is something the group is already aware of—why I'm here."

Sin looks down, and is about to hold her arm out to the side, until she realises she can't. Normally, Addy is sitting next to her and during the hard parts of group therapy, Sin will reach over and take Addy's hand in hers. She will pull strength from having that contact, but since Dr. Asshole pushed his chair in between them, that can't happen. Lenny, who sits on Sin's other side, next to me, must have noticed the same thing I did because he reaches out and takes her hand in his, sending her the strength she needs to repeat what we already know is a horrendous fucking story.

"I'm here because after years of dealing with abuse and anorexia, I felt that my only way out was to literally try to end my life." Gasps echo around the room as Sin opens up more than ever before. She's never said she tried to kill herself before. "I was probably close to killing myself with my eating disorder, anyway. My heart was in a lot of distress, but I didn't care. As far as I was concerned, it wasn't happening quick enough for my liking. So, I took a handful of pills… I don't even know what they were, I just threw them down with some liquor and crawled into bed to die. Obviously, someone found me and called the hospital. They worked their asses off to save me, and all I could say when I woke up was that they should have let me die. They decided there and then to commit me, and given that they found me home filled with drugs, they did it via a court order."

Dr. Manning is smiling from ear to ear, and I can't help but wonder what the fuck is wrong with him. There's a sombre silence around the room as we all take in probably one of the worst moments in Sin's life, and he's fucking smiling about it. "That's great, Sin. Now, why don't you tell us your diagnosis and your vices." There's a happy tone to his voice that doesn't fit with the moment, and we're all looking at him as if to say, 'What the fuck are you so cheery about?'

"So, obviously suicidal ideation and attempt was the main diagnosis, but since I've been here we've been working on anxiety, depression, and anorexia," Sin mumbles, losing that cheerful edge she usually has.

"Excellent," sings Dr. Manning, as he rubs his hands together like the world's shittest *Bond* villain. Did he really just say that what Sin is suffering from is excellent?

Everyone looks equally stunned, and Dr. Hughes has obviously seen the sheer horror on all our faces, as she steps in trying to cover for her socially inept boss. "I think what Dr. Manning means by that is it's excellent we could come up with a diagnosis, since that plays such a big role in determining your treatment path. Pinpointing exactly what your diagnosis is, as opposed to what your symptoms are, can be a completely different thing."

Sin gives Dr. Hughes a small smile, and I think her backtracking on that asshole's behalf has put everybody at ease. Except for Dr. Dickhead, who has a face like a slapped ass, as he glares at Dr. Hughes with laser focus.

"Thank you for that, Dr. Hughes." His voice practically drips with acid as he snarls at her, sounding anything but thankful. Dr. Hughes seems to shrink in her seat, obviously picking up on his not-so-subtle tone. Turning his attention back to Sin, he continues, "Now, tell us about your history."

The knuckles on the hand clutching Lenny's turns white, and he winces in pain, obviously impressed by the strength on the little waif of a girl. I watch as Sin bites her bottom lip and her whole body seems to shake. It's difficult to miss that this girl's clearly terrified.

"Erm… So, I-I… I'm…" Sin mumbles quietly, her voice quivering as she tries to find the words.

Addy has a murderous look on her face as she speaks with much more conviction that I would have ever expected from her. "Why does she have to do this if she doesn't want to? Can't you see how much you are hurting her? Surely that isn't therapy, it's torture."

Dr. Manning spins his whole body so that he's facing Addy, since he's sitting next to her and she isn't able to see him fully. I expect her to shy away and avert her gaze, but she raises her chin in defiance. A subtle gesture, but one everyone in the room notices. Anger is clear in Dr. Manning's voice. "Addison, this has nothing to do with you. Everyone will be expected to engage in the therapy fully. You can call it whatever name you like, but this is a very respectable technique, and I fully believe in it. Therefore, we will continue the session."

Addy isn't happy with the response, and to be honest, there's a lot of us that aren't. Addy turns her attention to Dr. Hughes, who is squirming and looking uncomfortable, as though she's caught in the middle of her parents arguing and she doesn't know which side she's supposed to take. "Dr. Hughes, didn't you say at the beginning that this is an experimental approach and our results would go towards research?"

"Yes, that's correct," Dr. Hughes replies, her eyes glancing over to Dr. Dickhead before flashing back to Addy.

"Well, surely if it's experimental, then we have to give consent to take part? That means we can opt out, surely." Everyone in the circle suddenly looks hopeful, because what Addy's saying makes sense, but before Dr. Hughes can answer, Dr. Dickhead cuts in.

"Enough. I am in charge here and we are completing the session. You have two choices here, Addison. You either shut up and let Sin finish her story, or you take over and tell us yours. What shall it be?" His voice is sadistic, the air of authority back again, and I can see he absolutely hates having his authority threatened.

Addy is about to argue back, given the look of fury etched across her pretty face, until Sin speaks first, "It's fine, Addy. I will tell my story."

"Are you sure?" Addy asks, as she looks at Sin with concern on her face. She really cares about her, even if she sometimes gives off an indifferent vibe.

Sin nods, and Dr. Dickhead actually laughs before telling her to continue with her story. I can't help but think of all the ways I can remove his balls and feed them to him.

Taking a deep breath, Sin tells her story. "I'm going to break it down, as it will be a long one if not. When I was a child, I wasn't really wanted. I was the baby of a family of six, and at certain points in my childhood, I considered whether my family knew I existed. It wasn't that they abused me as such, they just treated me like a ghost, and they severely neglected me, both physically and emotionally. They starved me of love and attention, and so when I was fifteen and I met my ex, I was an easy target."

Sin pauses, then takes another deep breath, and I see Lenny squeeze her hand for support. She gives a small smile before continuing. "At first he was lovely, adoring, and so fucking kind. He made me feel like a princess and I fell for him hard. Now I know it's a well-used grooming technique, but at the time I didn't know any better. He told me I needed to be skinny, and he pushed so hard I developed an eating disorder. He introduced me to drugs, getting me hooked on them to the point I craved them on a daily basis. That's when he said I need to pay for the drugs. But he wouldn't allow me to go out and get a job. He'd already cut me off from any family and friends that still knew and cared that I existed. He said my only option was to prostitute myself. I needed more drugs to get me through those horrendous moments, and it became a vicious cycle."

Sin drops her head before reaching up with her spare hand to wipe away a stray tear that had fallen. I notice Addy doing the same thing, and I can see that she, too, is feeling Sin's pain. In fact, we all are. This quirky little pixie girl, with her bright and bubbly energy, has known more pain and hardship in her eighteen years than most people feel in a lifetime. And I know I'm not the only person in this circle whose heart breaks for her. The silence in the room is almost palpable, as we all give Sin a moment to compose herself.

Unfortunately, Dr. Dickhead doesn't seem to have the ability to read other people's emotions—an unfortunate trait for a psychologist—and he just barrels right into the next question. "Brilliant. Thanks for sharing that, Lucinda. Now, my question to you is, do you think your past was responsible for your suicide attempt?"

Sin looks around at the group, shame evident as she decides how to answer such a personal question in front of others. "I think it definitely plays a part. Had I not experienced what I went through, I would never have got to the dark place I was in."

Nodding his head, Dr. Manning looks over at the group, addressing us all. "What do you all think?"

Addy is the first to speak up, her protectiveness of Sin overpowering her desire to slink back into the shadows where she normally resides. I've been in group therapy with Addy for the last few weeks now, and this is the most she has spoken compared to all the other sessions combined. "I don't think we have any right to discuss it. Sin has her reasons, and they are personal. You can't possibly expect her to talk about such a personal situation."

Dr. Manning's brow furrows and his steely gaze is aimed at Addy. He looks furious, and I expect her to shy away, but she holds her back straight. To anyone who doesn't know her, she looks confident, but I can see her anxiety shining through. The way her fingers fiddle with each other discreetly, giving her hands something to do. When she isn't talking, she's chewing on her lower lip as her nerves take hold. You can even see a slight tremor in her hands. She's terrified of standing up to Dr. Manning, but I'm so fucking proud that she is. Although, this is ruining my plan. I don't know how I'm going to argue with her when I couldn't be more proud of her and agree with every word she says.

Fuck... I have to implement my plan today. I have no other options. I just need to wait for the right moment, and hope I don't hurt Addy too much.

"The whole point of the group session is to learn from the experiences of others, Addy. So, we will discuss Sin's suicide attempt and look at her reasons, and then when we come to you, we can talk about when you tried to kill yourself and the reasons behind that."

Gasps echo around the circle, and my own shock

joins them as all the colour drains from Addy's face. Fuck, she's never mentioned a suicide attempt before. Even with all the self-harm I see each and every night, it's never fit with the Addy I know. Don't get me wrong, I know she is shrouded in darkness, and there are some days she struggles to even function, but I've never thought her capable of truly harming herself. So, learning she has tried to end her life makes me question how much I really know about her.

"What happened to confidentiality?" Addy mutters, her eyes glazing over with unshed tears, and my heart breaks for her. I want to say fuck them all, walk over and take her into my arms, but nothing good would come from that.

"We maintain confidentiality within the group, Addy. So, don't try to use that as a cop-out. Back to my original question. Is it Sin's past that's to blame for her suicide attempt, or her present?" Dr. Manning either doesn't realise Addy is in pain, or he simply doesn't give a shit. He clearly needs to get results from this shitshow of a research project, and he will stop at nothing to get the results.

"Her past," Addy mumbles, not even bothering to expand.

Seeing my opening, I jump in. I try to give Addy a sign, a small smile and a wink, but I'm not sure if she sees me or not. Her head is downcast as she tries to hide away from the raw wound Dr. Manning just opened in front of everyone.

"I think to blame her past is a cop-out. It wasn't past Sin that tried to kill herself, it was this Sin. She may have been influenced by all the bad shit she went through, but if you were going to blame those instances, then why didn't Sin try to kill herself the first time she was prostituted, or the first time her ex abused her? For those to be classed as catalysts, surely they would have to be recent events. There will have been a reason why Sin chose that moment. Her past may have influenced it, but it wasn't the cause. If Sin knew how to deal, maybe it wouldn't have happened." As soon as the words leave my mouth, Addy's eyes shoot up to meet mine.

"Are you saying she tried to kill herself not because of all the bad shit that happened to her, but merely because she doesn't have the coping skills to survive?" Addy snaps, and even though she's asking about Sin, I can tell she's referring to herself.

Fuck, now is the time to backtrack. I can see how much I'm hurting her, and it fucking breaks my heart. As I glance over at Dr. Hughes, I can see she's watching our interaction with interest, and I know this is my moment. I will just have to apologise afterwards.

"Yeah, I think that. I had bad shit going on in my life from the age of eight, but I didn't turn to drugs to cope at that age. Something triggered me at a much later age. Yes, the shit I went through in my past played a part, but it was the crap I dealt with that happened with my ex that caused me to turn to drugs. If I'd had a better coping mechanism, or the strength I had when I was eight, things could have been different."

"So essentially, my past means nothing?" Addy snaps, and even though that's not what I'm saying, she's just picking up on the worst parts, I run with it.

"Not nothing, but it's not as relevant as you're making it out to be. Think about a time in your past, the worst moment when you first experienced the pain that brought you here. It was a couple of years ago, I think I remember you saying. Did you have the same nightmares you do now back then? If that was the worst time in your life, surely your nightmares should have been happening then too?" I ask. I regret it instantly.

Addy's face drains of colour and her eyes appear to be looking right at me, but it's like she doesn't see me. She's looking right through me, like I don't even exist. And fuck, does that not feel like a knife to my heart. Everyone is staring at Addy, waiting for her to answer me, and she opens her mouth a couple of times but nothing comes out.

Sin, noticing how much pain Addy is in, jumps in. "Ads, have you been having nightmares again? Is this like the ones you had when you first got here?"

Shit, I expected Sin to jump to her defence, not question her further. Addy's already vacant eyes fill with unshed tears, and she's frozen. Never have I been more pleased that Dr. Manning speaks. "Addy, focus. We've discussed your nightmares in detail, and you informed me that the treatment is working. Is this not the case?" His voice comes out harsh and snappy, almost like he's pissed that she discussed her nightmares with anyone else, but the idea she told me really seems to grate on him. The laser-focused glances he throws my way would be enough to kill if his gaze was harmful. The level of disdain is clear on his face as he looks at me. He always has an air of self-importance, which causes him to look down on others, but this is different. The way he's looking at me right now is pure hatred, and I do not know why.

Dr. Hughes jumps on the end of Dr. Manning's sentence, clearly trying to soften his harsh tone. "Addy, I know it's difficult to talk about things that scare us, or that affect us badly, but it's really important for your treatment, and your progress in this programme that you can confide in us and tell us what you are dealing with. You can't expect us to help you if we don't know the whole story." Even though Dr. Hughes does a much better job than Dr. Asshole, she still comes off a little judgy, and I can tell Addy hears it, too.

"I-I… I've got to go," Addy mumbles as she stands, her chair scraping across the floor to the point it grates through everyone. I can feel it ripple down my body as I shudder. Addy stumbles, not really knowing what to do. She wants to run, but the idea that everyone is looking at her is too much to take.

"Addison, sit down. The session is not over," Dr. Dickhead, in true form, stands and addresses her in his sternest voice. What he obviously doesn't know about Addy is that she hates when people are condescending and look down on her.

Standing up a little taller, Addy finds her voice, and I couldn't be more pleased. "No. I don't agree with what you are doing here. I will talk about my issues when I feel up to doing so. I've talked about things with you in private because I trusted you, but you've just blown that trust out of the water by telling everyone stuff I thought was confidential. And as for what you said, Dr. Hughes," Addy says, as she turns to address a very shocked-looking Dr. Hughes. "As far as I'm concerned, I told my psychiatrist everything he needed to know. I told him about the nightmares that haunt me, and he gives me pills. He never asks me if they work, and so I never tell him how much worse the nightmares have got since I first got here. So, don't you dare say this is my fault. I told my healthcare professional, and it's his job to help me. Don't you dare lay blame on me."

Both doctors look shocked, like they don't quite know what to say. Addy might have found her voice, but the terror she's feeling is still very real. Her whole body is physically shaking, and her words, although she's loud and stern, it's easy to miss the slight quiver when she speaks. Her skin's drained of colour, and her vacant eyes are filled with tears that are rolling down her face.

Sin stands up and moves around Dr. Manning until she's standing right in front of Addy. Unlike Dr. Dickhead, she doesn't look like a threat; she holds her arms up, the universal sign she doesn't mean her any harm. With movements that are almost painfully slow, she moves one arm to rest on Addy's shoulder. She goes slow enough that Addy could have moved away or stopped her if she wants, and it was enough to not freak her out. I can tell Sin wants to hug her, but Addy isn't ready for that. She looks down at Sin, and all the pain is swimming in her eyes. She hates being this vulnerable at all, let alone in front of other people. I've only ever seen her like this with me, and my body literally itches to go to her. But I can't this time, because this time I'm to blame.

My body has been fighting addiction for the last couple of weeks, and I've almost become used to the annoyingly ever-present itch under my skin, letting me know I could really do with a hit right about now. Those feelings I've grown used to. I wouldn't say I'm on top of them, or a recovered addict. I'm still an addict who is barely hanging on to his sobriety, but I'm learning. Yet, the desperate need to go to Addy, to hold her. That itch is worse than any craving. Maybe she's become my drug. Maybe I'm craving Addy, and now I've ruined it and can't have her. My body is withdrawing. Though I feel this will not be an easy addiction to beat.

Sin slowly moves her other hand up and sweeps Addy's luscious brown locks out of her face. She leans down and whispers in Addy's ear, but it's loud enough that we can probably all hear. "Addy, I remember what it was like when you first got here. The first time you saw Slender Man in your dreams. You told me how he abused you, humiliated you, and even sexually assaulted you. Having to relive him every night was slowly killing you. But then you seemed to perk up. You told me Dr. Manning had found a treatment, and you never spoke of Slender Man again. You have to tell me, do you still see him?"

Addy seems to take a quick breath as she allows more tears to form. "He never went away. I stopped telling people because I knew they would just think I was going crazy. It's more than a nightmare. I know he's just an urban legend. My dad used to tell us the story when we were growing up. Logically, I know he's not real… but to me, he is. He feels real. The pain and suffering he inflicts feels real. So, yes, I kept that a secret, but I think I had a fucking good reason for doing that. Now you all know how fucking insane I am, and I'm going to be stuck here forever." Her words run together towards the end as she voices her real fears for the first time. Even I didn't know she believed her nightmares were real. I knew she was dreaming of being tortured and abused, but I had no idea she thought he was real. I believe that's called psychosis, and that's way out of my remit. I don't know how to help her. I try to tell myself that I've done the right thing here. I may have had an ulterior motive to make it look like we're not really friends, but actually it has got her talking about the real issues she's clearly suffering badly with.

I bullshit my brain into thinking I've done the right thing, but all that changes when Addy shrugs out of Sin's arms and turns to me. Her once emotionless eyes are now lit with flames as she stares at me, contempt evident in the way her face screws up as she looks at me. "It takes a lot for me to trust someone, and once that trust has been broken, it can never be repaired. You all know my business now, and hopefully I will be able to heal from this, or it might have traumatised me. I guess we will have to see. But one thing I do know, I won't ever put trust in the wrong person again. I want to make this very clear, and I wholeheartedly mean every word, and no intervention will change how I feel, so please don't try. Dylan, I trusted you, and you abused that trust. You have hurt me more than I thought anyone was capable of doing. I'm a person who has felt the worst possible pain imaginable, so I thought everything after that would be a walk in the park, would pale into insignificance. Yet you still managed to break my already fractured heart.

You've reminded me why I don't need or want friends. So, stay the fuck away from me. I will be civil in group, but otherwise, I never want to speak to you again."

Eight
ADDY

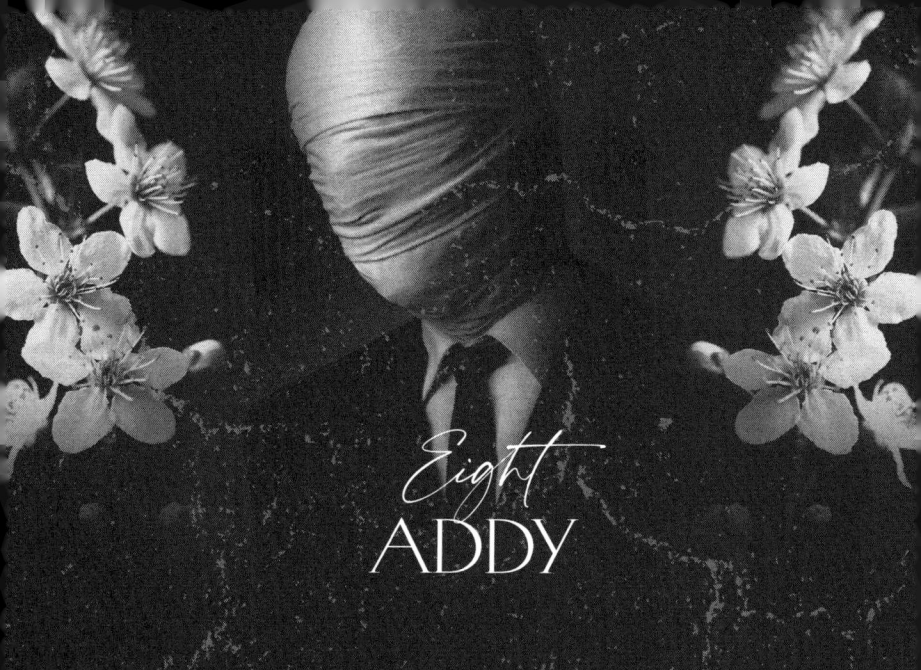

AFTER THE FUCKING DISASTER THAT WAS GROUP SESSION almost a week ago now, my routine has been severely disrupted. I guess when you confess you haven't been getting better and in fact you have been becoming more psychotic, that's not something the professionals can ignore.

They pulled me out of the group therapy, as they felt like I needed to work on myself before joining back with the group. I think they also worried things between Dylan and I would kick off. They have nothing to worry about from me. I made him a promise that we would never speak again, and I fucking intend on sticking to that. Clearly he's not got the message, as he tries to contact me several times a day. No matter where I am, he finds me. Like our souls are connected, and he just has to pull on that rope to find where I am, then he appears. Each time he tries to talk to me, he says the same thing. That I need to listen to him, to hear the full story. But, he's wrong. I don't have to listen to anything he has to say.

My sessions with Dr. Manning have been more awkward. He seems so fucking pissed that I told someone about my nightmares, and that I didn't tell him about the full extent of my psychosis. He started asking me weird questions, like if the man had a face, or if I could place his voice, if there was anything remarkable about him. It's like he's trying to find out how real I've made this guy in my head. I didn't know the answer to any of those questions, but they got me thinking…what if I pay more attention to the details? Maybe then, when I find out exactly what it is about this man that is tormenting me so much, then I can start to heal. He has to be more than a figment of the story my dad told me.

Dr. Manning is doing research, and he's coming to see me shortly to discuss a new type of medication. If I'm being honest, I'm so fucking done being a guinea pig. I just want to decline all the medication and do it my way, but I know if I do that, Dr. Manning will record me as being uncooperative. There are only so many times they can do that before I risk getting kicked out of the programme. I know that sounds appealing, getting out is what I've been yearning for. But I'm here by secure hold, which means if I'm non-cooperative, they can get a judge to declare me mentally incompetent, and Dr. Manning will take complete control over me and my life. It has to be him because I have nobody else. No relatives, no friends. Nobody.

I'm getting ready for bed when a knock sounds at the

door. I know it's not Dr. Manning, because he just walks in. Pompous twat thinks he's too good to knock. I send a silent prayer to whoever the fuck is listening that it's not Dylan on the other side of the door. I want to stand firm. I want to stay away from him. He hurt me so fucking bad; he doesn't deserve my friendship. But, I miss him. I miss his touch and the way he calmed me down after an episode. The feel of his hand trailing circles around my back and arm as he held me tight. He warmed me in places I thought were long since gone. The fire hasn't burnt in my core for a while, but he has a direct line, even from just the way his sexy silver eyes look almost molten when he looks at me. He looks at me like he wants to devour me, and sometimes, I think I might want to let him.

"Addy, it's me, Dr. Hughes. Please, can I come in?" Shit, I was so caught up thinking about how sinfully hot Dylan is, and how much I really need to forget all that and focus on what a dickhead he is. I was so caught up in him, I forgot someone was on the other side of the door until Dr. Hughes started shouting.

I pull the door open and give her a small smile. Gesturing with my arm, I invite her in, pointing over to the chairs and table by the window. She gives me a grin before taking her seat. Maybe she thought I'd turn her away? She's not technically my psychiatrist, that would be Manning. She runs my group therapy, and gets a say on that, but overall, Manning is my main carer, and he's the one responsible for my care pathway and my individual sessions. So, it's unusual Dr. Hughes would come to see me, particularly so late at night.

"Shouldn't you have gone home a while ago?" I voice what had been going through my mind, and she let out a small laugh.

"Yes, I should have, and I'm sure my cat will have plenty to say about my being late, but I needed to talk to you, and I want you to know that this conversation is completely confidential. I know after the group session you don't trust that, and have been struggling to open up since then, and I don't blame you. But the reason I came to see you so late, when there's nobody else around, is because I have concerns, and I can't turn a blind eye to them. I also can't tell you what they are until I have proof, and I'm sorry if that breaks what little trust you had with me, but I have to be honest with you."

Now she's piqued my interest. "So, you are looking into something presumably related to my care, but you can't tell me what, and you need me to not tell anyone you are investigating whatever it is you are looking into?"

Dr. Hughes nods her head, a sincere smile helping to settle my nerves. Dylan always used to speak highly of Dr. Hughes. He said she was one of the good ones. She genuinely wanted to see him get better, and she's not afraid to do the hard things to get there. She would call him out on his shit, and it's really helped. But that's what Dylan said. Can I take his word and believe that I should trust this woman?

"Yes. I can't tell you anything until I have sufficient proof. Or if my suspicions turn out to be unfounded, I will tell you that straight away. All I ask is that you keep our meetings private and not share them with anyone."

"Why do I get the feeling you were about to add,

particularly Dr. Manning, at the end of that sentence?" I ask, and she lets out the slightest chuckle. Her hand flies to her mouth, almost like the laugh escaping was unplanned, and she tries to hide her mistake.

"Yes, it really is imperative that he doesn't know." Her voice is sombre, and she looks around the room suspiciously, almost like she's worried there's someone watching or listening to our conversations. I know there are security cameras in the halls, looking at the doors to our room, but there are not supposed to be any cameras in our room. There's a couple of suicide watch rooms near the nurses' station, and if they deem you a suicide risk, then you have to sleep in one of those rooms, and there are cameras in there watching your every move. I get that… there's a use for them in those rooms. But to have them in our personal room feels invasive.

"Are there cameras in my room?" I whisper, needing to know the truth.

Dr. Hughes shakes her head. "No, I don't believe so. There are not supposed to be cameras in any of the patients' rooms, other than the suicide watch rooms."

"So why do you look so shifty?"

Her giggle returns as I reach over and take a sip of the hot chocolate I made to get me winding down ready for bed. It doesn't taste the way he makes it, and all it does is make me miss him more. But, it's part of my nighttime routine and so I have to stick to it.

"I'm sorry if I've put you on edge. That was never my intention. Can you tell me a bit about your nighttime routine? I've read some parts of your notes that discuss this routine, but there's also a lot of vagueness in your notes, and I would love for you to fill in the gaps," Dr. Hughes explains, as she crosses her legs, clearly getting more comfortable. Even after working more than a twelve-hour day, she still looks perfectly put together. Her pencil knee-length skirt still looks smartly pressed, her flowery blouse is perfectly in place. Even the ponytail she's pulled her hair into doesn't have a strand out of place. This woman is the epitome of perfection and a classic beauty, but I don't think he sees that. Her passion lies in helping others, or at least that is what Dylan told me. Now is the time to find out if that's true or not.

Taking a big, deep breath, I tell her the whole sordid tale. From the first time Slender Man invaded my nightmares, right through until last night. I tell her about how real he is to me, and all the ways he torments and humiliates me. I show her the cuts, bruises, and scars that adorn my body, that I've inflicted upon myself while in the throes of a delusion. I tell her about seeking help from Dr. Manning initially, and how he told me that talking about my delusions with others was a guaranteed way to keep myself locked here indefinitely. She looked most shocked when I told her about all the fucking experimental shit I let him pump into my body, hoping I can force Slender Man to stop haunting me. I tell her all about the stories Dad used to tell, and how I think this is his way of haunting me, punishing me for the terrible sin I committed. I let it all out, and I can't stop the tears.

When I finally look up, I notice Dr. Hughes has tears flowing freely down her beautiful face. Her mouth flops open, then closed, like she's trying to find the right words. But what do you say to help someone who has been tormented by her own mind for so long she's reached breaking point? Because that's exactly where I am right now. I don't know how much more I can take.

It can't help but think back to the small respite I got when I was with Dylan. He couldn't take the pain away, but for a short time, he let me into his bubble and he kept me safe. He held me and gave me a safe space to forget about all the shit in my life. Then he went and took that all away. Even if he believes he has a good reason, I don't. He broke my trust, and he started the discussion that saw my biggest secret let loose in the world. He risked me ever getting my freedom from this place, and that's something I don't think I can forget.

Finally able to find her voice, although thick with emotion, Dr. Hughes replies, "I'm so sorry, Addy. I had no idea you were suffering so much. We have weekly meetings where the more extreme cases are discussed, and you were never mentioned at it. The mere fact he's using experimental drugs on you should be something the whole team is aware of. Particularly since I facilitate your group therapy. Did you say Dr. Manning administers the drugs himself?" she asks incredulously as I take another sip on my now lukewarm hot chocolate, trying not to think of the memories it brings.

"Normally, yes. Or one of the other nurses, whose name I can't remember, he does it a couple of nights per week. Is that not normal? He said with them being experimental, he's the only person authorised to administer them, and obviously the nurse must be too." I rack my brains, trying to recall anything he's said about the meds, anything at all that might be useful for Dr.

Hughes, but I just can't think of anything.

Her face crinkles just for a moment before she pulls her professional mask back into place. But, just for a fraction of a minute, I saw the concern laced in her features. "It's not protocol, but that doesn't mean Dr. Manning doesn't have a very good excuse for his behaviour. It may be something to do with the rules of the trial. I'm not entirely sure, but I promise you, I will look into this." Whilst her words try to sound strong and sure, I can hear the uncertainty in her voice. She doesn't believe the words coming out of her mouth any more than I do. I do not know why Dr. Manning is keeping my care a secret from everyone else. Maybe he's giving me drugs he shouldn't, experimenting off the books to see what works and what doesn't. Perhaps he's only trying to do the best for his patient. Nevertheless, other healthcare professionals should be involved. Or at the very least, I should be fully informed about the decisions made for my care. That's when it occurs to me, he doesn't have to tell me shit. They declared me mentally incompetent when I was sectioned. As far as the law goes, while I'm here under a secure hold, he's the person who makes decisions in my best interests, because there is nobody else. He doesn't need my permission, or to even tell me what he's doing, and that scares the shit out of me. Maybe now I've confided in Dr. Hughes, she will help me gain control of my life again.

"Can you help me?" My voice sounds desperate, almost pleading, and I know she's my last chance. I can't keep going like this for much longer, feeling betrayed by my brain. If I don't get free soon, I don't think I ever will.

"Addy, what you are describing is a very complex version of psychosis that seems to manifest only when you're asleep. I will be completely honest and say I've never seen dissociative or psychosis episodes present in this way before, nor have I heard of this. That's not to say it doesn't exist, it could just be very rare. Dr. Manning has over a month's head start on me, and will no doubt have already done research around the presentation, but that doesn't mean I won't do my own. I will look into it myself first, then I will approach Dr. Manning to find out what he knows and which treatment plan he's using. I will work as quickly as I can, because I know how much this is hurting you. I can't promise to have answers right away, but all I ask is that you trust me when I say I am looking into this. I want to help you. Hell, I want to help all my patients. I don't want people coming into our facility and feeling like they get worse. You should be getting better, and I will do my damnedest to make sure you do." Her voice is passionate and rings around the room, sincerity bouncing off all the walls. Leaning forward, she lays her hand on my arm and gives me a small smile. I think this woman genuinely cares, so the least I can do is give her a couple of days to get things sorted.

Just as I'm about to reply to her, the handle on the door creaks and we spring apart like teenagers who have been caught doing something they shouldn't. Dr. Manning waltzes into my room without knocking, the way he does every night. He stops in his tracks when he sees Dr. Hughes, his suspicious gaze raking over her body.

"Amy, what are you doing here?" he snaps,

addressing Dr. Hughes by her first name, no doubt as a way to undermine her authority. He loves reminding people he's the psychiatrist in charge of this facility, and other than a facility manager that I've never seen before, he's the person in charge. And fuck, does he like to let everyone know that.

"Stephen," Dr. Hughes says politely, one side of her mouth pulling up into a cocky grin as she uses his move against him. His eyes narrow and his brow furrows, his displeasure more than evident. She ignores him and continues, "I was just checking how Addy is. She's not had a few good days, and I wanted to make sure she was okay to return to group tomorrow."

His nose crinkles like he's just smelled something foul. "I'm her primary physician, that's my decision," he snaps, venom dripping from each word. What a tool.

Dr. Hughes seems to shrink down, clearly not enjoying being told off by her superior—especially in front of me. Taking a deep breath, I decide to step in to help her. "It was my fault, Dr. Manning. I approached Dr. Hughes and said I felt ready to return to group therapy. I didn't know I needed to go through you, as Dr. Hughes is the psychiatrist in charge of the group. So, it's my fault."

Out of the corner of my eye, I notice Dr. Hughes releases a big sigh of relief, but I keep my eyes trained on Dr. Manning. His laser focus never leaves me, and if looks could kill, I'd be six feet under by now. He looks suspicious, like he's not sure he can believe our story or not, and for the first time I question why he's acting so oddly. Why is he suspicious of us? Is it really him that has something to hide? Maybe he doesn't want Dr. Hughes to find out what medication he has me on, or to see my care plan, because it will be there, in black and white, hard proof that he is failing. No matter what he tries, Slender Man is stronger. That must be an embarrassment for a world-class, lead psychologist.

"Fine, well… we can discuss this tomorrow." The hint for Dr. Hughes to get out is implicit, if not verbalised.

I stare at Dr. Hughes, unable to hide the fear from my face. Now that I know Dr. Manning is lying to her about my care, I'm terrified of having anything to do with him. But, legally, he's my guardian and all of my legal and medical decisions go through me until I can gain back my competence. He's the person who decides that I'm competent—the irony of that is not lost on me! Seeing my obvious distress, Dr. Hughes discreetly lays a hand on top of mine and fixes my gaze with her determined stare.

"I'm so glad you are feeling better, Addy. We have got this, and I'm always here to help whenever needed. It will all sort out." She then turns to Dr. Manning, and adds on the last part, just for him. "Dr. Manning and I will discuss your case and see if two minds are better than one. Won't we, Dr. Manning?"

His jaw twitches and I can see he's not happy, but as quick as a flash, he hides the obvious annoyance that appeared first, and he smiles at me, then Dr. Hughes. "Of course. We only want what's best for you, Addy. Now, if you will excuse us, Dr. Hughes, I'd like to get this visit concluded so I can at least go home to see my wife today."

Without even thinking about what I'm saying, I blurt out words before I clamp my hand over my mouth to stop myself. "You're married?!"

Dr. Manning's and Dr. Hughes' laughter fills the room, though it's obvious Dr. Manning's is a little more forced than natural. I don't know why I'm surprised to find he's married. He looks to be in his early thirties, and he's not a bad-looking guy. Strong, chiselled cheekbones. Plump, pink lips, a pointed nose just a little too large for his face, and almost cloudy pale green eyes all make him look a little posh, and give him the typical rich guy good looks you expect English royals to have. His dark brown hair is more gel than anything else, but it's always styled so perfectly, not a strand out of place. He's so put together, it's almost laughable that he works in a place surrounded by broken people.

"Just because we spend all our time here, doesn't mean we don't have lives outside of Lakeridge," Dr. Hughes explains, as she stands and walks towards the door.

"Yes, you better get home, Amy. I saw you're down for the early shift in the morning," Dr. Manning instructs, sounding like a parent reminding their child about their responsibilities. The blush that spreads across Dr. Hughes' face seems to agree with my analogy.

"Sleep well tonight, Addy. Remember, sleep can't harm you. It's only your mind" I try to take on board what she says, to really believe it, but it's hard. I want to believe that all this bullshit is from my brain, that it's my mind manifesting as Slender Man. Yet, I don't believe it. I want to believe he's all in my head and that he's not real, but the more I see him, the more he touches me, and terrorises me, the more I believe he is real. Which leaves me fighting against my sanity.

Dr. Hughes leaves, and Dr. Manning gives me the lecture I've been waiting for. Telling me how important it is that I trust him and that I confide in him. That telling other people is fine, if that's what I want to do, but he makes it very clear he believes if I ever want to be sane again, then it's him I need to lean on. After what feels like his longest lecture to date, he pulls out the medication I've been taking. He reaches over to give me it, and I hesitate for just a fraction of a second, but it's enough he catches it. "Look, if you don't want to take part in this experimental trial, then say the word. Granted, it will ruin it for everyone, corrupt the scientific data, and possibly cause the whole trial to fall apart, but that is your choice."

Wow, talk about the fucking hard sell, but I know he's right. Just because this drug doesn't appear to be working for me, doesn't mean it's not working for the countless other people taking it. It wouldn't be in this stage of testing, being admitted to patients, if it didn't work. Or at least that's what I keep telling myself.

Taking a deep breath, I try to explain what I'm thinking without pissing him off. "I'm not saying I want to come off the drug, but I would like to know more about it. I can't even remember its name." I've been racking my brain, trying to remember how much he told me about the drug when he told me I was joining the trial, but my brain's been so foggy recently, it's a fucking miracle I remember my own name sometimes.

"Okay, well, tomorrow I will bring you all the paperwork that we went over when we joined the trial. Even though I'm in charge… of your medical decisions, Addy, I am a reasonable man. You only have to ask, and

I would be more than happy to go through everything with you." I don't miss the way his voice deepens and practically growls when he says he's in charge. Even though he adds on the end about my medical decision, we both know he meant it how it sounded originally. Dr. Manning runs this facility, and he lets no one forget that.

I take the medication without a fuss, ignoring the niggling in the back of my brain asking why I'm taking medication I don't know anything about, which could potentially be making me sicker. But, the reality is, if I don't swallow this pill, Dr. Manning will have me deemed combative and will have me strapped down to the bed and I will be injected with the drug. The decision should be mine, but it isn't. So, I take it willingly, and pray to whoever is listening that tonight is the night it works. That I've seen the last of the Slender Man.

It feels as though I've only been asleep for a short amount of time before my nightmare begins. I feel as though I'm woken up by the rattling noise of the door, but of course, that's all in my head. As the door slams shut behind him, and the closing of the lock echoes around the room, I try to tell myself not to be scared. That I can't fear something my head is creating, but I know that's a lie because the closer he gets to the bed, the more fucking terrified I am.

Then, that mechanical voice that literally haunts my dreams captures my attention. "Hello, Addy. I hear you have been a very naughty girl. I thought I clarified that you are not allowed to discuss my presence with anyone, yet you did it in front of a whole group of people."

I'm just about to question how the hell he knows about that, but of course he does. If the Slender Man is a figment of my imagination, then it stands to reason he knows everything I've been through. "I didn't mean for that to happen."

"Stand," he snaps, and I instantly rush out of the bed to stand before him. "Do you think that telling people will get you help? Do you think Dr. Hughes knowing will make things better?"

Before I even have a chance to answer, pain ricochets through my cheek as he slaps me. The force sends me off balance, and I feel as though my brain is rattling around in my skull, not to mention the burn I feel spreading across my cheek. Grabbing hold of my hair, he roughly pulls me over to the chair. All the pomp and circumstance he usually puts me through is long forgotten, and he drags me until he's sitting on the chair, and I'm bent over his knee like a naughty child about to be punished.

Wasting no time, he literally rips the pyjamas off my body, the torn fabric is thrown into the corner of the room, no longer serving any purpose. Normally when he spanks me, he drags it out for as long as he can, humiliating me with each blow. He has me count them and thank him for them, all while he massages my ass cheeks, trying to get my pussy as excited as possible. In his sick and twisted mind, he thinks if he stimulates me enough, I will enjoy it. He pretends I'm wet, even though I'm dry as a bone. No way could I ever get excited about this torture.

Changing from his usual routine, he slaps his palm

down hard onto my right ass cheek, and before I even have time to acclimatise to the pain, he repeats the process on the left. He rains down blow after blow, across both cheeks and my upper thighs. He uses his free arm to grab hold of my waist, his legs capturing my hands, as I scream and writhe around, desperately trying to break free from his hold. This isn't for some sick, twisted sexual pleasure like it normally is. This is about inflicting pain—punishment.

Tears are streaming uncontrollably down my face, mixing with the snot as I hyperventilate, trying to catch my breath in between the blows. The stinging is like nothing I've ever felt before, as he rains down blows on my already sensitive backside. When he's finally finished, he pushes me off his lap until I'm a collapsed heap on the floor, gasping for breath as I try to gain back some element of control.

"Have you learnt your lesson?" he asks, and even with the mechanical voice, it's easy to hear the condescending tone.

What fucking lesson? All I know is the sick, sadistic fuck just beat me. He can claim it was a lesson all he wants, but there's no denying the Slender Man has a rock-hard cock, thanks to his abuse of me. He gets off on causing pain and humiliation, and I just have to put up with it. My brain is so fucking messed up. How can a simple urban legend my dad once told me get twisted so badly it becomes this nightmare?

Wanting to avoid another beating, I answer with exactly what he wants to hear. "Yes, Sir. Sorry, Sir. I have taken my punishment like a good girl and have learnt my lesson. Please, don't punish me anymore." I'm straight up begging now, not sure my body can go through any more pain. It feels so real, so all-consuming. It's terrifying.

"Good, now we can move on to the best part of the evening. I'm going to fuck your ass, hard and fast, because that's what naughty girls like you deserve. But, since this is a punishment, I will not use any lube. However, before you complain and get yourself into more trouble, you took that punishment like my good girl, so I will allow you to suck my dick and get it wet. That's the only thing we will use, so if you don't want my cock to rip you open, you better get it nice and wet."

His words echo through my mind, freezing me to the spot. Every night seems to get that little bit worse, and this really tops things off. As I pull up onto my knees, ignoring the sharp pain shooting through my ass, I crawl until I'm in between his legs. My head bowed, I resign myself to my fate. As he pulls out his cock, I think to myself, *I don't know how much more of this I can take.*

I scream and shout, thrashing around on the bed as I desperately try to free myself from my dream. That's when I hear something, and I worry Slender Man is coming back. He's just left me battered, bruised, destroyed, and the thought that he might be back so soon is more than I can take. I scream, hoping like hell that someone, anyone, can hear me.

I hear the noise again, but it sounds different. I try to focus, and although I have no idea who it is or what they're saying, it's definitely not a mechanical voice. I latch onto the soft, smooth yet deep voice, and I let it pull me back to reality. I can't open my eyes yet, so fucking scared of what I might see when I open them. Instead, I just listen to the voice.

"Hey, Addy. Listen to my voice, pretty girl. I'm here. Come back to me."

I feel the bed beside me dip as the person lowers themselves down to sit beside me. I freeze, but there's something in the back of my mind that's reassuring me there's nothing to worry about. That the person really is here to help. But, the problem is, my mind is the last person I should trust right now.

Taking in the surrounding scene without opening my eyes, I can feel a hard body beside me. Close enough that I can feel their body heat, but they're not touching me. That's when I smell the familiar cocoa scent, and I know exactly who it is. I allow his presence, his scent, everything that is Dylan, to envelop me, and I can't deny that he's calming my racing heart. I know I should be mad at him. That I shouldn't forgive him for what he did. But, if just his presence alone can still my tortured mind, imagine what being held by him could do. We will have to talk, eventually. I probably should have heard him out all those times he tried to talk to me, but I wasn't ready. I'm still not. Talking can wait, but I need him to hold me.

Opening my eyes, I look up at him and see his silver eyes are glazed over with unshed tears as he looks at me with concern. Before I know what he's doing, he pulls his t-shirt off, exposing his fucking gorgeous inked chest. I want to look, but I'm too freaked out that this man is undressing in front of me. I try to scurry away, but he holds his hands out for me.

"Take this. It should cover you fully," Dylan says, giving me a small smile, but making sure to look nowhere other than my face. That's when I look down and see I'm completely naked, the bedclothes I wore last night over in the corner of the room torn to shreds, while the duvet is in a crumpled mess on the floor. I must have just been laying completely naked, screaming like a crazy lady on an unmade bed.

As I roll over to face Dylan, I can't help the hiss that escapes me as the pain from all over my body invades my senses. I reach out to take the t-shirt, my hand shaky and almost too weak to do it. My whole body trembles, whether it's from pain, cold, or fear, is undecided. The t-shirt feels heavy in my hands, and for a moment, I consider whether I actually need it, as the effort of covering my fragile body seems far too fucking much.

Dylan must sense my hesitation. "Would you like me to help you with that, pretty girl?" His voice is soft and tender, almost reserved from what I've come to expect from Dylan. He's looking at me like I'm a timid animal, about to scatter at any moment, and if I could move my body without causing unspeakable pain, I probably would. I guess it's safe to say the medication Dr. Manning tried is not working. This nightmarish hallucination seemed more real than ever.

"Please." It's all I manage to squeak out, my voice sounding rough and hoarse after all the screaming. Even though these walls are soundproof, there should still be nurses occupying this area, monitoring it and making sure I'm okay. Either they don't hear me at all, which is really worrying, or the even more terrifying thought is that they hear me and do fuck all.

Almost as though I weigh nothing at all, Dylan lifts me up, his warm hand gripping my hips in the most delicate of ways as he manoeuvres me until I'm sitting up. He's been respectful, very careful not to look at my naked body, but now that I'm no longer curled up into a ball, and my assets are on display for anyone to see, he's unable to look away. For a flash of a second, I see something that could only be described as hunger, but that's quickly replaced by concern and then anger. I hate to see him looking at me like he feels sorry for me.

Moving my arms slowly to try to cover up my body, I hope he has missed my cheeks flushing from the humiliation of having him see my naked body for the first time, and him being repulsed by it. But before I'm able to cover myself fully, he uses one hand to gently take my hands in his. All his movements are slow and gentle, and I know he's waiting for me to stop him at any moment. The fact that he's asking consent to just look at my body causes my heart to soar. I guess genuine, nice guys really do exist.

Using the arm that isn't gripping my hands, he gently strokes it across my battered and bloody skin. He starts on my arms, and moves over my collarbone, tracing wounds that travel over to my back. He leans over, and I twist slightly to make it easier for him. Part of me is screaming, telling me I have to stop him. I don't want Dylan, of all people, seeing how broken and marred I am. I never want him to look at me differently. But, the other part of my brain, the one that's winning right now, she is sick of all the secrets.

Even though Dylan was the one who blew things up for me last time, sharing my biggest secret in group—which is the reason I'm supposed to be mad at him—despite all that, I want him to know. There's a part of me that trusts him, despite what happened before. So, I let his gaze travel over my body, and I try not to wince or cry out too much when he reaches a particularly fresh or painful wound.

"Addy…" His voice is full of anguish, and it trails off as he loses the words that should follow.

"I know, I'm sorry."

"Why are you apologising?" Dyl asks, and honestly, I don't know. It just feels like the right thing to say, and so I just shrug. "Addy… these marks. There are so many in various stages of healing. These fresh wounds, in particular, will need cleaning."

I give him a small nod, but that's the most I can manage right now. He seems to realise that's what I'm hinting at, and as he chews on his deliciously plump lower lip, I can see he's mulling something over in his head. "Just ask what you are so desperate to ask, Dyl."

Letting go of my hands, he reaches up so that both hands are lightly gripping my cheeks, ensuring that I don't avert his gaze. I ignore the electric shocks cascading down my spine as his fingers touch my skin. He's sitting so close I can feel the warmth from his naked chest. I want to look him over, to analyse his ink, but there will be time for that later. Besides, this is obviously very important, and so I push away all the pain and try to focus on Dylan.

"Let me be very clear when I say this, I still think you are the most beautiful girl I've ever laid eyes on, and seeing you now doesn't change anything. But I have to ask… how did you get these wounds, Addy?" He seems almost sheepish at the end, but I barely register that he's finished speaking. My mind is still caught up on the fact that he just called me the most beautiful girl he's ever seen.

I want to believe Dylan is just flirting, trying to make me feel better, but that's just not the type of person he is. I know he calls me pretty girl, but I figured that was just a nickname. I have a surreal fangirl moment, where all I can think is Dylan fucking Matthews, drummer and songwriter for one of my favourite bands ever, The Catastrophists, just told me I'm the most beautiful girl he's ever met. He's travelled the world, no doubt having a new girl or two in every country, and I doubt he even remembers the ones he was with while high. Yet he's still sitting here, looking at me like I hung the moon. It's no wonder my heart's racing, my palms are sweating, and my stomach is doing tiny little flips. Not to mention the heat warming up my long-forgotten core.

He lightly strokes his thumb across my cheek, no doubt trying to pull me away from the very obvious daydream I was in just then. He's so close. I could lean forward, close the gap, and finally feel how soft his lips really are, but I fear he's rejecting me. Words are one thing, but actions are something else entirely. So, I decide to answer him honestly and hope like hell he still thinks I'm normal at the end.

"The marks are from when the Slender Man visits

my dreams. My hallucinations become so real, and I genuinely feel as though they're real, that I leave marks on my body. Some I can't even possibly explain how I got them, but it's always the same. Almost every night, I've been asleep for maybe an hour, if not slightly longer, and that's when he comes." I take a deep breath, leaning into the hand cupping my cheek, and I pull strength and comfort from the thumb delicately sweeping across my cheek. It's enough that I'm able to continue, his molten silver eyes watching me with rapt awe.

"I would say it happens around five, maybe six times a week, and there's no pattern. I know logically they are hallucinations that happen while I'm dreaming, but they don't feel that way. It feels like I'm really awake, and the real Slender Man is here abusing me. You don't have to tell me how crazy I sound," I add, trying to move my gaze from his, but he doesn't allow it.

"I never said you were crazy," he states firmly, pulling a small smile from my sombre face. "But I am worried about these marks. Can you tell me what happens in the dreams to cause these marks? That way, I can try to piece together what you are doing in the real world to damage yourself like this. Some of the wounds look pretty specific, but I'm not sure you could do that to yourself."

I know he's only trying to help, and Lord fucking knows I need someone to be in my corner, but I just don't know how going over all this is going to help anyone.

Reaching over, I take hold of the t-shirt, and Dylan seems to understand exactly what I want. If I'm going to open myself up to him, it will be vulnerable enough, without being naked on the top of it. Instead of letting me do it, he moves the t-shirt over my head, and as he pulls it down, I'm enveloped by a smell that is all Dylan—cocoa and peppermint. I try my hardest not to deeply inhale, making it obvious that I'm sniffing his t-shirt, so I try to do it discreetly. The moan I can't help but release is far from discreet, and thankfully Dylan doesn't say anything. Although I catch the slightest hint of a smirk on his face. It's actually quite nice that he feels he can be normal with me. I don't want him to change when he hears what I have to say.

"Can you hold me while I tell you?" I ask, looking up at Dylan through my eyelashes, desperately hoping the desperation wasn't too obvious.

Without a word Dylan shuffles until he's sitting at the top of the bed, his back resting against the wall, where there should be a headboard. He opens his arms for me and just like I've done so many times before on the sofa in the common area, I climb until I'm laying by his side, nestled into the crook of his shoulder. He wraps his arm around me, pulling until I rest my cheek against his bare chest. I lift the arm I'm not lying on and wrap it over his chest, loving the way my skin seems to tingle when it connects with his naked flesh.

We snuggle until we are both comfortable, and I feel fully enclosed within his arms, safe and protected. Listening to the rhythmic beating of his heart and the soft melody of his breathing, I feel my own beginning to calm, instantly becoming in sync with him, like we were made to exist together.

Fuck, I don't know what it is about tonight, but being around Dylan now, I feel more than I ever have before. I should feel mad, angry at him for what happened, but I don't. It's like my body is telling me he's capable of not only protecting me, but caring for me despite everything. And that is something I need. This visit from Slender Man was rough, probably one of the toughest I've encountered compared to before because he just seemed so angry at me. In the past, it had all been about him exerting his authority over me, and him using me as a fucking plaything, but tonight was more than that. He wanted to punish me, to teach me a lesson, without letting me know what exactly it was I had done wrong. Last night he pushed me further than ever before and if that's how my nights are going to be going forward, I don't know how many more I can take. Having Dylan here afterwards to calm me and help me come down from that pain is just what I need, but he can't be here every time, and even if he is, there's only so much I can endure and I'm close to my breaking point.

Dylan says nothing, he just lightly strokes my arm, and he uses his free hand to trace across my face. After a few deep breaths, I tell him everything. I don't just tell him about last night's visit, I tell him about them all. I try to keep them in, but the tears fall of their own accord, dripping onto Dylan's bare chest, but he doesn't say anything, he just lets me talk and cry.

When I finish telling him the whole sordid tale, I wait for him to say something, and I just lay there. I'm too afraid to look up, just in case he's looking at me differently. I feel him holding his breath under my cheek, and after a while the bewilderment gets the better of me. I have to know what he's thinking, and more importantly, I need to know if he's going to be looking at me differently from now on.

Pushing myself upwards, I sit on my knees next to him, until we are at eye level, and I pull the t-shirt down just to make sure it's covering all my girly bits. Not that it matters, since he's seen it all before, and I think him catching a chaste view of my bruised ass cheeks or my pussy is the least of my problems right now.

Finally, I look over at him and the first thing I'm shocked to see is the tears in his eyes. It's clear he's trying to hold them back, but the glazed look in his normally silver eyes makes them look almost molten. He's chewing on his lower lip, but not in the anxious way I'm used to. This looks more like he's biting hit lip to stop himself from talking. But, as he meets my gaze, what I love most is that he doesn't look at me with pity. Yes, there is an element of sadness there, but it's more like he feels sorry for what I've been through, not that he pities me. Yet, the main emotions etched across his beautiful face are anger and concern, and I need to know if he's angry at me.

"Can you say something now?" I ask, my voice coming out barely more than a whisper, as I feel more vulnerable than I ever have before.

Dylan gives me a small smile, and I watch as he opens his mouth a couple of times, but closes it again just as quickly. It's like he doesn't quite know where to start or what the right words to use are. I take hold of his hand in mine. I may not have much strength left, but I want him to know that he can tell me anything.

Looking down at our clasped hands, Dylan finally speaks. "Addy… I honestly don't know what to say. I want to tell you how very fucking sorry I am that you are going through this, but I know you don't want my pity and you don't have it. I'm also very fucking angry that Dr. Dickhead knows all about this, yet he's clearly not doing anything to help you. He's playing God, deciding what the best course of treatment is without talking it through with you. Just because you are in a secure facility, doesn't mean you should lose all your rights. I will be honest, I want to help you… but I have no fucking clue what to do. You are genuinely one of the nicest people I've ever met, and I'm so sorry I hurt you. On top of everything you are going through, that was the last thing you needed, and I have no idea how to apologise." His words get faster and he sounds more desperate and lost.

He genuinely believes that he's caused me pain, and he's beating himself up for that. It actually warms my heart to hear how sorry he is, and I can tell he genuinely is mad at himself for hurting me. I know he has his reasons, and eventually I will hear him out, but right now, knowing he's sorry is enough for me. It's been a very long time since anyone has ever given a shit about me, so hearing this beautiful guy, who feels so intensely, and takes on all my pain and wants to help me, feels fucking amazing.

I don't know where it comes from, and it's certainly not something I was thinking about or had planned, but out of the blue, I lean forward and press my lips against Dylan's. It's the slightest little kiss, and our lips only touch for a second before I pull away, and we both sit there stunned by my spontaneous action. My lips tingle, and it's almost like they ache to be pressed against Dylan's again.

His sparkling silver eyes look at me before he looks down at my plump, pale lips. The way he looks at me, I feel it right down in my core, heating me up and making me forget about the horror I just experienced in my dream. I pull my lower lip in between my teeth, trying not to squirm under his fucking sexy gaze. He looks like he's warring with himself, and I have no idea what he's thinking. Hell, I'm not even sure if I'm thinking logically. All I know is I want to feel his lips against mine again. So when he leans forward and captures my lips with his, I'm over the fucking moon.

As soon as our lips touch, and we press them together harder this time, it's like we are both electrocuted and brought to life. We shuffle and move with desperation as he pulls me until I'm sitting on his lap, straddling him. One hand is gripping my hip, pulling me against him, while his other hand is at the back of my neck, controlling my movements so he can deepen the kiss.

My hands instantly snake into his hair as I grip hold of it and pull him against me. My tongue sweeps across his lower lip to gain entry, and he's only too happy to comply. Our tongues battle for dominance as I take in his taste and the feel of his hard body against mine. We are so close, I can feel every ridge and every muscle. I can't get enough, and as he pulls me closer, my pelvis tilts and that's when I really feel him.

His grey sweatpants cover his rock-hard cock, and I can feel him rubbing against my bare pussy. I'm sore, battered, and bruised everywhere from where I've injured myself in my delusions. I don't even want to think about what I did to myself to make my pussy so sore. I try not to think about it, to just feel Dylan, but it all becomes too much.

Pulling my face back slightly, we still keep holding each other as we gasp for breath. I can feel him beneath me, and it doesn't scare me like I thought it would. Ever since I met Dylan, I've been worried he could be just another delusion. My brain is giving me everything I've ever wanted. He's literally the guy I dreamt about dating as a teenager, and now he's here with his tongue in my mouth, calling me the most beautiful girl he's ever seen. It sounds too good to be true, and I'm not going to lie, until this moment I thought it could be. But I know he's real. My brain isn't capable of creating something so beautiful and perfect. The only problem is that I feel tainted. I know Slender Man isn't real, and I haven't really been sexually abused, and that the injuries I sustain are caused by myself, but that doesn't change how I feel. The idea of anything happening with Dylan, not even an hour after Slender Man assaulted me in my nightmares. It feels wrong—icky, almost.

As if he can read my mind, he uses one of his hands to raise my chin until I meet his gaze and he settles my fears. "Hey, pretty girl, stop freaking out. It was just a kiss, and we can stop now. I know you have been through a traumatic event tonight and I would never take advantage of that. I didn't intend to kiss you, but when you kissed me, I couldn't hold back. I want you to know, whatever this is, we will take it as slow as you need. I just want to be here for you. I want to help you."

I can hear the kindness and the sincerity in his voice, and I really believe him. "But what about you? If Dr.

Hughes believes you are with another patient, you could be kicked out and sent to prison. Then you could lose your band. It's not worth the risk," I say, and am shocked when he shakes his head.

"Addy, I may not have known you for long, and honestly, I have no idea where this will go, but I already know you are worth the risk. I have to help you, and more importantly than that, I can't stay away from you. There's something about your lost, broken soul that calls to mine. Maybe together two broken people can become whole. I think I was always meant to find you." He tucks a rogue strand of hair behind my ear before pressing the slightest kiss against my lips. It's soft, tender, and so fucking beautiful. Even after he pulls away, it's like I can feel he's still there.

"I feel the same. There's something about you I'm drawn to. It's like we're magnets, and the world is forcing us together. I really hope you can help me, and maybe when we both get out of here, we can see if this is something real."

With a smile, he pulls me down until I'm laying in his arms, curled up like a ball. I don't want to move, I want to stay attached to him forever. There's a safety in his arms that I'm not used to feeling. We lay like that, companionable silence filling the air as we both just hold each other, and for once, when I feel sleep pulling me in, I don't fear it. I don't know why, but I do trust that Dylan will be there to protect me, even if the one he's protecting me from is myself.

Nine
DYLAN

The next few days pass by in a blur. Things have become so easy and natural between Addy and me. Each night, after her nightmare has scared the shit out of her and she's harmed herself even further, and the nurses give her permission to leave her room, she finds me. Either in the kitchen, or she comes to my room. Thankfully, when I first got here, I was still going through my diva behaviour and I demanded there be no camera's outside of my room, and given I practically have a whole corridor to myself to ensure not only my anonymity but also my safety, it's easy for Addy to sneak into my room.

We fall into the same routine, where I hold her while she finds the strength to come back to me, and I try to pretend I don't see the worsening marks across her body. They terrify me because I worry that one day just harming herself won't be enough. And when that day comes, I could lose her.

Addy informs me Dr. Hughes is looking into her case now, which is reassuring because I don't trust Dr. Asshole as far as I can throw him. I think he's more concerned with his ego, and how he looks to his peers, than actually doing his job and caring for patients. Whereas Dr. Hughes cares, of that I am certain.

This morning, when Addy crawled into my bed, I knew something was different. There's a brightness in her eyes I wasn't used to seeing. She told me that last night was one of the rare nights that her nightmares weren't filled with him, that she actually got a bit of sleep. I think back to this morning, and try to keep my dick from breaking, given how rock hard he is.

"Hey, Dyl, are you awake?" Addy whispers as she pushes the door to my room open. The only other sound is her bare feet making contact with the cold hardwood floor.

I roll over, not caring that she woke me up, and flick the small light on beside my bed. "Yeah, I'm up. Are you okay?" I ask, as I blink a few times, trying to get my eyes to focus on the new light.

As she gets closer to my bed, the small bedside light casts a glow over her petite frame, and while I try to see any signs of new injuries, I can't help but appreciate how fucking gorgeous this girl is. And she doesn't even know it. The baggy Nirvana t-shirt of mine that she's wearing dwarfs her petite frame, hanging down to her mid-thigh. Her long brunette locks fall across her chest, and even though it looks mussed up, it gives her that after sex bedhead look that only women can rock. Her emerald green eyes sparkle, which is something I'm not used to seeing. Don't get me wrong, even dulled they are beautiful, but with the glow back in them, they are quite the spectacle.

Her creamy white thighs that peek out from beneath my t-shirt make her legs look longer than they are. I can't help but wonder if she has any underwear on beneath my t-shirt, and that thought wakes my cock up in an instant, so I try to get him to show a little restraint.

As Addy climbs onto the bed, kneeling next to me, I try not to look down at her pussy. She's obviously here because she needs me, not so I can perve on how fucking insanely gorgeous this girl is. If I thought she looked good before, it's nothing compared to how she looks wearing nothing except my t-shirt.

"I actually had a few hours' sleep with no disturbances. I even dreamt like a normal person. Do you have any idea how fucking amazing that feels, Dyl?" she shrieks, her whole body practically humming with excitement as she bounces on her heels besides me.

"I'm so happy for you, Addy. How do you know it was a normal dream?" I'm not trying to rain on her parade or anything, I'm just trying to understand what she goes through a little more. The more I know, the easier it will be for me to help her.

A blush spreads across her cheeks and I hold my arms out for her to climb into them, like we've done for the last few nights. Although, this time, instead of resting her head against my chest, her body is suddenly flush against mine, and she crawls into my lap until she's straddling both thighs. My hands move to her hips, and I grab hold to stabilise her—or to feel that this is really happening. It doesn't feel quite real.

I know all the moves I would normally make. All the ways I would normally pull the woman into my hold, shimmying her body into position and grinding her against my hard cock. But it's like I have to — well, I want to — throw the rule book out of the window with Addy. Not just because we are both in a secure psychiatric facility, so now is hardly the time to think sexy thoughts — though they are there all the fucking time now! But Addy's mind is so fragile. At first glance, I would think she's a tough cookie with a lot more fight than you would think, and I would say she could easily kick depression's ass with a little help. But she has so much more going on. The nightmares are so intense, so graphic, and scary that she actually believes she's being assaulted. She actually believes a man with no face is raping her while she sleeps, and she hates her body so much she abuses herself. I have no fucking experience of being around women with complex mental health needs such as those, and so I feel the best thing to do is to just let Addy take the lead. It's not like I can ask Dr. Hughes for advice. That would just get me a one-way ticket out of here and straight to a regular prison.

Thankfully, Addy takes the lead, and she moves her body until she's sitting directly on my cock. I can feel the heat from her pussy, making me wonder once again if she's wearing any underwear underneath my t-shirt. If she isn't, then only my boxers and the small sheet covering my body separates us. She laces her fingers through my hair, pulling it just the way she knows I like, and I look up at her gorgeous eyes, and the mischievous glint I see there has me hard as a rock.

"Someone is in a good mood tonight," I joke, as I tighten my grip slightly on her hips.

She chuckles, and it rings out like music to my ears. I think this might be the first time I've ever heard her laugh. I'm talking real, unrestrained laughing, and that makes me so fucking sad. This girl deserves to laugh more, and I'm going to make it my mission to make her laugh every day. "I was going to say the same thing to you," *she jokes as she rolls her pelvis against my hard length, making her pun very fucking clear.*

"Well… you can hardly blame me for that. The most beautiful girl I've ever met is half naked, wearing my t-shirt, and she's grinding all over my cock. You are lucky I haven't blown my load in my boxers. If you tell me you don't have any panties on beneath that shirt, I don't know what I will do." *I stroke my hands down from where they were on top of her t-shirt, down to her naked thighs. If I slide my hands back up and under the t-shirt, I will have my answer, but I try to show restraint, just enjoying the feel of her silky skin beneath my calloused fingers.*

She freezes, removes her hands from my hair to cup my cheeks, guiding me to ensure I meet her gaze. "You really think I'm the most beautiful girl you've ever seen?" *she asks, her insecurity ringing out loud and clear, and it makes me so fucking mad that this gorgeous girl has no idea just how stunning she really is.*

I match her, moving my hands to cup her cheeks, making sure she keeps the eye contact she started. "Addy, hear me loud and clear when I say this. You are, without a doubt, the most beautiful girl I've ever met."

She averts her eyes, and I can see tears are filling them as she struggles to deal with the compliment. Her voice is barely above a whisper when she replies, "What about all my scars and marks? What about the fact that I genuinely believe I'm being raped by a faceless man every night?"

Using my thumb, I wipe away the stray tears that fall and I pull her closer to me, ignoring the way my boxer-covered cock sits more snuggly between her legs. "Addy, they just make *you even stronger. They are battle scars, reminding you that no matter what life throws at you, you are a survivor."*

Nodding her head, Addy agrees with me, although her tone takes on an edge I don't enjoy hearing. "I always survive, even when I shouldn't."

"What do you mean?" I ask, needing her to clarify that she isn't currently suicidal. I need nothing more than to keep this girl—my girl—safe.

"I should have died two years ago, but I didn't. I lost everything that day, and it feels like every day since then has been a punishment. God's—or whichever deity runs this fucked-up world—their reminder that you can't cheat death." She rests her forehead against mine, and I gently run my hands up and down her arms to soothe her.

"Do you want to talk about it, or do you want to go back to being happy and tell me about that instead? I'm here for whatever you need," I tell her, hoping she knows how much I really mean that.

Her head snaps up. "So, you are up for whatever I want?" That playful tone from when she first came into my room is back, as is the glint in her emerald eyes. Granted, the unshed tears are still there, but I can tell she's trying to push them back.

"Too damn right I am. So, what are you thinking?"

"I had just under six hours of uninterrupted sleep tonight, with no nightmares. I feel better than I've felt in a long fucking time. For the first time since I arrived at this shithole, I dreamt about something other than him, and for once, I want to live in my dream." Wow, that's a big thing for her to say, since her nightmares are the thing that she fears the most.

"Okay, so what was your dream about?" Please say it was about me, please say it was about me! *I think to myself,*

hoping like hell it was a sexy dream about us.

"I have no idea if it's another one of my delusions. If my brain can create Slender Man to torture me, maybe it created you to lure me into a false sense of security. Maybe it created you so that I could feel again, only for him to have more to take away from me." There's a sadness to her tone, and my heart breaks for her. She really has no idea what is real and what isn't. I don't know what it's like to question everything. To wonder whether the people in your life are real, or simply placed here just to torment you.

Leaning forward, I gently press my lips against hers, only for a moment. It's brief and soft, but it tells her everything I want to say. "I'm very real, Addy. I know you've been through a lot, and we can take things at your speed. But, there's one thing I want you to know. Even though we have to hide things from everyone for now, the time will come when we don't have to hide. I will claim you as mine, and I won't ever let you go. But for now, let's just take it a day at a time."

She doesn't hesitate; she throws her arms back around my neck and pulls me to her so that she can crash our lips together in a bruising kiss. Our tongues battle for dominance, and I can't hold back the groan when I taste her on my lips. I want more, so much more.

Using my hands, I stroke up her thighs, my fingers heating from the feel of her skin under my touch. I reach for my t-shirt, and I hesitate. Should I go under the fabric like I want to, or not move too fast and stick to above the clothes? Luckily, Addy decides for me by placing her hands on top of mine and gently guiding them beneath.

As my hand grazes over her soft skin, travelling up, I confirm my initial thought that she isn't wearing any underwear.

Our kiss deepens, and she removes her hands, letting me take control of where I want my hands to go, and she moves hers to my chest before inching them under the hem of my t-shirt and dragging her nails over my back. Fuck, does that feel amazing.

Needing more access to her, I grab hold of her hips and roll her until she's lying beneath me, my hard body pressed against hers. She lets out a surprised yelp as she digs her nails into my back. I break the kiss for only a moment, and as I'm about to move back in, she capitalises on it and tugs at the hem of my t-shirt. She's silently asking me to remove it, which I'm more than happy to do.

Once my shirt is off, I look down to see Addy looks mesmerised as she stares at the ink adorning my body. Her fingers reach out to trace along the numerous seemingly random designs. They all look like they are random, that they don't fit together, but to me they do. Every single one of them has a meaning, be that big or small. The ink adorning my body is like a road map of where I've been, and when I'm out of here, a tattoo to remember my time here will join the others. I don't just document the good, I do the bad and the painful because they help to shape who I am. Whilst being in rehab is one of the hardest things I've ever done, and something I would very much prefer never to repeat, it's still the reason I'm sober, and I plan on staying that way. So, in a year, or even ten years' time, when I'm having a wobble over whether I should use again, I will be able to look at the tattoo I choose and remember this time. Remember all the pain and suffering, and what I had to go through to get clean and to stay clean. I need future me to know not to fuck that up.

"They are beautiful," she says, her voice filled with awe.

"Not as beautiful as you," I reply, hating how fucking

cheesy I sound. But the truth is, I can't help acting cheesy and romantic around this girl. She deserves the world, and if you'd told me a couple of weeks ago that I would want to give a girl the world, I would have laughed in your face. I didn't even go back for seconds with the same girl. Yet, here I am, trying to woo her like I'm interested in something long term. Am I?

Fuck, I need to think about that answer pretty damn fucking fast because if I can't give this girl everything, then I need to walk away. She's been through more pain, loss, and suffering in her short life than most people ever encounter, and I sure as fuck shouldn't be adding to it.

As much as it scares me to think I might want a relationship when we get out of here, what terrifies me more is the idea of walking away from this girl. The thought of never seeing her again literally terrifies me. I want to be the guy to make her laugh, to make her smile, and most importantly, to make her realise that this life is real, and she really is entitled to good things in her life.

"You really mean it when you say we can take this as fast or as slow as I want?" she asks, unable to hide the trepidation in her words.

Nodding with a smile, I let her know I mean every word I ever say to her. "Of course."

She averts her eyes, and normally I would make her look at me, to make her face me rather than shying away, but I can tell that whatever she's about to say makes her nervous. Sometimes it's easier to say the hard things without keeping eye contact. "Can you show me how much you like me? I haven't been with a guy in a very long time, and even then it was only one guy for a few months. It was never anything special. I want you to show me what it's really like. That way, I will know you're not *a hallucination."*

Fuck, could this girl be any more perfect? I want to give her the world, but I don't want to push her. But, I can feel not only the sincerity in her voice, but the determination. She knows what she wants, she just needs my help. And let's be very fucking honest, doing this is hardly a punishment.

"Okay, but we aren't going all the way. This is all about you. You can tell me to stop, at any time, and I will. Okay?" I ask, and with a nod of her head, she crashes her lips against mine.

This time, my hand doesn't hesitate as I gently move underneath her top, scooping around the side of her boob until I reach her nipple. I gently take it between my thumb and forefinger and massage it until the nub hardens. Addy arches her back with a moan, thrusting her chest closer to me. Just as I'm about to do the same with the other nipple, Addy reaches down and pulls my t-shirt over her head and throws it onto the floor. I take a moment to admire the beautiful, very naked woman underneath me.

The longer I stare, the more I can see the blemishes and scars from all her episodes of self-harm. I look at the different shapes and sizes littered across her body, all in various degrees of healing, and I try not to see all the ways she's hurt herself. But mostly, what I'm trying not to see are all the scars that would be almost impossible to self-inflict.

I push all those thoughts out of my mind and focus on the girl before me, and on giving her exactly what she asked for. Parting my lips from hers, I lower my lips until I'm in line with her nipple, before slicking my tongue across her hard pebble. She arches her back, giving me the perfect opportunity to latch my mouth around her nipple, sucking it in and dragging out the most delectable groan of pleasure.

Alternating between sucking on one nipple whilst tugging on the other, I then swap over to ensure they both get the same attention. Addy falls apart beneath me, squirming away as her moans get louder. Thank fuck these rooms are all soundproofed, or we really would be fucked. Not that I care. Nothing is pulling me from this girl right now.

With my free hand, I lightly trace along her body, loving the feel of her silky smooth skin beneath my touch. It almost feels like her skin heats up, leaving a blazing trail wherever my fingers go. Until finally I reach her creamy thighs. As soon as I stroke my hand over the top of her thigh, her legs open farther for me. I look up at Addy, needing to know for certain that she's sure she wants this.

As Addy nods her head, I allow my finger to slide along her waiting slit, and as soon as I feel that she's wet, I can't hold back my appreciative moan. I swipe my finger along her slit a couple more times, just gathering plenty of her juices onto the tip, before pulling my hand away from her pussy. Making sure not to break eye contact, I slowly bring the wet finger towards my lips, ensuring she can see how my finger glistens with her juices before placing my finger in my mouth.

Fuck! Her delicate honey flavour with the slightest hint of salt fills my mouth, and I'm fucking salivating. One taste of this beauty, and I need so much more.

She looks enraptured as she stares at my mouth, her eyes blazed and full of hunger. "You taste so fucking sweet," I tell her, and I love the blush that spreads across her cheeks. This girl isn't used to receiving compliments, which makes me so fucking mad at the guy that came before me.

Leaning down, she captures my lips with hers, and I hear

the moment she tastes herself on my tongue as her pleasure-filled sigh fills the room. Lowering my finger back down to her slit, this time, I swipe it in a little deeper. As the tip of my finger reaches her entrance, I tease her by sweeping around her waiting hole, but never dipping inside. I then slide my finger up to her clit, pressing my finger against her engorged nub, and I love the response it pulls from her. Back arched, fingers gripping the bed sheet, as my mouth swallows her cries of pleasure.

Once I'm sure she's wet enough, I gently press one finger into her waiting pussy, making sure to keep my thumb lightly rubbing over her clit to ensure she feels everything. I slide my finger all the way in, and I can feel how tight she is. Even with only one finger in, I can feel her pussy gripping me tightly like a glove.

Moving my finger back out again slowly, this time when I push back in, I add a second finger. I move painstakingly slowly, needing to be sure I'm not hurting Addy, or moving too fast for her. As soon as both fingers are inside, I pause again, giving her time to adjust, but Addy has different ideas. Her voice is wanton as she thrusts her pelvis to give me her instructions. "Please, Dylan. Please move your fingers. I need more. I need to feel everything."

A smile spreads across my face as I look down at her beautiful face before giving her exactly what she asked for. My fingers thrust in and out of her pussy, my thumb continuing to flick over her clit at every available opportunity while my mouth captures and alternates between her nipples. Following her cries of pleasure, I work my fingers faster, loving the way she tilts her hips to meet my thrusts. Her fucking gorgeous body writhes underneath me, my boxer-covered cock is rubbing against her thigh. I know I said this was only for Addy and wasn't about me, but I'm really starting to fucking regret that now. My hard cock is straining to be free, and I can feel my engorged head is throbbing painfully. If I keep rubbing up against her thigh, whilst listening to the sounds of pleasure coming from this beauty's lips, I might come in my pants—something I haven't done since I was a hormonal teenager, desperate to see my first pussy.

I notice the moment it changes for her, when her moans become more frantic and the thrusts of her hips more uncoordinated. She's reaching that peak, and I want to see her fall apart. I gently curve my fingers as I increase my speed, and I feel the moment I hit that sweet spot as her pussy walls begin to tighten. I watch as her muscles coil, as she becomes tense beneath me, her breathing coming in pants now. With each exhale, she begs me. "Please... Dyl... I-I need... I-I want... please... more." Her voice is a combination of moans and pleading, and who am I not to give my girl exactly what she wants?

Pressing my thumb harder against her clit, I increase the speed of my fingers, thrusting them in and out, curling them in just the right spot. It's not long before I feel her falling apart. Her pussy clamps down on my fingers, squeezing them like a vice, as her body trembles. Her loud moans and breathy pants echo around the room and my cock pulses in my pants. It's taking all my willpower not to blow my load right now. I've never seen anything as beautiful as the blissed-out look on Addy's face as she comes on my fingers.

I wait for her to come down from her bliss, peppering little kisses across her jaw as I give her time to calm down. She tries to slow her breathing down, and once her muscles relax, I gently pull my fingers from her sopping pussy. My fingers are drenched in her juices, and she watches intently as I pull my fingers to my lips, desperate to taste her again.

Her hand reaches down to my cock, and I lightly grab hold of her with my free hand. I finish licking my fingers clean before I explain, "As much as I would love for you to get my cock out right now, that's not what this was about. I wanted this to be all about you. Maybe we can do that another time, but for now, I'm happy with it all being about you."

As much as I hate to fucking admit this, I don't think I've put a woman first when it comes to sex in a long fucking time. I haven't really needed to. They have all been willing to just throw themselves at me, never really giving a shit about me, just that they could walk away saying they fucked Dylan from The Catastrophists. So, if they were using me first, why the hell couldn't I use them—or at least, that was my dumb, drug-fuelled logic. I see now what an ass I was being, but I guess it takes the right girl for you to see the error of your ways.

"Nobody's ever really put me first." Her voice is so small and sad, and in that instance, I decide she deserves to be put first all the fucking time. I never want her to feel like that again.

"Addy, you will never come second to anyone or anything with me." I'm surprised to hear myself saying that, mostly because I've always put my music before everyone, but I guess maybe that's because I've never truly cared about anyone like this before. The only other people I really care about are my bandmates, whom have been my best friends since we were kids, but they came with the music, so I never had to choose before. I think for a while drinking and drugs took priority, but now I have a new focus.

"This doesn't feel real. I've been alone for so long. This feels like the exact thing my brain would do to make me think

I'm happy. The perfect delusion to make me feel good before Slender Man comes back and ruins it all."

Taking her cheeks between my hands, I angle her head until she's looking up at me and can't look away. "Addy, I promise you I am completely real. I don't know how to prove it to you, other than to ask you, have you ever had an orgasm like that before?" Her cheeks flush bright red, and she tries to avert her eyes, but I don't let her. I already know the answer, but I need her to say it.

"No, never."

"Have you ever been able to make yourself come like that?"

Shaking her head between my hands, she looks down as she confirms my suspicions. "No, never as mind-blowing as that."

"So, if you've never come like that before, or even dreamed of coming like that, how was your brain able to create something so amazing? I know it's hard for you to know what's real and what's a delusion, but you only have to trust your gut. Listen to what your instincts are telling you. They won't lead you far wrong," I explain, before pressing my lips against hers. I can tell there's something more she wants to say, but the longer we wait, the more the silence becomes deafening.

"There are times when he feels just as real as you do. The pain he inflicts, it's unbearably real. But I will try my best to push thoughts of him aside and just concentrate on you. Thank you for today. You made me feel things I didn't know I was capable of feeling." She reaches up and sweeps a lock of my hair out of my eyes and pushes it back with the rest. It must have flopped loose during all the excitement. The gesture feels so tender and loving, it makes my heart race. And for the first time since I arrived at Lakeridge, I have an overwhelming urge

to pick up my guitar and write a song. Looks like I've found my muse again. Now, if only we can work out a way to save Addy. But how can I save her from her own mind?

Ten
DYLAN

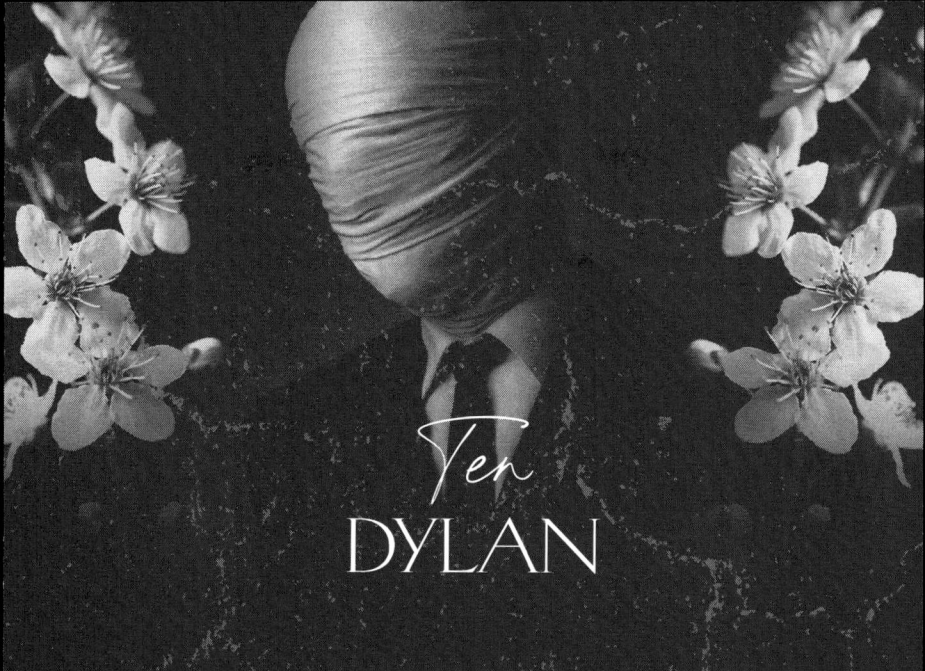

When I wake up the next morning, I expect Addy to crawl back into my bed again. Flashbacks of the night before have been invading my memories ever since, and I can't get control over my hard cock. He's constantly erect, thinking of all the things I want to do to Addy, but I know we need to take things slow. While she can't differentiate between reality and delusions, there's no way I should take advantage of her. I want her to know I'm real, but I don't know how to do that.

Looking at my watch, I see it's almost three in the morning, which is our usual meeting time. Rolling out of bed, I pull on my grey sweatpants, but don't bother with a shirt. I am still flirting with Addy, after all. So, showing her my lean muscles can't exactly hurt. Although, whenever she's seen me topless before, she's always been more drawn to the tattoos than the muscles. But, at this stage, I will take anything.

I head out my door, grateful again to Dr. Hughes for not insisting my room be locked. I make my way towards the kitchen, but just as I'm about to turn down the corridor that will take me there, I'm pulled in the opposite direction by a familiar noise. I freeze, listening to a blast from the past.

It's me—or should I say, it's The Catastrophists. But the song that's playing is "You're My Perfect", and it's a love song that we recorded in Jake's garage and put up onto YouTube when we were seventeen. It's the song that got us recognised after it went viral, but we never properly recorded it. In fact, that recording is the only time we ever performed the song live. The record producers wanted to sign us, but they felt the market called for a more rock type of music, which was perfect for us because we rarely did ballads. But this song, I always felt a connection to it. From the minute I wrote it, I knew it was a hit, and when the producers said they wanted us to stay true to our rocker style, we agreed, but not recording this song properly was always my biggest regret.

I want to say that I wrote the song after experiencing some great love, but that's not true. I've never really been in love. The closest I came broke my heart before I was able to fall properly. The truth is, I don't think I know what love is. I grew up without a family, and nobody ever told me they loved me. So, when I wrote the song, I pictured what it would be like to meet that perfect person. That one person in the whole world who completes you, and who makes you feel like you can take on the world together. They love you for who you are, and they never try to change you. To the rest of the world, you may be completely flawed, but to that one person, you are perfect. That's the kind of love I dreamt of, and I put it into that song. And as I hear the beautiful melody of Jake's voice crooning out, I gravitate towards the music.

The closer I get, the louder the song becomes until finally I'm standing outside of the room marked 'Dance Studio' and I can hear the song clear as day. I didn't even know Lakeridge had a dance studio. I mean, I knew dance therapy was one of my options, but I've never been this far down the arts corridor.

Even though the door to the studio is closed, there's a large window that can be used as a viewing area with seats facing the bright room. The lights are on bright, and the music rings out as clear as day, and I worry I'm about to disturb someone. But, I want to see if someone is dancing to my song. So, I slowly tilt my head, keeping my body behind the wall, so just my head is visible to anyone looking out of the window. What I see inside floors me.

It's Addy. Dressed only in my old Catastrophists tour t-shirt that hangs to her mid-thigh. Her long hair is pulled up into a messy bun on the top of her head, and she's wearing no shoes. I needn't have worried about her seeing me. I could have stood in the middle of the dance floor, stark bollock naked, and I still don't think that would have pulled her out of her dance. It's like she's transfixed by the music, and she's allowing the beat and the melody to take over her body as she just follows along for the ride.

The way her body moves is so majestic. Her arms stretch out, making the perfect shape, while her toes point in a way that shows she's received proper dance training. The way her body moves, bending and swaying with the music to create the most beautiful shapes.

She brings her leg up straight beside her head—and in typical guy fashion, I note she is wearing underwear this time—before standing on tiptoe on her other leg as she uses her arms to spin. She goes around a couple of times, dropping from tiptoe to the ball of her foot and back again as she gathers momentum for the one-footed spin. As she lowers her foot down, she propels herself into a jump, swaying to the music when she lands.

As the music picks up tempo, building up to the usual big finish, she pushes her body to match the speed of the music, flipping herself as I can almost feel my drumsticks colliding with the skins. It's like she was made to dance to this song. Actually, it looks like she was made to dance.

The song draws to a close, and Addy rolls her body across the floor, sweeping her leg out at just the right time, before flipping her body until she's standing up, striking a pose just as the music finishes.

I want to clap and cheer, to tell her how fucking amazing she is, and for a moment, I almost do. Until I see the floods of tears streaming down her face. This feels like a deeply personal moment, and I don't want to invade her trust, but at the same time, I want her to know that I'm here if she needs me.

Rushing into the room, I know she can hear the slap of my bare feet against the polished wooden dance floor. She freezes and rather than turning around, she just looks at me through the large mirror that covers the main wall opposite the viewing window. As the speaker system morphs into another one of my songs, one from my first—and arguably best—recorded album, she collapses to the floor and tears overwhelm her.

I rush towards her, and that's when I see small patches of blood seeping into the t-shirt she's wearing at the back. I know she will have new wounds, and I need to help her with them to clean them and stop the bleeding. But, even at Slender Man's worst, I've never seen her this full of pain. This is something else.

I drop to the floor beside her, and at first I don't touch her. I simply sit there, letting her know I'm here for her. I want to close the distance, to pull her into my arms, but it's not as easy as that. I don't want her to think I'm forcing her to do more than she's comfortable with, which is probably why I'm so fucking glad when she reaches out and grabs hold of me, pulling herself into my arms.

I wrap my arms around her as tightly as I can, and we just sit there with her head on my bare chest, tears running down my skin. My hand gently strokes up and down her back, and I try to ignore the way she winces when I hit an open wound, or the fact that I can feel blood seeping through the shirt and onto my hand. We sit like that, my songs echoing in the background, and I just wait for her to calm down. I don't want to talk before she's ready.

Eventually she stops crying, and looks up at me, her bright eyes now red-rimmed and swollen, her beautiful face blotchy and puffy. I push the hair out of her eyes and wipe away the last few remaining tears with the pad of my thumb. I don't know what it is, but this isn't like the other times I've held her while she cries. This isn't about

Slender Man, of that I'm fairly certain. I just have no idea why she's this upset.

I give her my signature cocky smile, just to let her know that she's safe talking to me, and to remind her that no matter what she tells me, nothing will push me away. She returns with a small smile of her own, but it doesn't reach my eyes. I take that as my cue to break the ice. "So, you are a fan, after all," I joke, and I shrug my shoulders as if pointing to the sound echoing all around us.

She lets out a small chuckle, and it's like my whole body relaxes. I can feel my tight muscles unfurling and starting to calm down. "What can I say? I'm a secret fan."

My stomach flips, and I don't know why or what it is about knowing she listens to my music, but it makes me feel ten feet tall. Obviously there are millions of people who listen to our albums, and who come to see us live, which is how we sell out tours in minutes, and each new song we release hits that number one spot. So I'm no stranger to having fans, but with her it's different. I want her to love everything about me, and my music is who I am.

"Addy, I had no idea you are a dancer. That, just then, was fucking beautiful, and I think you took one of my songs and brought it to life. Why didn't I know this about you?" I ask, thinking back over all our hot chocolate conversations, wondering if she told me, or at least hint at it, but she didn't.

With a small smile and a shrug of her shoulders, Addy averts her eyes before replying. "I'm not a dancer, or at least I'm not anymore." Her voice is small and sad, and I can feel my cold black heart—that is starting to thaw out just for her—starting to break. I hate hearing how lost and lonely she sounds.

"Babe, I just saw you. You can say the words, but your body tells a different story. You *are* a dancer. Why on earth would you think you aren't?"

She lets out a short, sharp, and very sarcastic sounding laugh as she shakes her head, her eyes glistening with fresh unshed tears. "That's the first time I danced since the night they died two years ago." Her voice is barely above a whisper, but I hear her loud and clear. "Do you know I should have died that night too?"

"Don't say that," I snap as I place my hands on her shoulders tightly, but she simply shakes her head.

"I'm not just saying it because I wanted to die along with my family, although that is true, too. I actually should have died, and it's my fault I didn't. I cheated death and I've been paying for it ever since. I think that's why Slender Man haunts me. He's my reminder that I'm living on borrowed time, encouraging me to end it all and go back to my family." The tears stream down her face now, and I can feel my own eyes welling up. The idea of losing her after I just found her kills me. But I don't know what to say.

"Addy…" My voice tails off as I struggle to find the right words.

"It's true, Dylan. Two years ago, a gas pipe in our family home snapped. The company said the pipe eroded, and it was nothing more than a horrible accident. But when the pipe snapped and gas leaked into our house, it didn't take long for it to catch onto an open flame. They think Mum must have been burning candles. She liked to light them to chill out after the kids had all gone to bed. As soon as the gas met the open flame, the house exploded. Mum and Dad were in the same room as the initial blast, and they were killed instantly. The kids were upstairs in their beds, and they died from smoke inhalation and burns. I'm not sure if they tried to get out or if they just never had time. I've never wanted to know. My room was directly above the blast, and so there was no way I would have escaped."

Reaching out, I wipe the tears as they fall from Addy's eyes, and I just hold her as tight as I can. I don't think there are any words I could say right now that would make her feel better. As long as she believes she should have died, she won't hear anything different.

"I can hear what you are thinking. You think I survived for a reason, but you're wrong," she snaps, and I wonder if I spoke aloud, but she's so lost in her own head.

"I never said that, Ads. But why do you think you were supposed to die?" I ask, hoping not to upset her too much with my questions, but I think she needs to talk about it. She won't ever start to heal from her trauma if she doesn't.

"I was supposed to be grounded. That morning, I'd asked Mum and Dad if I could go out. I told them about this amazing dance competition, but I may have left a few key details out. I told them it was an amazing opportunity, and that the winner would win a great prize. What I didn't expect was for them to look the competition up online. They found out it was actually an underground competition run by a local nightclub owner who holds street dance tournaments with a large cash prize. The money would have been enough to help get me through university. I had been offered a place at the London Contemporary Dance School—which everyone calls The Place—it's a specialist university in London. In fact, it's become one of the top schools for contemporary dance, now rivalling Juilliard in America. They only take a small cohort and when I was offered a place, I was thrilled, until I found out the fees alone were around ten grand a year. I knew I could get a job to pay my monthly bills and accommodation, but I didn't want my parents to cover my fees. We weren't exactly well off." Addy pauses, takes a big, deep breath, and I can see she's building up to the main part of her story.

Leaning over, she grabs the bottle of water from the side of the room. Taking a few big gulps, she offers it to me, which I accept. As I'm taking a drink, she continues with her story. "The first-place prize was fifteen thousand pounds, which would have set my first year up nicely. But when my parents found out it was taking place in a seedy nightclub with a less than stellar reputation, they told me no. It didn't matter about the money, they just didn't want me in that club. It didn't matter that I'd just turned eighteen. It wasn't somewhere they wanted their daughter going. I didn't care about the club's reputation, I just wanted to dance. When they said no, I argued. I shouted, I swore at them. I told them I hated them and they were ruining my future. I stomped off and refused to speak to them. That night, after they'd gone to bed, I snuck out. I should have been in bed, and I would have died with them. Instead, I've had to live with the knowledge that the last thing I said to my parents is that I hated them. Is it any wonder I'm being tormented by my own nightmares?" she sobs, and all I can do is pull her into my chest and hold her tight as she falls apart.

"Addy, I know you probably won't believe me when I say this, and I know I didn't have the pleasure of meeting your parents, but I'm sure they know how much you love them. I'm sure all teenagers shout and tell their parents they hate them at some point, you are just one of the unlucky ones who never got to put things right. But I know they know how much you love them. How can they not?" I whisper into her ear, hoping I've not said the wrong thing in any way. It's one of those scenarios where I know what I have to say, I'm just hoping she doesn't think it's the wrong thing.

"Thank you for saying that, Dylan. I'm not sure I believe it quite yet, but I'm trying. Did you know I haven't danced since that night?" she asks, and I'm completely shocked.

Pulling her back slightly, I angle her head so that she has no choice but to make eye contact with me. I hate how fucking lost her beautiful emerald green eyes are. "So, you didn't take your place at the big, fancy London dance school?" I ask, and she shakes her head.

"I won the competition. I performed the dance you just saw, and I won. But after they died, I just couldn't function. I didn't know how to live by myself. I had no other family left, nobody to help me, and I just felt so fucking lonely. Initially, they deferred my entry for a year and were very understanding about my situation. But when the next year rolled around, I still hadn't danced. I was out of shape, and in no way ready to attend. They said they couldn't hold my place any longer. It was like they'd given me a year to mourn, and couldn't understand when I still wasn't over their deaths a year later. So I turned down my place. I've just been surviving ever since."

Stroking my hand down her arm, I feel her shiver beneath my touch. "I would never have known you hadn't danced for two years after seeing that. You are a natural. You were born to dance, it's in your very make-up. Personally, I think you're doing the world a disservice by depriving them of your dancing. But more than that, I think you're depriving yourself. Your soul needs to dance."

As soon as I finish speaking, I stand up, pulling Addy to her feet alongside me. She looks confused, and her nose scrunches into the cutest pout. I just give her my signature cocky grin before saying, "Dance with me."

She takes a step back and looks up at me with confusion in her eyes before she chuckles. "What's so funny, pretty girl?"

"Erm… well… Can you dance?" She says it tentatively, like she's worried she might offend me—which she does. So naturally I play on that to watch her squirm.

"How dare you?! Are you implying I look like someone who doesn't know how to dance?" I try to push as much indignation into my voice as possible, and her eyes widen in shock.

"I'm sorry… it's just… I-I have—"

I chuckle as she stumbles over finding the correct word. When it doesn't come, I take pity on her and cut her off. We could be here all day while she finds the right words. "What I think you're trying to say is that I don't look like I know how to dance?"

"Don't get me wrong, I'm sure you can sway around to the music in a club. That's so easy that any guy can do it. But, being able to dance the way I dance requires a lot of skill, and people either have a natural talent for it, or they've been training for years. It's about learning to interpret the rhythm of the music." When she talks, it's easy to see how passionate she is about dancing. It makes me sad that she's been living without this in her life for so long. I've only been without my music for a few weeks, and I feel as though someone chopped off my arm, like I'm missing a vital organ. So I don't know how she's coping without it.

"I guess you could say I have a natural talent. As someone who creates music, I feel like I have a connection with the rhythm, even if it's not one of my songs. I can break down the different layers of the music, grabbing onto the parts that matter and running with it. I can assure you, I'm a good dancer. Are you going to let me show you, or are we going to sit here all day until we get caught?" I ask, and she shakes her head from side to side. It's not the confirmation I was looking for, but more like this is batshit crazy.

"What shall we dance to?" she asks, and I can't help but smile, knowing I'm about to have her back in my arms in just a moment. But I think the thing I like so much is that she's willing to share this part of her life with me.

"Since you seem to like my music so much, why don't you pick an old Catastrophists song. Make it a ballad from the first album. You won't find one on any other albums," I explain, and her eyes widen in shock before she hops on the spot, almost like she's struggling to contain her excitement over something. I raise my brow, silently questioning what she's thinking.

"I just realised I can ask you a question about your band, can't I?"

With a slight chuckle, I nod. "You have always been able to ask me about my band."

"I know, but when we were still getting to know each other, I didn't want to offend you, and I still don't, but I have a question that I can't hold off on asking any longer," she explains as she swings on her heels in excitement.

"Okay, fire away."

"Well, as I'm sure you've worked out since I have the damn thing on repeat, I personally think your first album was by far your best. I mean, some of the songs are so good, they are fan favourites. And don't get me wrong, your other albums have all been great, but they've all lacked the spark from your original album. Why do you think that is?"

I release the breath I didn't know I was holding, and reach out to pull her into me. I place my hands on her hips and pull her close before we begin swaying to the music—my music—that's playing in the background. As she wraps her arms around my neck, I begin explaining. "When we signed our first record deal, they basically bent over backwards to get us to sign, and a lot of the stuff we negotiated involved the type of music we wanted, including on our first album. There are actually a couple of songs that never made it beyond our YouTube channel that I think deserve to be recorded, but the label wanted us to maintain a certain image, which we agreed to because we desperately wanted to get a recording deal. Then, the further in we got, the more we had to conform to their expectations. I guess you could say I was made to write a certain type of song, instead of me being able to write whatever came to me. It felt forced to me, and I quickly began to hate doing it. I think that's around the time I started drinking heavily. We had everything we ever wanted, but the stipulations that came with it meant we weren't the band we initially set out to be."

I've never told anyone that before, but as I'm explaining it to Addy, it all begins to make sense to me. I began resenting writing songs because I wasn't allowed to use my creative freedom; I wasn't allowed to write the songs I wanted to write. That meant I wasn't getting the creative outlet I've always had before. I know I could have kept on writing for myself, but what would have been the point?

It occurs to me, I really should have this conversation with Jake, to see how he and the guys feel. Maybe if I'm feeling like the record label is cutting off our potential, and preventing us from being the band we set out to be, then maybe they feel that too. I don't know what we would do about it since we are tied to our label. Though I guess if we really wanted to, we could get out of it. But what would we do from there? Would we sign with someone else, only to have them tell us who to be? Which brings me to the even bigger question I've been trying to avoid asking myself. I don't mean to say the words aloud, but I do. "I'm worried that when I leave here, I won't want to go back to that world. I started drinking and doing drugs because of the pressures of being a rock star, and the fact that I hated having my creative muse stifled when I couldn't write or produce the music I wanted. Here it's easy to stay sober as I have no temptations. But if I go back into that world, there will be temptations all the time. I just don't know if I'm strong enough to overcome them."

I try not to look at Addy, keeping my gaze fixed on a piece of the wall on the opposite side of the room, as a way of hiding my embarrassment. It's hard baring your soul to someone. I guess that must be how she felt when she told me about her family.

Suddenly, I'm pulled out of my own head by Addy, grabbing hold of my cheeks, directing my attention to her. The look in her beautiful green eyes is pure fire, and my heart races as I take in the stunning girl in my arms. I've never felt like this before. I've never got butterflies in my stomach just from looking at a girl. I'm beginning to think my feelings for this girl are more than just sexual attraction. I didn't think my dark, black heart was capable of having feelings, but for her I would do anything.

"Listen to me, Dylan. You are a lot fucking stronger than you realise. You have chosen to get clean, and I have every faith that you will continue to do so when you get back into the outside world. And every time you stumble or think you might relapse, you talk to me. I will be there to help you during the times you can't help yourself. Okay?" She talks with such vigour, and I'm overcome with emotion. This girl wants to be with me when we get out of here, walking by my side through the journey, and I think I want to let her.

"You really want to help me when we get out of here?" I need to hear her say it.

"Of course. Why, do you not want anything to do with me when we get out of here? I know a screwed-up, ex-dancer with no life or purpose isn't exactly that type of girl a rock star should hang out with. So, I get it."

Now it's my turn to shake my head. "Are you kidding? Any guy would be fucking lucky to have you, which is why I was so confused that you would want me. I know in here we're in our own little bubble, and it's nice, and it works, but when we get back into the real world, I just worry that things will change. That you won't want me or my lifestyle."

"You are crazy, Dylan. I like you, and I have no idea what the future brings for us both when we get out of here—at this rate I may never fucking get out of here—but when we do, I would love to be part of your life. But I don't just want to be some groupie following you around, desperate for a little bit of your time and attention. And I sure as fuck won't ever share you with another woman." Her voice takes on a raspy growl at the end, making her sound super sexy and possessive. I love it.

"Addy, no girl could ever compete with you, so I wouldn't even bother trying. You are all I need. I would love it if we could make a real go of things when we are on the outside," I explain before pulling her in so that I can place my lips against hers while we continue swaying to the music.

As soon as our lips crash together, what's supposed to be chaste turns into a bruising, passionate kiss. Our hands roam over each other's bodies, as our lips meld together and our tongues battle for dominance. Addy moans against my lips, and it's the sexiest fucking thing I've ever heard. I want to push her up against the mirror wall and have her watch while I fuck her.

Fuck! That's when I pull away from her, and she lets out the sexiest fucking whimper as she looks at me with a furrowed brow, her confusion clear.

"If we keep kissing like that, I won't be able to hold back, and I don't want our first time together to be me fucking you hard up against a wall. Although, we should add that to our to-do list, for sure." Addy laughs, but I'm very fucking serious. We need a 'to-do list', or maybe we should call it a 'where to do it' list?

"What if I want you to fuck me against the wall?" she asks, her voice low and husky and full of sex.

I groan, and my throbbing cock is screaming at me to give her what she wants. But we both know that we are getting caught up in the moment. She deserves better, and I'm supposed to be better. If she was a random groupie, then I would have had no issues fucking her against a wall, taking all the pleasure I want without any concern for hers, before walking away and never seeing her again, let alone learning her name. Addy deserves better than that—even if my very sore blue balls disagree with me.

"Why don't we have that dance instead? So I can show you I can do more than just sway to the music."

With a nod, she lets go of me and walks towards the sound system. "Do you have a preferred song?" she asks.

I shake my head. "No, you choose."

With a smile, she messes around with the iPod attached to the speaker system. Within a few seconds, a slow, melodic sound fills the room, and Addy turns it up louder. I recognise the song instantly. "Make You Feel Me" is one of the first songs I ever wrote, and it's another that was never officially recorded. This is a live performance we recorded in Jake's garage, and has only been shown on YouTube. It's also one of my favourite songs that I've ever written.

As Addy reaches me and the beat of the drum begins, I take hold of her in my arms and we start to move. Placing my hands on her hips, I move them along with the beat, drawing her body closer to mine. From there we allow the beat of the music to consume us, and my feet and hips move in time with the rhythm. I move us around the open space, and Addy allows me to lead, following along like the perfect dance partner. Even though we've never danced together before, it's like we know each other's movements before they even happen. When I get ready to spin her, Addy allows her body to move in the direction I send her, as her feet follow along with my instructions.

We dance together for another couple of songs, until sweat is dripping down my back, and both our faces are flushed. As we are getting ready to draw the dance to a close, I decide to see if we really have built up the connection I thought I felt. I spin her out, keeping hold of her with one hand, and as I twirl her back towards my body, I reach down to connect with her thigh. From the moment my hand touches the skin of her leg, she knows what I am going to do, and she holds her body in exactly the right way as I push her into the air. She keeps her position, holding her body still whilst also creating the most stunning shape with her pointed toes and out-stretched arm. As she lands, I catch her perfectly before spinning her away. This time I let go and she spins farther away, increasing her speed with each twirl. Once she reaches the other side of the room, she looks over at me, silently communicating with me through her eyes. I nod my head, knowing exactly what she's about to do, and without hesitation she begins to run towards me. Her strides are long and graceful, and it only takes her a couple before she reaches her target. I'm still a good few feet away, but she doesn't hesitate, and she launches her body at me, maintaining the beautiful lines with her arms and legs. Holding my arms out, as soon as she's within reach, I grab her, spinning us around as she clings to me. As the music draws to a close, my spins slow but my hold on her remains just as tight.

The song finishes, and we stand there, panting for breath while staring at each other. Her hair clings to the top of her forehead where sweat has gathered, and her face looks flushed, but Addy has never looked so beautiful. I've always known dance to be such a personal thing, and I've never really danced with someone else. It's more just something I realised I could do as I wrote music and danced it out. Whereas this is a whole new experience. I felt a connection with Addy while we danced. It was like we were moving as one, pre-empting each other's movements and matching them. I've never felt closer to another person. It feels as though our hearts are beating together, perfectly in sync, like we were made for each other.

Once we've both caught our breaths, we still continue to stand in the middle of the dance studio, just staring at each other. I think each of us is waiting for the other to say something first, and just as I'm about to, Addy beats me to it. "Well… you were right. You can dance."

I can't help but chuckle, and her laughter rings out, too. "That was amazing, pretty girl."

A bright smile crosses her face. "I've never felt a connection like that with a dance partner before. Usually, it takes weeks of practice before we are on the same level, but with you, it was all so simple. You knew what you wanted us to do, and my body just responded. I don't even know how to describe the bond I felt with you."

Reaching up, I take a stray piece of hair from her forehead and place it behind her ear before cupping her cheek with my hand. "I felt so much when we danced, too. It's like you not only got me, but you felt my music too."

Addy averts her eyes, like she doesn't want to make eye contact with me anymore, and I wonder what I've said that's upset her. Clasping her hand in mine, I give it a little squeeze until I get her attention back. "What's wrong, pretty girl? Where've you gone inside that head of yours?"

As soon as the words leave my mouth, I realise I may have answered my own question. I think she's worried this isn't real, but I wait for her to reply, anyway.

"I'm scared," she whispers.

Reaching up to cup her cheek again, whilst squeezing her hand tighter, I make sure she's looking at me and can see all the sincerity and emotion in every single word. "I promise you, this is real, Addy."

"I know that. But I'm scared about how I feel. I've

been alone for so long. Every minute we spend together, I like you more and more, and that scares the shit out of me. I'm worried that I will grow attached to you, only to lose you like I lose everyone. I can't lose another person, Dylan."

A smile spreads across my face, and I can feel the relief in the pit of my stomach. Convincing her I'm real and not a figment of her delusions would have been a very difficult task. But telling her how I feel and promising to be there for her, that I can do. "Addy, I know how you feel. I have been alone my entire life. Nobody knows about my past, it's something I've worked hard to keep out of the media. But the truth is, I have no family. I never met my dad, don't even think Mum knew who he was. And Mum died of a heroin overdose when I was three years old. I was left alone with her decomposing body for three days before we were found, and I was close to death. I had no other living relatives that I knew of, and so they placed me in the foster care system. Long story short, I bounced around from home to home, never settling anywhere for longer than a few months.

"At fourteen, I moved into Jake's garage. His parents had no idea I was living there at first, but after a couple of months, they found out. I told them my story, and they fostered me. I agreed, but only if I could keep living in the garage. I had a nice set-up with the music equipment, and honestly, I didn't need more than that. I wasn't looking for a family, and living in their home would have felt like that. Still, they've always treated me like family, celebrating birthdays and Christmases with them, getting the same amount of gifts as they gave their other children. But I still couldn't accept it. I was a pain in the ass, but they still loved me. It's only through talking to Dr. Hughes that I realised that's exactly what makes them my family. I think I have a lot of making up to do with them when I get out of here. But, my point is, until recently, I had no idea I was capable of having feelings, or allowing someone to love me. So, I'm equally as terrified by the feelings I have for you, and how quickly they're growing. But the idea of not seeing you every day, of not holding you in my arms, that scares me more."

Her eyes fill with unshed tears, and I rack my brain, trying to work out what I've said that could have upset her. Until she speaks and I realise the tears are for me. "Dylan, I had no idea about your childhood. I'm so sorry. I don't even know what to say. Except that I promise to stand by your side for as long as you will let me. I think we stand a fantastic chance of being happy together. We just have to overcome all the obstacles to finally get there."

Wiping away the stray tear that falls, my heart breaks that this beautiful girl cares for me so much. "We will fight all our demons together. Now that I have you, I'm never letting you go."

"Good. Though, it might be a good idea if we go back to our rooms. We don't want anyone catching us, do we?" Addy states as she looks at her watch, and I do the same. As soon as we see that it's almost five in the morning, we spring apart.

"Shit. I feel bad telling you I won't ever let you go, followed by me having to leave," I joke, and Addy lets out a small laugh.

"Don't worry. I know what you mean. It's more

important that we don't get caught. You can't get kicked out of Lakeridge. I'm not worth that."

Shaking my head, I pull her against me. "You are totally worth it, but getting kicked out would mean I wouldn't get this time with you. So, I'm not going anywhere. Other than back to my room." I close the small gap between us and press my lips to hers. It's another kiss that's supposed to be short and sweet, but the minute I get a small taste of her, I want more and we deepen the kiss. I don't think I will ever get bored of this girl.

Eleven
DYLAN

AFTER THAT NIGHT, WE MET UP IN THE DANCE STUDIO A FEW times, even during the day. We both told Lyle that we wanted dance to be our choice of art therapy, which meant we could book the space for our practice time. I haven't told Dr. Hughes that we are dancing together yet. I've just told her that I discovered dance is a way for me to merge myself into my music. I'm worried if I tell her we are dancing together, so soon after her lecture, she will think that I'm using it as an excuse to be close to Addy—which, I guess, to some degree I am. But, it's also true that I'm getting a lot out of dancing and I really think it has the potential to help me heal.

I know Addy hadn't told Dr. Dickhead Manning. Probably for the same reasons I didn't tell Dr. Hughes. Although he has this superiority complex that he would use to judge her love of dance, I'm sure. I don't know how she allows him to be her main psychiatrist—not that she has a whole lot of choice in the matter. But he seems to care more about himself and his research than he does about caring for his patients on an individual level.

Every time Addy comes out of a session with him, she looks like she's been pulled through the wringer backwards. I know when I do my own therapy sessions that they can be tough, but never as soul-destroying as hers are. So today when I'm sitting in the main recreation room, just waiting for her session to be over, I'm shocked to see her come bursting into the room. Normally she's very aware of where I am, and even though she won't always come to sit with me, she will throw a cheeky smile my way. But today is the complete opposite. I think there could have been a line of naked people against one wall of the room and she wouldn't have noticed us.

Her face is flushed, and her eyes have got that blank look about them I hate. She doesn't hesitate; she sprints straight for the open back door and out into the garden area. I've seen her go out there before, but I've never followed her. Until today.

That look on her face has me desperate to find her, to make sure she's okay. I follow her around the side of the big house, towards a small patch of grass that is covered on all sides by large cherry blossom trees. Their beautiful pink and white blossoms all knit together, forming a canopy that shields the garden from the hot sun. I peek into the secluded garden to see Addy sitting in the middle of the grass, surrounded by the beautiful fallen leaves.

It's clear that nobody comes to this area of the garden, as the fallen leaves look virtually untouched.

There is a small wooden bench off to the side of the garden, but that's covered with old cherry blossoms too, so obviously Addy doesn't bother using that. Preferring instead to be sitting directly on the ground, and just as she's about to lie back into the grass, I take a step into the trees. My footsteps cause the surrounding branches to rustle, and instantly Addy shoots back up, glaring at who might have encroached on her private space. She looks startled, which I'm not surprised by, since nobody really comes outside.

"I saw you run out here, and I came to see if you are okay. Normally when you come here I give you space, but today seemed different," I explain, concern etched on my face. My jaw is tight, thanks to the fact that I've been grinding my teeth, worried about Addy all the time, and that look on her face when she ran out here isn't helping.

"You know I come here?" she asks, shocked and bewildered that I have noticed so much about her. She's never told me about how much she loves this garden before, but I'm pretty observant when it comes to Addy. I can tell how this place makes her feel.

"Pretty girl, without sounding like a complete psycho stalker, I watch you. I'm constantly checking that you are okay, and I've seen you go to the garden every day when the doors are unlocked. It always seems to give you some kind of peace, if how you look after you've been here is any indication. That's why I've never bothered you before. I know how important it is to have a safe space, and I hate that I'm invading yours, but I saw how you looked, and I got concerned. It seems like recently, every appointment with Dr. Manning is as bad as the last." My voice takes on a low, possessive growl as I talk about Dr. Dickhead. He cares more about his research and his status as a top doctor than actually treating patients and caring about them as individuals. I think he pushes Addy to get the results he wants to see, and he isn't remotely helping her.

"I don't mind you being here. In fact, I quite like that we now have a safe place where we can both come. And it's very secluded." I don't know if she's doing it on purpose, but her voice takes on a sexy, seductive tone, and my cock responds instantly. My brain tries to shut him down, telling him we are checking on Addy, not fucking her. Although the mere thought of fucking her causes my giant blue balls to ache.

"Addy, please don't tempt me. I just want to know if you are okay."

She rolls her eyes, and I groan as she replies, "I'm not okay. He opened up a wound I thought I'd finally got control over. He reminded me I'm all alone and probably always will be, since I have no real family remaining. Then he told me life is probably hard for me, given I don't know what's real and what isn't. He just reminded me of shit I thought I had control of, and that darkness spread quickly. Depression hits hard and fast when it's bubbling away under the surface, just waiting to strike."

"Fuck, there's no way he should be saying or doing any of that. What a complete dickwad. Listen, pretty girl, and listen good when I tell you this. I made a promise to you before and I'll say it again now. I will stand by you while you battle your demons, and I will be here to give you strength whenever you need it. If you need me, I will always be here. It will take a fucking lot to pull me away from you, and I can't tell you that this is all real, but I can show you."

With that, I lean forward and catch her lips with mine. It's a hard but short kiss, one that's over far too fucking quickly. I try to pull away from her, knowing that with each kiss like this, they are getting more and more heated, and there's only one way these kisses will end. I'm just not sure she wants us to have sex for the first time out in the open in the middle of a blossom garden where we could get caught at any minute.

I must have spoken my worries aloud, because Addy is quick to reply, "But that's exactly what I want. This place is special for me. It's somewhere I come to feel like me and to find peace and happiness. Making that memory here with you, I want that."

Fuck. Now my cock really is screaming. "Addy, I fucking want to do this with you so bad, but I'm scared." I pause, trying to find the right words without upsetting her, or having her think I don't want her. "You have been through so much in your nightmares, and I know part of that is sexual. I never want to hurt you. Sometimes during sex, I can get a bit rough, a bit dominating, and I wouldn't ever want to be a trigger for you. Don't ever think that your hallucinations prevent me from wanting to have sex with you, because I really fucking do. In fact, if we don't do it soon, I may lose a bollock."

She laughs, and it's music to my ears. I was worried my words would hurt her, but instead she gets that sexy glint in her eye. "Don't be scared. Maybe to start with, we can take it slow and see how I feel. If I tell you I want more, or I want it harder, you have to listen to me. Eventually, I want to experience what it's like to really fuck you, but for now, we can go a little slow. Is that okay?"

I nod my head so many times my neck starts to hurt. Geez, eager much! "When you say go slow, do you mean now? Here?"

"Yes, I do," Addy says, as she peels off the plain black t-shirt she is wearing, revealing her bare chest beneath. Fuck, she's had no bra on this whole time. If I'd known that, one of my bollocks really would have dropped off.

Wait! Does that mean she's not wearing any panties either? Looks like I need to find out.

I waste no time leaning in and capturing her lips with mine while my hands caress her body. The feel of her silky smooth skin beneath my calloused fingers feels fucking amazing. Together with the taste of her against my tongue, this girl has me enraptured.

I pull her down until she's laying on her back, and I'm on my side right up against her naked chest. My hard cock is straining to be free from my jeans and is pressing against her thigh. I continue running my hands over her body as my mouth travels across her jaw and down to that sweet spot I know she has just above her clavicle. As soon as I reach it, I suck hard, nibbling at the edges of her skin at the same time, and a moan rips from her, filling the surrounding air while she arches her back beautifully. All that does is remind me I'm not showing her pebbled nipples enough attention, and so with my free hand I roll one between my thumb and forefinger.

Her hands claw at the back of my t-shirt, and at first I think she's just so frantic with lust it's making her actions uncoordinated—which I'm damn fucking proud of—but then I see she's just trying to get my t-shirt off. Releasing the hold I have on her hip, making sure to keep her nipple in my other hand, I reach up and pull off my shirt from the back of my neck, in that sexy one-handed way that only men seem to be able to pull off.

As soon as my skin and ink are showing, she wastes no time pushing away from the ground and climbing on top of me. She straddles my hips, her back arched and her amazing tits pushed out in the sexiest way. Reaching up, I place my hands at the top of her thighs and begin moving them higher, until she distracts me.

Leaning down, her long brunette locks spreading around us creating our own canopy like the one the blossom tree creates, she peppers kisses along my jaw, past my neck, and down across my chest. She covers every inch of my exposed skin, and it's like her fingers leave a trail of fire that her mouth cools down instantly. She peppers kisses all along my chest, following the lines of my ink down my body. Her tongue circles around my nipple and I'm shocked by the sensations it causes. I've always heard that some men have sensitive nipples with a direct line to their cock, but I've never known it to feel electric. Yet, now they do.

When she reaches the top of my jeans, she shuffles down so that she's sitting on my lower thighs now and leans over to lick the little happy trail going from my belly button directly into my boxers. Once she gets to my jeans, she pops the button and pulls down my zipper. I have to bite down on my lip to stop myself from releasing a loud groan as my body craves more from her.

Once the trousers are open, she tries to shimmy them down, but without my help, and while she's sitting on top of me, she stands no chance. Placing my hands on top of hers, I stop her attempts. "Stand," I grunt, my voice deep, dripping with lust.

Instantly, she does as she's instructed, and as soon as she's on her feet, I do the same. Ensuring we maintain eye contact, I slowly begin pulling my jeans down, exposing my strong, muscular thighs and the large tent in my boxers. "Get yours off too," I instruct, struggling to sound like anything except the lust-driven caveman I am in this moment.

We watch each other removing our jeans and I can't hold back the appreciative moan that seeps out when I see my pretty girl standing in front of me in nothing but a pair of deep purple lacy, short-style panties. "Twirl," I say, as I rotate one of my fingers to indicate I want to see what she looks like behind. When she moves too fast, I grunt at her again. "Slowly."

I watch as she rolls her eyes at my inability to form words, but she does as she's told and slowly turns around. Clearly, all the blood is draining from my brain and heading south, making it impossible for me to form coherent, full sentences. As she rotates and I see the way the shorts ride up, exposing the swell of her gorgeous ass cheeks, I'm so far gone, it's a miracle I'm not blowing in my pants.

In my defence, I'm normally a guy who fucks almost every night. The longest I go without sex is maybe a couple of days. And I've been in here over a month now, with no relief other than my left hand. So, it's a fucking miracle I haven't come already.

Once she makes it back around to face me, I ensure her eyes are fixed on mine and I lower my boxers. As soon as she realises what I'm doing, her gaze drops to my crotch, and I watch her eyes widen as my boxers fall down completely. As she stares at my rock-hard cock, I watch her take her lower lip between her teeth and begin nibbling on it. I can't help myself, I reach down and take hold of my shaft. My cock is probably larger than the average male's size, particularly when it comes to the girth, and as I take hold of the base, my fingers only just meet. Addy watches, mesmerised as I slowly fist my dick, dragging my hand up to the tip, pushing beads of pre-cum out onto the head. She licks her lips, and it drives me fucking insane.

I repeat the process a couple of times, keeping my hand movements slow, and she's so hypnotised by my actions that she doesn't even realise I'm moving towards her until we are close enough to touch. "Panties off, pretty girl," I instruct, before adding, "make it sexy."

A sexy-as-fuck smile crosses her face, and I didn't think my cock could get any harder, but it does. She twirls until her back is facing me, turning her head so that she's looking over her shoulder, keeping eye contact with me at all times. Slowly, she starts to shimmy her panties down until they are sitting just below the curve of her ass cheeks. That's when she spreads her legs slightly and bends over, giving me the most perfect view of her pantie-covered pussy.

"Fuck," I groan aloud as I fist my cock more.

Reaching back whilst she remains bent over, she

slowly lowers her panties to reveal her glistening pink lips. I'm very aware that we're naked, out in the open, and that anyone could catch us at any time, but even though I know all of that, I just don't care. I want Addy, and if she's willing to give herself to me after everything she's been through, then I am more than happy to go through with it.

Kneeling down, I take in her cunt and the way it glistens with her juices. I also see the wounds dotted all around, along her ass cheeks and her upper thighs. Most are welt marks, like she's been whipped or hit with something. They are all in various degrees of healing. Some are perfect purple scars, like they've fully healed, whereas others are fresh red scabs, like they've only just happened. I want to touch every mark, soothe them in some way to make her better. Anger ripples through my body at the thought of anything marring her perfect skin. I know Dr. Dickhead seems to think she does this to herself, but I'm really starting to wonder if that's true. I don't know if she would be capable of self-inflicting these wounds.

I'm so lost in my own head, Addy must have got bored of waiting for me to do something, as her voice pulls me back to the present. "Are you going to just sit there all day staring?" There's a gravelly tone to her voice that just drips sex, and I know she's all in for this.

Without a moment's hesitation, I lean forward and drag my tongue through her slit. Our moans of pleasure rip from us at the same time. I taste Addy on my tongue, that sweet honey flavour with a hint of saltiness that I'd sampled just the other day when I sucked her juices off my fingers, and I can't get enough. My mouth literally salivates, desperate for more, which I'm only too happy to give. I dive back in, sweeping my tongue along her slit, dipping it into her waiting hole, before dragging it over to her engorged clit. Circling around the clit before flicking over the sensitive nub has Addy crying out in pleasure, her legs beginning to shake, and even though I'm holding onto her hips with both hands, I know she won't be able to hold herself in this position much longer.

Once I'm sure her pussy is dripping wet, I slowly insert a finger into her hole while my tongue flicks across her clit. As soon as she's used to having one finger deep inside her, I add a second, stretching her out as I scissor my fingers. I need her to be ready to take my big cock, but I'm also loving the way she's losing control. Her legs are shaking, her breathing is coming in desperate pants, and her cries of pleasure are becoming louder and more frantic. She's getting closer to that edge, and I'm desperate to feel her fall apart for me.

Nudging my fingers in and out of her wet pussy, getting faster with each and every thrust, I also flick my tongue across her clit rapidly to help her get there faster. Her pussy walls tighten, and she's getting even wetter than she was before. Knowing she just needs a little more to push her over that edge, I take my hand from her hip, hoping she can hold herself upright on her jelly legs for just a few minutes longer, and after sucking my thumb to get it nice and wet, I gently press it against her puckered asshole. Her head flies up, and she looks around at me, her eyes wide as saucers, but she doesn't indicate she wants me to stop. In fact, her words and cries of pleasure spur me on.

"Fuck. Dyl... I-I... I'm s-so close. Please... please, I need... need to come," she begs, and I can feel my cock straining even more. Right now I'm wishing I had a third hand so I could give him a bit of love too, but that will come. We are not leaving him with blue balls today. This is just the start of many orgasms for us both.

"Cover your mouth with your hand, Addy, and come for me. Now!" I command, as I push the tip of my thumb past her sphincter and into her ass. At the same time, I curl my fingers at just the right spot and I suck her clit into my mouth as hard as I can.

She quickly bites down on her hand as she screams around it, falling apart to my touch. Her pussy walls tighten, gripping my fingers tightly, while the muscles in her ass try to push out my thumb. Her legs are shaking, and her body sways as she struggles to keep upright in this position. As she comes down from the high, I slowly pull my hands away from her before taking her hips into my hand. Like she weighs nothing at all, I pick her up and lower her to the ground. Other than a small yelp of surprise at my actions, she doesn't protest me manhandling her, and instead she concentrates on getting her breathing back to normal.

We are laying side by side, and I love seeing the flush of her cheeks, and the look of pleasure that's still etched across her beautiful face. Knowing I did that is the biggest fucking boost to my ego that I could have asked for. My engorged cock bobs against my lower stomach, and I notice the tip is even more swollen than normal and looks an angry purple colour. Pre-cum pools on the tip, and my instinct is to fist my cock, to give it some relief, but I know if I do that right now, there's a very good chance I will blow my load in my hand. Instead, I focus on other things to try and get him to calm down a bit. But while Addy lays next to me, beautiful, naked, and dripping wet, it's no good. I will never be able to think of anything except her, the sweet taste of her pussy, and the beautiful, serene look she gets on her face when she falls apart for me.

Once Addy has gathered herself together, and her breathing is almost back to normal, she rolls onto her side, her finger tracing my ink once again. She leans forward to press her lips against mine in a slow, sweet kiss, and as her tongue dips into my mouth, her groan rumbles through me. "I can taste myself on your tongue," she whispers against my ear, before pulling the lobe into her mouth and nibbling on it.

"Do you like the taste?" I ask, my voice a deep rumble.

Nodding her head, she gets that sexy, mischievous grin on her face before saying, "Yes, but I think I would like the taste of you more. Can I try?" Her eyes flick down to my cock, that begins bobbing with excitement over her question.

I can't help but let out a slow, deep laugh. "Pretty girl, you never need to ask my permission to suck my cock. He's all yours whenever you want him." She licks her lips as she moves into position. I feel like there's a bit I need to add onto the end, but I can already hear my cock bollocking me for even thinking about it. But I need her to hear me say it. "Addy, just so you know, as much as I would really like you to suck my cock right now, you don't have to. You don't ever have to do anything you aren't comfortable with."

She's bent over now, her face mere inches from my cock. She's so close I can feel her breath on my tip, and it's making my shaft throb with need. Mentally, I'm shouting at myself for saying that, but she has to know this will always follow her speed. I won't ever make her do anything she doesn't want to. Thankfully, she wants this, and doesn't hesitate letting me know. Her tiny hand tries and fails to wrap completely around my shaft as she lowers her mouth to the tip. Just as she's about to take me into her mouth, she looks up at me through hooded eyes. "I know that, Dylan. Believe me when I tell you, tasting you is exactly what I want to do right now."

As soon as she finishes her sentence, before I have a chance to say anything, her tongue flicks over my tip, tasting some beads of pre-cum that have gathered there. With one taste, she instantly wants more, and begins running her tongue all around the head, before slowly trailing down my shaft along the throbbing vein that runs along the underside of my dick. As she licks back up to the tip, her grip on me tightens, and she begins to work her fist up and down. The wetness she just left behind acts as just the right amount of lubrication and as she wanks me, I can't hold back the guttural moan that rips from my body. She continues to move her hand up and down as her mouth fully covers my tip, her tongue sliding through my slit, driving me fucking crazy.

After a short while, she moves her hand away and begins lowering her head down my shaft, taking my cock deeper and deeper with every thrust. As she bobs up and down on my dick, I can't help myself and I move my hand to the back of her head, fisting her hair into my hand. I want to take control, to show her how much she is really capable of when she lets go, but I promised her I would take it slow to start with. So I settle for just pulling on her hair slightly, something she seems to love, if her well-timed moans are any indication.

She pulls back up, having only got around halfway down my shaft, and her tongue circles around the tip as she looks up at me seductively. "I can feel you holding back, Dylan. Show me what you like. I will tell you to stop if I want you to."

"Are you sure?" I ask, concerned we might be rushing this, but she just nods her head. "Fine, but if you can't talk, hit my thigh hard three times. I will know to stop then."

She doesn't even acknowledge I've spoken, other than a slight nod of her head as she lowers herself back onto my cock. This time, when she reaches mid-cock and pulls back, I gently press her head a little further onto my cock before letting her come back up for air. We do this a few times, just so she can get used to it, and then I get more forceful, pressing her head down more so that my cock slips deeper down her throat. I love the feel of that moment when it hits the back of the throat, triggering the gag reflex, and as Addy swallows in panic, her throat massages and grips at my cock, pulling it farther in.

This time when I pull her head off, she coughs and splutters, gasping for breath as she uses her hand to wipe the tears from her eyes. Spit hangs from my cock and I can see it twitching desperately for more. But I'm not sure if either of us can handle any more. I know if she keeps sucking my cock like this, it won't be long before I'm blowing my load down her throat, and I don't want to do that this time.

As soon as Addy has control over her breathing again, I'm shocked when she lowers herself down onto my cock again, looking up at me through her eyelashes. There's that mischievous twinkle in her eyes, and this time she pushes my cock deep into her throat without my hand guiding her. She presses, swallowing rapidly until her nose touches my pubic area and my cock sits perfectly in the back of her throat. She stays there for a couple of seconds, just looking up at me, and just when I don't think she can get any sexier, she begins to swallow and move her tongue against the underside of my cock. It's too much, it feels too fucking good. I groan loudly as I pull her head off my cock, and she gasps, desperately trying to catch her breath.

"I could have done longer," she pouts in between pants and I can't help but chuckle. I'm so fucking turned on by this girl right now. It hasn't taken her long to learn what I like, and now that she knows, I'm sure she will use it to control me. I may be the one controlling her movements, the one that looks to be more dominating, but we all know she's the one that's really in charge.

"Yeah, but if you keep doing that, I will blow my load down your pretty little throat," I groan as she continues to pout.

"What if that's what I wanted?"

Shaking my head, I reach over and grab hold of her hips, lifting her again so that she is straddling my upper thighs. My cock sits just in front of her pussy, and it won't take much manoeuvring to get her into the right position. "We will have to do that another time. Right now, I want to be in your tight little pussy."

She reaches down and begins gently stroking my cock, moving her spit to ensure all my cock is covered, ready for her. "I guess we could do that instead," she muses, making it sound like she isn't dying to climb onto my cock right now.

Fuck! My brain catches up with the situation and I realise we may not be able to have sex. "I'm sorry, pretty girl. I don't think we can do this."

"What? Why?" she interrupts, her brow furrowing as she looks at me with confusion over my sudden hesitancy.

"I don't have any condoms. It wasn't exactly high on my priorities when I was packing. Besides, I think when Dr. Hughes searched my bag, she would definitely have confiscated them," I joke, trying to ease the tension, worried I may have just upset Addy. Which is why I'm shocked to see her smiling that sexy, mischievous grin again.

"I have the contraceptive implant, and when I was admitted they did a full STD screening. I'm sure you would have had one too. I'm clean. I'm happy to go ahead, if you are." I can hear the hope in her voice and fuck is my cock springing back to life again.

"I'm clean too, but I've never had sex without a condom before," I tell her, watching as her face falls with disappointment. She thinks I'm saying no. I quickly stumble to put that smile back on her face. "That's not me saying no, pretty girl. I'm saying that I have never done it without a rubber before, so it kinda feels right that my first time bare should be with you. I feel more for you than I ever have anyone else. So, I love the idea of being able to properly feel all of you."

A smile spreads across her face and she leans down to press a quick but passionate kiss against my lips, before pulling back and whispering in my ear. "You had better fuck me then."

Fuck, if that isn't the sexiest thing I've ever heard.

"You are going to ride me to start with. It's the best way for you to lower yourself onto my cock slowly, at your own pace, making sure you get used to my size before I fuck you properly," I explain, and Addy's eyes light up as she nods her head.

Raising her body up slightly, she positions herself over my cock, as I hold it tight at the bottom of the shaft to help direct it. Using her fingers to spread open her pretty pink pussy, she slowly lowers herself down so that the tip is pressing against her entrance. Once she's in position, she lets go of her pussy lips and places her hands on my chest. Almost painfully slowly she lowers herself down, and inch by inch I can feel her tight, wet hole engulfing my dick.

I'm so tempted to grab hold of her hips and smash her down so that she's seated fully on my cock, but I know she needs time to adjust, and so I keep my hands just lightly on her hips to support her rather than control her. It doesn't take long for her to take all of me, and once she's fully seated on it, we both let out matching moans. I give her a few minutes to adjust to the size before I help to guide her movements.

Gently, I use the grip on her hips to pull her up a few inches, so that at least half of my cock is still inside, before I drop her back down hard, my cock slamming deep into her pussy. A cry rips from her lips and I can tell she loved it, as she is quick to repeat the movement without any help from me. This time she gets all the way up, so that only the tip of my dick remains inside, before she slams back down again hard.

She does this a couple of times, and that's when I tighten my grip on her hips and take over. I lift her up and slam her back down before quickly repeating the same actions, meaning she doesn't get any time to adjust once my cock is all the way inside. I speed up, bouncing her up and down on my cock, and my hips thrust upward to meet her, sending my cock even deeper.

The feel of her dripping wet pussy as it clamps down on my cock, quivering slightly when I hit that spot deep within, has me pulsing with need. My dick is throbbing, and I can feel my balls tightening, that telltale sign I won't be able to last much longer. I try to hold off as much as I can, but then Addy rolls her hips in the sexiest way, causing my dick to hit new depths.

I can feel her pussy tightening as she rides my cock closer to her orgasm. I can feel I'm close, and it's taking all my willpower to hold off. But there's no way on this earth I am finishing before Addy. So, I reach up between our bodies and find her engorged clit. With each thrust, I press my thumb hard against her sensitive nub, causing Addy to lose all control. Her movements become more frantic, and her pants cause her tits to sway as she arches her back beautifully. I use my other hand to keep guiding her down hard onto my cock, making sure to tilt my pelvis at the exact right time, thrusting my dick deep into her pussy.

It doesn't take long for her to start losing control. Her body shakes and her pussy clamps down hard on my cock. "I'm going to come," she screams, and for a fraction of a second I worry people might hear us, but as Addy begins to fall apart on my cock, all logic slips away.

The feel of her pussy spasming around my cock is enough to send me over the edge, too. My muscles tighten and my shaft erupts deep in her pussy. Our moans echo amongst the trees as we both ride out our orgasms together.

As Addy comes back down, her body seems to collapse, and she falls on top of me, her chest rising and falling with each desperate gasp for air. I stroke my fingers across her back, loving the feel of her soft skin as I try to regulate my breathing too. I feel my cock deflating, but I don't pull out. I'm not quite ready to let go of her warm, wet pussy just yet.

Addy reaches up and pushes the hair out of her eyes and she looks up at me, her cheeks flushed with that sexy, just-fucked look on her face. I can't help but puff out my chest a bit when I think I did that to her. With a big smile on her face, she kisses me. It's short and sweet, but speaks volumes.

"Fuck, that was amazing. I've never felt anything like that before." I love the way her voice is filled with wonderment, like she didn't know sex could be that good. It makes me want to throat punch any guy that has ever touched her before for not showing her a good time, like she deserves.

"Honestly, I've never felt anything quite like that before either," I confess, but she shakes her head like she doesn't believe me.

"It's okay, Dylan. I know you've been with a lot of girls. I can't change that, but you don't need to lie for me."

I take her cheek in my hand, guiding her so she's looking at me. Her deep emerald eyes glisten as she connects with me. "I would never lie to you. Yes, I've been with other women, but it has never been like that. I'm going to sound like an ass for saying this, but before, with other women, it was always just about sex. I never really cared if she had fun or if we had a connection. As long as I came, I didn't give a shit. But with you, it's so different. I wanted you to enjoy it. I want to feel a connection with you, and I think we did. I really like you, Ads. Like, a lot, and it scares me. But, I think you are worth it. So, I'm diving in headfirst, and I'm hoping I don't crash in the process."

"I felt the connection, as well. And, for the record, I really like you too. I think if we carry on like this, falling for you will be so easy. Of course, that scares me, but like you, I'm willing to risk it. We promised we would battle our demons together, but here amongst the cherry blossoms—which I will now think of as our place—I promise to give you all of me, no matter how fucking terrifying that is."

I can't help the shit-eating grin that spreads across my face. "Amongst the cherry blossom trees, I promise to take whatever you are willing to give me and look after it. I won't ever hurt you. I promise that whatever happens, we will face it together."

I don't know how long we lay there together, naked amongst our cherry blossom trees, just being together and hoping like hell we never get caught. Yes, I'm terrified of starting this with Addy, particularly given the vulnerable place she's in, but if she's brave enough to take the risk, then so am I.

Twelve
ADDY

The next few days after our session in the cherry blossom garden were like a whirlwind. I didn't think things with Dylan could get any better, and then we had that afternoon together. He made me feel things I didn't think I was capable of feeling, and it scares the shit out of me how quickly I'm falling for him.

The biggest problem is, now that I've had a small taste of what it's really like to fully be with Dylan, and he with me, we literally can't keep our hands off each other. Which is becoming a real problem, since we are trying not to get caught. There's also the small issue of my declining mental health to deal with, too.

The first few nights after that day in the garden, I'm actually surprised Slender Man doesn't bring up the fact that I had sex with Dylan. I know it sounds crazy, but he—or should I say, my brain—loves to pick up on my areas of insecurity, and he loves to exploit those in order to humiliate me. He loves to call me a whore or a slut, and so I'm very shocked that he doesn't pick up on that to use it against me.

That doesn't mean his visits aren't still horrific, and in some ways they are worse each time. Now that I know how sex should feel with Dylan, it feels wrong to even hallucinate being with someone else. I tried to talk to Dyl about it last night, but it didn't go as planned.

After an awful visit from Slender Man, I couldn't wait to run to Dylan. We had planned to meet at our usual time of three in the morning in the dance studio, but by two-thirty, I couldn't wait any longer. I took off running through the corridors, my bare feet hitting the cold floors as I head straight for his room. As always, his door is unlocked, and I'm shocked to see Dylan is asleep when I get there. Normally he's the first person there when we meet, so I'm surprised to see him sleeping.

I stand over the edge of his bed, torn between needing to feel his body against mine, and wanting to disturb the beautifully serene look on his face. I feel like a bit of a creeper, standing over his sleeping form, just watching him sleep, but there's something so beautiful about him. He looks so at peace as he sleeps, his dark hair all messy, with sleep in his eyes. One arm is tucked under the pillow, and he sleeps with his belly against the mattress with just his head looking to the side. His bare back is showing, and I take a moment to appreciate the ink that adorns his skin.

As I stare at him, it's almost as though our breathing syncs together and I catch my breath. My heart is still racing, not from the run, but from the terror of my nightmare. It's hard to miss the cuts along my arms, and I can feel fresh welt marks across my back and ass. I can also feel a soreness in my vagina that I don't like to think about. I get that the other wounds are caused by me clawing at my skin, or by me hitting myself with different objects, but what the hell have I done to myself to cause that type of pain? In my nightmare, Slender Man rapes me in the most brutal ways—in my pussy, my mouth, and my ass. He fucks me dry and rough until I'm bleeding and sore. It's never about pleasure for me, it's always just about him taking what I'm not willing to give.

I can explain exactly what happens to me in my nightmares, but how that leads to real life injuries is beyond me. I might be assaulting myself somehow, but that scares the shit out of me. I don't even want to think about what I'm doing to cause droplets of blood to drip from my most sensitive areas.

Every time it's happened, I know why Dylan is so scared to have sex with me again. He's worried he will hurt me, or that he will trigger something deep inside me, but I'm not concerned about that. Honestly, I just want him to help me feel something other than pain. I think if I really was being sexually assaulted by a real person, then my outlook may be different, or it may not. I hope to God I never have to find out. But since this isn't something real, and is all either created by my mind, or self-inflicted, I feel like the best way to beat it is by creating better memories, filled with pleasure instead of pain.

Just as I'm about to decide whether to climb into bed with him, the shrill sound of an alarm screams out from the clock beside his bed. Without even opening his eyes, he groans and reaches over to silence it. His hand bobs around on the bedside table a couple of times until he finally reaches the off switch. He doesn't open his eyes, and I can't help but smile at how cute he looks as he desperately tries not to open his eyes.

"So this is how you always make it to the room before me?" I ask, and Dylan's eyes fly open as he jumps up in his bed with a yelp. I can't help but chuckle at his startled impression.

"Fuck, pretty girl. You just scared the shit out of me. Is everything okay?" His voice takes on a panicked tone as his eyes rake over my shaking body. He doesn't even wait for me to reply. He reaches out and pulls me down onto the bed with him.

I can see him looking at the cuts on my arms, and he notices how I wince when my back crashes against his body. I feel him pull up the large t-shirt I'm wearing—another of his old Catastrophists t-shirts—and I reach behind to stop him, but he leans over to whisper in my ear, "Please, just let me look."

He doesn't move the t-shirt up any farther until he sees me nod my head, giving him my permission. That's what I like about Dylan, he would never do anything that I didn't want. He wouldn't try to talk me into something, he always respects my decisions. Which is probably why I trust him so much to see my wounds.

I hear him hiss as he sees the wounds adorning my back and as he traces lightly across them, it's my turn to hiss. "These need cleaning so they don't get infected. Will you let me grab a cloth to clean them?" he asks, and I bite my lip, unsure if I should say yes or not. "I will try not to hurt you, I promise."

"Okay," I whisper, and he climbs out of the side of the bed and moves towards the en-suite in the corner of the room. He returns a short while later with a damp washcloth and I pull the t-shirt off for him.

At first I'm a little embarrassed to be so naked and exposed to him, not because I'm worried about actually being naked with him. It's more that I'm scared of what he will see. When we are fooling around, I know he notices the marks on my skin. I feel the moment of hesitation he has when he sees them, but all it takes is a quick sexy comment or a deep moan at the right time and that's more than enough to pull him back into the moment. But with this, his attention is on something I continually try my best to hide.

I wear long sleeves even on the hottest days of the year. I wrap up my wounds constantly to stop them from bleeding out onto my clothes. Not because I'm worried about damaging them, more because I'm worried about people asking what's causing the wounds. I don't want people to see the harm I'm capable of inflicting upon myself. Whereas, right now, all of Dylan's attention is placed on the one area I try to avoid him really looking at.

"Argh," I wince as I feel the cold liquid connect with an open wound on the top of my back.

"Ads, do you have any idea what may have caused these?" he asks, careful to avoid asking what I have used to inflict the injuries.

Shaking my head, I tell him, "No, sorry. I only know how they happened in my hallucination. I have no idea what I did to cause them."

He continues dabbing along the open wounds across my back, and each time he reaches a new raw area, I have to hold back a hiss or a cry of pain. I know what he's doing is for the best, but that doesn't mean it doesn't fucking hurt.

"Why don't you tell me what happened in your hallucination, and that might help make sense of what I'm seeing?" Even though I have my back to Dylan, I can hear the hesitation in his voice. He wants me to open up to him, but most of the times I've mentioned Slender Man before have just

been in passing comments, never in full detail. I think part of it is that I've lived it once. Why the hell would I want a repeat of that? And the biggest part is I just don't know if I'm ready for him to see the worst part of me.

He looks at me like I hung the moon most of the time, like he's the luckiest guy in the world, and even though I think he couldn't be more wrong, I'm not ready for him to stop looking at me that way just yet. Showing someone your darkest side, the worst part of you, and hoping they're still going to look at you the same way afterwards seems like an unreasonable ask. But I trust Dylan, so I begin telling him what happened.

"It always starts the same way, with Slender Man coming into my room shortly after I've fallen asleep. He's always fuzzy, like my brain just can't quite grasp at the frayed edges of reality to see who he is underneath the blank face. He starts by humiliating and belittling me. He ensures I'm naked and sitting in the submissive pose he taught me the first time he showed up. He always finds something that I've done wrong to punish me over—which isn't surprising given he's got unbridled access to my deepest, innermost desires. Today there was nothing in particular that made him want to punish me, he just did it. He beat me with his belt, calling me a whore or a bitch. I can't even count how many times he whipped me. All I know is that when he didn't get the reply he wanted from me, he turned so that he was whipping me with the buckle of the belt instead. That soon got me to cry out. You see, that's what he likes most. He loves to hear me cry, begging him to stop." I shudder, hating voicing this aloud, but I know Dylan deserves to hear the truth at least once.

"Addy…" His voice trails off, and I can hear the sadness, all the unsaid words he wants to add.

"Once he's broken me physically, that's when he moves on to the real torture. He usually makes me do something humiliating, or he will bend me over his knee to spank me like a naughty child. It's never about anything sexual at that point, it's always about pain, humiliation, and him showing he has power over me. That's usually the time when he really starts to hurt me. He might beat me again, using something different that time, or he will just move on to sexually assaulting me, which is what he did last night. Luckily, last night he only abused my mouth and pussy, because there have been times when he's forced himself into my ass, with no lube or preparation, and I feel as though I'm being torn in two. But tonight he just wanted to take pleasure from me for his own gain. Last night was all about getting him off, which actually is the best-case scenario," I mutter, thinking to myself as I tell the story.

I feel Dylan freeze, his hand hovering next to my back as opposed to continuing to clean the wounds there as he was. *"How is giving him pleasure the best-case scenario?"* he asks, sounding bewildered, like maybe I really have lost the plot.

"That's the quickest way for him to be done with me. When he's got what he came for, he usually leaves. But if he's more concerned with forcing me to feel things, trying to force my body into betraying me, those nights are always far worse. Obviously now I've been with you, I know what it feels like to truly enjoy sex, and he's never made me feel the way you do. I want to make that statement pretty fucking clear. But he still knows that my body will react even if I'm scared, in pain, or humiliated. Even if I don't want it to, or I try to force it not to, with the right amount of stimulation, of course my body will respond, eventually. Those are the nights I dread the most." I let the words hang between us, waiting and wondering if this will

be the time it's all too much for him. Is this when he leaves? But he doesn't, he instead goes back to dabbing the wounds along my back.

"I hadn't really thought about it like that. I can't imagine any part of it being good, but I guess you have to hope for the easier parts."

I nod, smiling at the way he gets it—gets me. That's exactly what I try to do. I'm not seeing the good side, or trying to find parts I enjoy, but if the nightmares are going to come—and they always fucking do—I may as well pray for the easier version. The one that makes me hate myself the least at the end of it.

"You're right. None of it is easy, and if I'm being honest, I was quite shocked this session was so tolerable," *I confess, as I reach around with one hand to rest it against his thigh. It's like I need to be touching him to ground myself while I try to gather myself.*

"What do you mean?" *I should have known he would want more details.*

"Ever since we had sex, I've been waiting for him to punish me. He spends all his time humiliating me, causing me pain, and making me feel like a whore. So, I just can't understand why he wouldn't use the fact that I had mind-blowing sex with someone else against me," *I explain, as I lightly trail the tips of my fingers over his strong, hard thigh.*

"What? So, it's like he doesn't mention it, or he doesn't know it happened?" *Dylan asks, as he turns me in his arms until I'm facing him. He then indicates for me to give him my left arm, which I hold out for him straight away, and he begins tending to the wounds up and down my arm, including the ones dotted across the top of my chest.*

I take a moment to think about his question. I've never really thought about it before, preferring to not focus on the events after they've happened. But, the more I think about Slender Man's behaviour, and I question how much of my life he uses against me, I realise that what Dylan is hinting at is correct. It seems like there are parts of my life, the parts that I keep a secret from the world, that he doesn't have access to. Which is really fucking confusing given the same brain that holds all my secrets also created him.

"Honestly, now you mention it, it's not something I ever considered before. It's like the stuff that I keep a secret from the world, the stuff that only you know, he doesn't know about that. The things he uses against me are things about my past. He uses that to draw on my fear and pain. I quite like the fact that he never mentions you," I admit. I feel like Dylan is this secret that not even Slender Man can take from me.

Dylan's face scrunches up, his brow furrows as he looks at me with confusion in his silver eyes. "Have you ever wondered how he doesn't know about me?" Dylan asks, as he lets go of my hand before picking up the other as he tends to those wounds instead.

"Honestly, no. I try so hard to not think about you when he's around. Ever since we took things further, and I started developing real feelings for you, I've been literally praying that he never finds out. You are a bright light in my world that's shrouded in darkness. If he brought you into this, and tainted what we have, I think I would lose a lot of the hope I feel. It's bad enough that I feel like I'm cheating on you, without him bringing it up and playing on that fear." My voice drops low, barely above a whisper, as I confess the thing that's been weighing on me the last few days. I keep my eyes averted,

choosing to look at the wounds he's tending to rather than to see the look on his face.

Dylan freezes his movements and just waits for me to look up at him. It doesn't take long until I give in, and even though I see he's smiling, I can tell it's forced. It goes nowhere near touching his eyes, and there's no cocky lilt to it I love. Dylan's forced smile kills me more than if he was sad. He's trying to put on a brave face for me.

"Why do you feel like you are cheating on me?" he asks, his head leaning to one side like it's a serious riddle he's struggling to understand. How can he not see where I'm coming from?

"Dylan. In my hallucinations, he penetrates me, forces me to endure horrific sexual acts. He makes me pleasure him before he fucks me any way he likes. In the real world, of course, that would be classed as cheating. So to me, because it feels so real, it feels like cheating."

Shaking his head, Dylan reaches out and cups my cheek in his palm, stroking his thumb across my face in a soothing gesture. "Even if what is happening to you is real—because to you it is very real—I can promise you, I will never see it as cheating. You aren't choosing to engage in anything with him. None of it is your choice, and that makes it assault, not cheating."

He speaks with such conviction, I almost believe him. Fuck, I really do want to believe him, but sometimes I worry that the things he says literally are too perfect. Maybe my brain keeps Dylan and Slender Man separate because they are using them both in different ways to torture me. Slender Man is playing on my hopes and fears, humiliating me and torturing me. But it's Dylan who really has the power to hurt me. He's broken past all the defences I spent a long fucking time building, and he's wormed his way into my heart. I've given him everything he needs to break me beyond repair. I just have to hope that he doesn't. But doing that means I have to hope he's real, and as perfect as I think he is. Because if he truly is another figment of my overactive imagination, then it won't be long until he hurts me in the worst way possible.

I'm pulled out of my memory and back to the present when the chair scrapes beside me. Sin sits down, and I see her cast a glance down at my sleeve-covered arm. It's the middle of summer, and one of the hottest days so far this year. To say it's hot would be a massive fucking understatement. Guys are walking around with no shirts on—which sometimes is not a pleasant sight—and women have their summer clothes on. So the fact that I'm wearing long sleeves makes me stick out like a sore thumb. But the cuts on my arms keep bleeding, and I need to keep them bandaged, so that nobody sees them. Once they are healed a bit, I can take the bandages off and I won't cover them as much. Everyone already knows me as a self-harmer, so I don't know why I bother to hide.

"I heard from Lyle that you have signed up for dance therapy," Sin says, practically buzzing with excitement from the chair opposite me. It's so hot sitting here by the window doing my puzzle, but I need people to think I'm behaving like normal. So, in around ten minutes' time when I sneak off to the blossom garden, nobody will question it. I have arranged to meet Dylan there when he gets finished with his session with Dr. Hughes.

Shaking my head, I tut at Sin. "I don't know who the bigger gossip is, you or Lyle. So much for patient confidentiality," I mutter, though I don't really mind that she knows. It is a bit of a worry that Lyle so easily gives away patient information. Working in the office exposes him to all our personal information, including how and why we came to be residents of Lakeridge, and it's concerning that he may not be keeping that information confidential.

Sin rolls her eyes at me. "Well, he didn't really tell me as such. He asked me to give you your new timetable, which I left on the door of your room, and that's where I saw you now had dance therapy time scheduled. I didn't know you dance. You will never guess who else signed up for dance therapy… Dylan." Her pause is barely long enough for her to take a breath, let alone for me to answer, before she's shouting out Dylan's name loud enough to draw attention to us.

Shushing her, I try to get her to stop jiggling up and down as she's drawing unwanted attention our way. My friend, as well as being a massive gossip, loves to people watch. It doesn't surprise me she's worked out there's something going on between Dylan and I. I just hope I can convince her to keep it to herself.

"Yes, I know. I can hear the cogs in your head turning from here, Sin. Don't jump to conclusions. We are friends, and that is all." The lie rolls off my tongue, but it feels bitter. Like I'm doing us a disservice by saying that. "Even if we wanted more, we couldn't. It's against the rules, and we can't risk Dylan getting kicked out and sent to a real prison."

Sin's eyes go wide, her head nodding. "We definitely can't have that. Your secret is always safe with me. You've seemed happier since he got here."

I may as well have not bothered lying, since she already seems to know and won't be deterred. I give her a small smile. "I am happy."

"Has he gone?" she asks, and we both know she doesn't need to elaborate. We know who she's talking about.

My face falls and I shake my head. "Please don't tell anyone. I promise, I'm dealing with it."

Sin reaches out and places her hand on top of mine before giving it a squeeze. I'm shocked as she doesn't normally touch me without giving me enough warning or asking me. Most of the time she avoids it altogether, knowing how much I prefer to have my own space, and how much I dislike being touched by others. What is more shocking is that I'm not as bothered by her touch as I used to be. Maybe Dylan really is helping me to heal.

"I hope so. You really do deserve to be happy," she says with a smile.

I go over the question in my head a few times, wondering if I should say it, and what saying it aloud will make her think. But in the end, I decide I have to know. "I know this is going to sound like a crazy question, but I have to ask. Is Dylan real? I don't trust that someone as perfect as him could really be interested in someone as fucked up as me. If my brain can create Slender Man to torment me, what's to say it didn't create Dylan to cause me pain in a different way."

Sin gives me a small smile as she looks at me with her bright blue eyes. "He's very real. Trust in how you feel, Addy. I know your brain makes it difficult for you to differentiate between reality and delusions, but I think deep down you know. You know how you feel for Dylan, and that's not something you can make up."

She holds her arms out, silently asking me if she can give me a hug, and with a nod of my head, she pulls me against her chest. "Thank you," I whisper, barely loud enough for her to hear, but I know she does.

"You are my best friend, Addy. You are always here for me, and I will always be here for you. Just remember that."

I hug her tighter, and for once I really feel all the love and support she has for me. It's almost overwhelming to know this little pixie of a girl who has been through so much in her young life is capable of caring so much about me.

Knowing I have someone else in my corner really is a great feeling. It's also something I haven't ever allowed myself before. Now that I have Dylan and Sin, I feel a lot stronger than I ever have before. But that doesn't stop the fear and doubt from creeping in. It constantly reminds me that there's a reason I have kept people at arm's length before. Letting people in just gives him new ways to hurt me. I worry that while my brain is still occupied by

Slender Man, I won't ever have what it takes to fully let Dylan in. I don't know if I will ever be capable of feeling love, not when my brain is so full of pain.

I don't want to run from Dylan; I want to run to him, but that goes against all the things I've learnt to survive Lakeridge. I need to get my shit together and fast because I worry it won't be long before I have no choice except to push Dylan away. Unless I find out first that he's not real, and I break beyond repair.

Thirteen
DYLAN

It's weird to think that I've been here for almost three months now, and it's been over six weeks that I've been secretly seeing Addy. We've managed to keep it a secret, except for Sin knowing. When I learnt that she'd found out, I was worried she couldn't keep it a secret. She's not best known for her discretion. But true to her word, she hasn't said anything to anyone.

Things have been going great between us, and we try to steal as many moments together as we can. I can feel myself falling for her, and I know she feels the same way, but there's something holding her back. I can feel it. It's like there's still a part of her, no matter how much I try to reassure her, that believes I'm not real. She can't tell the difference between delusion and reality, and she questions whether the time we spend together is real.

I have to admit, no matter how much I hide it from

her, that is one thing that kills me the most. I want her to have faith in our relationship, to put her trust in me and know that I would never hurt her. I can understand why her brain works the way it does, and why she fears it so much. But, if I'm being honest, I'm starting to wonder if it's all in her head.

Each night, when she sneaks into my room, or we meet in the dance studio, she has fresh wounds. I check them, clean them, and make sure they aren't too deep. But as I'm doing it, I look at them, their placements, what could have caused them, and it gets me thinking. Some of it just doesn't add up. I see some of the wounds and I worry she can't possibly have self-inflicted them, but that leads me down a scary path. If Addy isn't doing these things to herself, then someone else must be. But that would mean that Slender Man is real, which is an absolutely fucking insane idea. And the more I think about it, the more I feel like maybe I'm going a little insane too.

Can I really be thinking that Addy is being assaulted by a real faceless man? I try to think what the other explanations could be, but I just can't get past him being faceless. Addy is sure it's not a man in a mask. She's touched his face, stared at it intently while he punishes her, and nothing. There are times when she thinks maybe she can see piercing green eyes that seem so familiar, and that's when she starts to think she's really going crazy. How can a man with no face have an eye colour?

I've been going over and over it in my mind, and the one thing that I am sure of is that I need to help Addy. Clearly, the treatment path she is on now isn't the right one. Dr. Manning has been treating her for a little over four months, and if anything, she has got worse, yet he doesn't seem to give a shit. All he's concerned about is the trial medication he keeps giving her. I think he's looking for a result, waiting for it to happen so that he can make this massive breakthrough and publish a paper that gets him even more recognition. But that will not work with Addy. In my opinion, he's given the drug more than enough time to work, and it hasn't. He needs to document the side effects and move on to the next drug, but for some reason, he doesn't want to do that.

I know what I need to do. I need to bring it up with Dr. Hughes to get her to look into it further. She needs to take over Addy's care, but that would mean her going against her boss. And it would mean me telling her that Addy and I are closer than we should be. That's a big risk for me because if she decides I've broken the rules—which I clearly have—then she can have me moved to a regular prison. I'm not sure I could survive that, or stay sober.

So, for now, I need to shelve that idea and come up with another one... but what that is exactly is a fucking mystery to me.

"Morning, Dylan. How are you today?" Dr. Hughes asks, as she comes strolling into her office for our one-on-one session. I notice the two takeaway Costa coffees in her hand, and I'm over the fucking moon when she hands one to me. "It's a caramel latte."

"You remembered?" I ask, in awe that she remembered the type of coffee I told her I was craving in one of our sessions last week. When it comes to sobriety, there are a lot of things that I crave, or would love to have, but a proper coffee was high on my list. I was surprised it actually ranked higher than booze when we were talking about it. Maybe this whole sobriety thing is working?

She hands me the paper cup, and I don't even hesitate before taking a gulp. It's not as hot as it normally would be since she's obviously had to pick it up on her way to work. That perfect bitter taste combined with the hint of sweet caramel assaults my taste buds, and I can't help but groan.

Great, now I'm making sex noises in front of my therapist over a coffee.

"Thank you," I mutter with my mouth still desperately latched onto the cup as I take another sip, savouring it a bit more this time.

"You are welcome. You are doing so well, Dylan. I figured you deserve a treat."

"So, this isn't you buttering me up for something, is it?" I joke, but the minute Dr. Hughes averts her eyes, I know I've accidentally stumbled on the truth.

She clears her throat before talking. "Have you heard any of the other residents talking about what tomorrow is?" she asks, and I rack my brain trying to think of anything, but I've got nothing, and so I shake my head.

"Saturday?" I answer with my usual sarcasm, and Dr. Hughes rolls her eyes at me in response.

"Tomorrow is Family Day. It's where people who have reached a certain stage in their recovery can invite members of their family over for a visit. We had one last month, but you were not at a stage to attend it."

Nodding, I remember very clearly. Dr. Hughes told me the event was happening and made it clear she didn't think I was strong enough yet to be introduced back to elements of my old life. Not that anyone would have come to see me. No point having a Family Day when you don't have any family. Instead, Addy and I played pool and took advantage of having the recreation room almost to ourselves. The secure wing, which never gets visitors, is out of the way, and there were only a handful like Addy and me who weren't allowed—or just didn't have—family visiting. Some sleep all day, while others mope about trying to see what the others in the main room next door are doing for this special day. But not Addy and I. We just had fun and made use of the time we had together without prying eyes. I'm guessing tomorrow will be another day, just the same.

"Well, I think you've reached the stage where you are strong enough for us to introduce you to some elements of your old life. So, I give you permission to have family over to visit tomorrow, but only one or two. I don't want you to be overwhelmed."

I can't help looking at her like she's grown a third nipple right in front of me. This woman knows more about me than almost anyone else, second only to Addy. Yet she really thinks I have family who want to visit me in this shithole. "Thanks for the offer, but I don't have any family, remember?" I can't help but sound hostile towards her. What can I say, not having a family is a bit of a sore subject for me.

"Well, that's funny because I've already had someone RSVP."

My eyes widen, and I can't hide the shock from my face. "Who?"

"Jake," she says, much to my amazement, before adding, "how does that make you feel?"

I almost want to roll my eyes at her typical psychiatrist response, but honestly, I don't know how I feel. I know me getting clean and sober meant a lot to the band, but I never considered they would support me with this. I kinda feel shitty now for not thinking they would support me. The truth is, they've always been on my side, even when I was so high that I couldn't see that. I often mistook their help or their concern for meddling, something I now deeply regret.

Jake has been by my side since we were kids. Hell, he's the person I ran to when I had nowhere else to go. We formed The Catastrophists in his garage, and we bonded through our love of music. He never walked away from our friendship. That was all me.

"Honestly, I'm not entirely sure. I made a lot of mistakes the last few years and I have a lot to apologise for. I often think maybe it's a bit too much, that I've done too much to be forgiven for it."

With a small smile, she begins making notes on her notepad before finally replying. "I guess it's one of those situations where you never know until you try."

I guess she is right. I don't know how I feel about seeing Jake again. Maybe I won't know for sure until he's here. It will also depend a lot on how he feels. He's the person I wronged, after all.

Suddenly, the idea of tomorrow doesn't sound as appealing. As much as I would love to see Jake again, I'm crippled by fear of what might happen. Plus, I have to give up on my day with Addy. I know she will be supportive of me seeing Jake, though. She always says she would give anything to have her family back. Jake is my family, and I should do everything I can to hold on to him.

Time seemed to drag after the therapy session yesterday, after finding out about Family Day. As I predicted, Addy was in complete support of me seeing Jake. She actually felt kinda sad that she was missing out on meeting him. It didn't even scare me that I wanted to introduce Addy to him. She's going to be in my life when we both get out of here, so I guess Jake will meet her eventually. But today is about us rebuilding—or starting to rebuild—what I broke over the last couple of years with my addiction.

I must have walked miles this morning, just pacing up and down, looking at the giant clock on the recreation room wall. The minutes seem to tick by painstakingly slowly, and with each minute that passes, my nausea increases. My palms are sweating, and my heart is racing. Even Addy cannot calm me down, though she's doing a great job of trying, until the nurses came in and made anyone not taking part in Family Day leave the rec room.

I know she will only be next door, and if she goes into the garden, I could go to her, but the idea of being separated from her at the height of my anxiety is not great.

"Hey, Dylan, look at me. Take some big, deep breaths. You have got this. He's your brother, and he loves you. No matter what you have been through before, that is all in the past. He's here, which means he cares. Everything else can be fixed. Okay?" she placates, discreetly giving my hand a squeeze in a way that nobody can see as our bodies are blocking them from view. We've done so well keeping our secret, and we don't want to blow our cover now.

"Thanks, Addy. I... You know you mean the world to me, right?" Fuck, had I just been about to say those three little words? Now is not the time for that. I mean it when I say she means the world to me, and that falling for her would be easy, if I haven't already. The problem is, I have never known love. I've never been in love, and I've never been loved by anyone, so I have no idea if what I feel is how it should feel. Maybe I'm overthinking it and I should just listen to how my body feels? That's a discussion for another day. Right now, I need to focus on Jake.

Just as I think his name, Dr. Hughes comes strolling through the main recreation room doors, deep in conversation with Jake. They're both happy and smiling, talking to each other like they are old friends. I can't hide the pang of jealousy I feel, but I can't really explain why I feel jealous. Maybe because I want it to be that easy with Jake? Or maybe I feel possessive over the doctor? She is my therapist, after all. Fuck, I'm messed up.

They stop a few feet in front of me, and as soon as they see me, the laughter and conversation die down, replaced by awkward silence. Jake's face looks almost blank as he rakes his gaze over my body—no doubt checking to see if I still look like an addict.

When I was admitted I was thin, and I looked gaunt. Drink and drugs had taken hold of me, and I used booze as a food group instead of actually eating. I wasn't spending as much time in the gym as I am now, and I looked a bit like a rake. Now I've bulked up to the lean body I had back before the drugs. I now focus on healthy eating, with the odd treats. I run for more of a mental health requirement than a physical health thing; it helps me to clear my head and focus my thoughts. Then the dancing I've been doing with Addy has really helped tone me up, too.

I can see the shock in Jake's eyes as he no doubt sees the friend he used to know rather than the drug addict he left here a few months ago. We both stand there in silence, while Dr. Hughes flicks her gaze between the two of us like she's at a Wimbledon final. She's clearly waiting for one of us to make the first move, and when her piercing stare settles on me, it's clear she intends on me being that person.

"Hey Jake." Well, it's not my best opener, but I think it does the job.

Jake smiles, the big, lopsided grin I'm used to seeing from him, and he doesn't hesitate before reaching out and pulling me in for a tight hug. The moment his arms are around me, I feel my body sag as all the tension and nerves I felt over this moment melt away.

"I'm gonna leave you two to it, and I will come back and see how things are going shortly," Dr. Hughes says as she walks away. Jake shouts goodbye to her retreating form before turning back to face me. I lead him over to two empty armchairs in the corner of the room, and I watch as Jake hesitantly takes in his surroundings.

I don't blame him. This is a run-down psychiatric

facility, after all. The walls could do with a new lick of paint since the one currently on is peeling off. Everywhere looks like it could do with a good scrub clean. All the furniture looks like it's older than me. And that's before he even gets onto judging the people. It doesn't help that the nearest person to us is Barry, who spends all his time rocking in the same chair, muttering to himself about anything and everything. Thankfully, Toby, who likes to take his underwear off and wave it around his head, at least every couple of hours, is locked in his room. He's not exactly a poster child for this place actually working. I guess you could say I am.

"It's so great to see you, Dyl. The doc says you are doing great. You are sober, not needing any medication to help with that, and you're even engaging in different therapies to help control your addiction. I'm so proud of you," he states, puffing his chest out like a proud dad would.

I can feel my cheeks flush. I don't really do well with genuine compliments like that. "It's not easy. Every day is a struggle, but I'm doing okay. I worry about how I will be when I leave here. In here it's easy to stay clean, there's nothing to tempt me. But on the outside, I will be surrounded by the same temptations, the same lifestyle. I worry I will fall back into the same habits."

Jake shakes his head. "I don't think so. The old Dylan would never have said what you just did. You want to be sober, which you never did before. You have more fight in you than I've ever seen before. I don't know what's got you fighting so hard, but hold on to it."

I can't help but think of Addy, and I wonder whether

I should introduce her to Jake. I know he will love her, but I'm just not sure if it's the right time. "I will do. I guess I owe you and the guys a big apology. I've been reflecting on what an asshole I was to you all, and I don't think there's enough time in the world, or the right words to apologise to you for all the hurt I caused."

Jake smiles again, and I'm honestly shocked he's taking this so well. "You don't need to apologise to us. We are family, so we stand by you, even when you are being a first-class dickhead. We love you, Dyl, and we just want the old you back. You can make it up to us by writing us a kick-ass song for our comeback album."

At the mere mention of music, we go off on a tangent, talking like nothing has changed about music, and songs we've heard and love. I don't know how long we sit there for, just putting the world to rights and talking about our shared passion—music. It bonds us in the same way it did when we first met as kids. I guess you could say it reminded us of what brought us together in the first place.

It's not long before it's time for Family Day to end, the day having gone by far too quickly, and after the way I've bonded with Jake again over the last couple of hours, I make a snap decision to trust him with my biggest secret.

"Jake, I need your help with something, but you have to promise me you will tell no one about this, especially not Dr. Hughes," I explain, and I can see the confused expression cross his face.

"Why do I get the feeling I'm not going to like this?" he asks suspiciously.

Shaking my head, I tell him all about Addy. How we met, how important she is to me, and the problems she's going through. I explain about Dr. Dickhead, and how I think he's putting more effort into boosting his career than he is actually caring for her. I ask if he will do me a massive favour and do some digging into Dr. Manning. I need to know if he really has Addy's best interests at heart, and whether the trial drug he's giving her is seeing success anywhere. I know it's hard since we don't even know the name of the drug, but Jake will be able to hire people who will investigate and find out. I would do it myself if I could get access to the outside world.

At first Jake listens with interest, but the further I get into my story, the more his face falls until he's openly scowling at me. "Are you kidding me right now? Here's me thinking you are doing so well, putting all that effort in to get clean for the band, and all this time it was for some pussy," he snarls, and it takes every bit of self-control and anger management that Dr. Hughes taught me to ensure I don't spring off this chair and land my fist on his nose.

"Don't ever call her that again. This isn't just some fling, or about sex. I really like her. I worked my ass off to get clean for me, nobody else. I want to be back in the band, of course I do. The Catastrophists were all I knew, but now I have more. Addy is my life, and I have to help her. Even if it means risking the band, my future, my freedom, and you—my family. That isn't me choosing Addy over all those things. That's me telling you I would risk all of those things to help her. That's how much she means to me."

With each new sentence, I can see his confusion growing, only to be replaced by one of pure shock. "You really like this girl that much?"

"Yeah, I really do. Hell, maybe I even love her. You know, I haven't exactly had many role models to tell me what love is really supposed to be like. How am I supposed to know for sure if I love her?" I ask, allowing myself to be truly vulnerable in front of him, and hoping like hell he realises how much I've changed. He's right, the old me would have never talked about anything like this.

"I think the fact that you are even considering it tells me you are probably already there, you are just scared. This girl must mean a lot to you if you're willing to risk your future." His eyebrows raise in question, and I know what he's asking me. Is she just another addiction I've used to replace the ones I had to give up? When I get out of here and back to my old life, will I still want Addy to be a part of that?

"I don't see a future that doesn't have her in it, and if we don't help her, I fear that's exactly what could happen. You should see the marks all over her body, Jake. It breaks my fucking heart that I can't save her." My voice cracks as I voice something I've never said before. I wish I could save her, but at this point, I don't know what I'm saving her from.

Shaking his head, Jake stands up and I realise there probably isn't much longer left with him. "Okay, I will think about it. I can't make you any promises, Dyl."

I give him a smile. "That's okay. You have had to endure years of failed promises and let-downs from me. I can live with a maybe. Come," I call, as I head towards the back door.

We get out into the garden, and surprisingly there are

a couple of residents and their families sitting on the posh patio furniture I've never seen before. They're beautiful wicker sofas with bright blue cushions on that look almost new and clean. Normally there are a few plastic chairs that look like they could barely hold my weight, and they could have started out white but are now more of a murky grey colour. They are long gone, and the posh furniture is out. Apparently, Lakeridge likes to make an effort just for Family Day.

I don't bother looking around the garden; I pull Jake along behind me as we turn the corner and enter the cherry blossom garden. Just as I predicted, my girl is lying on the floor, looking up at the treetops. She's wearing a pair of denim cut-offs that stop mid-thigh, and one of my old Catastrophists t-shirts that she's rolled up and tied at the side so that you can see the small strip of skin between her top and her jeans. Her long brunette hair is splayed out around her in natural curls, and her face is make-up-free, but aside from looking a little pale, she looks beautiful.

As soon as she sees us enter her sanctuary, she looks shocked, and she springs to her feet, smoothing down her clothes and trying to stop her hair from having that sexy, messy look that I love. She shoots me with a death glare that clearly says she would have liked a bit more warning, but I ignore her, giving her a big, reassuring smile.

"Addy, this is Jake," I say, pointing behind me at my best friend, who is taking in Addy and her buzz of nervous energy. "Jake, this is the girl I was telling you about. Addy."

Jake steps forward, ever the gentleman, and he holds

his hand out with a bright smile—one our PR team taught him years ago—while he introduces himself. "Lovely to meet you, Addy. I'm Jake."

Addy laughs, or more accurately, she snorts before quickly covering her mouth with her hands, her face flushing red with embarrassment. "Erm… I-I know who you are. I'm a-a big fan," she mumbles as she reaches out to shake Jake's hand. I think she probably holds on for a little too long, and Jake looks at me like I really have just introduced him to a crazy person. I'm not missing the irony of that statement, given our location.

"Wow, I never got that kind of reception when I first met you," I only half joke, and Addy just rolls her eyes.

"If you weren't so much of an asshole when you first arrived, maybe I would have been nicer," she snaps, still shaking Jake's hand. That's when she looks down and realises she hasn't let go yet. Jake is just too nice to say anything. Addy quickly drops his hand like he burnt her and takes a step back, shrinking away with embarrassment.

Jake laughs as she calls me an asshole. "I know what he was like when he arrived here. Asshole is an understatement."

Now Addy laughs, and just like that, the two most important people in my life begin to get along. Both relax and talk to each other normally, and I feel like my life is becoming complete. Maybe now that Jake has seen how much she means to me, he will agree to help her.

"Addy, I have to ask, what do you see in Dylan?" Jake asks, though he doesn't sound as suspicious as the question sounds. More like he's genuinely curious.

"Honestly, he's the light in my darkness. I spend a lot of time not knowing the difference between reality and delusion, and he helps me with that. He stands by my side, supporting me. Not only that, but he's also willing to risk his own future just to make sure I'm okay. To me, that's a pretty perfect guy. I'm lucky I found him, and there are some days where I'm not sure I would still be here without him." Sadness engulfs me as she vocalises something I've long since suspected. Being stuck in a delusion based solely on pain and abuse, losing vast portions of sleep, and enduring your body being battered and bruised each and every day would take its toll on anyone. I'm lucky she's stayed with me this long. I have to save her before the darkness becomes too much and Slender Man takes what's mine.

"Sounds like you are both lucky to have found each other," Jake says, giving us both a smile, and we both nod in agreement. Before either of us can say anything more, the bell to indicate the end of Family Day rings loud and Addy and Jake say goodbye. They both say they hope to see each other again, and I genuinely believe them.

Walking Jake back to the rec room, I'm overcome with emotion as I say goodbye to my brother. "Thank you so much for coming, Jake. I can't even begin to tell you how much it means to me. And thank you for being so kind when you met Addy. You don't have to give me an answer about helping her now. Just think about it. Would that be okay?" I ask hopefully.

"I promise to think about it. I liked her. She seems nice, and she really cares about you. It's impossible to deny the bond you've both forged. I just hope she's as good for you as you say she is. I will keep your secret, though. It's the least I can do," he adds before pulling me in for a hug.

I thank him and wave him off as a nurse leads him out of the building. Just before he reaches the exit, Jake turns around and holds his arm in the air with all his fingers down in a fist except his index and his pinkie finger—the universal sign for rock music. It's something we used to do when we were kids and we wanted to remind ourselves that it was all about the music. I raise my arm in a matching salute, and he leaves with a big smile on his face.

Watching my best friend—my brother—leave smiling, my heart swells. Tears pool in my eyes as I realise that despite all the damage I did through years of substance abuse, it can all be fixed. Maybe I can have it all? Maybe I can be in The Catastrophists, have Addy by my side, and stay sober? That's my dream, and I sure as fuck am going to do everything in my power to make that happen, even if that means risking it all. I have to help Addy. It's the only way for me to be sure that we can spend the rest of our lives together. But to do that, she has to be one hundred per cent sure I'm real, and she has to fight against Slender Man—fight for us.

Fourteen
ADDY

Ever since the family open day, things have been going well with Dylan. He's been opening up a lot more, talking about what he dreams of in the future. It feels so weird every time he says he dreams of a future that involves me. Until a few weeks ago, I didn't even see myself having a future, but now he's talking about me going on tour with The Catastrophists. He wants me to choreograph the entire tour, as well as dance on it. I mean, that's a dream I didn't even know I had anymore.

When me and Arabella were younger, we used to talk about going on tour with bands. I always wanted to be a backing dancer, and she wanted to be a singer. Eventually she wanted to be the one at the front of the stage, and she was probably good enough too. I never had dreams like that. I have always been quite happy being the person in the background, a bit like Dylan in that respect. He's happy to make the music and then sit at the back on his drums while the show plays out before him. He doesn't need to be the frontman.

It's lunchtime, and I keep looking at the clock waiting for Dylan to arrive. I booked the dance studio for the next two hours. Not that many people come here or that it gets fully booked, but we're supposed to reserve the time, so I did. I've been warming up by myself for the last fifteen minutes, waiting for him to get here. We have told no one that we are dancing together yet, but we haven't exactly hid it either. We dance together here during the day. Our last rehearsal, Sin even came to watch. Dylan is normally always early to things like this, which is why I'm worried when he isn't here, and the more time goes by, the more worried I get.

Five minutes later he comes bursting through the doors, in his baggy shorts and t-shirt, his hair dishevelled, and his face flushed with sweat. "Sorry, pretty girl. I went for a run and completely lost track of time," he explains, as he takes a drink from his water bottle before placing it next to mine in the corner of the room.

"It's not like you to get caught up." My brow furrows as I try to take in whatever I'm missing, whatever he's not saying. Something has obviously thrown him off track, and it can't be Jake's visit, as that was a couple of days ago. Maybe something happened in his one-on-one session with Dr. Hughes? Though he never normally comes out of those sessions feeling shitty.

"Yeah, sorry. It's been a long day." He takes a deep breath, like he's trying to pluck up the courage to tell me what he's hiding. I lay a hand on his arm as reassurance, and that seems to be enough. "I told Dr. Hughes that we are dancing together. She immediately said we had broken the rules and that I couldn't date another resident. I spent ten minutes convincing her we have just bonded over dance. So she is coming to watch us. If she thinks we are using this dance time for anything other than dancing, I'm out of here. I guess that was on my mind while I was running."

I shake my head, infuriated that she would reduce our relationship to something so trivial. That's when I see her sitting where Sin sat yesterday, her normally kind face taking on a judgemental stare.

"We better put on a good show for her, then. Stretch out quickly and I will put the music on," I instruct, and take a moment to appreciate his ass as he bends over to stretch. I chastise myself, remembering to keep my head in business mode right now. Ogling his more than perfect ass, while fun, is not what a dance partner would do.

Scrolling through, I find the song we have been perfecting for the last few days. It's one of my favourite songs by The Catastrophists, and knowing Dylan wrote the song gives it so much more meaning. "Only You" talks about what it will be like when we find that one perfect person who we have been searching for all our lives, and how we finally feel complete when we meet. When Dylan wrote the song, he didn't know me, and he sure as fuck didn't think he believed in soulmates. If you ask Dylan, he wrote this song because he was told by his label to write a love song, but Dylan didn't know what love was, and so he wrote about what he thinks it will be like when you meet the one. It's like he wrote it for us, for this moment, without even realising.

The music starts and we both get into position. Whilst I was predominantly trained in Latin and ballroom, I loved adapting to a more street style of dance, and Dylan is without a doubt a self-taught, naturally talented street dancer. So whilst there are elements of this dance that we have choreographed, there are sections where we freestyle and that's when we have the most fun.

We start moving along with the slow melody of the music, and Dylan sashays me around the dance hall like we are dancing to a classic American Smooth style. Our backs are straight, but tilted backwards slightly, our arms locked in a hold, and my legs are perfectly pointed. We follow along with the music for a few seconds before the song shifts into an uptempo melody, the loud pounding of Dylan's drum providing the beat we move to. Gone are the perfect lines and holds. Instead, we draw our bodies together, touching in all the places that matter as we move our hips in time with the beat.

We jump up and down, leaping and swaying from one move to another, working together to create the most beautiful shapes. Then, as the music changes once more, we begin the freestyle element and I stand back and watch as Dylan takes centre stage for once.

His body pops to the beat as he moves in a way that is mesmerising to witness before dropping to the floor and spinning. Once he jumps back up, he holds his arm out for me to grab, and without hesitation, I let him spin me into the centre of the room.

Combining my love of ballet and street, I pop in a way that complements Dylan, whilst also throwing in a few classic ballet shapes and turns. It's been a long time since I've done some of them, and I'm not even going to say how sore my toes are. They're bleeding and blistered, but that's the feet of a dancer. Eventually I will get back to the stage where I don't even feel them anymore, and I can't wait for that.

Once the music changes again, we both pull ourselves back together and finish the routine with what can only be described as a bit of dirty dancing. My back is to Dylan's front, my ass grinding against his crotch while his hands sweep along my sides. Everywhere he touches, I feel alive, like his very touch sets me on fire.

We are so lost in the dance, I don't think we even realise that the music has finished. We just continue to sway, holding each other. Well… that is until a slow clap draws us apart. In fact, we jump apart like guilty teenagers who have just been caught doing something we shouldn't.

"Wow, you guys, that was amazing! I don't even have words to describe how beautiful that was. You are both very talented," Dr. Hughes says, as she walks towards us still clapping, a look of shock and amazement on her face.

"Do you believe me now, Doc? That we bonded over dance, and that's all there is to it?" Dylan asks, and I avert my eyes, hoping she can't see the lie that must be there.

"It's clear you both have a connection, but I will trust you. If you say this is only dance, I will believe you. But let me make one thing very clear: I will have a very low threshold of suspicion. If I even half suspect there's anything more going on, I will have no choice but to report it. I also have to inform Dr. Manning, as he's

Addy's primary physician."

"No," I snap, interrupting whatever other warning she may have for us.

"I'm sorry, Addy. I have no choice. He's my boss. I will clarify that I am monitoring you both and that you both have permission to continue dancing together, but that is all. Is that okay?" she asks, and I can't help but shake my head in despair.

"I guess it will have to be," I snap, not meaning to sound as harsh as I do. I look over and expect Dylan to have grabbed hold of me by now. Usually when he can see I'm struggling, he will reach out and just place his hand on my arm, or my leg, and that's all I need to take strength from him. But his hands are balled into fists at his sides. That leads me to think he wants to reach out, but he doesn't want Dr. Hughes to get the wrong idea. Smart! Though it doesn't help me right now.

"What is it you are so worried about if I tell Dr. Manning?" she asks, genuinely curious.

"Honestly, I don't know. He just gives me a general bad feeling. He looks down on me, and I don't think he would see any therapeutic value in dance, particularly dancing with Dylan," I explain, and Dr. Hughes nods her head rapidly like she really understands.

"You have my word. All will be fine. Now continue enjoying your practice time together. I can't wait to see what you come up with next," she says, as she walks towards the door. Just before leaving, she turns to look at Dylan over her shoulder. "Proud of you, Dylan. I didn't think you would ever find an art therapy. But you found one you are great at. Keep it up."

With that, she closes the door and walks down the corridor, leaving us to our routine time. Once we are sure she's gone, we dance exactly the way we want to dance, caught up in each other's arms. As we sway along to the music, we forget all about our worries, and just let the music and the dance consume us.

A loud crashing sound jostles me awake, and it sounds like something is about to rip the bedroom door off its hinges. I jump up instantly, knowing exactly who it is. I had been hoping for a night off, but I should be so lucky. From the moment he first stormed into my room, I knew tonight was going to be different. There was something different, almost like a buzzing of electricity filling the air. But it's more than that. He's different. He's angry in a way that I've never seen before, and I have no idea why. Or, at least, to start with, I didn't.

I jumped out of bed, pulling Dylan's t-shirt from my body, making sure to take in a deep inhale of his scent to help give me strength to do this, before throwing it to the floor. Completely naked, I kneel on the floor next to the chair beside my window, pulling my arms behind my back, sticking my tits out, while making sure my eyes are downcast at all times. I listen as he strides across the room, his shiny black shoes the only thing I can see as he towers over me.

CRACK!

I hear the slap of skin against skin a fraction of a second before an intense pain ricochets through my skull.

My cheek which took the brunt of the backhand flames and stings, but there's a deep ache that spreads through my face. I reach up and feel blood dripping from a cut just underneath my eye on my right cheek. He must wear a ring, and when the back of his hand made contact with my cheek, the ring must have sliced my skin open. Even using my hand to apply pressure to the wound doesn't help to dull the pain.

"I always knew you were just another dirty slut," he slurs, his voice sounding booming and angry, and surprisingly this time, the voice doesn't sound like it's coming through a simulator. It sounds like a man's voice. It's impossible to tell if I recognise it or not, as it's so distorted with rage.

Before I have a chance to reply—not that I would have known what to say—he rains blow upon blow down on my body. A slap with his right hand, followed by a slap from his left. He's using me like a punching bag, and pain vibrates all over my body. It's screaming at me, telling me how much pain I'll be in, and how much trouble I'm in. But that I already know.

It doesn't take long before his blows knock me off balance and I fall to the floor. At that point, he kicks me twice in my stomach and once again in my back. I scream out in pain as I try desperately to curl my body up into a ball to protect myself as much as I can. All the while, I can hear his maniacal laugh echoing around the room.

"Please... Please, no more. I can't... I can't take any more. I'm sorry. Whatever I've done, I'm sorry," I sob, tears strolling down my face as pain racks my body.

"You should have thought about that before you

disobeyed me, you whore." His voice, whilst definitely the most human it's ever been, it almost sounds like the growl of a monster.

"I didn't… how did I… disobey you?" I ask, keeping an arm over my head and one wrapped around my stomach to try to protect myself. Even though the blows have stopped, I have no idea when they will start again. All I can hear are his puffs and pants of exertion hovering over me.

"I told you the day we first met that you are mine now. You are my slut, to use any way in which I please. Your holes belong to me. That is the only reason for you to exist. And you agreed to this, remember?" His evil sneer drags up the awful memories of that first night. I had been so certain he was real, and he beat the shit out of me, and raped me in the most violent way, bending me to his will until I broke. I remember the exact moment when I agreed to be his whore. I would have said or done anything in that moment to make the pain stop, to make him go away.

He's visited countless times since then, and each time I start off so sure he's real, just like right now. I can hear his heavy breathing, just like you would a real person who is exerting himself. I can smell the awful odour that comes from his mouth when he speaks, even though I can't even see his mouth. His face is blank, and the more I stare, the longer he's here, the more I'm sure he's an illusion. A way for my brain to punish me in the most horrific of ways.

Nodding frantically from my foetal position on the floor, I confirm that I remember, and he laughs—but it's not a funny laugh. He sounds manic and almost deranged. "If you remember the promise you made to me, why would you then go and whore yourself out to Dylan Matthews?"

I freeze, my world finally coming crashing down around me. I had been so sure I could hide Dylan from that part of my brain; I do not know how, but I went almost six weeks without him finding out. Now he knows, and I'm sure the punishment will be severe.

"Now that we have confirmed you are a cheating slut, we need to discuss your punishment. What do you think is a fair punishment?" he asks, his voice sounding almost pleased, and I know why. This is a new game he started a couple of days ago. He gets me to name my own punishment, but if it's not as severe or worse than the one in his head, not only will he do the punishment he was thinking of, he will also do my punishment too. So essentially, I get twice the torture. Or I name something that was even worse than he came up with, and he takes great pleasure re-enacting my own punishment. It's a fucking sick game, and I don't have the energy to play it today.

I remain silent until he kicks me in my lower back again, causing my scream to ring out, as I move my hand to stroke the throbbing area that his boot had just connected with. "You better answer me, whore."

My sobs continue, and it's hard to form coherent sentences with all the pain and fear vibrating through my body. "I don't know, Sir. Nothing happened with Dylan. We are just dance partners. I swear."

I don't know why I'm bothering to negotiate with him. He's clearly not capable of being rational or discussing things. I almost laugh at myself, because what it boils down to is that I'm trying to rationalise with the irrational, delusional side of my brain. It's a lost cause.

"If you were just dance partners, you wouldn't have hid it from me. You would have asked my permission," he growls before reaching down and grabbing a big chunk of my hair. With it firmly in his fist, he pulls up, dragging me until I'm sitting on my knees again, and I'm screaming from the burning on my scalp. There's no way he hadn't pulled out large chunks of my hair when he did it.

I keep one hand wrapped around my body, trying to protect my vital organs, and cover up some of my nudity, while I use the other to wipe the tears and snot off my face. I'm still sobbing uncontrollably, blood seeping out of different wounds all over my body, as my muscles scream at me to make the pain stop. I wish I fucking knew how.

Keeping my eyes down, just like he taught me, I feel the touch of his icy cold skin against my chin as he raises my head to make sure I'm looking directly at him. Then, completely out of the blue, he pulls a gun from his back pocket. I recoil, suddenly feeling even more afraid than I ever have before. The silvery metal of the barrel reflects in the harsh moonlight, and I try to tell myself repeatedly that it's not real, but it's like I'm just not hearing it.

He opens the chamber, spins it around so that I can see it's empty. He then pulls out one gold bullet and places it into the chamber, before spinning it around, a giant smile spreading across his face. "I think we should play a game. You are going to name a way for me to punish you, and if I like it, then that's good, but if I don't, I will shoot. You get to name three things, which is potentially three times I will shoot you. So, what is your first punishment going to be?" he asks, the gun pointed directly at my face. My body is shaking so badly, I can barely hold myself upright on my knees.

I think back to all the ways he's punished me in the past, and try to imagine which he's enjoyed the most. It's difficult to even predict what's going on in his head, so I decide to go with the punishments I will hate the most. I would rather suffer pain than die. "Erm… you could… fuck my asshole dry until I scream in agony."

Even though it's clear he has no face, the fuzziness around his blank mask makes that very clear. It's almost like I can sense him smiling. "Very good. I like that one. What next?"

Fuck, that was by far my worst. Now I need to think of other things he enjoys doing to me. "Whipping my body with your belt," I mutter, my voice barely above a whisper, as all the energy is rapidly leaving my body.

Without even a moment's hesitation, I hear the click as he pulls the trigger on the gun. Thankfully, it was an empty chamber, but that still didn't stop the heart attack it feels like I just put my body through. As soon as I heard that click, for just a fraction of a second, I worried I was going to die. My heart stopped, before starting up again at a rapid pace. I cry out in relief, and my body sags lower onto the floor, exhaustion kicking in further.

Slender Man loves to see my body betraying me, which is why he grabs me by the hair and pulls me back up onto my sore, aching knees. "One more, whore. What's it going to be?"

I can hear the excitement in his voice, like he's just

waiting for me to make the wrong choice. Honestly, my brain is so exhausted, I can't even think straight. He wiggles the gun in my face, and I don't know where my burst of anger comes from, but I am just so sick of being hurt and tortured. "I don't fucking know, and I don't fucking care. We both know you are going to do what the hell you want, so let's get it over and done with so I can get rid of you. Then yeah, I'm going to go back to Dylan. You can tell me to stay away from him as much as you want, but you can't change the way I feel about him. I think that is what you are really mad about," I scream, trying to use my last push of energy to get up off my knees. I will be able to protect myself better if I have my feet firmly on the floor. Sadly, Slender Man definitely doesn't appreciate me talking back to him.

With a roar of anger, he pulls the trigger not once, but twice, in quick succession. But instead of flinching or crying out in fear, I simply stand there, staring down the barrel of the gun. I don't know if I've just lost all energy to care, or if I really am okay with dying. I think there is a part of me that hopes for that bullet to come flying towards me. I want Slender Man to end my life, because at this point it would be a small mercy. Don't get me wrong, the thought of leaving Dylan really does hurt, possibly more than all the pain Slender Man can inflict. Dylan has been abandoned his whole life, and I'm not sure I can be another person who does that to him.

Before I can even let out a grateful sigh of relief, a sharp pain erupts around my temple, my vision begins to blur. I blink rapidly as I fall to the floor, just in time to see that he hit me with the butt of the gun. I can feel the warm trickle of blood flowing down my face. Fuck, I think this might actually be the time he kills me. All I can do is lie here, my body aching and throbbing with immense pain, and think of Dylan. Even just the mere thought of him, it shines a light on my darkness. Right now, I may be under the cover of darkness, but he's the shining light I need to get out the other side. I vow to hold on for Dylan.

It's at that moment that I'm reminded that Slender Man really does know all my thoughts. "Let me make this very clear, slut. I forbid you from having anything to do with Dylan. If you even think of muttering a word to him, I will haunt him. If you think the pain and suffering I cause you is bad, wait until you see what I do to him. Do I make myself clear?"

I nod, and as he goes to slap me, I quickly reply verbally, just the way he likes. "I understand. I won't go near him."

"You better not. Don't even think about cheating or trying to go behind my back because you know you can't hide from me. I'm part of you," he laughs maniacally, and I cower back from him. We both know this is only the start of the night for me. I have a long punishment ahead, and now I don't have the thought of seeing Dylan to get me through. This really might be the night he kills me.

I don't know how long Slender Man abuses me for; it feels like forever, and it got so painful I ended up drifting in and out of consciousness. When I finally woke up a short while later, I could barely move without causing myself pain. Given the sharp stabbing pain I feel when I take a breath, I wouldn't be surprised if I'd broken a rib or two.

Looking over at the clock on the wall, I see that it's just after four in the morning, which means I'm an hour late to meet Dylan. Maybe that's a good thing. I need to find a way to tell him we can't ever see each other again, and when I'm feeling like this, it's hardly the time. All I want right now is for him to take me in his arms and hold me until I feel better.

I must have dosed off slightly, comforted by that thought, and so when I wake up to the sound of Dylan's panicked voice, I'm torn between pulling him closer and pushing him away. I think, just for this one time, I'm going to let him take care of me. I can break both our hearts when I'm a little stronger.

Dylan runs around a bit, looking frantic, as I drift in and out of sleep. Or maybe I'm losing consciousness. I wouldn't be surprised if I have a concussion given the amount of times I got hit around the head. Dylan must have been in my en-suite, because when he comes back in a few minutes later, he tries to get my attention. Realising he's fighting a losing battle, he clearly decides to move me himself. As gently as he possibly can, he scoops me up into his arms in a bridal hold, and he carries me into my en-suite. He must have begun drawing me a bath because by the time he gets me in there, the tub is almost full of steaming water.

"Do you want to test if the temp is okay?" he mutters in my ear, as he places one of his hands in the water to test for himself.

"As long as it's boiling hot, that's all I need." My voice sounds distant and vacant, and I don't miss Dylan's frown.

"Do you mind if I carry you in?" he asks, ever the gentleman getting the permission he needs.

I nod, and slowly Dylan lowers me into the tub. His arms submerge in the water with me, and he doesn't appear to care that the sleeves of his t-shirt are getting wet. I watch as the water surrounding me slowly turns an awful pinkish colour, and that's when I realise I must be bleeding more than I thought. I both love and hate the burn of the water as I submerge myself in it. I hate the way it makes my wounds sting as it cleans them out, but I love the fact that it's actually helping me feel clean.

A strange noise pulls me out of my head, and I look over at Dylan who is sitting with his back against the bathroom wall. His knees are up against his chest, and his head is resting in one of his hands, the other is reaching out and holding on to my hand. I hadn't even realised our fingers are clasped together, but suddenly the idea of parting from him feels more terrifying than anything else I faced this evening.

It's not until I really look at his face that I realise Dylan is crying. There are tears running down his beautiful face, and he just looks so small and helpless. Like I'm finally seeing the scared little boy who doesn't know what love really is, or if it's something he's capable of. The mere fact that he's crying over this moment, over seeing me this way, that tells me he's more than capable of love.

"Dylan," I mutter as I give his hand a gentle squeeze. I'm not sure if I'm reassuring him, or just trying to get his attention, but when he looks up at me, I realise now is as good a time as any. There's never going to be a right time, or a good time, to hurt the only man I've ever cared about. But if I want him to be safe, I have to set him free.

Before I'm able to say anything, Dylan beats me to it. "What the hell happened, Addy? This doesn't look self-inflicted. This looks like you've had the shit kicked out of you. I really think we should call Dr. Hughes, or the nurse, until the docs come in. Hell, at this point I would even take Dr. Dickhead. You could have serious injuries, Addy."

I shake my head violently to express how much I don't like that idea, but I instantly regret it when it feels like my brain is rattling around inside my head, being battered and bruised. "No. I don't want anyone else getting involved. You promised, Dyl."

"That was before I found you like this. What the hell happened, Addy?" he pleads, desperately hoping I will open up, just a little, to tell him what happened.

Since it's all ending shortly, I may as well do myself a favour and drag out every minute with him. "If I tell you, you have to promise not to get angry or sad." Dylan shakes his head. "I can't promise that because I am already angry and sad. You have no idea how fucking painful it was to see you passed out on the floor, blood dripping from different cuts across your fragile body. For a moment, your breathing was so slow and shallow, I thought you were fucking dead, Addy. My heart literally broke. I can't lose you."

Fuck, this is not how I expected this to go. I need him to go back to being angry and mad at me for the wounds

I've inflicted on myself. If he's mad at me, it will make what I've got to do a tiny bit easier.

"It was because of you. Slender Man knew we were together, or at least he thought we were, until I confirmed it. That's when he kicked the shit out of me. He tortured me, played Russian roulette with a gun, and made me pick my own punishments. I tried to fight back, but there's only so much you can battle against your own mind." I splash the surrounding water, whirling around some of the heat into places where it's cooling.

"He's never mentioned me before?" Dylan asks, as he scurries closer to the edge of the bath, his brows pulled together like he's trying to solve a really hard maths equation.

"No, I always thought that was weird. Now I know it was just my brain luring me into a false sense of security," I growl, so fucking angry at the whole situation.

"What do you mean?"

"I mean, my brain knew what it was doing all along. It made me think I was safe, that Slender Man didn't know about you. You were a bright light in my dark days. You gave me hope, and the more time I spent with you, the more I fell for you. But it's all been leading to this moment. The moment where my heart gets truly broken. I can't be with you, Dyl. Hell, I can't ever see you again or Slender Man will come and haunt your dreams. While we are together, your life—and mine—is in grave danger," I confess, and I can see the confusion on his face.

"Addy, you can't possibly believe that. If you are the one creating Slender Man, then how can you possibly inflict him on me? The most you could do is physically hurt me yourself, while you think you are him, but I don't think that's how it works," Dylan muses, and I know he's right. Slender Man is in my head. That means there's no possible way for him to come to life and start terrorising Dylan, but that doesn't mean Dylan can't get hurt. If I'm capable of inflicting this much self-harm while I'm in one of my psychotic states, what's to say I won't hurt him? And given the sadness that's spreading across Dylan's face, it's obvious he feels the same.

"It doesn't matter how it works. Please, you have to leave. We can't be seen together. It's too dangerous," I explain, looking around the small bathroom just to make sure there's no sign of Slender Man. I wouldn't put it past him waiting in the wings, stalking me until he finds me breaking the rules, just the way he likes it.

"Addy, I think you need some serious help. I need you to let me help you," Dylan begs, tears flowing freely now, but I shake my head aggressively, annoyed that he isn't listening to me.

"No! Dylan, I want you to leave. I need you to stay the hell away from me," I shout, my voice breaking at the end. I try to hold back the tears as best I can. But, as Dylan stands up, all fight leaving his body, I realise this really is the end and I can't stop the tears from falling.

Dylan reaches the bathroom door, stops, and turns his head to look over his shoulder. I hate the pain and heartbreak that ooze from every pore. But more than anything, I hate that I'm responsible for that look. I feel like I've just kicked a puppy, one I was really starting to love.

"I will always be here if you need me, Addy. I think…

I think I love you." As soon as those three little words are out in the open, neither of us can take them back. I'm shocked he was the one to say it first, given I've suspected that's how I feel for a while. It's just a shame that hearing him say it now is the worst possible time. Never have words cut me so deeply.

He doesn't even wait for me to reply. He leaves the bathroom with tears flowing down his face. This pain is worse than anything Slender Man could have ever done to me. Sobs rack my body as I lay in the bath, hating myself with every fibre of my being. I always thought it would be Slender Man who broke me, who knew it would be Dylan.

Fifteen
DYLAN

I WANDER BACK TO MY ROOM, LOST IN A DAZE AS MEMORIES OF Addy's broken, battered, and bruised body fill my mind. When I saw her lying there on the floor, so small and fragile, I was terrified I was too late. I fell to the floor to wake her up, and all I kept thinking was how much of an asshole I am to have waited so long.

When she didn't show up at our usual time, I told myself she was having one of her rare good nights, and that I needed to leave her to sleep. But the longer that went on, the more I paced. Maybe I knew something wasn't right? I guess in a way my gut was telling me to find her, and so I did.

The more I looked at her wounds, the more I'm convinced that Addy isn't doing this to herself. Some of those wounds, it would have been next to impossible to self-inflict. My pretty girl is around five foot four, with a petite body to match. There's no way she has the strength and the endurance to continue beating herself to the point of cracking her ribs—and if the bruising that was beginning to appear was any indication, she had at least one rib fracture.

Not only that, I'm sure on her back I saw a large shoe print, and there's no fucking way she could have done that herself. There's also the fact that Slender Man chooses now to make a big deal about me. Addy and I have been having sex regularly now for at least a month, and it's clear we are both developing strong feelings. If Slender Man is a creation of her own making, surely he would know all her secrets. Yet, he only mentioned me after we told people we were dancing together. The timing just doesn't fit. I think there's so much more going on here, but I don't know what.

The idea that someone is breaking into Addy's room every night and attacking her is preposterous. There are cameras everywhere, and nurses who patrol the halls, not to mention the other patients. Maybe someone could get away with it once or twice, but nearly every night for months just doesn't seem possible.

I also have no explanation for why Addy sees a faceless man, or why she believes he's a figment of her own imagination, brought to life to torture and torment her as a punishment for surviving when her family didn't. This all can't be one giant bout of survivor's guilt, mixed in with a bit of post-traumatic stress disorder, could it?

I realise the time has come when I have no choice but to risk everything. I can't help Addy on my own, and even if she really means what she says, and it is over between us, I still need to get her the help she deserves. Besides, I meant every word I said when I walked out of that bathroom. I do love her, and I will always be there for her. I didn't really know how much I meant it until I said the words out loud. I guess sometimes it takes the fear of losing someone to realise how much you truly love them.

The rest of the morning passes by reasonably quickly. With it being a Saturday, we all have recreational time in the morning. I spent mine running, since it was the only way I could think to relax—other than dancing. But sadly, it didn't work. I know what I need to do, and as I sit on the bed in my room and pull out the guitar Dr. Hughes had given me a couple of weeks after I completed my detox, I finally feel at peace.

I've been avoiding music throughout the process of getting sober, afraid that most of my talent is connected to the drugs as opposed to me. Or maybe I needed the drugs to perform? All of it was complete bullshit. Fear created in my own head to hold me back. From the second I picked up the guitar, it was like I was finally coming home.

My fingers move of their own accord and a melody erupts out of the strings with no hesitation. As soon as I'm in the swing of things, I start to sing. The words come to me, like they've always been a part of me, just waiting for this moment to make themselves known. That's how I always feel when I'm writing a song. Like it's always there, it's just been waiting for me to bring it to life.

This song is easy and flows out of me like a bird

soaring through the sky. Talking about finally finding the love I didn't truly believe I was ever worthy of, it's so natural to finally sing the words and to talk about how I feel. I don't know if I will ever be able to share this song with anyone except Addy, but if I do, I know it will be the best song The Catastrophists ever release. "Finding My Forever." If only the song were true, and my forever hadn't just kicked me out of her life.

The afternoon runs away from me, and it's not until I see it's almost five in the afternoon that I realise I've almost missed my window of opportunity. Placing my guitar in its case, I run through the house, only one destination in mind. I weave around the few patients that are milling about and get chastised by a few nurses for running in the halls, until I finally find the corridor I need. I mentally chant, hoping I haven't missed it today.

Please still be here. Please still be here.

"Come in," shouts Dr. Hughes as soon as I knock on the door.

My heart finally starts to beat again, only now it's racing over the anticipation of what I'm about to do. I have no idea if I'm doing the right thing, but I know I need help, and whilst I'm stuck in here, Dr. Hughes is the only person who can help me. I'm not sure I can wait another couple of weeks to hear from Jake, to see if he can help.

I burst into Dr. Hughes' office, and she gives me a big smile, even though I can see she's packing her bag and getting ready to go home for the evening. That's what I love about her. She always puts her patients first, no matter what. Or at least, I'm hoping, as that's the compassion I need to draw on to get her to help me.

"Dylan, what can I do for you?" she asks, putting her bag down and walking around to stand in front of her desk. She leans against it slightly, waiting to see if I'm going to stop pacing long enough to have a seat. Right now I have too much pent-up energy to do anything except walk.

"I need your help. I need you to understand that if I'm willing to risk everything, to put my whole future on the line, that I would only do that if it was important." The words tumble out quickly, and I can see the doctor is struggling to keep up.

"Dylan, just breathe. Now, start from the beginning," she says calmly, as she points to the sofa, indicating that I should sit down. I follow her instructions, slowing my breathing down as I take a seat.

"I want to make a deal with you, and I know you will not like it."

"Okay, tell me more," she says, as she takes a seat opposite me.

"Promise you won't say anything until I finish speaking and give me your word that you will at least hear me out."

She nods, and I give her a small smile as a thank-you. "I will promise you that."

I then proceed to tell her everything. About how Addy and I have been in a relationship, and everything I've learnt and seen for myself about Slender Man. I can see the disappointed look in her eyes, but I don't care. Addy needs help, which means I need someone who can help me save her. It's getting to the stage where if we don't get her some real help, she may not be with us much longer.

"I know you are mad I broke my promise, and I know I should have stayed away from her, but I couldn't. She means everything to me, and I have to help her. I suspect that someone is involved, that she is being hurt by a real person. So here's the deal I want to make with you. I want you to help me access the security cameras near her room and if they're suspicious in any way, then help me try to catch the person in real life. If I can prove that someone is responsible for Addy's injuries, then you have to let me finish my sentence here with Addy. But, if you can't find proof Slender Man is anything except a delusion in Addy's head, one that is now clearly affecting my own, then I will willingly let you kick me out of Lakeridge and send me to the local prison." I try to sound as confident as I can, but in all honesty, this could go either way. I guess I deserve to be punished for breaking the rules here. But caring for Addy takes priority.

"As pissed as I am that you've broken the rules, I think I suspected something was going on between you when I saw you dance. Rarely do two people who don't have feelings for each other dance with so much passion. I know why you want to help her, and I have been doing my own research, which has pulled up a few red flags for me. I've been trying to do this diplomatically, to avoid getting myself fired, but I guess now we have no choice but to dive in headfirst. We will go tonight, but I will take you up on your deal, Dylan. If this is all in your head, you will have to serve your sentence elsewhere."

I nod, completely fine with that, as long as Addy gets

the help she needs.

"Okay, we will meet back in your room in a couple of hours. Until then, I will check the footage."

I shake my head aggressively. "No, I need to see it. I need you to take me with you."

"Absolutely not, Dylan. That is a secure, staff only area, and I will not break that for anyone. I will report back to you fully, but that's the best I can do."

I guess that will have to be enough then. I don't know if I want her to find something on the tape, or if I want to be the one to find the answers. I think Addy will appreciate any help, but that doesn't stop me from wanting to be her knight in shining armour. She always calls me the bright light in her darkness, but now I want to be the one to take the darkness away completely. We have a plan. Let's just hope we find something, or I may have just ruined the rest of my life.

Sixteen
DYLAN

The wait for Dr. Hughes to come back feels like an eternity. I have no idea if I'm doing the right thing, or if I've just sealed my own death warrant. Because the reality is, if I get kicked out of Lakeridge and end up in a real prison, that's my life over. Not only will my very delicate sobriety be at risk, but my life will be over as I know it. I made a promise to finish my six months here, and if I can't come away after six months with full sobriety, then the boys are allowed to kick me out of the band. It's in the contract we signed. If I slip up, or if I don't finish my time here, that's the end of my role in The Catastrophists.

The idea that they could even continue on without me is indescribable. But, to be fair to them, they've put up with a lot from me over the past couple of years, and I think this is just the cumulation of that. They want to help me more than anything, and I can see that now. I can see this as the big, grand gesture I needed to make a change with my life, but that doesn't mean I enjoy being threatened.

While I pace up and down my room, my palms sweating and my heart racing, I continually tell myself I've made the right decision, and that this needed to happen. But with each nervous step I take, I question everything I've ever seen or heard where Addy is concerned. Have my feelings for her blinded me against what is really there? It scares me that it's easier for me to believe that someone is really breaking into her room each night, attacking her, torturing her, and then leaving and getting away with it like it never happened. It's easier for me to believe that than think Addy is capable of committing the level of self-harm I've witnessed on her body. Really, I have no idea if Addy is capable of hurting herself to that extent. People can do anything when they don't have the constraints of their minds to hold them back. Maybe I just don't enjoy thinking that she might be so far gone that it's not possible to bring her back?

Nobody wants to think that someone they love is suffering so badly with their mental health, stuck in the confines of their own mind, and yet there's nothing you can do to help them. If I'm being truthful, there's also a part of me that worries I'm going a little insane, too. I mean, everyone is so sure that Addy is telling the truth, that what she's experiencing is simply really strong delusions and acts of self-harm. Nobody has ever considered that the Slender Man might be real, and I know why. I can hear how it sounds. The idea that a faceless man breaks into a secure mental facility almost every night to torture the same girl, before leaving with no trace and never getting caught for months now, sounds fucking bonkers. But, that's really what I think. I've analysed every inch of Addy's beautiful alabaster skin, taking in each and every cut, welt, and bruise, and there are just too many that can't be explained. That's why I knew I had to take this risk. Even if she meant what she said when she ended things. I have to help her. I guess that's when you know what love really is. Love hurts. It makes you do stupid shit, but it feels fucking amazing.

There's a gentle knock on my door before it swings open, and Dr. Hughes rushes inside. She's peering around, hypervigilant, and looking like the world's shittest criminal. This well put together professional woman, scurrying about with a general air of rebellion, just doesn't fit together. I can't help but smile as she breathes a sigh of relief when she closes the door behind her. This woman clearly wasn't made for breaking the rules.

"Fuck am I glad to see you, Doc. I've been going out of my mind. What did you find?" I ask, as I finally stop pacing and stand in front of her.

I watch as her face crinkles, like she's not quite sure if she wants to tell me or not. Her eyes have a fire in them like I've never seen, and it's obvious she's angry. But there's also a sadness there, and I'm guessing that's the part she's reluctant to tell me about.

"Shall we sit?" she says in the tone she usually reserves for when we're having our therapy sessions.

Moving towards the two comfy chairs that are

under the window, Dr. Hughes takes a seat in one and gestures for me to take the other. I hesitate for a moment, wondering if I'm too wound up to sit, but she gives me that pointed stare that makes it clear it wasn't really up for debate.

I flop down in the seat, but cannot stop my knee from jigging up and down, the anxiety needing to take some form. "Don't keep me in suspense, Doc."

Dr. Hughes gives me a small smile, but it's one that doesn't quite reach her eyes. It's more to comfort me than because she actually feels it. "I checked the security cameras, Dylan…" She trails off and my heart races. If she doesn't tell me something soon, we might need a fucking defibrillator.

"And?" I snap, my nerves getting the better of me.

"The cameras in and around her room are all damaged. They appear to have been damaged for a while. It's unclear whether or not they've been reported. I didn't want to ask any of the nurses since that could alert people to what we are doing. From what I can see on the notes I've read, there have only ever been two people who administer the medication to Addy: Dr. Manning and Lance, the nurse. This isn't anything too unusual. When we work with experimental or research medication, only people who are named as part of the project can administer the drugs. The main problem for me is that when I did some research into the drug trial, I couldn't find it. We should register all trials with the research council, but I couldn't find this one on their website. To do a proper check, I would need the paperwork linked to the trial, as that has contact details for the person responsible for running the trial, but that information is kept in Addy's hospital file, which Dr. Manning keeps locked in his desk," she explains, and I can't quite get my head around everything she just said.

"What does that all mean, Doc?" I wouldn't say I'm unintelligent, but I guess maybe my brain isn't quite firing as quickly as it could be right now. It's consumed with questions, fears, and concerns. Have I made the right decision, being the main one.

"It means that there's enough suspicious activity for me to investigate your claims. There are too many things happening that shouldn't be, and if one of my residents is really in danger, that's something I can't ignore." With each word that comes out of Dr. Hughes' mouth, it's clear how much she truly cares about her patients. I may be scared shitless of this whole thing, and of finally getting answers one way or the other, but I'm not even slightly concerned about my choice of accomplice. Dr. Hughes cares more deeply about others than anyone I've ever met, and I suspect when this is all said and done, I'm going to owe her big time.

"Fuck! So what do we do next?" I ask, thousands of ideas all rolling around in my head at once. I have no fucking clue where to start.

"There is no 'we', Dylan. I will do this next part alone. But first I need to know if Addy has mentioned a pattern. Like, for example, how long has she been asleep when he appears?" she asks casually, brushing right over the fact that she's trying to cut me out of the plan.

Anger bubbles under the surface, my face distorting to reflect the annoyance I'm feeling right now. "You can fuck right off. I am going with you. Not only do I need to be there for Addy, but there's no fucking way you are going on your own. What if it turns out I'm right and someone is really abusing Addy? That means you will be forced to confront him—and we have no real clue if it is just one man—but there's no way I'm letting you do that alone. It's not safe, and we don't trust anyone else enough to bring them on board just yet. You know, it makes sense to be safe."

I can see Dr. Hughes' face change as she mulls it over. She's torn between dragging a patient into a potentially dangerous situation and going into that same scenario on her own. There's only one logical answer, but I watch her contemplate it, anyway.

"Fine. You can come, but you have to promise to stay away if there's any sign of trouble. You're there for Addy, and that's all. Do I make myself clear?" Her voice has more than just her usual air of authority. She's stern and full of conviction.

Nodding, I give her the biggest smile I can muster, given the circumstances. "Thank you. You have no idea how much this means to me."

"I think I do, Dylan. You were willing to risk everything for this. She must mean a lot to you." I'm not sure if Dr. Hughes is asking me, or merely musing aloud. But she would be right.

"I think I love her," I mutter, barely above a whisper. I know I said the words to Addy when she rejected me, and at that moment, I absolutely knew how I felt. But that doesn't mean a lifetime's worth of fear and phobias have just gone away overnight. Of course I'm still worried that

I don't really know what love is, or what it even means to be in love with another person. I also don't want to even think about how painful it was to walk away from her, knowing I may never hear her say the same words back.

"What makes you say you think you love her? Why aren't you certain?" she asks, and it's like we have dropped back into one of my counselling sessions. I guess her inquisitive and caring nature is just part of what makes Dr. Hughes so good.

"How about a lifetime of fear and insecurity? Or the fact that I've never loved anyone before, or had anyone ever tell me they love me? How can I possibly be sure I'm in love if I don't even know what love looks like?"

A light chuckle that sounds like little high-pitched bells echo across the room as Dr. Hughes shuffles forward in her seat until our knees are almost touching. She leans over and places her hand on top of mine, and it's amazing how comforting such a simple, innocent gesture can be. "Dylan, I would say that if you are willing to give up everything that has ever meant anything to you to help Addy, then that sounds a lot like love to me. Love means putting the needs of someone else before your own, and I think that's exactly what you've done here. You know there's a chance I could kick you out of Lakeridge, and I know what will happen with the band if that happens. Music is all you've ever known, and probably the only real love you've ever felt. So the fact that you will risk that for her, because you need to see her get better, that's love to me."

We talk a little after that, but it's clear we are just filling the time. I explain everything Addy has ever told me about Slender Man and his visits. Addy is usually in bed by ten, as Dr. Manning usually comes to administer the meds around nine-thirty in the evening. The only time I'm sure of after that is when she comes to meet me at three in the morning. Giving us a five-hour window. The nurse does their last physical walk-around checks between ten and eleven, and after that the corridors are all secured, and the residents are supposed to be monitored by security cameras.

There are some residents who have medications and checks at around two in the morning, and I don't think anyone would be stupid enough to attack Addy while the nurses are doing their checks. Which narrows down our window to anywhere between eleven and two. We decided to opt for midnight.

As we go over the plan again and again, I just hope that it all comes together. Not just for my own future, but for Addy's, too. As much as it would kill me to know someone really was assaulting Addy, and she's been going through this torture night after night right under everyone's nose, it would also be a bit of a relief. If it's a real person, we can put a stop to it all today. Yes, Addy will need a lot of fucking therapy and support to get over the trauma that's been inflicted on her, but at least she can start to recover from that. If this turns out to all be a delusion, combined with a fair few coincidences like the failed security cameras, that's something I'm not sure we can treat.

Since I met Addy, the delusions are only getting worse. The beating is getting harsher, and the wounds that adorn her body are increasing in quantity and severity. If she continues on at this rate, it won't be long before the delusions claim her life, and I most definitely can't deal with that. I've lost so much in my life already; I can't lose her too.

A loud ringing pulls us both out of our small talk, the shrill sound scaring the shit out of me. Dr. Hughes looks down at the mobile phone she placed on the table beside us earlier. She must have set an alarm to let us know it's midnight. Time to put this plan into action.

We both stand and walk to the door in silence, but before she pulls it open, Dr. Hughes looks over her shoulder, her face a mask of seriousness. "I mean it, Dylan. You will not in any way put your life in danger, and you will do whatever I tell you to. Is that clear?"

I nod, letting her know I agree to her terms, although I'm very careful not to make any promises I can't keep. I have no idea how I will feel if we really do find out someone is attacking my girl, and therefore I can't make any promises that I can't keep when it comes to dealing with the scumbag who abuses vulnerable girls.

I follow Dr. Hughes as she opens my door and walks through the corridors. Surprisingly, she holds herself with much more certainty and conviction than she did when she first snuck into my room earlier. She looks like just another doctor walking around her place of work doing her job. Never mind that it's gone midnight and she should definitely be at home. If anyone were to see her, I don't think they would question that she's doing anything other than her job. I might be the one that gets into trouble for walking around after lights out. Not that I've ever been caught or stopped yet.

We get to the corridor next to Addy's and I can feel my heart beating in my throat, my mouth suddenly feels really dry, and my body is vibrating—a combination of anticipation and nerves. Dr. Hughes freezes and turns to face me, whispering as she does. "If there is someone in the room, we will need to try to get undeniable proof, Dylan. So, I'm going to open the door just a bit, and use my phone to record whatever is going on in there. I know your instincts will tell you to barge in, but we have to do this properly. If someone is hurting Addy, there's no way in hell am I letting them get away with it because there's no firm evidence."

I hadn't even considered that. She's right. With the way my nerves are at the moment, I would probably barge straight in there to find out once and for all what's going on. But Dr. Hughes is right, we can't do that. So, I give her a nod to tell her I understand, then I take some slow, deep breaths to try to calm myself. It's difficult, but with each deep inhale, I feel the oxygen filling my lungs, and as I release and my diaphragm relaxes, my heart slows down back into a normal rhythm.

Once we reach Addy's door, I notice the small window in the middle of the door, the one the nurses are supposed to use to check on us overnight, has been covered over. Luckily, the cover slides over the window from our side of the door, which means someone must have closed it before going in. It's against the rules for residents to close it. Even I was told no when I tried to persuade them to let me close it. I got away with a lot when I first got here, playing on the celebrity card, but that was one thing they wouldn't negotiate on. Nurses being able to see into the room at all times is a safety feature, and one that isn't negotiable.

Dr. Hughes reaches up and slowly slides the flap open, and I think we both freeze, unsure of if anyone could hear the slight scraping sound. Crouching low, I almost frog crawl until I'm on the other side of the door. We don't speak. The only sound that can be heard is our shared breathing, which is quicker than normal.

We stare at each other, silently communicating over what to do next. Dr. Hughes points at her eyes, then at the newly exposed window on the door, and holds up three fingers, making it clear she's counting down. I nod but make sure to point to my own eyes, too. I need to look in there just as much, if not more, than she does. I have to know what's real. With a small nod, she begins the countdown on her fingers.

As soon as all three fingers are down, she moves her hand and we both lean in at the same time. My heart is pounding so much I can hear the whooshing sound of blood running through my ears. My palms are sweating and my hands shake. I don't know what I want to find, but I'm ready for answers.

I don't know why I close my eyes when I lean in, but obviously Dr. Hughes didn't as I hear her sharp intake of breath and feel it on my face. My eyes fly open and what I see devastates me.

My beautiful Addy is kneeling on the floor, in between the knees of a man dressed impeccably in a suit. Addy is completely naked, and as she bobs her head up and down, it's impossible to miss what he's making her do. What kills me the most is that at the same time as

Addy is blowing him, he's whipping her back and ass until her skin is raw.

The room is soundproof, so we can't hear anything, but I can almost feel Addy's pain and anguish from here. I look up, hoping to see the identity of her tormentor, and am shocked to see that Addy was right. Slender Man is dressed in an impeccable black suit, crisp white shirt, and a matching black tie. But his face, rather than being completely faceless like Addy described, he's actually covered in bandages. It looks like the asshole has literally just wrapped medical bandages around his head, leaving the most minute slits so that he can see out of them.

My blood boils and a rage like I've never felt before simmers beneath the surface. I have no idea who is in there, who the man behind the bandaged mask is, but I fully fucking intend on finding out. As my hands ball into fists, I move to open the door, but Dr. Hughes stops me.

Placing her hand on my chest, she gently pushes me backwards before placing her finger in front of her mouth, making it clear I need to not alert anyone to our position. As she does that, she takes the phone out of her pocket and begins filming. It feels as though we stand there for fucking ages, and even though it's probably not that long, it just feels wrong to be standing here doing fuck all while Addy is in there in pain.

My nerve endings prickle as rage builds. My teeth grind together so loud I'm surprised everyone can't hear it. I keep clasping and unclasping my fists, as the desperate need to punish the person behind the mask grows like a toxic poison, spreading through my veins. I try to hold it back as long as I can, but when I see him change up the position of his belt, so that he's now whipping her with the belt buckle, that's when I lose it.

I not so gently push Dr. Hughes aside, and as I go to grab the door handle, she tries to stop me. But I've stood by for long enough. I push the door open so hard it slams against the wall; the shock reverberates loudly around the room. Once I'm inside, the soundproofing no longer protects me from the gut-wrenching screams and howls of pain coming from Addy, who is being silenced each time he shoves his cock down her throat. I've never known true anger until this moment, and I'm not even ashamed to say I let my emotions get the better of me.

Launching myself into the room, I try to be as gentle with Addy as I can, but it's like I've got tunnel vision and a red mist has descended. I pick her up but before I'm able to move her safely out of the way, a sharp crack slices down over my arm and I drop Addy onto the floor beside us, pain from the belt hitting me stabs across my arm.

That's when I throw myself at him, as he tries to whip me again with one hand and put his cock away with the other. Thankfully, he hasn't quite mastered the art of multitasking, and I'm able to land two quick punches to the head, which knocks him off balance. I take that opportunity to grab the belt out of his hand and I roughly throw it far away from us.

As I turn to throw the belt, he manages to land a punch to my side, and I can't help but laugh. There's barely any force behind it at all. Typical that it's a weak fucking man who takes pleasure in overpowering a woman. Well, he's not going to get away with choosing my woman.

I turn and reach for the lapels of his jacket, trying to pull him off the seat so that I can overpower him, but he's not stupid. He knows that's the last thing on this earth that he should allow because once I've got him secure, I'm ripping the bandage off for the world to see.

As I try to grab him, I reach over with my spare hand to land another blow against his cheek with a roar of aggression. Somehow, he manages to push me away as I swipe across his jawbone. It catches me off guard and I stumble to the floor. He capitalises on that by standing up quickly and kicking me twice in the stomach.

Screaming, I don't even really feel the pain. I'm just so full of rage and an overwhelming urge to get answers. I roll and try to get up off the floor, but before I can, I watch almost in slow motion as he lifts the plant pot off the table between the chairs and crashes it onto the top of my head.

Blinding pain sears around my left temple, and spots invade my vision, causing me to blink rapidly. This doesn't help, it only adds to the nausea that's swirling around in my thankfully empty stomach. The edges of my vision are turning black and the more I try to focus or stand up, the worse the skull-shattering pain becomes. That's when I feel a warm liquid begin to trickle down just past my eye, and I lift my shaky hand to the wound, wincing as I make contact. My touch makes the stinging pain burn, and the throbbing inside my head worsen as I touch the blood running down my face.

It's like my body is trying to tell me what's going on, and how much fucking danger I'm in, but my brain is still trying to stop the blinding pain from worsening, whilst also trying to vomit or faint. The ringing in my ears is so loud, I can't even hear the other people in the room with me—well, not until they really start screaming.

I roll over quickly as soon as I remember where I am and the real danger we are all in, though as the nausea makes my stomach flip and dry heave, I wish I'd moved a little slower. I rub my eyes enough to finally focus them, only to watch as Slender Man—or whoever the massive cuntwaffle that is pretending to be him is—punches Dr. Hughes right on the end of her nose, blood pouring everywhere, before he kicks her in the stomach, which propels her across the room until her back makes a sickening *thud* when it hits the wall.

The horror of seeing Dr. Hughes' crumpled body lying motionless in the corner of the room with blood seeping out around her like a crimson aura, spurs me on enough to finally get to my feet. My whole body burns, my hands are shaking, and my legs feel almost too wobbly to hold me up for any significant length of time. Taking a few deep breaths, I ignore the stabbing pain I feel in my right ribs with each inhale and I try to focus my body. As I do, that's when I see Slender Man is holding up Addy, who is very naked with blood running all over her beautiful alabaster skin, and he has a sharp weapon against her neck. As I focus on the point where it's pressing against her neck, small blood droplets oozing down over her chest, I realise he's holding a piece of the broken plant pot, using the jagged edges as a weapon. But I notice the part he's clinging on tightly to, that's also sharp and is causing his hand to bleed. But for me, that's a good thing. It means the asshole standing in front of me is not something supernatural. He's not an unbeatable nightmare. No, this is a fucked-up coward of a man who is hiding behind some bandages and people's fear. But if he bleeds like the rest of us, then I can make him suffer.

I don't know where the sudden bloodlust comes from. I have never even been in a proper fight, unless you count one or two times when I got my ass kicked in our early career for opening my drug-fuelled mouth to the wrong person. But once we got popular enough to need security, they handled all my fights after that. I don't even train using a punching bag in the gym like some men do. But, as I stand here, making eye contact with the only woman I've ever really loved, seeing the terror in her eyes, I know I would burn the world down to protect her.

I try to get Addy's attention, but I don't know if fear—or something more—has her frozen. Her fragile body is trembling as sobs rack her body completely. Her face is a mess of blood, sweat, tears, and snot, but none of that matters to me. I just need to get her out of this situation.

"Let her go, you asshole. Don't you think you've done enough damage?" I shout, taking a step forward. I hoped he wouldn't notice my move, but he did and I'm rewarded for my efforts by a squeal from Addy, though I can't see why she would cry out in more pain. The sharp object against her neck hasn't moved.

I try to quickly do a thorough assessment of her body whilst looking for what could cause her pain. There are more cuts, bruises, and welts along her chest than I can count. She's got a couple of fresh cuts along her temple and cheek, which are trickling blood. The wound on her neck where the jagged piece of pottery stabs against her is only superficial right now with just a few drops of blood seeping out. But as I run my eyes over her curves, that's when I see his other hand is pressed against her hip. A smaller piece of plant pot that looks just as sharp is pressing into Addy's side. By the looks of the position, he's not too far away from causing major damage to her kidney if he pushes it in deep enough. At the moment, it's not too deep, although there's a lot more blood flowing from this wound than the one at her neck, and terror consumes me. It was hard enough taking him on before when I thought he just had one weapon, but now he has two and he's using the love of my life as a human shield because he knows I won't hurt one hair on her head. But, I think what he's severely underestimated is how far people will go for the one they love.

"Look, we can still all walk away from this. I just want to make sure Addy is safe. So, if you pass her to me, I will let you walk out of that door. This doesn't have to end badly." I try to speak logically and calmly to negotiate with this asshole. My words may say one thing, but I think we both know I didn't mean them. No way in the world was I allowing this cunt to walk free from here, particularly not until I've identified him.

Slender Man growls like a wild animal, a caged bear trapped and cornered who is desperate for freedom. I'm very aware that the more desperate he becomes, the more dangerous he will be.

"We both know you have no intention of just letting me walk out of here, but let me be very clear with you. If you don't let me leave, I will carve up your girl here right in front of you. So, here's what you are going to do," he instructs, and I try to work out if I've heard the voice before, but it's impossible. He must talk through a voice box simulator as he sounds like a mechanical computer-generated voice.

Fuck! The only way I might find out who this guy is will be to take his mask off, but I can't do that without risking Addy's life, and he knows it. I try to think of a plan while he continues. "You are going to move over to that far wall, and you are going to turn your back until you're facing the wall. I'm going to move towards the door with Addy in tow, and you will not move a muscle. If you are capable of doing that, then I will give Addy to you as I leave. But you can't follow me." Despite the mechanical, almost dull sound of his voice, I can almost hear the desperation and malice dripping from each word.

I may not like it, but this may be the best plan we have. As soon as Addy is away from him, I can then charge him. I don't give a shit if I get injured, but I will take him down if it's the last thing I do. This guy is not leaving this room, and he sure as fuck isn't going anywhere until I know exactly who he is.

I try to make it look like I've given up in the hope he will play right into my plan. I look at Addy, hoping she can see the determination in my eyes and know there's no way I'm giving up without a fight. But she's sobbing too hard to even see me. Not only that, but her eyes appear almost glazed over, like she couldn't properly see me even though I am standing in front of her. Her pupils are blown and her normally bright green eyes now appear dull and lifeless. She looks like she's high as a kite, but I've been around a lot of drugs, and the majority of people, even those who are spaced out on a combination of the toughest drugs, can pull themselves out of their high if they see danger. I'm not saying that's how it is for everyone, but for a lot it is.

Once I am standing in the farthest corner away from him, he begins to walk towards the door, but with a hostage in tow, a weapon in each hand, and thanks to the blows I inflicted on him when I first burst in here, I'm not remotely surprised to see him struggling, swaying from one foot to the other.

Slowly, he moves the hand on Addy's hip back to his pocket, and he securely tucks the sharp plant pot piece into his trouser pocket before using his now free hand to grab hold of Addy's arm. As he pulls her towards the door, his vision flits from me to Addy and then to the door. He needs to see where he's going, but he doesn't want to take his eyes off me, knowing how much of a danger I am to him, and he would be right. Thankfully, he has no choice, and while his gaze is turned towards the door, I see my opportunity and I don't hesitate.

Pushing myself forward, I ignore the way my body screams at me or my head throbs, not to mention the nausea and spots along my vision that are threatening to take control, but I remind myself of the reason I'm doing all this. The pretty girl standing in front of me, so consumed by fear and confusion that she looks as though she has no idea what's going on around her. I guess that's a good thing, because I don't want her to see me lose my shit the way I'm about to.

As I throw myself at Slender Man, it's like everything

moves in slow motion. He realises at the last second exactly what I'm doing. Thankfully, he pushes Addy out of the way so that he can use his full force to deal with me. I hear her scream, but I'm assuming it's just from the landing. I can't pull my gaze from Slender Man, as I need all my faculties to take him down once and for all.

I launch myself at him so hard, my feet literally leave the ground as I fly through the air when I charge at him. The full force of my body hitting him is just the right amount to knock him on his ass, and I fall on top of him. Sharpness burns along my side, no doubt from the impact, but I push away all the pain I feel and focus on the one job at hand.

He tries to scramble from under me, but I pin him in place, using my strong thighs to clamp around his as I straddle him. He flails around with his arms, and I feel a sharp sting across my arm. When I look down, I see that he's still got the plant pot piece in his hand, and he's managed to slash me a few times.

I only have one free hand, as the other is pressing down on his shoulder to stop him from moving too much, but I take advantage and smash my fist into his bandage-covered face. Blood begins to seep into the bandages, crimson pools spreading out over the fabric, and I feel a sick sense of pride at seeing that.

His arm falters, his head no doubt swimming from the blows I just delivered, and I capitalise on the opportunity by using my free hand to grapple with his. He doesn't put up too much of a fight. His hand sliced up from the jagged edges, and it's only made worse as I rip the makeshift weapon from his hand. As I hold it in mine,

I'm torn over what to do. There's a part of me that wants to slam it right down in the middle of his bandaged face, to make sure he's never able to do this to another human being ever again. But, despite the rage coursing through my body, I know I can't kill him. It's not who I am. Besides, I want Addy to have the pleasure of witnessing this asshole get every punishment he deserves. So instead, I throw the weapon as far away from us as I can and return my attention to him.

It's like he knows exactly what I plan to do, as he thrashes about, desperate to push me off him so he could break free to no avail. The hand that I just pulled the weapon from is the only free limb he has, and as he tries as hard as he can to punch me with it. The problem is that he was weak to start with, and now, after the fighting and the injuries he sustained, he's even more pathetic than before. I'm able to grab his hand and secure it beside his body, trapping it with my thigh. He doesn't put up much resistance. Now that he's trapped and I have both my hands free, I do what I've wanted to do since the moment I walked into the room and saw the pain and suffering he was inflicting on my beautiful Addy.

I claw at the bandages, trying as hard as I can to rip them from his face. My fingernails catch on the skin beneath, causing him to hiss in pain, but I don't care. He deserves everything he gets.

It takes me longer than I thought it would, but when I finally get the bandage off, and fully expose who Slender Man really is, it's like my eyes can't quite believe what I'm seeing.

Dr. Manning.

Dr. Dickhead.

The man charged with caring for Addy and making decisions on her behalf.

A red mist descends over me and a rage like nothing I've ever felt before descends and I just lose it. My blood whooshes through my ears, deafening me as I punch Dr. Manning as hard as I can. I'm vaguely aware of movement out of the corner of my eye, but all I'm focused on right now is punishing Dr. Manning for betraying the trust Addy, and all the other patients at Lakeridge, placed on him.

Blood spurts from his face, and my knuckles ache, but I don't stop—I don't think I can stop. I feel his body go limp beneath me, and I know that I've done enough, but still I raise my arm again to land another blow. That slight pause, where I ask myself if I really need to do more, is all it takes for me to take in the surrounding scene.

As well as a loud ringing that sounds oddly similar to the type of emergency bell you would hear in a hospital, there's also someone pulling on my shoulder. I look over to see a very battered-looking Dr. Hughes attempting to pull me off Dr. Manning. I can see her lips moving, but the loud noise and all the adrenaline is making it difficult to focus, so I lean closer to her.

As soon as I hear Dr. Hughes say Addy's name, it's like I'm snapped out of my trance. "Dylan, please. You have to stop. Addy is injured and scared. She needs you. Please."

I look over the corner of the room, just as the room floods with staff members who are answering the emergency call bell. They all appear to freeze when they run into the room, taking in the scene around them, the bloody destruction as they jump to the wrong conclusion.

Addy is in the corner of the room, curled up with her legs towards her chest, gripping onto her side as blood pours out of the wound, painting her pale skin scarlet. Her eyes are wide and terrified, like she can't quite believe what she's seeing around her. There's blood leaking out of the side of her mouth, and she looks to be gasping for breath.

Fuck! I'd been so caught up in identifying the prick behind the mask, I never even thought of Addy or how scared she must be.

Two nurses move towards her, while Lance and the security guards, who have incorrectly assessed the situation and have decided I'm the threat, fan out around me so that they can come at me from all angles. I notice a sharp needle in Lance's hand—the drugs they use to sedate people who kick off. I don't want to be sedated; I need to be with Addy. I've been so caught up that I've failed her.

I watch as the nurses pull her hands away to reveal two deep stab wounds on one side, but on the other side, closer to her back, there's a piece of plant pot sticking out of her, right over where her kidney would be.

Lance moves towards me with the needle and I hold my hands out and up, like someone being arrested by the police who wants to show they aren't a threat. "It's not me. I'm not the threat here," I shout, but they continue to close in on me.

I'm vaguely aware of Dr. Hughes behind me shouting, but there's so much chaos in the room that nobody can really hear anything. I know Lance is almost close enough to make his move, and if I want to remain conscious so that I can tell them what really happened and stay with Addy, I'm going to fight to keep him away from me, which I admit, doesn't exactly look good.

Just as Lance gets ready to strike, and I curl my hands into fists to protect myself, Dr. Hughes throws herself into my path, blocking Lance from being able to reach me. It's only then do we start to hear what she's saying. "No! Dylan isn't the danger here. Do not tranquilise him. Dr. Manning is the one who needs to be arrested. Call the police and two ambulances here urgently," she shouts, and when Lance hesitates, she adds, "that's an order!"

I've never heard the small, usually meek and polite woman use that tone before, but nobody messes with her. Within minutes, they spring into action, moving me out of the way so security can place secure restraints on Dr. Manning, who is still out cold. As soon as Dr. Hughes has done her part, she collapses to the floor and Lance rushes to her side, assessing the bleeding cut along her head.

Another nurse approaches me, taking in the blood covering my body, but I shoo her away. I'm not even sure how much of the blood is mine. I know my body burns and with each step I take, the pain becomes more intense, but I would battle anything to get to Addy.

I push past them and drop down to see my pretty girl. I sit on the floor beside her crumpled, broken body and I notice that her breathing is slowing down and becoming shallow. Her wounds are too deep and she's losing too much blood. If we don't get her to a hospital soon, Slender Man will have won and he will have taken her from me.

As gently as I can, I reach out and wipe the tears away from her face, which gets Addy opening her startled eyes. Her mouth tips up into a ghost of a smile as she looks at me through her glassy green eyes. "Dylan. You came for me?" she whispers, before starting to cough at the exertion as blood splutters from her mouth.

"Pretty girl, I will always be here for you." Fuck, I hate seeing her like this. Her body is broken and failing her. She's always been so fucking strong and it kills me to see her like this. Knowing that everything she's endured hasn't all been in her head, and that all the fucked-up shit she thought was fake has actually been real the entire time, it only makes her that much fucking stronger.

"I knew you would be my…" Addy looks up at me and reaches out to touch my cheek before her words tear me to pieces. "My heaven."

"No, Addy. We aren't in heaven. You are not dying, do you hear me?!" I state firmly, a rogue tear slipping out of the corner of my eye. Fuck, I really hope I haven't just lied. I can't even begin to think about her leaving me. We are supposed to have forever together. We have had nowhere near long enough.

"You have always been too good to be true, Dyl. Are you really real?" she asks, the pain and anguish croaking out of every word.

"Addison Mitchell, let me make this very clear.

I'm real and you are not dying. We are supposed to be together, and I need you to hold on so that we can start our forever. I made you a promise, and you made one to me. I need you to survive. Please, Addy. I can't survive without you," I sob, pulling her further into my hold without moving her too much. Her blood is covering my t-shirt, and I can feel the warm liquid soaking against my skin.

I look around at the nurses, a frantic look in my eyes as I silently ask them to help me. I don't want Addy to see how scared I am, and I sure as fuck can't start screaming about getting her an ambulance urgently, as that won't exactly help. We can all see her slipping away before our eyes, and nobody knows what the hell to do.

"Dylan. You are a lot stronger than you think. You can survive without me. Promise me you will stay sober, no matter what." I wipe the tears that begin to fall from her eyes, as I bite down on the inside of my lip to try to stop my own tears from falling.

"Pretty girl, just because I can survive without you, doesn't mean I ever want to. I love you. When I said that, I meant it and I plan on telling you every single day of forever, Addy."

Her eyes blink open a couple of times, and it's clear she's struggling to keep them open for any significant length of time. But somehow, she manages to meet my gaze and hits me with the biggest smile she can manage. "You know, when I first met you, I never thought I'd be saying this… but I love you, too."

Her eyes flutter closed and her arm drops down from my cheek, hitting the floor with a thud as her breathing slows. A scream rips from my gut as I feel the most pain I've ever felt. Just a second before, I felt like I was on cloud nine, finally hearing the words I've waited my entire life to hear, only for them to be tarnished. I cannot—I will not—lose her.

Seventeen
ADDY

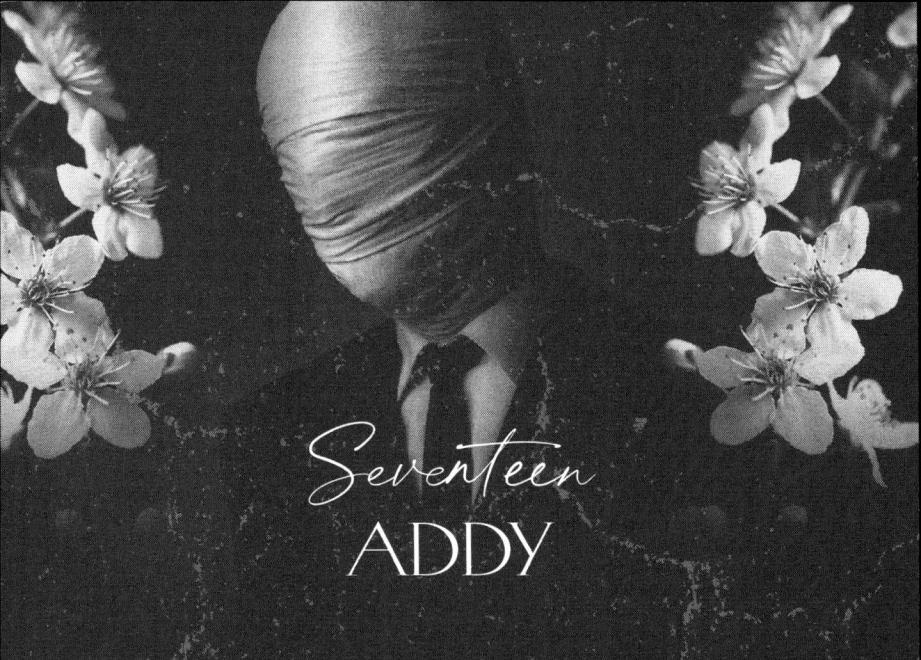

A LOUD INCESSANT BEEPING SOUND WAKES ME UP, AND I CURSE the noise. For once I was in a deep sleep, and I was dreaming happy dreams. Thoughts of Dylan and I saying that we love each other underneath our cherry blossom trees, and promising each other forever. Never at any point did I question whether the dream was real or a delusion. It's like I just knew it was a dream, but one that was based on reality. I could feel it deep within my soul that we were meant to be together. So naturally, I would have liked to stay in that dream forever.

I can hear the noise, but my body feels different this time as I try to pull myself awake. I know it's not normal for me to get this good of a night's sleep, but normally I'm up and moving. Though today, I'm struggling to even open my eyes. It's like I have heavy bags attached to them and I can't even drag them open.

I try to think back to before I went to bed. Did I have a particularly bad visit from Slender Man? Was I hurt? But, most importantly, why the fuck can't I remember anything?

Mentally, I try to assess my body for injuries while I think back to what the last thing I clearly remember is. As I try to move my position slightly, I'm overcome by aches and pains all along my body, but most specifically my front-left and right sides and also towards the back. I know whatever wound I've suffered is severe, but I can feel there's something—possibly painkillers—flowing through my body, preventing the pain from becoming so unbearable I sink beneath it.

Why can't I remember what happened?

I force my eyelids to open, and a bright light assaults my eyes, forcing me to blink rapidly to try to acclimatise to it. When they finally get used to the lights, that's when I'm able to take in my surroundings, and the first thing I realise is that I'm no longer at Lakeridge. I know that place; I know all the rooms, but this is a hospital room.

The smell of antiseptic wafts over my nose, and that's not the same as Lakeridge, which has a more musty smell than anything. The walls are a crisp white colour on three sides, but the one opposite me is painted a bright lemon colour, no doubt to make the room look brighter. But the paint looks new, whereas at Lakeridge the walls stopped being white some time ago, and nearly all the walls have cracks or chips showing that the facility has needed a good lick of paint for a long time. Then there's all the machines and wires around me. The big machine to my left is the one responsible for the incessant beeping, that I now know to be my heart rate. There's also a monitor below it, but I'm not sure what that hooks up to. Then on my opposite side are a couple of IV tubes that are pumping things into my body.

I can see out of the corner of my eye that I have an oxygen tube running across my cheeks and into my nose. At least I'm breathing on my own, so I can't be that bad, I think to myself.

I try to open my mouth, but it is so dry it feels like it's full of cotton wool. So, I focus my eyes again, and take a proper look around the room, rather than just moving my eyes from left to right like I did just a moment before. I look down towards the end of the bed, and I'm shocked to see there are get-well-soon cards filling a table, not to mention a couple of large balloons beside it. But no water. So I keep looking.

That's when I look down beside me and see Dylan. He's sitting in a chair beside my bed, but he's leaning over, laying his arms on my blanket and resting his head on top of them. It's clear from the little snores coming from him, he's definitely asleep. My heart soars when I see him, and that's when a memory hits me out of nowhere. It's me telling Dylan that I want nothing to do with him, that I can't ever properly be with him. I watch all over again as his face distorts in pain and he breaks before my eyes. That's when he tells me he loves me, and that even if I really mean it and we can't be together, that doesn't change how he feels.

Holy shit! Why is he still here, sitting beside my sick bed, clearly worrying about me when I broke his heart? Did we make up again after that?

I don't want to wake him. Not only because he looks at peace, but as soon as he wakes up, we will have to talk. I need to know why I'm here, but I also need to find out what happened. There must have been a good reason for me to hurt him like that, and I'm just hoping that reason has suddenly gone away, because the idea of living without him is a pain that no morphine can alleviate.

I try to take in the rest of the room, desperate to find some water for my dry mouth, and that's when I notice Dr. Hughes is curled up on a reclining chair in the corner of the room. She, too, is fast asleep, and when I see the clock on the wall behind her showing it's two-thirty in the morning, I'm not surprised everyone is sleeping.

To the left of me is the table I've been looking for, with a glass of water with a straw in it. I try to lift my arm, but each time I move, a new pain batters my body. I can't even imagine what the hell I've done to myself this time to end up here. Because that has to be the cause. It has to be a Slender Man visit that got out of hand, and I've injured myself so badly that I needed to visit a proper hospital. Although I am surprised Dr. Hughes allowed Dylan to come with me.

She looks so young curled up on the chair. Her beautiful blonde hair hangs loose around her face in her perfect bob. She's dressed in sweatpants and a baggy hoodie, which really is not normal for her. In all the time I've known her, I've only ever seen her dressed in smart business attire. Seeing her like this reminds me of when you're a teenager and you go into town and see one of your teachers outside of work. You know they have a life, you just don't expect to see them having it. I know something big must have happened for her to be here instead of at Lakeridge. I just wish I could remember what.

Shuffling to my left, in the water's direction, I can't help the hiss that escapes my lips as I feel something in my back, like a knife is being stabbed into my kidney area. The hiss is enough to disturb Dylan, and he snaps his head up quickly, creases from where he was laying have imprinted on the side of his cheek and the dark bags under his eyes tell me he hasn't got any decent sleep in a while. But, the way he looks at me when he sees I'm awake is something I won't ever forget.

His beautiful silver eyes, although they're surrounded by dark circles, shine brightly as he looks at me like he's not really believing what he's seeing. The corners of his lips tip up into the biggest smile, and a little dimple appears that sets my heart racing. At exactly the same moment, the machine I'm hooked up to beeps loudly, causing us both to laugh.

Reaching up, he runs his fingers through his hair before scrubbing at his eyes. "Are you really awake?" he asks.

I try to talk, but my mouth is so dry only a croaking sound comes out. I try again to reach for the water, but Dylan is up in a flash, reaching over to grab the cup. He holds it in front of my lips and moves the straw for me to grasp. I take in a big drag of water and as soon as the cool liquid hits my dry mouth, it feels amazing and I pull for more. A loud moan echoes around the straw and Dylan groans.

"Don't make noises like that, pretty girl. You are

killing me!" he murmurs, as he squeezes my hand, like he's checking I'm really here and awake.

I finish several big gulps of water, enough to stop my mouth from being dehydrated and feeling dry. I pull away from the straw and look over at Dylan. He places the glass back on the table, and I reach up with the hand that isn't covered in wires to place a hand over his cheek.

"I'm so sorry, Dylan," I croak.

Even though he's got a beautiful smile on his face, I can see the pain in his eyes. I need to know what exactly happened, as I'm worried I have so much to apologise for.

He shakes his head vigorously before reaching out and touching my cheek softly. He strokes under my eye and I realise the tears I had tried so desperately hard to control have started to fall. As always, Dylan is there to wipe them away and help me see that life isn't all bad.

I do not know what the hell I've done to deserve a guy like him, but I'm grateful he's still here. I can still see the look in his eyes when I broke his heart, and it's like a knife to my chest. After everything I put him through, why the hell is he still here? Not that I'm complaining, I just need to know.

"Addy... babe, you have nothing at all to ever apologise for." He sounds so determined and sure, and the finality in his voice tells me he really means what he says.

"Dylan, the last thing I remember is telling you we had to end things. I saw the pain in your eyes, and I know I had my reasons for doing that to you, but I had to protect you. I know I sound crazy, but I care about you far too much for anything bad to happen to you." I know it's a pathetic attempt at an explanation, but it's the best I have right now.

Reaching out, he takes a stray piece of hair that's fluttering in front of my face and tucks it behind my ear before returning to stroking my cheek. His touch sets my skin alight and I can feel it right down in my core. Sadly, there's no way to hide how I feel given all the monitors I'm hooked up to, and the more Dylan gets me excited, the louder and more determined the beeping sounds on the monitor.

He chuckles and I can see the cocky little grin that spreads across his face, like he's proud of himself. I want to hit him playfully, like I usually do, and tell him to stop being cocky, that he doesn't really affect me that much, but sadly there's evidence to the contrary.

Dylan's smile quickly turns from cocky to forced, and I know it's because he's getting ready to have a difficult conversation with me. But I don't mind, I just have to know the truth. I hate having gaps in my memory. I squeeze the hand that's still tightly clasped with mine, indicating for him to continue.

"So much has happened since what you last remember, Addy. I know you didn't mean what you said, and that's why I ignored you. But, I have to ask, why did you break things off? Why not just tell me about whatever was bothering you?" he asks, as his thumb traces lines across my cheek and down my jaw in the most soothing way.

"It's hard for me to explain, but you know how I told you that for the longest time, my brain had managed to keep you and Slender Man separate? It's almost as though he didn't know about you, which I know is fucking insane given my brain created him, so he should know all about me. But the night before, when my delusion started, he knew about you. He was pissed, and I really thought he was going to kill me. It was probably one of the worst sessions, and the harm I inflicted on myself afterwards was horrendous.

"But then he started threatening you. Saying he could get to you, which, on reflection, I know sounds insane because a delusion can't just jump from my head and suddenly start appearing in your head. But at the time, it sounded so real. He sounded so real, and I got caught up in that. I'm so sorry. You are right, I should have talked to you about it. I just didn't want to admit that I was potentially getting more insane."

I can see the sadness in his eyes, but it's not pity. I know even on my worst days, Dylan would never feel sorry for me. He knows how important it is for me to never feel that from him. But that doesn't mean I can't tell that he's hiding something from me.

"Addy, I would never think you were getting more insane, and I kinda figured that's what happened," he says, biting on his lip as his brow furrows.

"What is it you aren't telling me, Dylan? I know something bad must have happened for me to be in hospital. I can tell we're not in Lakeridge anymore. I need you to tell me before the thoughts running around my head overwhelm me." I can't tell him about all the different flashes of memories, all the different scenarios I have running through my mind, because I know most of them can't be real. Most of the memories are fragmented, like little clips here and there. Like me telling Dylan I loved him and him promising me forever. Or finding out Slender Man is real. But I've had these dreams so many times before, and just because I want them to be real, doesn't mean they are.

Dylan takes his hand from my cheek and begins running it through his hair. How does he manage to make it look even sexier the more messy it gets? It's quite a talent he has there. Even the way he crumples his face, twitching up his nose as he contemplates what exactly he should say, looks so cute. I want to reach out to straighten the furrow on his brow, to put him at ease, but I don't know how.

"Addy, I-I…" his voice stutters and trails off as his molten silver eyes drop from my gaze and he stares at where our hands are clasped together. I need him to keep going, but I don't know how to push him, or if I should. Maybe on this occasion ignorance really is bliss?

I'm so caught up in all things Dylan—like always—that I almost miss Dr. Hughes sitting in the chair with her knees bent up against her chest while her arms wrap around her body. It's so weird to see her as anything but professional. I expect her to be perched on the edge of the chair, like she would be during a session, with her back straight as she asks me how I'm feeling. But it's clear from the bags under her eyes, her blotchy pale skin, and the giant bruise around her eyes that she isn't here as my professional psychiatrist. That's when I notice the wristband on her arm, and I realise she's a patient here too.

My mind catches up quicker now, and I look down

again at Dylan and my clasped hands, and that's when I see he's also wearing a hospital identity band. All three of us are patients. What the hell happened? Why are they in my room, when they obviously should be resting in their own? I have so many fucking questions, and I need answers. I'm not a fragile china doll that will break easily. I've been through more than most people can endure, and I've survived. Whatever happens, I will survive this, too.

"Addy, you're awake. How are you feeling?" Dr. Hughes asks, her voice sounding hoarse and raspy, like she's been a smoker for sixty years and her cough is finally getting the better of her.

Dylan looks over at Dr. Hughes and gives her a look that says he couldn't be more grateful for her chipping in.

"Erm... aside from being very, very confused and in some pain, I'm not too bad. What happened to you both? Are you patients here too?" I ask, although their hospital ID bands do kinda give the game away a little.

Dr. Hughes stands, wobbling slightly as she does, and within seconds Dylan lets go of my hand and rushes to her side, giving her a hand to hold on to. She pushes it away, or at least she tries to, but Dylan is very determined. I try to pretend my stomach didn't just do a flip that could only be caused by jealousy. Fuck, I'm messed up. How can I be jealous of him doing the right thing?

He helps Dr. Hughes into the chair next to him, and as she sits down, her face contorts in pain and she groans lightly, clutching at her side. Other than the bruises on her face and the cut over her eyes, it's impossible to assess her other injuries because of her baggy clothes. She looks up at me, and it's almost like she's scared to talk to me. Fuck, did I do this to her? It's obvious someone has beaten the shit out of her. Did I do it while I was in one of my dissociative episodes? Is that why I can't remember?

"Dr. Hughes… I have to ask. Did I do this to you?"

Both Dylan and Dr. Hughes shake their heads, although she stops after the first time, pulling her hand up to her temple as though even just that slight movement caused her head to hurt. I can't imagine how much pain she must be in, but if it's anything like the intense pounding I can feel in the periphery of my head, I feel for her. With my headache, it's like I can feel it and I'm aware of it. As though it's knocking on the edge of my skull, just waiting until the pain relief drops its protective barrier, and then it will strike, stabbing away at my head with not a care in the world. Thankfully, whatever pain relief I'm getting is just enough to keep it at bay for now.

"No, Addy. This wasn't you." She pauses, and looks over at Dylan, who gives her a small nod before she continues. "Addy, there's a lot to talk to you about, and I'm not entirely sure if now is the right time. You've only just woken up and I would prefer a doctor to give you the all-clear first, but Dylan doesn't think you will want to wait that long. He thinks you're strong enough to handle the truth now. But, I want to ask what you think. There's no harm in waiting until you're a little stronger."

I can't help but smile at Dylan, who has taken hold of my hand and clasps it with his again. I didn't even notice. It's like he's a part of me, and having him touching me just feels normal. I love that he knows me so well. "Dylan is right. Not knowing is so much worse. As you know, my brain can create any and all scenarios. I have all these flashes in my mind and I have no idea what's real and what's fake. I need to know."

She lets out a sigh, like I gave her the answer she was hoping I wouldn't give, but we all knew I would. As she talks, I take a deep breath and try to settle my nerves. My heart is racing quicker than it was, and both Dylan's and Dr. Hughes' gazes flick up to the monitor as they look back at me with concern etched across their faces. "It's gonna be a bit hard to explain, but I will go through it all with you as best I can. If at any point it gets too much for you, we will stop. Okay?" she asks, and I nod my head in confirmation.

"I promise, I'm strong enough. I can handle it," I confirm, and Dylan chuckles from beside me.

"Oh, we know you are a tough cookie, pretty girl. But you don't have to be all the time. I've got you," he says as he squeezes my hand reassuringly whilst flashing me that sexy grin I love. We all ignore the way the heart monitor spikes again, and I push away the desire I have to lean over and plant a kiss on his lips. We will need to wait until we are alone for that.

"Go on, Dr. Hughes."

She takes a deep breath before starting her story. "Addy, have you ever heard of the drug LSD?"

"Of course. It's an illegal drug used to get high," I reply.

"That's right, but when it's taken in high doses regularly, it causes hallucinations. It can also make people very open to suggestions."

"But I don't do drugs. I never have," I snap, even though I don't really know where she's going with this.

I know I should keep quiet and let her explain, but if she's trying to accuse me of doing drugs, I need to set the record straight on that.

Dylan clears his throat, pulling my attention from Dr. Hughes to him. No doubt he's trying to move my angry gaze away from her. "Nobody thinks you do, Ads. Please, just let Dr. Hughes explain."

I nod for her to continue, my face a blank mask as I wait to hear what she has to say. "I don't really know how to say this, so I'm just going to jump right in. Slender Man is real. He has never been a hallucination. This whole time, he's been real," she explains, and I feel like the world around me is crashing in. Blood rushes to my ears, causing a pounding in my head, and I feel like the room around me is spinning. The monitor beside me bleeps, but I don't care. I blink a few times and place my free hand against my temple, hoping to make the throbbing and dizziness in my head disappear.

"Ads, are you okay?" Dylan asks, the concern evident in his tone.

"Please, just keep going. I need to know everything," I say, even though I'm not sure I truly mean it. I'm scared shitless of what they just said. He's been real the whole time. All those times I thought I'd injured myself and I hadn't. Someone else did it to me. All the nightmares of being raped, tortured, and abused in the worst ways possible—they weren't nightmares. It was all real. I had reached the point where I didn't think I could survive what I was putting myself through. Now I know that it really happened. Does that make it better or worse? I have no fucking clue.

"Dylan came to see me and told me all about your relationship. He said he was confident that Slender Man was a real person, and that he needed to help you. There was a lot he couldn't explain, but he was willing to take the risk of getting you the help you needed. So, we made a deal. I would spend one night humouring him and investigating his theory. If we found out Slender Man wasn't real and he was a delusion, then Dylan agreed to being kicked out of the facility, which would mean him serving the rest of his sentence in a real prison. However, if we found Slender Man was real, I had to promise to get you the help you need, and let Dylan continue on at the facility, knowing full well he won't stop seeing you. So, I agreed to hear him out," she explains, and I can see Dylan blushing out of the corner of my eye.

I turn to him, not really believing what I'm hearing. "You risked everything for me?" My voice becomes high-pitched at the end, turning the statement into more of a question. I have no idea why he would risk so much for me.

Dylan shoots a smile my way that makes my heart flutter—and he hears it, too, on that damn machine. "I would risk everything for you. Every time I saw a fresh wound, I questioned if you really could have done that to yourself. I honestly didn't believe you were capable, but I believed the experts. So, I didn't look too hard, and whenever I saw a wound that couldn't be explained—as there were some that obviously couldn't have been self-inflicted—I ignored them. You have no idea how fucking sorry I am for doing that. I should have told Dr. Hughes about my theory sooner, but I honestly didn't want to risk losing you. So, when you broke things off, I knew I had nothing to lose anymore, and all I wanted to do was help you."

This time, I don't give a shit that Dr. Hughes is watching us, or that the damn heart machine is beeping louder than an annoying kid's toy at Christmas. I reach over and grab the collar of Dylan's t-shirt into my fist. I pull on it until he's right in front of me, and I press my lips against his. It's soft and sweet with a promise of more, and it's over far too fucking soon. As I pull away, I'm rewarded by the biggest dimpled smile I think I've ever seen on Dylan's face.

"I don't know what I've done to deserve you, but thank you." He laces our fingers together again, giving it a big squeeze and I can see the sparkle in his molten silver eyes—it's a promise of more. When we are both feeling better, and when we don't have an audience, we both plan on showing each other exactly how thankful we are for each other.

Dylan turns to Dr. Hughes, not even bothering to hide his cocky grin. "Sorry about that, Doc. Now, why don't you get to the big bit?"

Dr. Hughes shakes her head with a small chuckle, and I know she's thinking the same thing that I am. Only Dylan could get away with being that cocky. "Are you happy for me to continue?" she asks me, and I draw strength from the feel of Dylan's hand against mine. I feel his warmth and his love, and I hold on to that tightly.

"Please do." I nod.

"This is the bit that is quite hard to hear. I will fill in all the blanks, but this is the main bit. We found out that you were being drugged with quite high-dose LSD. As a result, you believed the trauma you were experiencing was all a hallucination, as that's what he told you. The few memories that you had that you couldn't explain were your brain's way of pushing past the LSD. I know you said that on a couple of occasions, instead of having no face at all, you felt Slender Man had a bandaged face, and that you thought you could see eyes, and that's exactly what you could see. It was a real man, wearing a bandage around his head to cover his face, and using a voice distorter to hide his real voice from you. Combined with suggestions that your dad's ghost story was coming to life and the LSD, you believed it was true."

Fuck! So, all this time, whenever I had a suspicion that it didn't quite fall into what I knew, it was because I was pushing past the delusion.

Taking a big, deep breath, I ask the question that I can tell we've all been avoiding. "Do I know him?"

Dylan freezes beside me, his jaw slamming so tightly shut it's a miracle it hasn't shattered. I'm most surprised to see the sadness in Dr. Hughes' eyes, like she's almost ashamed to tell me the answer. They cast glances at each other, some kind of silent communication taking place. I can tell by the way Dylan is glaring at Dr. Hughes, he's not happy with whatever she's about to say.

"Honestly, Addy, the police have asked us not to tell you until they've had a chance to question you. They are worried you have no idea who is responsible, but if we tell you, that could change your story," Dr. Hughes explains. I can see Dylan is about to say something, anger flaring across his face, but I cut him off.

"All I can tell the police is the truth. I have no fucking clue who Slender Man is, or who he could be. I don't have a single suspect. But, I'm guessing by the cuts along Dylan's knuckles, and the injuries you both have, that you confronted him, which means there is little doubt who is responsible. So surely you telling me won't make a difference. I'm not going to turn around and say I knew it was him all along because I didn't. I believed he was all in my head, and honestly, I think it's going to take me a fucking long time to stop thinking like that. But, in order for me to ever stand a chance of healing, I have to know who he is."

Dylan looks over at Dr. Hughes and with a nod of his head, she lets out a frustrated sigh. "I am so sorry to have to tell you this, Addy. I hoped I wouldn't have to and that we could let the police have this horrible job, but you are right. You deserve the truth, and my reasons for not wanting to be the person to tell you are purely selfish due to my own shame. The person drugging you, making you believe Slender Man was real, and who abused, tortured, and raped you is Dr. Stephen Manning."

Her words echo around the room and I feel frozen. I knew I never had a strong connection with him, and that I always kinda felt like he was acting in his own best interests—or that of the research—as opposed to for me. But never in a million years would I have suspected him. How could someone charged by the courts to act in my best interests be so evil?

I don't know what to say or what to think. Knowing Slender Man isn't real, and that this whole time it's just been a regular weak man who gets a thrill out of hurting women. That knowledge stabs me through the gut.

We spend the next few minutes discussing what actually happened the night they confronted him. Tears begin to fall as they tell me about how he had hurt the people I cared about in order to try to get away with it. Dr. Hughes explains she has a bleed on the brain from a blow she took to the head, and she's being admitted for observation. Dylan has been admitted for treatment of his injuries too, although his are more defensive cuts and bruises.

They also tell me all about the stab wounds I sustained when he tried to get away. I had to have my spleen removed as well as one of my kidneys. Luckily, I still have one healthy kidney, and so I shouldn't notice any adverse effects from that. Let's just hope the remaining kidney stays healthy for the rest of my life. Though it's something I will always have to monitor and watch out for. I hate the idea that I will have to monitor things for the rest of my life, all because of the actions of one evil man. Because that's all he is, just a man.

I choose not to give him any more power over me. No matter what happens in the days, weeks, or years to come, he has had control over me for the last time. I will not allow him to take anything more from me.

Now that she knows I'm going to be okay—at least physically—Dr. Hughes heads back to her own room. Dylan refuses to leave my side. Even when the nurse offers to bring in a roll-up bed for him, he refuses. Though, I hate the idea of him sleeping on the chair for another night, so I ask him to crawl into bed with me. At first he's hesitant about knocking into me, or pulling out a wire, but I honestly don't think I can survive another night without him by my side.

Never one to disappoint me, he shuffles into the bed, moving as slowly as he can to get close, but it still isn't close enough. I close the distance, turning slightly onto my side and resting my head against his chest. Thankfully, the nurse just administered a top-up of my pain relief, and so I only feel the slightest bite of pain when I curl up against Dylan. Though, being close to him, feeling his heart beating beneath my cheek, is the perfect type of analgesia.

He wraps his arm around me, and I take comfort in his warmth as he runs his fingers lightly up and down my arm. He leaves a trail of heat along his path as my body warms beneath his touch. Luckily, they unhooked me from the heart monitor to go to sleep, since I'm more stable now, which means I can at least maintain a bit of mystery over how I'm feeling. Though, I think Dylan knows that even the barest feather-light touch sets my soul on fire and I feel a deep yearning for him. Not necessarily in a sexual way, although if I didn't have some pretty serious abdominal wounds, I wouldn't say no right now. It's like my soul cries out to his, and two people who have never felt whole finally do.

"Dylan," I ask, cutting through the peaceful silence that fills the dark room with just a sliver of moonlight shining into the room, lighting up his beautiful face.

"Yes, pretty girl." Fuck, my heart does somersaults every time he calls me that. I don't think I will ever not want him.

"How can you still look at me the same way you

always have? You know what I went through was real. All the things I told you Slender Man subjected me to... it was all real. Doesn't that change how you view me?" I ask, and I feel him freeze beneath me, his hand stopping mid-trail.

"Honestly, of course it changes how I view you," he mutters underneath me. My stomach sinks and tears fill my eyes. Thankfully, he can't see my unshed tears, but I think he senses a change in my mood because he takes hold of my head into his hands and shifts my head so that I look up at him. Even though we can barely see each other, the moonlight shines over his face and it's enough to see he's smiling at me, which just makes no sense. "How can I not see you differently when you have survived so much? You are, without a shadow of a doubt, the strongest woman I've ever met. You have survived more than most people could endure, and you do it all with a smile."

"Fuck, you terrified me then. Don't scare me like that," I chastise playfully as I slap my hand against his chest, which only makes him chuckle more.

"Pretty girl, I love you, and that won't ever change. If anything, I hate that I didn't help you sooner." His voice breaks at the end, and I can tell he really does feel that way, which makes my heart ache.

I reach out to touch his cheek, and he meets my gaze again. "Dylan, you have nothing to be sorry for. Nobody had any idea about what was happening to me, but when you suspected, you risked everything for me. I don't think I've ever thanked you for that. I love you so much, and I'm extremely lucky that you cared enough to risk it all for me."

Reaching up, I press my lips against Dylan's and just like always, the second I taste him, I'm desperate for more. The kiss becomes bruising and I try to climb further into Dylan's lap, only to feel a sharp tug on my stitches. A sound that can only be described as a mix between a moan of pleasure and a groan of pain rips from me, and Dylan holds me still with a chuckle.

"There's a part of me that loves to hear that sound, pretty girl. But I don't like the pain part. All I can promise you is that once you are better, I will make up for it a million times over."

"You promise?" I ask.

"Abso-fucking-lutely, pretty girl. I love you and I promise you forever. If you will have me," Dylan says as he presses a kiss against my forehead.

"I will never not want you. I love you too, and of course I want to spend forever with you."

I place my head back against his chest, listening to the beat of his heart while I allow it to lull me to sleep. I know I should fear sleep, but it's like I can't fear anything with Dylan by my side. He will hold me up when I'm down and he will give me the strength to stand on my own when I need to. My world has been filled with nightmares for so long, now I'm finally ready to live my dream, with Dylan by my side. I'm excited for what our future together will bring.

Epilogue
DYLAN

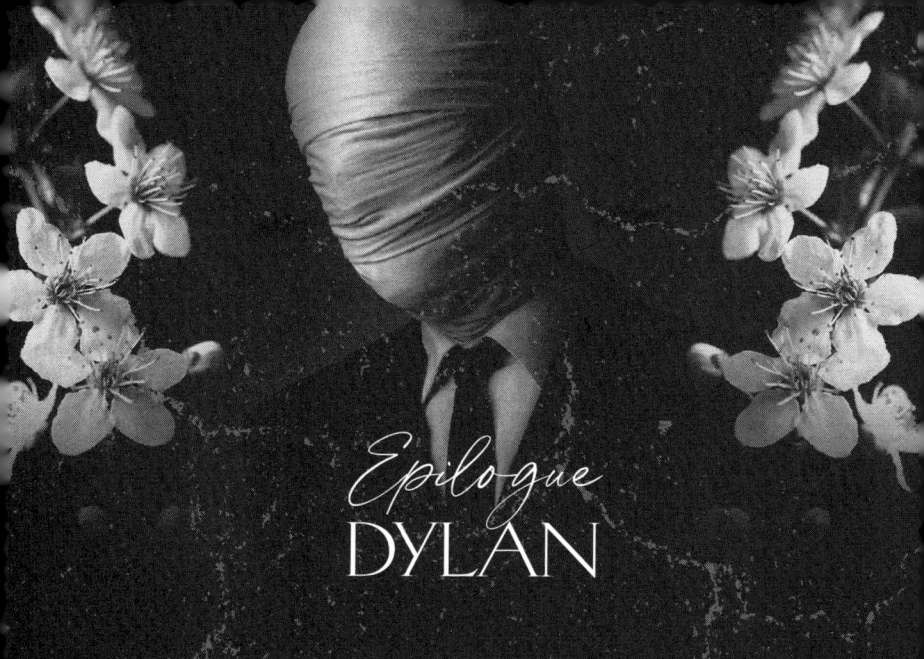

"Morning, Drummer. Wake up, sleepyhead," Lance calls into my room after he slams open the door in such a way that nobody in the facility should still be awake after feeling the bang and vibrations as it reverberates off the wall.

Groaning, I roll over and pull the cover over my head. It's the same thing I've been doing for the last few days—I lost count after two days and they all started merging together. I know the routine by now, so I cover my eyes to protect them from the bright lights that will invade my room any second when he switches on the big fluorescent light on the ceiling. When that doesn't work, he tries something different each day. Yesterday he pulled the duvet covers off me and got a great view of my pale white ass shining back at him. He clearly didn't know I sleep naked, but I have to admit, it was a lot of fun watching him discover that I do.

I wait for whatever he has planned, and when I don't hear anything, that sparks an element of suspicion. So, I open my eyes just slightly to find Lance has taken a seat in my armchair underneath the window.

"So much for doing work, Nurse Lancey," I grumble, as I roll over onto my back and shuffle up slightly so I'm sitting with my back against the wall where a headboard should be.

Lance just stares at me, his face a mask of indifference. He almost looks like he's bored of being here, but we all know that's not true. He loves his job. So much so that when he found out what had been happening with Slender Man and Dr. Manning, Lance was gutted. On a few occasions, Lance actually administered the LSD to Addy after Dr. Manning told him it was a specialist trial drug. He sobbed uncontrollably when Dr. Hughes told him. Not only did he apologise to Addy for drugging her, he also apologised to us all for putting us at risk. He felt guilty that he didn't see what was going on.

Lance is the chief nurse here at Lakeridge, which means he manages every nurse that works in this facility. Most managers don't do clinical shifts, particularly the nights, but Lance always said he wanted to be a different kind of leader. He still does all the paperwork and management stuff, but he also makes sure he allocates himself a few unsociable hour shifts.

I once asked him about it and he said, 'I would never ask one of my nurses to work a shift I'm not prepared to work'. It's the same with overtime. Unless someone really wants it, he will make sure to take his fair share.

So, you can imagine how cut up Lance was to discover what had been going on right under his nose. The whole incident, and the surrounding investigations, all proved that not only him but also the nurses he's in charge of, failed Addy in some way. And not just Addy, this whole facility. People started questioning that if that particular level of abuse could occur under everyone's nose, what else could be happening at Lakeridge that nobody knows anything about?

Initially, Lance offered his letter of resignation, realising that someone would have to take the fall for failing to protect the residents, but Addy made sure that didn't happen. Yes, the nurses should have checked up on her and they should have reported—or at the very least, followed up—when they learnt the security cameras around Addy's room were broken. But, not only were they extremely busy and under-staffed, they also thought they had informed a senior clinician, Dr. Manning. The fact that he did nothing to fix the issues, as they interfered with his meticulous planning, didn't fall on the nursing staff or Lance.

"Are you getting up?" Lance mutters from his place across the room, pulling me back to this moment rather than my awful memories of that time. I can still see Addy lying there in my arms, bleeding to death, and there was nothing I could do. I can relate to Lance's guilt. He failed to protect his patient, but I failed to help the woman I love, and that's a bitter pill too hard to swallow.

"Leave me alone. I want another hour or two," I groan as I pull the duvet cover up higher so that it's covering all of me except my head.

"Trust me, you need to get up and have a shower to make yourself stink just a little less," Lance jokes, and I can't help but chuckle.

The last few weeks since we found out about Slender Man and Dr. Dickhead, everyone has been a little weird with me. It's almost like they're being extra nice to me in the hope I don't push to get them fired. Strangely, I don't like that kind of attention anymore. When I was first admitted, I wanted the staff to bend over backwards to accommodate my every whim, but now I'm quite happy to keep my head down and just finish my stay here. So, having them be overly nice to me doesn't feel right, and I keep trying to tell them that. I think they're maybe also keeping an extra eye on me to make sure I don't relapse in any way—not that I could find an illegal drug in this place, even if I wanted to.

"Fuck off, Lance. I'm tired, okay," I grumble, not meaning to sound as harsh as I do, but he just chuckles and rolls his eyes.

"I warned you," he mutters under his breath, just loud enough for me to hear him.

I'm about to snap back, to ask him what he's talking about, when there's a gentle knock at my already open door. Dr. Hughes curves her head around the doorframe and gives me a big smile. As always, she's dressed in a perfectly pressed black skirt, with a light blue blouse she's tucked into the shirt. The jacket she usually wears with the suit has been shrugged off, and you can see the stripe lines where she's ironed everything perfectly.

Her bobbed blonde hair sits perfectly just above her shoulders and there isn't a lock out of place. She's wearing a bit of make-up, but only enough to make her look like the perfect professional, nothing more. Normally when she comes into my room to find I'm not ready, she wears a mask of disapproval, but today it seems nothing can hide the giant smile that's plastered across her face.

"Dylan, why on earth are you not showered and dressed?" she snaps, before turning her attention to Lance—his smug face drops as her glare catches his eye. "And you, Lance. You were supposed to make sure he's up and ready."

I can't help but chuckle. It's funny watching Dr. Hughes in her new leadership role. Ever since Dr. Dickhead was arrested, the big managers of the facility that we never see asked Dr. Hughes if she would agree to a trial period of running the facility. If it goes well and they like her, they will offer her the job. At the moment, they still haven't decided, meaning she's having to cover two roles, but you can tell she loves it. Management would be stupid fucks if they don't hire her.

Lance seems to shrink in his seat, desperate to avoid Dr. Hughes' scowl. "I tried, but he's not listening."

Rolling her eyes, she asks him, "Did you tell him why it's important he doesn't smell like rotten food today of all days?"

Now it's my turn to be offended. "I don't smell that fucking bad."

"Dylan, can you even remember the last time you showered?" she asks, and the fact that I have to rack my brain to find the answer tells me she's probably right. I should have showered. But it's not too late.

"Fine, I will go now," I groan as I throw the duvet

cover off the bed, exposing my almost completely naked flesh.

The cold air hitting my bare legs sends a shiver up my spine. Thankfully, I'm wearing boxers today, as my cock doesn't do well in cold weather. Not that I usually have him on display, but if he's gonna come out, I would want him to be at his best, which is most definitely not while it's cold.

"It's too late now," Dr. Hughes moans, and now it's my turn to be confused.

I look over at the clock on my bedside table and see that I still have almost forty minutes before I have to attend group therapy, so I don't know what they're all waffling on about. They're both staring at me, looking like I'm the one who is forgetting something. I rack my brain, but I'm too tired to think of anything.

"He has no idea what today is, does he?" Lance asks Dr. Hughes incredulously, and she responds with a chuckle.

"Well… why don't you just tell me what today is so we can get on with it," I grumble with the same annoyed tone I've permanently had attached to me for the last week.

"Dylan, today is your last day here. It's your graduation party," Dr. Hughes sings as she claps her hands together, a bright smile on her face.

As soon as the words register, I spring up from the bed. "I'm really going home today?" I ask, looking from Dr. Hughes to Lance, worried this might be an elaborate prank.

"Why? Do you want to stay with me, Drummer?"

Lance asks, and I can't help but scoff at him.

"You can fuck right off. As much as I've loved hanging out with you two every day, I plan on getting as far away from this place as I can and never looking back."

Dr. Hughes nods her head. "Good! That was our aim all along, Dylan. Now, get dressed because you have one last short one-on-one session with me while Lance does your final drug test. If you are clean, we can talk about the community outreach programmes I've set you up with, and all the meetings that are available in your area, as these will be a big help when you're in the outside world and you're afraid you might use. Having a support team is essential." Dr. Hughes may sound to an outsider like she's nagging, but in reality, she just really cares. She's worked hard to get me sober, and she wants to do everything in her power to help me stay sober. But we both know the only person who can guarantee I stay clean and sober is me.

"Thanks, Doc. I will definitely go to some meetings and find a sponsor. I think I need that. Do I really get to leave today?" I ask, my insecurities flooding back to the surface.

"Yes, but only if you pass this test. So, let's piss in the cup so we can both get this over with," Lance jokes in his usual gruff tone. He stands up and points towards the en-suite, causing us both to groan. Dr. Hughes makes a hasty exit, but Lance isn't allowed to go anywhere. The rules state he has to witness me providing the sample, keep his eye on it the whole time, and then perform the test. That way there's no chance of it being tampered with and the courts know the results are genuine. As a result, every couple of days for the last six months, poor Lance has had to watch me take a piss. So, knowing this is the last time someone is going to observe me taking a piss is fucking awesome.

I don't need to wait for the results to know I'm clean. But, as I'm talking to Dr. Hughes in her office and she confirms it, I feel a sense of relief. I've been clean and sober for six whole months. Don't get me wrong, I'm still terrified that when I go into the outside world, I won't be able to stay sober, but I've spent the last couple of weeks preparing for it so I knew this day would arrive. How did I forget about it?

That's an easy answer. For the last week, my life seems to have passed by in a blur. Not depression or sadness, just a deep yearning as though I feel something is missing, something that I need in order to be complete. But today is the day I get it back, and I can assure you, I will never part from it again.

My morning with Dr. Hughes went well and passed by at a mind-numbingly slow speed. I desperately watched the clock, although I'd no idea why because I knew I had no plans for this afternoon, other than if the drug test came back clean—which it did—then I would be graduating. So, if my graduation follows the pattern of the others, there will be a small ceremony and party to say goodbye to everyone. Though, for me, there will be some people I can't imagine saying goodbye to.

Sin drops by my room while I'm packing, crazy

excited I am finally going home. She's had a few slip-ups recently which have put her release on hold, but I know she will get there. She's a lot fucking stronger than she looks. These last couple of months, I've got to know her and we've grown close as friends. It will be weird not seeing her little pixie face every morning and listening to her gossip and pretend I'm listening and actually give a shit.

She's practically buzzing with excitement as she bobs up and down on the spot at the entrance to my room. "Come on. Dr. Hughes says I'm responsible for making sure you get to the party. So, let's go!"

She reaches out with her hand to grab mine, and I take one final look around the room. I packed everything back into the suitcase that I brought with me. It's weird, but I feel like I'm going home so much lighter than I was when I came in. I mean that figuratively, since literally, I have more than bulked up, thanks to my exercise regime. I mean, my soul feels a lot lighter, and that's why I think I'm capable of staying sober.

We arrive at the door to the rec room, and I'm surprised to see it's shut. I can't remember if I've ever seen it closed before. "Well… what are you waiting for? Open it," she sings, practically pushing me through the door when I take a little too long for her liking.

As I stumble through the door, I'm overwhelmed by shouts and screams of "Surprise!" echoing all around the room. I blink a few times, not believing what I'm seeing. The whole recreation room has been decorated, filled with black and gold balloons that say various motivational quotes such as 'you did it', 'congratulations', and my personal favourite 'you're going home'.

Well… it was my favourite until I saw the girl standing in the middle of the crowd, looking like a fucking supermodel, holding a balloon that says 'I'm so proud of you, Dylan'. For the first time in just over a week, I can feel my heart starting to beat again.

They discharged Addy from Lakeridge eight long, lonely days ago. After our little hospital trip, she made great progress physically, healing up in no time. However, her mental health was understandably very shaken. Everything she thought she knew was a lie, and the biggest challenge she faced was learning how to trust her brain again. It's not something that happened overnight, and it was made worse by the real nightmares she started having about Slender Man. Only this time, I was allowed to hold her in my arms all night and let her know she wasn't alone.

At first, Dr. Hughes was vehemently against it, since it breaks several rules. Though she agreed to honour the agreement we made in the bet, and she promised me Addy and I could carry on seeing each other discreetly, but apparently that didn't cover staying in the same bed. All that changed when Dr. Hughes saw how much it helped her with the night terrors. Without me there to hold her, she would scream, shout, and thrash around as the nightmares took hold. But, with me there to gently bring her back to the present, she recovered a lot quicker.

Don't get me wrong, even now Addy needs a lot of psychological support, and has regular outpatient appointments with Dr. Hughes. This isn't the norm. Usually, Dr. Hughes would be expected to discharge

Addy into the care of the community psychiatric team for them to provide her with the follow-up care. Addy could only stay in Lakeridge while she was a danger to herself and to others, which she never truly was. Yes, she had a suicide attempt, which is what got her admitted in the first place. But had this place not been a run-down sack of shit with only one decent psychiatrist, she may have been home a few days later with some treatment. Instead, Lakeridge allowed Dr. Dickhead to take over her care, and he nearly broke Addy. But he didn't expect her to be such a survivor.

As soon as I see Addy, I waste no time moving towards her and she runs to me, letting go of the balloon. She throws her arms around my neck and jumps into my arms, wrapping her legs around my hips, grabbing hold like a spider monkey who won't ever let go—not that I would ever want her to. We press our mouths together in a bruising kiss and my lips tingle as I taste her. It may have only been just over a week, but I feel like a starved man tasting a chocolate cake for the first time. It's delicious and I can't get enough.

It's like we're in our own little bubble as I feel her body pressing against mine, our tongues battling for dominance, and I feel alive again. My skin prickles, like it's heating up all over just from being near Addy. I can't get enough of this girl.

"Put her down, Dylan," a booming voice sounds from behind me, and normally I would ignore everything to be with Addy, but I'd recognise that voice anywhere. I'm just shocked to hear it here.

Releasing my lips from Addy's, a little groan slips

out of her and it's almost enough to draw me back in. But, as I look over her shoulder, I'm shocked to see not just Louis—the owner of the booming voice—but Jake and Henry are here too. As I look around the room, it's so weird to me to see patients, staff, and my band all intermingled together. Yet, everyone seems completely at ease, and they all look happy. Maybe they're glad I'm going.

Addy slips out of my hold, much to my annoyance, before whispering in my ear, "We have forever. Go and see everyone else." She places a kiss on my cheek and, with a bright smile, she steps out of the way completely. Fuck, could this girl get any more perfect?

Slowly, I move towards my bandmates, two of whom I haven't seen for the entire six months I've been in here. I've only seen Jake once. I'm a little nervous as I approach them. I know I probably shouldn't be, but I have a whole fucking lot to apologise for, and I don't really know how to start. They're more than just my bandmates, they're my friends… my brothers, and I've treated them like shit the last couple of years. Finding the words to say that and to apologise is difficult.

"Look at you. Jake said you bulked up, but I didn't think he meant this much," Louis exclaims, as he pulls me in for a hug without hesitation. I release the breath I didn't know I was holding as my brother wraps his arms around me.

Within seconds I feel as though I'm being crushed as Henry and Jake both circle around me and throw themselves on top of us to get in on the hug, too. "Argh, we've missed you, man," Henry says from behind me, his head resting against my back—or at least I think it's him since I can see Jake's head on my shoulder.

"I've missed you guys, too. Look, I don't even know where to begin with an apology…" I start, thankful I can't look any of them in the eye when I say this. I think some things are easier to do when you don't have to look at the person.

Jake interrupts me, pulling away from the hug as the rest of the boys follow. "Good, because we've talked about it and we don't want an apology. You were going through some shit, and yes, it made you a bit of a dick to be around for a while, but that's just the nature of being unwell. Now that you are better and we have our brother back, that's all that matters. We don't want to hash over the past. We just want to start fresh."

Dr. Hughes, who had been floating around in the background, comes over to stand next to Jake, and I catch the blush that spreads across my doctor's cheeks when Jake throws a smile her way. Looks like my doctor has a bit of a crush. Or maybe it's the other way around and Jake's the one with the crush?

"It's great that you boys could be here today to see Dylan graduate. I just want to say, on behalf of everyone here at Lakeridge, that we really will miss you, Dylan," Dr. Hughes says as cheers ring out from the people around the room, which shocks me. I didn't realise I was so well liked.

Lance steps forward and takes over from Dr. Hughes. "Even though you were a massive pain in most of our asses the first couple of weeks, we've all watched you grow. You have fought your demons, and nobody is saying you will be free of them. Sadly, they will follow you around for the rest of your life, but we hope that the skills you have learnt here at Lakeridge are more than enough to help you stand strong when you leave here."

Fuck, I'm getting choked up and I don't know what to say. Should I say something or are they not finished yet? Everyone is looking around like there should be more to come, and that's when, begrudgingly, Lyle, who is standing beside Dr. Hughes, stumbles forward. He was too busy giving Jake the stink eye to realise he missed his cue.

Lyle talks and it sounds as though he's reading from a script in his head, his voice monotone and focused. "Even though we like to think that the skills we taught you are the reason you will be successful on the outside, we know there's a far bigger part to thank. We should have known that you would break all the rules—and believe me, I still think you should be punished—" Dr. Hughes clears her throat purposefully, keeping Lyle on track and causing everyone to chuckle. "Even though you broke all the rules, for you, it was actually a good thing. You found something here that Lakeridge couldn't give you. You found someone to fight your demons with, and who will stand by and support you, no matter what. And in return, you have given her the exact same love and care."

Addy walks over to me and places her hand in mine, squeezing it in that reassuring way only she can. Her smile is bright enough to light up the Las Vegas strip, and it baffles me I'm the person responsible.

Sin, who is still practically hopping from one foot to

the other, moves to stand in front of us both, and tears are already streaming down her face. "We didn't do much of a graduation party for Addy because she asked us not to. She wanted to celebrate her graduation with you, since her new life can only really begin with you in it. It's clear to everyone here that the two of you have found real, true love here amongst the darkness, the pain, and the grief. Every one of us comes in here hoping to leave a different person, but with you two, it's like you came in as two broken pieces and you're leaving as one whole person. You both make up the missing pieces in each other's lives, and you make each other stronger. Your love is an inspiration for us all, and I know that I personally have learnt not to settle until I have the kind of love you two have."

Addy lets go of my hand and pulls Sin in for a hug as tears flow down both girls' cheeks. They continue to hold each other as Jake steps forward, a sad look on his face, though I have no idea why. This is supposed to be a happy occasion, yet he doesn't look happy. "Last time I was here, Dylan, you asked me for my help, and I didn't want to give you it. Honestly, I was an asshole, and I should have listened to you. I hired a private investigator, but I left it too late. They found information which the police have found useful, but it didn't come to light until after you caught him on your own. I failed to see how much Addy meant to you that day, and I will always hold some level of regret, wondering if I'd only listened to you, could I have helped keep Addy safe sooner?" Jake's voice breaks and Addy's breath hitches.

"Jake, you don't have to—" Addy reassures Jake, but

he cuts her off.

"I know you are going to say it's okay, Addy, and I thank you for that, but it's not okay. What it boils down to is that I didn't listen to my brother when he asked for my help. I can blame Dylan's past and the substance abuse, but really, it's all on me. I judged him as the old Dylan, and didn't trust that he'd changed, and I want to make a promise to you both that it won't happen again."

Louis and Henry step forward so they're flanking Jake, each putting a hand on his shoulders to show their support. I move towards them to show them my thanks, but Louis begins to speak, and as soon as he does I know he's talking for the band. I've seen him use this professional tone too many times before. "As a band, we will always support you, but as your brothers, we have to make sure you stay clean and sober. We have discussed this at length, and after talking to Addy a bit this week, we think we have a good idea of how you feel. You really have a good one there, Dyl." Louis winks at me before continuing. "We have decided that we can't put your sobriety at risk, and our current lifestyle is only going to tempt you. Besides, when we got talking about it, we all realised that we weren't happy about the direction the band has been heading. We aren't making the music we want to make. So, if you agree to it, we would like to part ways with our current label, and start our own label. We can do the work we want to do, make the music we want to make, and we can control the gigs, so we don't take on any more than you are comfortable with. What do you say?"

I can't help but smile as my heart races. I look over

at the girl who has made all this possible and I notice the flush spreading across her cheeks at all the attention. It's strange for me to think she's been hanging out with the guys without me, but it's also kinda cool. Both The Catastrophists and Addy are the biggest parts of my life, and having them together will do nothing but good things for my health and happiness.

"Of course I'm in!" I shout, before high fiving each of my brothers.

"Well, since you are going to miss the talent show next week, why don't you and Addy show us your routine now? I think Jake knows the song," Dr. Hughes says, giving my bandmate a nod. He leans under the table beside him and pulls out his guitar that I didn't see stashed there. It only takes a few seconds before Sin is rushing over to him with a seat before moving everyone back so they are pressed around the edges of the room.

"Looks like we are dancing," Addy says with a smile, as she takes off her shoes. Addy loves to feel the floor beneath her feet when she dances, using it to accentuate every move she makes. I'm more of a street dancer and prefer to dance in trainers.

I pull my girl into my arms and place a kiss against her lips. It's short, sweet, but promises so much more. I look over at Jake, unsure of which song he's going to play, but Addy and I have been freestyling together for so long it won't matter. We will just listen to the music, allow it to consume us as we move.

The soft strum of the guitar strings starts, and I recognise it straight away. It's the song I wrote for Addy. I've never played it for her before, but I wrote it in my song book. She must have seen it and given it to Jake as nobody else touches my song book.

As the words I wrote just for her begin to fill the room, sounding even more beautiful coming from Jake's raspy tone, Addy takes hold of my hand and moves it to her waist. I'm frozen just from listening to the words that mean so much to me come to life. Getting to dance with the girl I love, to the song I wrote just for her, really is something magical.

Staying as close together as we can, I move Addy around the room like she's a little doll, and she holds on. Our moves are the perfect mix of slow, sensual, and sexy as Addy creates the most perfect shapes. Her back presses against my front, her ass right over my cock as she sways her hips in just the right way. Thank fuck I'm wearing jeans, or my erection would be very visible. But I just can't resist how fucking gorgeous she is.

As the song changes tempo and becomes slightly more upbeat, I hear Louis and Henry begin to clap or bang on any available surface, clearly picking up on the harmony and filling in the bass and rhythm needed around it. This is always how we used to make music. I would come up with the melody, the song, and they would fill the rest in around it. This just proves it's the perfect way for us to make music.

Following the beat, I begin to move Addy faster across the floor, spinning her and throwing her into the lifts we've practised so many times before. Each time I throw her up in the air, only to catch her in a whole new position, the room erupts in gasps as they watch on in awe. I can only imagine how we look dancing together.

I'm guessing they can see what I've always seen. Two people who can function independently, but who are better together.

As the song draws to a close, and we end on our big lift, the crowd surrounding us burst into applause, but all I can see is Addy. I slide her down my body so that her feet touch the floor, her head coming to my chin. She looks up and her emerald green eyes sparkle with unshed tears, and my heart sinks as I think maybe I've done something wrong. I reach out to wipe the rogue tear that falls from her eye and she smiles at me.

"Pretty girl, what's the matter?" I ask, concern seeps into my words as I think through all the possible reasons she may be upset. I settle on just asking her.

"I'm not upset, Dyl. These are happy tears. I heard you playing that song and I loved it. I showed it to Jake, who agrees it has so much potential. I didn't know if you ever planned on showing anyone the song, but I knew it had to be out there. At first I was worried you would be mad," she explains as more tears roll down her face.

Shaking my head, I'm shocked that I gave off that impression. "No, absolutely not, pretty girl. I loved dancing to it with you. Jake did it so much justice."

She leans over to whisper in my ear and as her warm breath touches my ear, a tingle spreads down my spine, causing me to shiver. "Don't say anything, but I think you sang it better. But I am a bit biased, I guess."

I pull her lips to mine as the surrounding crowd disperses. Dr. Hughes announces the buffet is open, and Lance puts some music on the sound system. I'm not saying it's the most lively party I've ever been to, but it's definitely the best this psychiatric facility has ever seen. Just as I'm fully taking in how much I've missed her this last week, she pulls her lips away before looking around like she's doing something she shouldn't. Everyone is distracted. They're all either talking to each other or they're at the buffet eating. So, when Addy pulls my hand, I follow. Let's be honest, no matter what the circumstances, I would follow this girl anywhere.

She pulls me out of the back door, looking around to make sure nobody has seen us, and I don't need more than one guess to know where she could be taking us.

Pulling me into the cherry blossom garden, as soon as we are hidden by the leaves, she pulls me against her and kisses me in the way I've been desperate for since I realised she was here. The taste of her on my tongue ignites a fire deep within, and the sexy-as-fuck little moans she releases have my cock standing hard to attention.

My hands grip her hips tightly and I pull her against me tightly, so she can feel my cock pressing against her stomach. Like the little minx she is, Addy turns around and grinds her ass over my cock while looking over her shoulder and giving me the sexiest grin.

Reaching back, she grabs hold of my denim-covered cock and squeezes lightly, ensuring he's well and truly hard. She then turns around and pulls off her t-shirt, revealing a sexy black lace bra. Whenever we've been together, it's always been while we were both in Lakeridge, and when she was admitted, bringing sexy underwear wasn't exactly high on her list. So this is the first time I'm seeing her in anything so stunning, and it complements her body perfectly.

"So, what do you say? Do you want a quickie for old time's sake here in our garden? Then you can take me home and fuck me in every room of our new place," Addy says as she cocks her hip, making her look even sexier. Hearing her talk about our new home sends shivers down my balls, too.

When Addy left here, she didn't know what she was going to do. She has a flat she bought with some of the money from her family's life insurance, but she hates it there, and all it does is bring up unhappy memories. I was worried about her going home to an empty apartment and stewing over her past, so I offered her a key to my flat. Well, when I say a key, I clarified that when I leave here, I never want to spend another night sleeping without her. I've barely slept this last week worrying about how Addy is. Although her night terrors are more under control than they ever have been, she still gets them, and I worried that being on her own would cause her more worry. If the black bags under her eyes are any indication, I was most likely right. But, I plan on rectifying that when I get home by keeping her by my side.

Until we get home, and I can show my girl how much I love her, I think one final trip down memory lane won't be too bad.

"I think I may actually miss this place," I mutter, and Addy laughs.

"Nah, we will have so much more fun in our own home," Addy says playfully, throwing a wink my way before shimmying out of her skin-tight jeans.

Fuck, if I thought the bra was sexy, it's nothing compared to the lacey little shorts she's currently wearing.

"I don't know. All the walls here are soundproof, which is definitely useful," I joke as I stalk towards her, pulling off my shirt at the same time. She starts to retreat slowly, like a prey caught in their hunter's crosshairs. She thinks she can run from me, but she can't.

"Yeah, I thought that too. So, the band may have helped me soundproof the flat. They think it's so you can make music in the comfort of your own home, but I know different. Now, no matter what room we're in, you can make me scream as loud as you want." Addy turns around so I have a view of her magnificent figure from behind, including the curves of her ass as the hem of her shorts ride up slightly.

Her long, wavy brown hair flows down her back and she reaches around to unhook the bra before pulling it away and dropping it to the floor. I can't see anything because she's facing the other way, but my cock is pulsing with need at just the thought. I waste no time pulling my jeans down until we're both standing there in just our underwear, staring at each other with lust flaming in our eyes.

"Fuck, I don't know if you know this, but I fucking love you, Addison Mitchell," I growl, as I pull her to me, spinning her so that her chest crashes against mine.

"I do know it. Just like I know that I fucking love you, Dylan Matthews." With that, she presses her lips hard against mine and I scoop my hands under her ass, lifting her until she's in my arms. Hearing those words makes my heart soar.

To think that just six months ago I was still a broken boy who didn't know what love was. I'd never been in love, or been loved by anyone else. Hell, other than my bandmates, I didn't even have a family. Now I have everything I never thought I wanted. I have friends, family, and the girl I love by my side. I used to lose myself in drink and drugs, desperate to hide and escape from the world, but now I never want to live under the cover of darkness again. Now, together with the people I love that love me back, I want to stand in the light and live life to the fullest. No matter what demons are thrown our way, I know we will both be able to face them together.

The End

Thank You
ACKNOWLEDGMENTS

Thank you so much for taking a chance on Under the Cover of Darkness. I had so much fun delving into the world of Lakeridge and exploring the Slender Man urban legend. I can't tell you how much I absolutely loved writing Addy and Dylan's story. There's a beauty in their story that needed to be told, and I hope you fell in love with them as much as I did. I planned on this story being a standalone, but there's a very good chance that this isn't the last we've seen from The Catastrophists!!

This book seemed to take a lot more for me to write, and I think it's because of not only the darkness in this book, but also the beauty. Life got in the way a lot, but when I finally got this book finished, I couldn't be more pleased with it. There are lots of people I need to thank for helping me with this book.

Dani, thank you so much for not only coming up

with such an amazing concept of twisting urban legends, but then letting me be part of it. Not only was this your brain child, you created the graphics, and covers. You are crazy talented, lady, and I'm very thankful for you!

Zoe-Amelia and Kerrie - My Betas - as always thank you so much for reading through my words and helping make them shine. Not only do you always agree to help no matter how busy you are, you love my characters just as much as I do. Thank you for being awesome!

Rumi - my amazing editor - you have an incredible ability to help make my words better, and you always do an amazing job no matter how much of a crunch I put you under. Thank you for always helping me!

Mr Luna - while I was writing this book, there were days when I didn't think I would get it finished. There were days when I thought I'd taken on too much and couldn't do it, but you always knew I could. You are always my biggest cheerleader, and will drop anything to help me out if you can. I'm so lucky to have you on this crazy journey with me. No matter where life takes me, I know I'm already the luckiest girl in the world to have you by my side.

Debs - my best, longest friend - you inspire me each and every day. I can't even imagine how hard it is to be faced with darkness on a daily basis. You are so strong, and what you've overcome is something you should be proud of. You are always there when I need you, and no matter the distance between us, or how many times you ignore my texts when you're stressed, I know we have each other's backs. You are my best friend and I'm lucky to have you.

Ena, Amanda, and all the Bloggers and Bookstagrammers - thank you so much for helping to get Under The Cover Of Darkness seen by as many people as possible. I'm grateful for your support and I can't thank you all enough.

To my LUNAtics - thank you to each and every one of you for taking a chance on my twisted love story. I hope you loved Dylan and Addy as much as I do. You guys are the reason I can keep on writing, and I'm so incredibly humbled every time I hear that someone is reading and loves my books. Thank you to you all!

About EMMA

Emma Luna is a USA Today Bestselling dark romance author from the UK. In a previous life she was a Midwife and a Lecturer, but now she listens to the voices in her head and puts pen to paper to bring their stories to life. In her spare time, when she should be sleeping, she also loves to edit, proofread, and format books for other amazing authors.

Emma's books are dark, dangerous, and devilishly sexy. She loves writing about strong, feisty, but underestimated women, and the cocky, dirty-mouthed men they bring to their knees.

When Emma isn't writing, promoting, or editing books she can be found napping, colouring in adult colouring books, and collecting novelty notebooks. She also enjoys coffee and gossiping with her mum, playing or having hugs with her gorgeous nephew, who is the light of her life, and curling up on the sofa to watch a film with Mr Luna. Oh and for those of you that don't know, Emma is a hardcore Harry Potter fan—Team Ravenclaw!!

Thank you for taking a chance on a crazy Brit and the voices inside her head. That makes you a true LUNAtic now too!

If you want to find out all things Emma Luna you can join my newsletter here:

https://www.emmalunaauthor.com

If you have facebook, you can join my reader group for exclusive news and giveaways:

https://www.facebook.com/groups/emmaslunatics

If you would like to check out any of Emma's other books or stalk her in more places, you can find everything you need here:

https://www.linktr.ee/emmaluna

https://www.emmalunaauthor.com/
https://www.facebook.com/EmmaLunaAuthor/
https://www.instagram.com/emmalunaauthor/
https://www.bookbub.com/profile/emma-luna
https://www.amazon.com/Emma--Luna/e/B082GNYLM4
https://www.goodreads.com/author/show/19880511.Emma_Luna
https://www.tiktok.com/@emmalunaauthor

Other books BY EMMA

Sins of our Fathers Series
Book One - Broken
https://geni.us/SouF-Broken

Managing Mischief
Book One - Piper
https://geni.us/MM-Piper

Beautifully Brutal Series
Black Wedding
https://geni.us/BW-BB
Dangerously Deceptive
https://geni.us/DD-BB
Trust In Me
https://geni.us/TiM-BB
The Ties We Break

https://geni.us/TTWB-BB
Fighting To Be Free
https://geni.us/FTBF-BB

Willowmead Academy -
Co-write with Maddison Cole
Life Lessons
https://geni.us/WA-LifeLessons

Twisted Legends Collection
Under the Cover of Darkness
https://geni.us/TL8-UtCoD

Standalone
I Was Always Yours
https://geni.us/IWasAlwaysYours

Printed in Great Britain
by Amazon